# Doodlebug Ranch

*To Audrey*

*Keep the old West alive*

*[signature] 11/17/11*

# DOODLEBUG RANCH

ROBERT OLIVER BERNHAGEN

Mill City Press

MILL CITY PRESS, INC.
212 3RD AVENUE NORTH, SUITE 290
MINNEAPOLIS, MN 55401
612.455.2294
WWW.MILLCITYPUBLISHING.COM

ISBN-13: 978-1-937600-32-7
LCCN: 2011940161

PRINTED IN THE UNITED STATES OF AMERICA

Dedicated to the enthusiastic and supportive readers of

# GRASSHOPPER FLATS.

*They nudged me into completing the saga of James Monroe Henry.*

# Prologue

On Saturday, March 4, 1885, on a chilly but sunny day in Washington D.C., newly elected President Grover Cleveland delivered his first inaugural address to the country. More than 150,000 people witnessed his first inauguration on the East Front of the Capitol. The large bandstand that had been constructed on the Capitol steps was covered with red, white, and blue bunting as well as draped American flags. Later that evening, a huge fireworks display lit up the sky and a ball was held for the public at the Pension Building on Judiciary Square. While folks in D.C. were celebrating and enjoying the weekend's festivities, it was a day of sadness and somber reflection at the Box H ranch in northern Arizona. They were attending yet another funeral.

The Box H ranch was a middling-sized ranch of about six thousand acres located some thirty miles west of Flagstaff. It was nestled at the foot of Bill Williams Mountain, at an elevation of seven thousand feet midway between Kaibab Lake and Dogtown Lake. The mountain was named for the famed trapper, western guide and renowned recluse, William Sherley Williams. Old Solitaire, as he was known, was killed by the Utes in 1849 and the mountain was named for him in 1852.

The ranch was heavy in tall pine trees, short junipers and grassy meadows.  The land was flat to gently rolling and at most times of the year, held ample water for the local wildlife and some two hundred head of livestock.  Deer and elk were plentiful as were the wolves, bears, coyotes and mountain lions that fed on them.  Migrating geese and ducks stopped by the seasonal ponds on their journeys to and fro.  The skies were blue and sunny most of the year although the winters could be brutal.  It was great cattle country and all things considered a right fine place to live.

There were no fireworks or cheering crowds at the Box H on that drizzly Saturday afternoon.  Another member of the Porter Henry family was being laid to rest in the burial mound behind the ranch house.  Her name was Miriam Henry and she was just two weeks past her third birthday.  Prairie fever had taken her like a phantom in the night. She fell suddenly ill one day and died the next.  Her father, G.W. was consumed with guilt and remorse but there was naught to be done by anyone.

Life on the frontier was indeed harsh and cruel.  Blood, sweat and tears were the currency of the Old West.  Porter Henry had already lost his wife, Miriam, and two young sons to the fever.  Now he had lost his grand daughter too.  G.W., his eldest son, along with his pregnant wife, Susanna, and their six year old son, Franklin, stood dutifully by his side.

Porter's youngest son, Monroe, and his only daughter, Taylor, had left the ranch and gone off to Santa Fe almost three years earlier.  They had not been heard from in over two years.

The solemn gathering at the funeral made them all wonder about Monroe and Taylor.  Where were they?  Were they still alive?  Had they received the news of the Miriam's death and if so, why hadn't they contacted the family?

Porter was afraid that he might pass away without ever seeing or hearing from them again.

"Towns like the Flats sprung from nowhere, dried up and blew away like dust in the wind."

# Chapter I

## "Headin' back to Grasshopper Flats"

### SPRING 1886

After ever'thing that happened, I was "sure as sunrise" certain I would never return to Grasshopper Flats. In fact, I figured to walk 'cross the burning coals of hell in my sock feet before I'd go back there again. Yet here I was, Henry Charles, in the spring of 1886, headin' slowly but surely in that direction.

That first time I ventured to Grasshopper Flats was on Sunday, April, 7, 1878. That exact date is easy to remember since it was also my personal "Declaration of Independence" day. I'd left my home and family to sally forth to "see the world and seek my fortune". After all, I was sixteen and cock-sure I could handle anything the world could throw at me. Well, the awful events of that first day in the Flats changed darn near ever'thing. I received some hard lessons from the school of life and failed 'em all.

First off, I managed to gamble away all my saved-up money before getting stupidly drunk and deathly sick on a gawd-awful concoction they called "Injun whiskey". I lost all my breakfast as well as most of my dignity on account of that devil's brew. I was too sick to die and too drunk to care.

Next, I got myself hard-slapped by a pretty gal and beat up by an old bear hunter. Finally, I concluded my day in Grasshopper Flats by being shot at by the town drunk and run out of town in a hail-storm of laughter and bullets.

When I returned four years later, I managed to get over that pretty gal, became friends with the old bear hunter and found the town drunk to be a recovered sheriff. At long last I was able to put those awful memories to rest. Of course, the gamblin' and drinkin' problems are still works in progress.

While coming to grips with that part of my life, I found a new identity and better yet, a promising financial future. It was to take me over three hundred miles away to the city of Santa Fe and a world I'd never known. Yeah, the poker game of life can deal you some strange cards.

After four long and eventful years in the New Mexico Territory, I'm finally headin' back to Grasshopper Flats with my tail firmly planted twixt my legs. My once great prospects and good fortune have turned to naught but dust and are out there somewhere... just blowing in the wind.

### SUMMER 1882

On the day we left the Box H for Santa Fe, Taylor Henry and I had little to say to each other. Most of the time, we rode along in silence since we were still confused and confounded by our new relationship. For most of our lives, we thought of ourselves as brother and sister. Then just a few short weeks ago, we found out that I was born a "sagebrush" orphan that the Henry family had adopted. I was a replacement for their young son who had died of prairie fever. I was the born-son of Charles Ulster Farley and not Porter Henry so Taylor Henry and I were not blood kin and had to get used to the idea of being "jus' friends".

Up to that point in my life, I thought of myself as James Monroe Henry. Oh sure, ever'one called me "Monroe" rather than James but that's because I had an older brother named James Madison. He died of cholera but the folks still held him in their hearts and prayers. They named each of their children after dead presidents. My oldest brother is known as G.W. which is short for George

Washington. I had older twin brothers named after John Adams and Thomas Jefferson as well as a younger brother called A.J. for "Old Hickory", Andrew Jackson. All three of 'em were long dead and buried but never to be forgotten. Even their lone daughter, Taylor Henry, was named for Zackary Taylor. I reckon the folks just left out the "Zackary" part since she was a girl and bound to add another name to hers in the future.

After Charles Farley died, I decided to legally change my name to Henry Charles so I could honor both of my fathers. Good old Charles left me all his worldly goods which included a substantial bank account in Flagstaff and a gambling casino in Santa Fe known as "St. Charles Place". I was headed for Santa Fe to take over the business while Taylor was going along for the adventure of it. She had just turned eighteen and had never really been off the family ranch. It was easy for us to do things as brother and sister but a might more complicated traveling together as "jus' friends".

## SPRING 1886

Dawn was just sneakin' up over the horizon and the wind was chilly. Old man winter wasn't quite done with us and you could feel it in the air. I was half awake and half asleep but quite unwilling to get out from under my warm blanket. As usual, my mind had been meandering through events in my past and plans for my future.

Suddenly, I came full awake with an icy chill up my spine. Something or someone was "out there". Without moving a muscle and with my eyes still closed, I searched for what I could sense but not explain. I was unable to hear or smell whatever or whoever was watching me but I could "feel" their eyes. My horse Goner was also aware of the intruders and was gently tugging on his tether line. For what seemed an eternity, I waited patiently for something to happen. Finally, the wind shifted just enough for me to catch a whiff of wet fur. The morning dew had betrayed the invaders and the additional stench of rotted meat confirmed my suspicions. We were being stalked by a pack of coyotes and their last meal had been long dead when they ate it.

I was relived that it wasn't two-legged varmints but I'd have to get up and deal with 'em anyway. A single gunshot would have done the trick but it was way too noisy and certain to attract unwanted attention. I decided to stand up and run, with my blanket waving behind me, in ever widening circles around the smoldering campfire. All the while, I was growlin' and snarlin' the best I could. I must have been quite a sight but Goner paid me no mind as I raced past him. Neither a pack of mangy "ground vultures" nor a slightly crazed cowboy was going to disturb that mustang's breakfast. Fortunately, the coyotes wanted no part of me and scattered like scalded dogs.

Well, when the "prairie wolves" were finally routed I was huffin' and puffin' like an old bull in a meadow full of seasoned heifers. I checked my meager grub sack and chuckled at how disappointed the coyotes would have been iff'n they'd got to it. It was plain to see that I'd have to hunt up some eatin' meat if I planned to make it all the way across the badlands to Flagstaff.

As I "gophered" through my saddle bags for the last of my coffee and a hard tack biscuit, I couldn't help but imagine how it must have been for the settlers in that small wagon train some twenty-four years before. They must have been in this same general area at the same time of year. My father, Charles, had gotten up and gone before the sun to hunt down breakfast but since I was just six months old, it was most likely I was sound asleep on my cradleboard in the wagon.

The Navajo's would have hit us at first light before most folks were awake and aware. I'll bet some of 'em died right where they slept. It was my good fortune to be taken prisoner by the marauding Injuns rather than being slaughtered along with the other folks in the wagon train. I couldn't help smiling at my Henry rifle while remembering that it was also taken on that fateful morning and how fate had reunited us.

I "made it and ate it" in a hurry since I wanted to get on the road again as soon as possible. Goner was fully fed and seemed eager for the trip home. I don't know how horses know when they're homeward bound, but they do. He seemed to remember every step of the way even though it had been four long years since we'd passed this way.

The sun was full bright and the air was crisp from the cool evening. It was a perfect time of day for riding. I scattered the remains of my campfire, packed up the rest of my gear, hitched up my Colt revolver and we lit out at a spirited pace.

The high desert of Northwest New Mexico Territory was a vacant and lonesome land. My Pa used to say that desolate land was only good for growing prairie grass and Gila monsters. I kept my sights set on Mount Taylor which loomed in the distance as an eleven thousand foot trail marker. It was part of the San Mateo Mountains and just like Taylor Henry; it was named for good old Zackary Taylor. The Navajo's still called it *Tsoodzil*, the turquoise mountain, one of the four sacred mountains that mark the boundaries of the *Dinetah*, the traditional Navajo homeland. Guess that mountain was sacred to the Acoma, Laguna, and Zuni people too. It seemed to me that Injuns tended to place their Gods on mountains so they were in sight yet just out of reach. I knew the Hopi felt thataway about Mount Humphrey which was north of Flagstaff.

As the morning passed away, I started looking around for water and game. Both had been mighty scarce but I knew that as we climbed higher into the mountains we would find all the water and game we could wish for. I stopped around noon so Goner could drink from a small mountain lake and graze on the fresh grass that covered the shoreline. I laid out a small campsite in case I decided to stay the night and then I set out on foot with my Henry rifle to see if I could scare up any critters. I was tired of jerky and biscuits and wished for some fresh meat to add to my grub sack.

A fresh game trail led me into a deep and winding canyon and then I saw 'em. Three huge turkey vultures were circling above something or someone several hundred yards farther down the canyon. Carefully, I made my way into the canyon by staying close to one side and keeping a watchful eye on the other. The steep canyon walls looked to be about fifty foot high and I was an easy target for anyone on top so I made my way like a fox sneaking in a henhouse. As the canyon twisted and turned, I got an awful uneasy feeling in the pit of my stomach. It felt like I was walking into a trap. The last turn confirmed my instincts; it was a box canyon with no way out.

The prairie buzzards were circling lower and lower as there was something hidden behind a large boulder that commanded their attention. I surveyed the area for a full minute before I was reasonably certain that there was no one else around. Finally I raced the last hundred yards to the boulder as the first vulture landed atop it. I paused to catch my breath and consider my options. My advance scared the birds off but all three stayed close and primed for an assault. I crouched down and carefully edged my way around the boulder. Finally, I could see what had attracted the vultures; an Injun was staked out on the canyon floor.

The young brave was still strainin' and pullin' against the tie-down ropes but was badly cut up and quickly running out of struggle. I started towards him when I caught a flash of sunlight off metal and instinctively leapt backwards. The lance that was meant for my ribcage barely missed as I stumbled and fell in a cloud of dust. A terrifying war cry was followed by a young Navajo warrior rushing at me with his knife held high. I drew my Colt pistol but it was too late as he was upon me. I dropped the revolver when I blocked his thrust and we wrestled around on the canyon floor. We rolled over and over as he tried desperately to plunge the blade into my chest. I was so intent on taking the razor-sharp dagger away from him that I failed to note the size of my attacker. He'd come at me like a mother badger protecting her young but the intensity of his assault belied his small stature. He could be no more than five foot five and less than one hundred twenty-five pounds while I was six foot two and two hundred twenty pounds. Evidently, the Navajo hadn't noticed either or just didn't care as he continued to try to take my scalp.

Finally, my size and strength overcame his determination and I was able to wrest the knife away and return it to him blade first. The crazed warrior died with his eyes wide with hatred. I was covered with blood and sweat but otherwise unscathed.

I staggered to my feet and stood over his body with the bloody knife still in my hand. The young Navajo was clearly unprepared for our life and death struggle but he died with honor. I hoped he made it to the happy hunting ground.

I picked up my Colt and walked over to the staked Injun. He was short in stature but well built with a round face and long black braids. I judged him to be a Hopi warrior but if true, he was a long way from the Hopi Reservation. His eyes were alert and he was watching me with an expression somewhere betwixt apprehension and fear. When he noticed the bloody knife in my hand, he took a deep breath and closed his eyes.

Desperately, I tried to remember the Hopi word for friend but it'd been a lot of years since Hopi Joe had tried to teach us his language. I could only recall one word that might be right.

"*Wikwawa?*"

His eyes opened and a smile started to form on his face. In a whispered voice he cautiously returned the greeting… "*Wikwawa*".

Slowly and carefully, I cut his bonds and watched as he struggled to get to his feet. He had many knife wounds but they were not deep. They were most likely a form of torture. The Navajo's wanted to inflict "much pain but no death" on their enemy and the smell of fresh blood was certain to attract predators like coyotes and vultures.

I helped him to his feet and supported him as we started to walk back down the canyon. He kept trying to speak but his voice was little more than a whisper. Finally I understood him when he was able to say "*kuyi*".

Somehow I knew that Hopi word too. He needed water.

When he could no longer stand, I gently lowered him to the ground. Then I repeated "*kuyi*" several times and pointed in the direction of my campsite. He nodded his head that he understood. As I walked away from him I kept repeating "*wikwawa*" and "*kuyi*".

I retraced my steps through the canyon and down the game trail to where Goner was waiting for me. Actually, he was so busy eatin' and drinkin' that he probably hadn't even noticed I was gone. I hastily filled three canteens and two water sacks, mounted up and headed back to the canyon.

My Hopi friend was right where I left him and he barely moved when I rode up. I trickled small amounts of water into his mouth until he came around. He responded by sitting up so he could take the canteen from me and drink on his own. After several long gulps of water he drained the canteen and lay back down with his eyes closed. I could see he was in a lot of pain but was never gonna show it. Ever' so often his eyes would open just a might so he could see what I was up to. The Hopi warrior was still kinda wary of me and my intentions but seemed grateful for the help. He finally spoke as I was going through my saddle bags looking for a piece of jerky.

"*Kwakwhay Bahana*"

I didn't understand him. "*Bahana?*"

"I thought you knew my language."

Hearing him speaking English kinda confused me. "Well, I don't. Just a few words is all."

"*Bahana*" means white man. I thanked you… for the water… and for saving me. I owe you my life."

I couldn't help but remember the time my adopted parents saved a young Hopi warrior and how he returned their kindness by delivering me to them.

"You don't owe me nothing. No man should be left to die like that. Why did the Navajo stake you?"

He needed more water so I handed him another canteen and helped him take a slow drink. When he'd had enough, he spoke with great anger in his voice. "The Navajo have hated my people since the beginning of time. They wanted me to die slowly and with much pain."

"They? There was more of 'em?"

"A raiding party… six, maybe eight."

That changed ever'thing. I looked up and down the canyon and listened for any sounds that the raiding party was returning.

"We can't stay here. If you can get up on my horse, we can go back to my campsite and I can treat your wounds."

My Hopi friend nodded in agreement and I helped him up on Goner's back. I led the way back to camp while he did his best to stay upright in the saddle. The agony of his wounds was apparent on his face but he never spoke of it nor cried out. The short distance seemed to take forever but we finally made it to camp just as he passed out. I kept him from falling off and carried him to a shady spot by the waters edge.

I heated water over a small campfire and cleaned his wounds with rags from my saddle bags. I had no good way to stop all the bleeding so I made some hot mud packs and covered the cuts to let the mud dry. I didn't have an Injun's knowledge of healing but I did the best I could. Finally, the bleeding stopped and he seemed to rest easy. I covered him with my blanket and fueled the fire before considering our situation.

The Navajo raiding party was certain to come back so we had to light a shuck and get out of there as soon as possible. I thought about Goner carrying double or building some kind of *travois* and then it came to me. That young Navajo warrior must have been left behind to make certain my friend died before he could rejoin the raiding party. He had to have a horse somewhere thereabouts. I mounted Goner and raced back to the box canyon.

The turkey vultures were already at work on the Navajo as we rode up. They flew off when we got there but continued to circle overhead. I dragged the body over to the stakes and tied him down. With any luck, the hoverin' predators would surely make him unrecognizable to any curious Navajo that might come looking for their friend. It might just buy us some time.

Long ago I taught Goner to "whinny" on command and I got him to do so again. The old trick worked and his call was answered by the Navajo pony which was tied up in a sheltered draw about fifty yards away. Along with the gray pony, I found a bow and quiver full of arrows as well as a half-full grub sack. The "grub" was mostly berries and nuts with a small amount of dried meat but it was more than I expected.

I untied the pony so Goner and I could lead him back to my campsite. When we got back, I tethered both horses and checked on my patient. He was still passed out but looked to be doing alright. The mud packs were holding and he didn't seem to have a fever.

I decided to try hunting again as we both could use fresh meat. Rather than cause a noisy ruckus with my rifle, I figured to try out the bow and arrows. I was reminded once again of Hopi Joe. He taught all of us Henry boys to use the bow and we were all pretty good with it. At close range, it was as effective as a rifle and completely silent.

Before heading out, I practiced by shooting two arrows at a large juniper tree. The first missed but the second stuck solid. I figured that was good enough and went out looking for game. After an hour of chasin' and stalkin', my third and fourth arrows missed their mark but the fifth was dead center and brought down a good sized white-tailed deer. I hoisted it over my shoulders and carried it back to camp.

My wounded friend looked to be passed out but I found him awake and alert when I laid down the deer by the campfire.

"Great white hunter comes back?"

I was surprised and relived to hear his voice. "Yes, and I've brought fresh meat for supper. I hope you like venison."

"You always hunt with bow?"

"I thought it would attract less attention. That raiding party might just be headin' back this way."

He seemed to consider what I said and looked away before he answered. "Navajo are gone. They are cowards that steal in the night and run."

"Steal? What did they steal from you? And why are you so far off your reservation?"

He didn't answer right away and continued to look down as if he were unwilling to look at me or answer my questions.

"I was sent by the chief of my village to the people of Acoma pueblo. I took three pack mules loaded with gifts and trade goods. To all of the peoples, gifts are given in a circle so the Acoma people presented me with gifts.  Then I bartered our pottery, baskets and moccasins for their fine jewelry and silver.  I stayed with them for seven moons and was returning with the gifts and goods for our people.  The Navajo stole it all and left me to die in shame and dishonor."

As he turned away from me, I noticed a head wound that I hadn't seen before.  It looked like he'd been hit from behind with a war club or tomahawk.  His hair was matted from the dried blood but I could see the raw scalp beneath.  I fetched the warm water and rags and gently cleaned the wound.  I didn't know what to say and he couldn't or wouldn't give me any more information so I went about the business of guttin' the deer for supper while my patient fell back asleep.

I tried to figure what came next.  It might be a day or two before my Hopi friend could ride and I couldn't just leave him here alone so I was sorta stuck.  If I could be certain that raiding party wasn't comin' back, I could rest a little easier but as it was, I had to be on guard ever' minute.  In my experience, Injuns were notional and their actions could seldom be foretold… even by other Injuns.

I was careful to keep our fire low so supper took awhile.  When it was ready, I woke my patient to see if he would join me.  Being Injun proud and stubborn, he did so reluctantly and remained silent.  I did notice that his wounds hadn't affected his hunger any and I took that for a good sign.  Finally, I decided to draw him out.

"Where did you learn to speak English?"

He seemed amused by my attempt at conversation and continued eating while he considered his answer.

"Four years ago, when your President Arthur signed the treaty with my people to set aside the lands for our reservation, my father taught us all to speak your language so we would be able to understand your people."

"Well, I'm Henry Charles, what do I call you?  What's your name?"

Again, he seemed amused by my questions and thought awhile before answering.

"Toho."

"Joe?"

"No, Toho. It means great cat… mountain lion."

I tried to pronounce it and he corrected me until I got it right. We both shared a laugh and relaxed a little. When I finished eating, Toho was already asleep. I bedded down in the shadows and kept a lookout for as long as I could.

I tried to keep one eye open most the night and didn't really get to sleep till it was damn near dawn. I woke with a jolt to find Toho already awake and carefully removing the mud packs to inspect the damage. He'd gotten the fire started to boil water so he could brew a potion with some cream colored flowers that folks called Cliffrose. That figured to be a Hopi concoction to cleanse and heal-up his wounds.

Then I spied my bandana wrapped around his head in order to hold some sort of poultice in place. He must have slipped it off my neck while I was sleeping. The faded red bandana didn't matter one whit but I was embarrassed to admit that I hadn't woke up when he removed it.

Toho seemed too busy to eat so I made a small breakfast and I watched him as he treated his wounds. He would need a heap of healing to be fully recovered but I could tell he was grimly determined to go after the Navajos right away. The Hopi were generally considered to be a passive and friendly people but Toho was acting more like an avenging Apache. He was ready to kill or be killed; there was no mistakin' the look in his eyes. When he finished with his "doctoring", he struggled to his feet and faced me.

"Thank you for your help but now, I must go."

He picked up the Navajo's grub sack, the bow and quiver and staggered towards the gray Injun pony. He barely made it and had to hang on the pony to keep from fallin' over. I walked over and boosted him up on his mount and handed him one of my canteens. He was more comfortable riding bareback than in a saddle anyway so he was right at home on the Navajo's pony.

"Here, you're gonna need this."

I could see the pain in his face but he smiled anyway and accepted my gift.

"Yes, I will. Thank you again, Henry."

Riding all hunched over, he headed back towards the box canyon. After cleaning up the campsite, I saddled Goner and followed
after him. It wasn't really my fight but I didn't have it in me to let
him go after a raiding party all by himself.

While Toho tracked the Navajos, I tracked him. I tried to stay
close but never too close. Their trail was just north of due west so
they figured to be headed for Chaco Canyon. The Navajos were
now on their own land and they were welcome to it. It was high
desert country and just about as bleak and dry as an old burro bone.
Sagebrush and cactus were all that grew here and animals of any sort,
other than lizards and snakes, were nowhere to be found. Although
it was still springtime, the dry heat made traveling difficult. Water,
or lack of it, played tricks on a person's mind and made it hard to
follow a trail what with all the dust and sand.

In spite of the exhausting journey through this hostile territory,
Toho seemed to be getting stronger rather than weaker. I found remains of his meals that spoke of his ability to hunt down whatever
crawled or slithered across his path while I was still getting along
with jerky and biscuits. Somehow, he was able to uncover ever' drop
of water that he came across while I was rationing the water from
my canteens and water sacks. My admiration and respect for him
was growing with each day. After four days of chasin', he finally
caught up with the Navajos at sunset and I was close behind.

We were just entering the southern entrance of Chaco Canyon.
Just to the north, Fajada Butte rose some four hundred feet from the
canyon floor and made a fine guide post. The darkened shapes of
the rocks stood out against the dark blue skies. It was eerily beautiful and foreboding all at the same time.

A tendril of smoke betrayed the presence of the raiding party
amongst the rocks and boulders that peppered the foothills and the
fading sunlight allowed us to approach without being seen. Toho
chose to circle their encampment and climb to the higher ground

behind. I tethered Goner and crawled across the canyon floor while cradlin' my Henry rifle.

From my position, I could see most of the camp. The raiding party had a pretty good fire going and there were at least five of 'em 'round it. It looked like they were "drinking whiskey and telling tall tales" as my Pa used to say. Their ponies and pack mules were tied up off to one side and there were two lookouts, silhouetted by the campfire light, atop boulders on either side of the camp. It seemed like they were watching and listening to the others more than they were looking out and that would surely be to our advantage. I waited for Toho to make his move and I didn't have to wait long.

He rose from behind a rock outcropping and launched an arrow at one of the lookouts. Toho's aim was true and the arrow went clear through the neck of the Navajo. Being unable to call out, the dying warrior struggled with the arrow before falling off the far side of the boulder away from the others. I held my breath and waited but none of the celebratin' Injuns seemed to hear anything or take any notice.

What with the flickerin' light from the campfire, I could barely see Toho as he moved cat-like into better position to get a bead on the remaining sentinel. One of the warriors around the fire tossed a half full bottle of whiskey up to the lookout and he was drinking from it when Toho's arrow struck in the middle of his back with a loud thud. He made a pitiful gurgling sound and dropped the bottle which shattered on the rocks. The dying Navajo staggered a few steps before falling off his perch, bouncing down the side of the boulder and almost ending up in the campfire. This time, ever'one noticed.

The raiding party scattered like a stomped-on ant hill. Two of 'em scampered to my right and two hurried off to the left as if they intended to outflank or surround their unseen attacker. The fifth one was shouting out what sounded like orders while charging straight up the hillside towards Toho. You could tell he was their leader since he was sportin' a tattered cavalry jacket and hat. From where I was watching, things were just about to get interesting.

I was crouched down just to the left of the encampment so two of the warriors came running right towards my position but they were looking up the hill and didn't see me. The first one started climbing the rocks but the second was running drunk so he stumbled and fell. He babbled something to the first one and then struggled mightily to stand up. The firewater had made him clumsy and care-less. I figured this was gonna be my best chance so I took it. Five days earlier I'd taken a knife from a Navajo and right then, I found the perfect way to return it. I crept a few feet closer and let it fly. My aim was true and the blade lodged deep in his chest. He uttered a guttural groan and collapsed in a heap. As I'd hoped, the first one was too far away or too busy to hear anything. Near as I could count, there were three down with only four to go.

If Toho had wanted to die in battle like a true warrior, he was surely going to get his chance. There were four angry drunken Navajos closing in on him and he was just standing his ground and waiting. For my part, I was hoping to sneak up behind 'em and help even up the odds a little.

The two Navajos that headed off to the right found him first. They split up and rushed at him from opposite sides. He was taken by surprise but managed to get off one arrow that stuck in the thigh of one of his attackers before becoming engaged in a hand to hand struggle with the second. By this time all four of the Navajo's were whoopin' and hollerin' the way Injuns do so I was able to locate the others. I shouldered the Henry and waited for a clear shot. It was getting darker by the minute and I could barely make out the shapes from the shadows.

The Navajo just ahead of me musta sensed something and sud-denly turned around. When he saw me, he let out a blood-curdlin' scream and raced back towards me with his war club held high. I let him as close as I dared and then stopped his advance with two rapid chest-centered rounds from my rifle. The shots echoed off all the rock formations and sounded like a twenty-one gun salute. Now ever'one knew I was there.

In all the excitement, I hadn't noticed that the leader of the raiders, the one who'd gone straight up the hillside, was toting a Spencer rifle. When I did take notice, he was pointing it in my general direction. Before he could squeeze off a shot, I dove for shelter just in the nick of time. His first bullet struck a rock behind me and ricocheted off several others. That fifty-six caliber round sounded like a cannon ball going past. As I scrambled behind a rock outcropping, he fired again and this time the bullet broke off a chunk of rock just above me. It fell on my head like a hod full of bricks. I was dazed and confused as I tried to stand but lost my balance and fell to the ground. My Henry rifle was nowhere in sight so as I lay on the ground, I carefully drew my Colt and waited. My head was still spinnin' but I was able to focus my eyes. When I saw the barrel of his Spencer coming around a large boulder I just aimed the pistol and fired at it. The Navajo walked right into the forty-five slug as he turned the corner. One round wasn't enough so I repeated the action two more times and hoped that would be enough.

He was as tough as old rawhide and died in sections. The first shot stopped him cold and knocked off his cavalry hat. The second sent him to his knees and caused him to let loose of the Spencer. The third one finally put him down for good. It seemed strange to be shooting at a cavalry jacket but there was no cure for it.

While I was busy fighting for my life, I figured Toho must have been doing the same so when I regained my senses, I made my way over to where I'd last seen him. I was bleeding from my head wound but didn't have time to fuss over it. The last I knew, there were still two more Navajos to be dealt with.

I was mighty cautious about my approach since I had no way of knowing who'd survived the scrappin'. When I finally located Toho, he was draped over the body of a dead Navaho and seemed about to pass out from exhaustion. There were no weapons about so he musta beat him to death with his bare hands. It sure seemed like he'd managed to overcome both warriors and live to tell about it.

I fetched water from their campsite and returned to tend to my crazed Hopi friend. As I was holding his head so he could drink, he mumbled something and pointed past my right shoulder. Instinct took a'hold of me and I rolled to my left and drew my Colt at the same time. Sure 'nuff, coming right at me with his tomahawk held high was the Navajo with an arrow in his right thigh. He was dragging that leg and mad as hell. I put him out of his misery with two quick rounds to the chest. He was dead before he hit the ground and the battle was finally over. Meanwhile, Toho had passed out again and missed all the excitement.

The next morning dawned bright and sunny and found us recovering from our battles. I was missing a chunk of my scalp and Toho had some new knife wounds to add to his collection. He made a poultice for my head and cleaned and bandaged his new wounds as best he could. Since the Navajo encampment suited our purpose, it made good sense to stay for at least a day or two and fully recover but neither of us were about to stay in hostile territory any longer than we had to.

After taking notice of a half dozen ravens overhead, we collected the seven bodies in one spot and covered them with good sized rocks and boulders. No sense in drawing too much attention before we were safely away from the area. In good time, all the carrion eaters would get their share.

It figured that the raiders were renegades off the Navajo reservation. They were probably nothing more than whiskey-driven young warriors out to plunder and murder anyone who crossed their paths. Redskin, white-eye or Mexican made little or no difference. Judging by the blond hair on one of their scalp trees, they had surely encountered some white settlers along the way. In this God-forsaken land, life and death were only separated by luck and circumstance.

Toho figured we had eight to ten days of hard travel to reach his village on the First Mesa which was part of the Hopi reservation. I rummaged through the supplies left by the raiding party and found dried mutton, pinion nuts, fry bread and, of course, two more bottles of whiskey. What little water they had was barely fit for the horses and mules. Their knives, tomahawks and war clubs were of little use to us but Toho did keep the Spencer rifle and a half-full sack of bullets.

I cooked up some of the fry bread and mutton for breakfast while Toho checked the pack mules. He seemed satisfied that all of his gifts and trade goods were present and accounted for. After eating, we had nothing to do except sit around and mend.

Since Toho wasn't much for idle chatter, I stayed pretty quiet and let him pick his time. He seemed to be troubled by something more than just his wounds.

"Now you have saved my life for a second time. How can I ever repay you?"

I had to chuckle at that one. "I think we saved each other last night... or don't you remember that last one with the tomahawk?"

He tried to make sense out of what I said but couldn't so I explained what happened. He listened with interest and nodded his understanding but went silent again. His honor had been restored by recapturing the goods and killing the Navajos but the deep obligation he felt to me was bothering him. I couldn't think of any way to relieve him of that feeling.

Goner seemed to get along with the rest of the *remuda* so I just made sure they all had what little water and grazing grass that arid land could provide. I took particular notice of one of the Navajo ponies. She was a pure white pinto filly with a black and brown blaze and mane. Toho also noticed and spent several minutes examining her.

I was trying to clean up the dried blood from my poor rumpled hat when Toho finally spoke again.

"Henry is a fine name. My father is blood brother to a white man named Henry."

I couldn't believe what I heard. Could it be possible?

"Was his last name Henry? Is his full name Porter Henry?"

Toho stared at me with a look of disbelief.

"Yes, but how do you know this?"

I was almost overcome with emotion. I still couldn't believe what I was hearing.

"Porter Henry is my father. I've known your father since I was born. He was part of our family when I was growing up. I've always known him as Hopi Joe."

"My father's name is not Joe. It is Toho. I was so named in his honor."

"Don't ya see? My folks must have misunderstood and called him Joe because it made better sense to them. I called you Joe at first… remember?"

Toho nodded in agreement while considering what I said and then laughed out loud. "My father would never have told them. He has nothing but great love and respect for your family."

"Since you're his son, I figure you're part of our family too."

Toho looked at me with disbelief in his eyes. "That would be a great honor."

I couldn't wait to tell Toho the story about how my folks had found and saved his father. I'd heard it so many times growing up.

"Twenty-four years ago, when my folks were coming west with a wagon train, they found your father badly wounded and staked out to die. He'd been left there by the Navajo, just like you were. Ma treated his wounds and they transported him in our wagon all the way to his village."

Toho was listening to what I said but seemed to have a face full of questions.

Since he didn't ask any of 'em, I just continued.

"Somehow, your father understood that my folks lost a boy baby and how that loss had affected my Ma. After recovering from his wounds, he found a white baby that was taken to a Navajo village and somehow managed to snatch that baby away and give him to my folks. I reckon it was his way of repaying them for saving his skin. You know, giving a life for a life."

I was so caught up in the tellin' of the story I didn't notice that Toho had looked away as if he was reluctant to face me.

"I was that baby! I was raised as Porter Henry's son but I wasn't really. I'd been taken from my real father by the Navajo during a wagon train massacre. I could have been raised as their slave or worse. Your father surely saved my life."

I waited for a reaction but none was forthcoming. Toho continued to look off in the distance as if lost in thought.

"I guess you could say that by saving your life I was repaying him. That would make us even."

He finally turned around with a stony face.

"I too have heard the story of the white baby from the wagon train but it was not the same as you tell it."

I was confused and taken aback. "What's not the same?"

"It is not important."

"It is to me. My whole life got turned upside down because of that story. I have to know if it's the whole truth."

Toho considered his answer and did so carefully while I tried to calm down.

"My father always told us that the white baby was called Monroe Henry and not Henry Charles."

"That was my name, Monroe Henry. I only changed it to Henry Charles after I found my real father. His name was Charles."

Toho stared into my eyes for a few seconds and then placed his hands on both of my shoulders and said, "Then you are truly my white brother."

It was clear that Toho had more to say but it was also plain that at this time, he wasn't about to say it. As much as I wanted to ask, I decided to wait. After all, we were headed for his village where I would see Hopi Joe and get the rest of the story.

After just a few hours of rest and boredom, I think we were both ready to hit the trail. My headache wasn't going away and neither were his wounds but traveling wasn't gonna make us any worse. Besides, the stench of the bodies had attracted the attention of a small pack of coyotes. They were cautious and skittish but they were also hungry so they kept inching their way ever closer. I threw a couple of rocks in their general direction and then decided I'd had enough. I gathered my gear and prepared to leave. Toho seemed to agree as he followed my lead.

As I was loading Goner and talking to him, Toho asked me about Goner's name. I explained that I rescued my mustang stallion from a snow bank when he was a scairt colt and Pa said he would have been a "goner" iff'n I hadn't. I guess the irony was lost on Toho as he had nothing further to say.

When I carefully packed the two bottles of whiskey in my saddle bags, Toho took notice. "Firewater no good for Injun or white man."

"That's true enough but this is only for medical purpose. I won't drink it."

"Whiskey is not medicine. It makes Injun crazy and sick."

"Sounds like you know first hand."

Toho nodded his head. "Father made me try it so I would know not to."

Now that made sense and sounded like Hopi Joe. My Pa always said Injuns couldn't hold their liquor and should be kept from it. Of course that applied to most white men too. I was reminded of my first taste of Injun whiskey eight years ago in Grasshopper Flats. It was a rotgut concoction of alcohol, chewing tobacco, lye soap, red peppers, sagebrush and strychnine which made me sick just to think of it.

We finished loading our supplies and prepared to head out with our three pack mules and seven ponies. For some Injun reason, Toho handed me the rope that connected all of the pack mules while he fashioned separate ropes of different lengths for each of the Injun ponies and held all seven in his right hand. That white filly was on the shortest rope and was positioned right behind his pony.

As we hit the trail, the sun was high, the air was still and it figured to be a long hot ride. The ravens had come back and were circling overhead while the coyotes seemed to be slinking in from all directions, so much for not drawing too much attention.

As dry as it was, we surely raised a plume of dust as we made our way through the canyon. Without any hint of a breeze to move it along, the dust just hung in the air like a swarm of sand gnats. If anyone had been looking for us, we'd have been easy to spot.

A few hours later, we made it to the Chaco River. It wasn't much of a river in dry season but what little water there was, was wet and welcome. The river ran due west through the badlands so we just rode along the bank. We rode from sun up to dark out and pushed our horses and mules as much as we dared. We also kept a watchful eye on our back trail but saw no one following us.

After three days, we entered the foothills of the Chuska Mountains. The land gradually went from arid and flat to lush green and hilly. Pine and juniper trees were ever'where and I saw signs of bears, mountain lions, bobcats, coyotes and foxes. As we neared Wheatfield Lake, I spied a beaver dam, several raccoons and a porcupine. It was a whole different world from the badlands.

After a restful and restoring night by the lake, we pushed on to the east end of Canyon de Chelly. I was concerned about all the Navajos that lived in the canyon but Toho reassured me that most were peaceful farmers and sheepherders. The Treaty of 1868 had ended the constant fighting and only young renegades, like the ones we ran into, ever went out on the warpath. I double-checked the loads in my rifle and pistol just in case.

We entered the canyon by *Tsaile* Lake and rode at full gallop. Toho showed me some of the old Injun ruins in the Mummy Cave and the Big Cave as we proceeded down the *Canyon del Muerto*. Off to the south, he pointed out the sandstone pillar that was known as Spider Rock. He said it rose about eight hundred feet up from the canyon floor.

"The Navajo believe that Spider Woman lives on the top of that standing stone. They warn their young ones that she has been known to come down from the top on her web ladder and take away children that misbehave."

Toho had to laugh before continuing. "They also claim the top of the rock is white from the sun-bleached bones of children that were taken."

"You don't believe that hogwash do ya?."

"The Hopi believe that at the beginning of time, *Kotyangwuti*, the Spider Woman, controlled the underworld which was the home of the gods while the sun god, *Taiowa*, ruled the sky. Using only their thoughts, they created the Earth between those two worlds. She taught the people to plant, weave and make pottery. When sorcerers brought evil to the Third World, Spider Woman showed the people how to reach the Fourth World where we live to this day."

Toho didn't wait for my comment as he urged his horse to a faster pace. I looked around and found out why. We were being chased by a growing group of Navajos. Whether they were hostile or just curious, we weren't waiting around to find out.

We rode as fast as we could but our speed was limited by the pack mules so the riders kept gaining on us. Toho slowed his pace and released two of the ponies. As they headed off to our right, several of the pursuing warriors went after them. After another minute or so, Toho released two more of the ponies and the rest of the Navahos went after them. I reckon he had this all planned out before we left. Those ponies were a great prize for those Navajos and they got 'em without a fight.

We finally reached the mouth of the canyon and the Day and Damon trading post at *Chinle*. The new proprietor, Michael Donovan, was set up for bartering or *huuya* as Toho said it. After the usual haggling, he traded two of the remaining ponies for silver jewelry and rock candy. He said the candy was a treat for the children of his village and the jewelry was Hopi money or *siiva*. He refused all attempts to trade for the white pinto and made it clear he had special plans for that pony.

The next morning, we left *Chinle* heading west for four more days of hard riding. Toho remained a man of few words as we rode and at night, we were both too tired to talk much. He was only concerned with getting back to his people and I was just along for the ride. Luckily, we avoided contact with any other Navajos.

Our journey took us past Black Mountain and *Balukai* Mesa before entering the Hopi reservation and making our way to First Mesa and the Village of *Walpi*. It was situated atop a mesa some three hundred feet above the valley floor. Slowly and carefully, we climbed the steep slope of the mesa until we reached the flat top. We caused quite a stir as we rode in.  Men, women and children came from all directions to greet Toho and stare at the white stranger.  But to one man, I was no stranger and certain to be welcomed with open arms.

# CHAPTER II
# "Santa Fe, end of the trail"

**SPRING 1886**

Hopi Joe was standing in the middle of the village as we rode in. I'm certain he was equally proud and relieved that Toho had returned safely from his long journey. Word of our arrival spread like a wildfire and brought out the entire village to welcome us as well as inspect the gifts and trade goods we were delivering. What with all the whoopin' and hollarin', it felt like we were leading a parade.

I'd heard about the Hopi's pueblo villages but had never seen one. All the lodges seemed to be made of dried adobe and were connected on both sides to others. They were even stacked atop of one another. I reckoned that the door openings separated the rooms for each family.

After we dismounted, Toho made his way through the throng and was given a bear hug by his father. I stayed by the horses and mules while they spoke. I couldn't understand any of what they said but I gathered by the way Toho was gesturing and pointing at me that he was telling Hopi Joe ever'thing that happened. The noise quieted down as ever'one strained to hear his story and when he finished, a huge cheer went up from the crowd. They all went to celebratin' as Hopi Joe made his way to me and we embraced.

"It is good to see you, Mon-roe Henry. Toho tells me that you saved his life as your father saved mine. Our families are truly bonded by blood."

I wanted to explain what happened and I wanted to ask questions but there was no time as Toho started to distribute the gifts and trade goods and the party was on.

Amid all the celebrating, Toho lead his gray pony and the white pinto away from the frenzied crowd and hitched them near another pueblo lodge some thirty yards from where we were. He gazed back at me and nodded his approval and then went inside. A few moments later, he came out with what appeared to be a young Hopi woman; however she was wearing some kind of shawl that covered most of her so I couldn't tell for certain. It looked like he was presenting the pinto as a gift and she seemed very excited and receptive. In all the days we spent together, Toho had never mentioned anything about a having a woman but then again, neither had I.

When things settled down a bit, Hopi Joe lead me to his clan's *kiva* and we descended into the underground stone room where we were joined by many of the elders of the clan. We sat in a large circle around a fire pit and were served food and drink by young maidens in festive dress. I sat on one side of Hopi Joe while Toho, who finally joined us, sat on the other side. We were served a lamb stew made with hominy and green chilies along with a blue cornbread known as *piki*. After almost a month of eating my own trail cooking, I'd almost forgotten what good food tasted like but I caught on real quick and I ate 'till I was about to burst.

Ever'one was in the best of spirits and the air was alive with conversation but it was all in Hopi so I was kinda left out. Noting my discomfort, Toho spoke in English to his father.

"Henry does not understand, father, we should speak in his language."

Joe laughed and smiled at me. "Yes, we should. It has been a long time since I tried to teach him our language and I'm sure he does not remember."

I looked at Toho. "I remembered *wikwawa* didn't I?"

Toho paused before answering. "Yes you did and exactly when I wished to hear it. But you are more than a friend, Henry. You are my brother and I owe you my life."

Hopi Joe put his arms around both of us and said, "And now, I have two sons."

After all the eatin' and drinkin', Toho excused himself so Hopi Joe and I were finally alone. It was my turn to ask questions.

"Joe, Toho and I spoke of the time, twenty years ago, when you rescued me from the Navaho and presented me to my parents. He seemed to have heard a different story than the one I heard. What haven't I been told?"

Joe was taken aback by my question and seemed to consider his answer carefully. He bade me to sit beside him before speaking.

"It was not a different story, but perhaps a longer one. We already had two white children in our village before your parents saved my life. They were discovered in an abandoned wagon along with their dead parents. The man and woman had died from the fever and the children were taken with it. Whenever a traveling family got the fever, they were forced from the wagon train by their God-fearing companions and left to continue on their own. The two children, a boy and a girl, looked enough alike to be twins but the boy was older.

Hopi Joe paused again and lit his "cloud blower", which was nothing more than a short, funnel-shaped clay pipe.

"When I recovered from my wounds, I thought to give the boy child to your parents but he was weak from fever and near death. The girl was healthy but your mother wept for a lost son and not a daughter. When we heard of a white boy baby in the hands of the Navajo, I decided to steal him away. It was a simple thing to do as the Navajo left him alone with an old squaw. For a short time, there were three white children here until you were taken to the Henry family and the sickly boy died. Toho was also a small child at that time and played with you. You have truly been brothers since then."

I thought about what he said and remembered Toho had called me his white brother but that led to another question.

"What happened to the white girl?"

"We raised her to be one with us. Her name is Chosovi, the bluebird, to honor her blue eyes. She is to be joined with Toho now that he has returned from his journey."

Toho was getting hitched? Now that made sense. It figured that he brought back that pretty pinto pony as a wedding gift for her.

Sensing that my questions were answered, Hopi Joe had a few of his own.

"What about you, Mon-roe? What have you been doing these past four years? Your father says that he has not heard from you or your sister, Taylor, in a long time."

I tried to explain to Hopi Joe that I wasn't much for letters but Taylor had written to Pa. When she didn't get any letters back from him, she stopped. We just figured Pa wasn't much for letter writing either.

He nodded his understanding of what I said but his manner suggested that he didn't believe me. I assured him we were both doing well and the business was successful. He didn't seem to believe that either. I guess I was never much good at tellin tall tales. Pa always said honesty was in the eyes and mine were full of it.

I feigned weariness and Hopi Joe summoned a young warrior to take me to my sleeping quarters. He took me to a small building made out of what looked to be stone fragments bound together with mud plaster. The roof was made of pole battens and grass thatching which was covered with dry earth. The floor was hardened dirt and rock. He gave me a blanket and indicated that I was to sleep on that dirt floor.

I was tired but mostly, I wished to get away from Hopi Joe and his questions. His direct question about the last four years hit me betwixt the eyes like a hard left jab. Had it really had been four years since Taylor and I left the ranch and headed for Santa Fe?

## SUMMER 1882

Taylor and I had a rather uneventful journey from Flagstaff to Santa Fe. The weather was fair and we didn't have any unwanted run-ins with Injuns or critters. We talked about our past and our hopes about the future but except for the weather, we didn't talk about the present. I was really attracted to her and I sensed that she felt the same but our relationship was far too complicated. I guess we both figured that ever'thing would work out eventually.

Our last night before reaching Santa Fe was spent around a campfire with the wind blowing up a blue northern. The sky got a blue-black color and the temperature dropped like a chunk of granite tossed down a water well. Since it was still the summer season, we were caught unprepared and it felt like winter was upon us. So there we were, huddled together, wrapped up in a large Mexican blanket we were sharing, staring at the fire and finally forced to confront our feelings.

Once we got finished complaining about the weather change, we remained adrift in our own thoughts for a long while until I broke the silence.

"Do you think you'll be able to call me Henry rather than Monroe? It is bound to be confusing for awhile."

Taylor nudged me with her elbow in a playful way. "Yes... Henry, I'll do my very best to remember. Just don't ask me to become Taylor Charles. I'm staying Taylor Henry. I can still be your sister. We'll just say we had different fathers and that's the truth."

"You do realize that once folks in Santa Fe accept us as brother and sister, we can never be anything else....iff'n we'd ever have a mind to."

That sort of took Taylor by surprise and she had to chew on it for awhile.

"I never thought of that. What'll we do?"

I'd given this some thought but I wanted to see what Taylor might have to say.

"Well, we can go as friends or as total strangers. Either way, I'll see you have money to get by and a good place to stay but we'll certainly have to live apart."

I could see her mind going through all the different stories we'd have to tell and how hard it would be.

"Monroe, if we go as friends, we'll have to explain the hows and whens of our friendship. We'd have to lie like crazy and be good about it. I don't know if we could do all that."

"Well, first off, you'd have to get my name right. That might be the hardest part for you."

Taylor nudged me with her elbow again but it wasn't quite so playful.

"Oh, Henry… you know what I mean. Folks might not believe that we were just friends and the blue-nosed ladies of Santa Fe might think of me as a wanton woman instead of a chaste young lady. I think we should just go as brother and sister and be done with it."

"Wait. What if we enter town separately and act like total strangers? I could arrange to get money to you secretly and we could meet openly in a week or so and then become friends in front of everyone. Then no one in town could question your good moral character."

"I guess that would work but we'd have to be extra careful until we were formally introduced. Why aren't you worried about your moral character?"

"I don't plan to have one. Remember, I own a saloon and gamblin' casino so all the fine-feathered folks in town will already look down their blue noses at me."

"So if you're gonna be running all the drinkin' and gamblin', I would imagine there'll be some saloon girls and trollop's involved too. How do you intend to handle them?"

"As often as they'll let me."

With that comment, I received another elbow and got knocked clear out of the blankets. Taylor ignored the cold long enough to jump atop me and beat my chest with her fists. We ended up rolling around in the dirt and laughing like the brother and sister that we still were.

With the sun about half-set behind us, we finally rode into Santa Fe the next afternoon. As we rode in, we became aware of the snow capped Sangre de Cristo Mountains to the north and the sandy barren valley in which the city had been built. The buildings were a mixture of the different cultures that had dominated the area. There were small Indian-style pueblos with flat roofs and adobe construction, large Spanish *haciendas* with arched roofs, protective courtyards and large porches, and the odd mixture of Territorial designs brought by the recent American settlers. The streets, which were narrow and interrupted by many alleyways, fanned out from the central plaza. Taylor told me she had read all about the plaza and how it was once an old fort. It was set up at the end of the Spanish Royal Road to Mexico City which they called *El Camino Real*. I just figured it for the end of the Santa Fe and the Old Pecos Trails. She said they had some fancy buildings there like the Palace of Governors and the San Miguel Mission,

It had been a long three weeks on the trail and we were both more than eager to get out of the saddle and into a hot bath before sleeping in an honest-to-god bed. I'm just as sure that Goner and Domino were itching to get us off their backs and stable food was a big step up from the prairie grass and sage brush they'd been eating. We boarded them in the local livery and went out to see Santa Fe.

First off, we stopped at several boarding houses that advertised rooms for rent. Taylor went in by herself as I waited around outside. I felt kinda foolish but we'd agreed we shouldn't be seen together since we were pretending to be strangers. After finding them "too expensive" or "too dirty", she eventually found one to her liking above a dry goods store owned by a family named Olson. They told her they had recently arrived in Santa Fe from Sweden. Taylor said the room was clean and the couple was friendly enough and might have a job for her so she was satisfied. We said our good-bys and I headed in the direction of "St. Charles Place".

By now, the sun was full-set and there was just a whiff of dusk lighting my way. The streets were bustling with all manner of folks going about their business. To them, I was just another cowpoke looking for whiskey, women or both. I carried my saddle bags over my shoulder and my Henry rifle in my left hand. My right hand swung free over my Colt revolver. I felt comfortable and confident as I made my way through the crowd.

I could tell I was heading the right direction when I heard the boisterous piano playing and a rowdy crowd singing along. Although the evening was still young, St. Charles Place was already up and running for the evening. Knowing Charles, I would have expected nothing else. As I got closer, the noise got louder and louder and was about earsplittin' by the time I got to the front doors.

The gambling house was two stories tall and built in adobe style. It had a parapet roof and kinda looked like a smaller version of the Alamo Mission in San Antone. There was a narrow walkway down the left side of the building and a wooden boardwalk out front. The batwing doors swung freely as men walked in and out.

From where I was standing I could see the joint was packed wall to wall with drinkers and gamblers. A very large woman was behind the bar swapping drinks with the customers and a red-headed piano player was beatin' the keys. I couldn't figure out why ever'one was shouting at the top of their lungs until I moved a little to my right and saw what they were shouting about.

Two men were fightin', knuckle and skull, and were really going at each other. Customers kept moving in and about so it was hard for me to see but a tall heavy set white fella looked like he was getting' whipped by a short dark skinned man. The crowd was mostly white, Mexican and Indian but they all seemed to be backing the Negro. The big white guy, who was at least six foot-five and three hundred pounds, was decked out like a muleskinner and probably smelt like one. The dusky fella, who was about five-foot seven and maybe one hundred fifty pounds, was dressed all in black, with *conchos* on his vest and a fancy silver hatband on his flat-topped gamblers hat.

It was a classic fight; the puncher agin the boxer. The big fella charged around like a wounded buffalo swinging wildly while the little guy ducked and danced just out of reach. That reminded me of my old friend, "Chip" O'Leary, who taught me how to use footwork and defense to exhaust a bigger opponent. His instructions had served me well and seemed to be working here too. The big muleskinner was just plumb tuckered.

Ever so often, the Negro would hold his ground and counter punch but with little effect. The big fella was just too big. I figured that he might have to hit him with a table leg until a furious flurry of well aimed and well timed punches ended the affair with the burly white man flying over a faro table and through a plate glass window to end up face down in the street.

Half the damn crowd rushed out the doors to see if he'd get up and they liked to run me over. I stood there with the rest of 'em and waited. The beaten pugilist had the good sense not to get up although it might have been by condition and not by choice. After a few minutes the crowd got tired of waiting and most of 'em went back in the casino. Others simply drifted off into the night. I started to go in when I heard the barmaid's boomin' voice.

"Excitement's over boys, let's get back to drinking. The first round's on me."

A rousing cheer was followed by a mad dash to the bar. The portly barmaid was pouring shots and beers faster than a politician shaking hands on Election Day. I waited till the stampede died down and walked to the far end of the bar. I decided to be just another customer awhile before I told them who I was so I ordered a beer and sat back to watch the action.

From my saddle bags, I pulled out my copies of the letters Charles sent to his bar manager, Paddy O'Shea, and the pit boss, Beau Didlet. He made it clear to them that they held their jobs as long as they wished but if anything happened to him, I was his son and the new owner. I'd instructed my attorney, Cecil Abernathy, to send them notice of Charles' death and the notice that I was headed for Santa Fe. Reckon they were as curious and anxious about me as I was about them.

The casino had returned to normal with the faro tables and roulette wheels raking in the money while onlookers surrounded all the poker tables. The Negro fella settled in at one of the poker tables and graciously accepted congratulations for his boxing skills. Then he began shufflin' and mixin' the cards with the same skill he'd shown as a boxer.

I was wondering about my bar manager and pit boss. Where were they when this ruckus started? No one seemed to be in charge except for the burly barmaid. It made some sense that they weren't here yet since it was still early in the evening.

I was suddenly startled by the loud "bang" caused by the batwing doors being slammed inward against the door frame. There he was, the semi-conscious muleskinner, staggering back and forth in the doorway with a huge skinning' knife in his right hand. It seemed to me that the man was barely able to stand upright.

"I'm gonna skin me a nigger."

The crowd went drop dead silent for a moment and then the piano player let loose with a Cajun funeral dirge about saints marching in. The drunkards in the audience laughed and sang along but there was nothing funny about what was about to happen. The dusky card-slinger carefully rose from his chair and slowly stalked his wounded opponent. In a cat-like fashion, he moved ever nearer the doorway as he gauged the situation. All of a sudden like, the wobbly muleskinner seemed to black out and pitch forward to his hands and knees but the knife remained in his huge fist.

The crowd cheered the apparent victory and the victor raised his arms in triumph. When he turned away, the muleskinner stopped playing possum, rose to his knees and pulled back his arm to throw his knife. Quicker than lightning, the Negro reached behind his neck, pulled a pearl handled ice pick from his collar sheath and threw it with incredible accuracy. It went all the way through the big fellas right wrist. He screamed in pain, dropped his knife and tried in vain to remove the pick from his wrist.

In a deliberate fashion, the Negro fella took several steps forward and kicked the muleskinner full in the face. Blood and teeth went ever'where as the unconscious man went ass over teakettle backwards. The crowd was dead silent again and all eyes were on the two of them. The Negro placed his foot across the man's right arm and with some effort, pulled his ice pick free. Then he knelt beside the fallen man and started to wave the pick above his face. I wasn't sure what was about to happen but I wanted no part of it. I took a drink from my beer, laid my rifle on the bar and removed the leather thong on my pistol holster.

"I think that man got his due, why not let him be?"

Now all eyes were on me. I hadn't planned to interfere but I couldn't help myself. The muleskinner, no matter what he'd done, was out cold and helpless and I was the only one around that seemed willing to speak up for him.

The Negro still had his back towards me but he stopped waving the ice pick and considered his words carefully.

"I was just fixin' to carve my initials on his forehead. I wasn't gonna hurt him none."

I knew he wanted me to speak so he could judge where I was standing so I moved behind some other customers and started to circle him.

"Maybe you could have a few of the boys' drag him out of here and be done with it. You've proved your point and he's paid for his bad manners."

"Why should you care what happens to him?"

"I figure he's ugly enough without adding your initials to his facial features."

My attempt at humor relieved the tension a little as many of the customers choked back a nervous laugh. I was just about to enter his field of vision so I back tracked and kept moving.

"What do you say? You back off and we can all get back to drinkin' and gamblin'."

While he was considering, the barmaid spoke up. "I strongly suggest that you do as he suggests, 'Pick'."

She was cradling a Colt revolving shotgun like a baby in her arms and looked like she knew how to use it. I knew that gun to be a fearsome weapon holding five rounds of ten gauge shells in it. "Pick" tilted his head so he could see her and asked with a chuckle in his voice.

"When have I ever heeded your suggestions?"

The barmaid was quick to respond. "Well you better take this one, lad, 'cause I'm betting that you're going up agin our new boss man."

She shifted her gaze in my direction and smiled. "And I'd be mighty surprised if he wasn't real handy with that Colt revolver he's fondling."

"Pick" decided to heed her words and slowly returned his ice pick to its sheath. Then, he rose to his feet and turned to face me. He looked me up and down for a few seconds and then broke out his very best phony smile.

"Well I'll be damned, Paddy, I think you're right. He has Mister Charles' features as well as his annoying sense of fair play."

With that settled, the tension left the gambling hall like air from a balloon and folks starting babblin' all at once. Conversations flowered and drinks were downed as ever'thing returned to normal. The piano man started to play "The Jolly Beggar" and every Irishman in the crowd started to sing along. Four men dragged the muleskinner outside so I made my way back to my spot at the bar and took a long drink of my beer. "Pick" started play at all the gaming tables with a wave of his arm and reluctantly walked over to join me. The barmaid reached below the bar, pulled out a brand new bottle of Irish whiskey and blew the dust off it. Then she grabbed three shot glasses and made her way to where we were waiting at the far end of the bar.

The rotund woman opened the bottle with her teeth and poured three shots of the finest whiskey the joint had to offer. She pushed two of them towards us and raised hers in a toast.

I'm Paddy O'Shea and this here's Beau Didlet. He's also known lovingly by one and all as 'Pick'. And I'm guessing that you would be calling yourself Henry Charles."

"Just Henry to my friends and I'm proud to know ya both."

Beau and I shook hands slowly and deliberately before raising our glasses to join Paddy in her Irish toast.

"To Mister Farley Charles. Here's hoping he arrived in heaven an hour before the devil knew he was dead"

We finished our drinks and agreed to meet the next morning to discuss the business and look at the books. Beau said the right things and shook my hand but his look of defiance when he did so, spoke volumes. Our little dustup over the muleskinner was gonna eat on him. He might have been Charles' choice as pit boss but he wouldn't have been mine. When he returned to his poker game, I was left alone with Paddy.

"Please excuse my confusion but I was sort of expecting a Patrick O'Shea."

Paddy flashed a knowing smile and with a twinkle in her eye she answered. "Aye, so was my father. Of course me mum hoped for a Patricia. What they got was neither or both, depending on how you look at it."

She trudged down the bar and filled orders while cursing or cajoling the customers as she felt necessary. From the back she looked to be a man with her short hair, broad shoulders and bow-legged walk but head on, she looked like a fleshy angel with chubby cheeks, ample breasts and a twinkle in her eye. I wasn't sure what she meant about neither or both but one thing was certain; I'd never met anyone quite like her.

After making her rounds, Paddy returned to my end of the bar and poured herself another drink of the Irish whiskey and offered me a refill. Knowing my limited capacity for hard liquor, I respect-fully declined her offer.

She downed the drink in one gulp and poured herself yet another. "Just leaves more of this amber colored joy juice for me."

Paddy swallered the second drink and wiped her mouth with the back of her hand. She stared at me for a few seconds as if she were trying to read my mind or perhaps look into my soul.

"So what happened to Mister Charles? The letter we got from your fancy lawyer fella just said he was dead… and you were com-ing here to take over."

I kept my answer short and to the point. "Sore loser shot him dead across a poker table."

Paddy put the cork back in the bottle and picked up all three glasses in one beefy hand. "Bet the darlin' man was trying to talk his way out of it wasn't he?"

"Yup."

She slammed down the bottle and the three glasses on the bar. "If I told him once, I told him a thousand times that some cowardly bastard would shoot him if he didn't shoot first. What happened to the cowardly bastard?"

"He's dead."

Paddy started back down the bar but turned to face me. "By your hand?"

I took a long draw of my beer which finished the glass. "Yup"

Paddy nodded her agreement and went back about her business. She was gone for awhile and returned with two small kegs of beer, one under each arm. I finished my beer as I watched the gambling and drinking that was going on. Beau seemed to be in full charge of the gaming as he kept a sharp eye on all the tables. The dealers were well aware of his attention and looked to be uneasy because of it. His gaze passed me several times but he showed no reaction or acknowledgement.

When Paddy returned to my end of the bar she brought me another draft beer, mounted a stool behind the bar with some effort and sighed, "Time to take a load off."

When I didn't comment, she seemed to get irritated. "Have ya got nothing to say, laddy?"

"Well, I'm here to learn and I've found that learnin' comes faster from listening than with talking."

"Well you certainly weren't blessed with your father's Irish tongue. He had *Bua na cainte*….the gift of gab. You're sitting there as quiet as a stone."

Paddy continued to study my face but the corners of her mouth looked like they wanted to smile. She sure was right about Charles; His mouth ran like an unstoppered whiskey keg at an Irish wake.

"That's true enough but few have his gift."

"*Aye*, he was an exceptional man....Mister Charles Ulster Farley."

Her use and knowledge of Charles real name took me by surprise. Charles said that he had used the name Farley Charles ever since he settled in Santa Fe. That was why his gambling casino was named St. Charles Place and why I had taken the name Henry Charles.

"Who else knows his real name?"

"No one 'cept for little ol' me. Your Father and I were very close, you know."

Paddy enjoyed her advantage and milked the situation. "Let's just say that there is very little I didn't know about your Sainted Father. And... there is very little that I do know about you."

"What else can you tell me about Charles?"

Paddy considered her options and then continued with a sigh of resignation. "When Charles came to Santa Fe, he was without resources other than his horse and rifle. He was forced to work the streets with a thimble-rig to earn his keep.

My questioning face led her to explain further.

"It's a street scam using three thimbles and a cork button. You might have seen it done with three walnut shells and a pea. However manipulated, the shell game is the same the world over. Since the Indians hereabouts had never seen it, your Father made a decent living teaching 'em the finer points.

Once he had a stake, Charles worked off a table in local saloons. He had quite the nimble fingers and gave up the shells to deal 'Three Card Monte'. His Irish tongue and fine Southern manners put men at ease while he picked their pockets."

Again, I was confused and Paddy knew it.

"Don't ya know a thing about the sweet science of gaming? 'Three Card Monte' is just a version of the old shell game using cards instead of thimbles or shells. We Irish call it 'Find the Lady' and the French call it *Bonneteau* but it's all the same. The dealer, or 'tosser', starts with three cards, one of which is a queen. The cards

are shown to the player, or 'punter', as they call him, and then thrown
face down on the table. The dealer tosses the cards back and forth
while the punter tries to watch the card he thinks is the queen. Then
the 'punter' is invited to bet on which card is the queen. It seems an
easy game and the poor sucker is often allowed to win some small
wagers. The 'tosser' congratulates and cajoles him into making ever
bigger bets until the last hand where he loses everything."

Paddy knew what she was talking about and I was an eager
listener.

"Charles put together a team to work the scam. That's how we
all got together. Beau acted the part of his shill. He would place
bets and Charles would allow him to win so others 'punters' thought
the game could be beaten. I was the roper and lookout. I encouraged suckers to try the game by telling 'em how easy it was to win
and kept an eye out for trouble. We had a big tough bloke named
Manfred to handle unhappy losers but one night, he got stabbed by
one of 'em and died. That's when Charles gave up the con games
and went to playing straight poker."

Paddy got up to serve a few customers and came back with another beer for me. I was still working on my second and could
certainly feel its effect. She seemed to be enjoying our conversation
so I continued with my questions.

"How did Charles happen to team up with Beau?"

"Monsieur Beau Didlet pretends to be of French Creole descent
from the island of Martinique but he's naught but a lousy Cajun half-
breed from the bayous of Louisiana. I hear tell his father caught and
killed alligators for a living. Stabbed 'em in the head with an ice
pick wouldn't ya know? His legal name is Otha Bates but don't you
ever whisper a word of it to him. He's real partial to Beau or Pick.

No matter, he grew up with the cons, scams and swindles of
his people and was well aware of the shell game that Charles was
running. Beau actually beat Charles by 'picking the pea' so they decided to become partners. They needed each other and were a good
team but they never really got along. Charles was raised in the old
South and wasn't all that comfortable with a Negro partner while

Beau doesn't cotton to taking orders from any white man. Take it from me, laddie, the day was acomin' when there would have been a violent split in that partnership."

Suddenly, Paddy was talking like a round boulder rolling down a steep slope. She kept picking up speed and the stories came fast and furious. Some were funny, some weren't, but all of the tales had one thing in common. They made it perfectly clear she was trying to warn me about Beau. He'd survived a hard life by being cunning, cautious and unbelievably cruel. She seemed certain he wasn't about to let anyone or anything stop him from whatever goal he'd set his sights on.

For my part, I couldn't see why Charles ever partnered up with him. Guess it made sense with the shell game and just continued when Charles got his gambling hall. From Paddy's way of looking at it, Charles never liked or trusted him and kept him on a short leash. I reckoned I was obliged to do the same.

When Paddy finally ran out of her stories, I got a word in edgewise.

"Well, now I know about Beau but how about you? How did you get involved with Charles?"

Paddy folded her arms and leaned back on her stool. She was sporting a wide grin like a mouse-fed alley cat.

"Now that's a lovely story that I'd be glad to tell but then you'll have to tell about James Monroe Henry."

Her use of my real name really took me by surprise. How the hell did she know that? Unable to speak, I just finished my second beer and nodded in agreement.

Relishing her victory, Paddy commenced with her tale.

"As I told you before, Father wanted a son to carry on his name and bloodline. Since I was only four years old when me mum died, he decided to raise me as the son he would never have. He cropped my hair and dressed me like a young lad so I could work the potato fields with all the other men and boys. Even though I grew big and strong like I am now, I was forever being taunted by the other lads. It was hard being a girl while trying to live like a boy.

When I reached the change at thirteen, I'd had enough and told everyone, including my dear Father, that I was going to dress and act like a young woman. He responded by sending me to a convent. As you might expect, I wasn't exactly accepted there, either. Sister Mary Margaret did her Catholic best to beat both genders out of me but failed miserably. After less than a year, I ran off to face the world on my own but by then; Ireland was in the grip of the Great Potato Famine so there were no jobs to be had and even less hope of ever finding one. I'll wager you didn't know that almost one fourth of all the people in Ireland left during that awful time?

In the spring of 1847, at the tender age of fifteen, I boarded a 'coffin' ship bound for British North America. After almost three months on the bloody ocean, we finally landed in Quebec but about half of the passengers were ill with typhus and cholera so they quarantined our ship at Grosse-Isle. I pretended to be dying from the fever so that my fellow passengers, acting like the good Irish Catholics they were, could throw me into the St. Lawrence River. Once they did, I swam ashore, stole a small boat and rowed across that freezing river to freedom in America. That's how I got to your country, laddie."

The more she talked, the more I drank of my third beer. I was so intrigued by her story that I ignored my strict rule about alcohol intake. I was drinking way too much, way too fast.

Paddy paid me little mind as she continued with her story. "I wandered around New England for almost ten years without finding a true home, real friends or a grand purpose. Sometimes I appeared as a young man and sometimes as a young woman. Both sides of the coin suited me and let me tell you I never heard a complaint from any of those I bedded....nosiree bob."

That thought sent me to drinking 'til I drained that third beer. Right then I understood why she said her parents got both or neither. Without dropping a line from her ramblin' tale, Paddy brought me yet another beer and slammed it down on the bar with enough force to splash foam all over me.

"Some upstanding Puritans in Massachusetts took exception to my way of life and encouraged me to head south so I dressed up like a man, got work as a deck hand on a river boat and headed down the Ohio River to the Mississippi. I ran the river for about five years and loved the life. I ate, drank, fought and loved like a man and held my own with the best of 'em. Thought I'd stay that way forever till '62 when the Union Army tried to draft me. I got away from the recruiters in Cincinnati by dressing like a woman and found kitchen work aboard the 'Sultana'. Glory, what a wondrous steamer she was. We traveled the Mississippi from St. Louie to New Orleans and back again. Since it was during the war years, we were commissioned by the War Department to carry troops and supplies so you might say I did get drafted after all."

Paddy laughed at her own yarnin', got up and went back down the bar to serve customers once again. I was trying to keep up with her stories but the beer and whiskey were having an effect on my concentrating. I did, however, take notice that Beau walked outside and was gone for about five minutes and wondered what could divert his attention from the games.

It sure seemed to me like Paddy was taking the long way 'round to answer my original question. Before she finally answered it, I got to hear all about the explosion that sank the "Sultana" on April 27, 1865. Since that one month saw the end of the Civil War, the assassination of President Lincoln and the death of John Wilkes Booth, like most Americans, I'd never heard of the "Sultana" disaster. Paddy said about eighteen hundred passengers and crew died that awful night. Most all of the passengers were Union soldiers returning home after the war. Many were just released from Confederate prison camps like Cahawba and Andersonville and were severely weakened by their incarceration. Paddy was one of very few who survived and she spent time recovering in a Memphis hospital. Although the official report called it an accident, she was certain it was the final act of some diehard rebel sympathizers who couldn't accept the fact that the war was finally over.

Then wouldn't you know, she hired on as a man again.  This time it was with the Union Pacific Railroad and she was present when they drove the Golden Spike in Promontory, Utah on May 10, 1869. Her life story was sounding like a history lesson.  At long last, she made it to Santa Fe and met Charles.

"Charles was still working the streets with Beau when I first saw him.  He was such a beautiful man that I dressed in my best womanly garb to attract his attention but he would never give me an eye. I was so tickled by the smooth and easy way he trimmed the suckers that I took to steering 'em to him anyway.  That's when he took notice of my assistance and hired me as a roper.  Heaven knows I'd have done it for free but getting paid to work with Charles was about the best thing that ever happened to me.

Paddy finished her story about the same time I found the bottom of my fourth glass of beer.  She took it from my numbing fingers and fetched me another.  The look on her face made it clear that it was now my turn.

"Now I want to hear all about James Monroe Henry and how he became Henry Charles, the owner of this fine establishment.  And since we're speaking of it, you should dress the part.  Get outta them cowboy duds and dress like the fine young gentleman that you are."

If her intention had been to get me drunk before my turn to answer questions, then she almost got her wish.  I was still aware of what I said but I was having trouble getting it out.  I reckon thinking clearly while speaking seemed to be out of the question.

"I grew up as Monroe Henry.  I never knew about Charles or our... relationship."

I got the giggles as I thought about how Charles and I really did get together.  Paddy sat back, folded her arms and frowned at me. She was intent on information and felt I was just fooling with her.

"The Pinkertons found out that I was a sage-brush orphan... (Burp) ....so they notified Charles and we met in Animas City.  Seems he had 'em looking for me ever since I got taken by the Navajos....

some twenty years ago.... and that's how I became his son... (Burp) ...until he died and left me this here saloon." (Giggles again)

Paddy wasn't exactly thrilled with my drunken response and pushed for more. "You said you shot the man who killed him?"

"Dat's right. Shot him two or tree times...I forget." (Burp)

Paddy finally gave up and laughed at my clumsy attempt to speak.

"Well there's one thing for certain; you can't hold your liquor like Charles could. Are you sure you're Irish?"

"Why I'm as Irish as Paddy's pig." (More giggles) "Have you got a pig?"

Being a big hearted Irish barmaid, Paddy couldn't stay mad at me. After all, she was the one who got me drunk in the first place. She pulled the half-glass of beer from my hands, slapped a key down on the bar and pointed to the second floor above us.

"I think you should call it a night. Charles' room is the first door on the right at the top of the stairs out back. This here's the key. You'll have to walk around to the right, down the alley and up the back stairs."

I was in total agreement with her and picked up my rifle and saddle bags as best I could. As I started for the front doors, Paddy had one last story to share.

"Just so you know, laddie. Charles was more than me boss and friend: he saved my life a few years back and I am forever beholdin' to him and his. You'll find me backing any play you make in this place."

I nodded my understanding and walked through the doors and down the slat-board sidewalk. I could feel Beau's eyes watching every step I took until I rounded the building and headed down the alley.

The moon was full bright so I could see where I was going but in my condition, I missed the body lying crosswise ahead of me and stumbled right over it. If I hadn't been so drunk, the stench would have warned me in plenty of time. The body had to be the mule-skinner and he was surely dead. I rolled him over to be certain and was instantly sick and sober. He'd been filleted and gutted from his gonads to his tonsils like a catfish headed for the fry pan. From the look of agony on his death face, it figured that he'd been alive and aware the whole time. It'd been done with his own blood soaked knife which lay under his body along with bits and pieces of his entrails.

Now I'd seen a lot of men die but never this level of cruelty and brutality. I gagged and retched over the body until I had nothing more to give. Whoever did this had a tab to pay and right then and there I felt obliged to collect.

# CHAPTER III

# "Hopi days are here again"

**SPRING 1886**

The thought of the gutted muleskinner woke me from dreams and brought me to my senses. I found myself wrapped in a woolen blanket, lying on the dirt floor in a small room with no windows. Moonlight snuck through the doorway to reveal the starkness of the interior. It was certain the Hopi didn't believe in providing grand lodgings for their visitors.

The cold floor and thin blanket made going back to sleep somewhat difficult and the vision of the gutted body just added to my discomfort. I was also concerned about lying to Hopi Joe. It wasn't that I didn't want to tell him the truth; I guess I just didn't want to face it myself. I no longer owned St. Charles Place and Taylor was no longer my sister or even my friend. If I couldn't actually admit the truth to myself how could I recount it to anyone else?

A slight rustle in the wind and a faint shadow across the moonlight made me aware of someone's presence outside my doorway. I had no reason to fear anyone in the Hopi village and could not imagine who else would be there but I located my pistol and loosened it in the holster as a matter of common sense.

"Monroe Henry… are you awake?"

It was a whispered voice and definitely female. I had absolutely no idea who she could be.

"Yes, I am now."

"My name is Chosovi. I need to speak with you."

I remembered Hopi Joe saying she was the white girl raised by the Hopi. She had blue eyes like mine and was supposed to be getting hitched with Toho. I couldn't wait to meet her.

"Well, come in."

There was a pause for a few seconds that made me wonder if she was still there outside the doorway but then she answered.

"No, it would not be proper for me to be in a room alone with you. I should leave."

I crawled over to the doorway and leaned against the inside wall so that we would be closer since we were both speaking in a whisper and it was difficult to hear.

"Then why come here at all? What did you want to tell me?"

"Toho and I will be joined tomorrow. He has asked that you be allowed to stand by my side during the ceremony as befitting a member of my family. Since my Hopi parents have passed and you are the only other white person here, it would be acceptable to the people."

"I would be honored to stand up for you and Toho. Is that all you wanted to tell me?"

"No, there is more."

This time there was a longer pause and I waited like a buzzard over a dried up water hole. Whatever she wanted to say, it was taking her a while to get up the courage to say it."

"Toho thinks that you are my family. That you are my born brother."

That hit me like a horse hoof in the head. That's what Toho wasn't telling me before. He thought that Charles' son was the one who had died. Before I could ask more questions, a small package wrapped in oil cloth was tossed into the room and Chosovi vanished as quickly and quietly as she had appeared.

When I opened the oil cloth, I found a small leather bound journal or diary. The cover seemed to be in pretty good shape but the pages were old and brittle. I tried to make out the writing but the scant light provided by the sliver moon wasn't enough to allow for reading. No matter, it could wait till morning. I wrapped up in the blanket and tried desperately to go to sleep but my mind was alive with conflicting images. I tried to concentrate on Toho, Chosovi and the old journal but I still couldn't shake the image of the gutted muleskinner as I tried to go back to sleep.

## SUMMER 1882

When I finished with all the puking and retching, I staggered around the back of the building and up the stairs. Following Paddy's directions, I stuck the key in the first door on the right at the top of the stairs. The door creaked open to reveal a rather large anteroom or parlor area. It was occupied by an ornate oak desk, three matching chairs and a small settee. A separate door opened to an adjoining bedroom which featured a huge canopy bed with numerous feather pillows and a royal blue bedspread. There was another door on the far side of the room but it turned out to be a closet. I'd only seen one other bed like that one and it was in a whorehouse in Animas City. Charles sure lived high on the hog.

Someone had kept the room clean and fresh as if awaiting his return. There was fresh water in the ewer and a porcelain wash basin that I made immediate use of. I cleaned up the best I could and headed back down to the casino. This time I stepped around the body without further complications.

When I passed through the front doors, Beau and Paddy were at the back of the bar and involved in what looked to be an argument. They stopped quarreling when they saw me come in but I could see they weren't finished with whatever they'd started. Beau returned to his poker game without a word or glance as Paddy rushed to the beer keg to pour me a glass. I stopped her with a wave of my hand and shouted as loud as I could.

"I just stumbled over the body of the muleskinner out in the alley. He's dead now but he was alive when somebody gutted him like fresh kill. No man deserves to die like that. Whoever did this is an inhuman monster that must be caught and brought to trial. I'm

offering one hundred dollars for information that leads to the capture and the conviction of the killer."

That brought a loud cheer from the crowd and a stampede for the
doors to see the corpse. Those that made it to the body had the same
reaction I had and the whole thing turned into a fiasco. The vomit-
ing, cursing and shouting were clearly heard inside the casino where
Beau, Paddy and I were the only ones remaining. I walked over to
the bar to confront Paddy.

"If I remember right, you said you'd back any play I made in
here. Are you with me now?"

Paddy was quick to respond. "Yes, indeed. What you describe
is beyond even my rather macabre imagination."

I turned to face Beau who had not moved from his table. "How
about you?"

After he gave his answer due consideration, he stood up and
spoke in a measured voice.

"That man was a feral pig but as you say, no one deserves that
kind of death. I will help you find the killer and see justice done."

With that pronouncement, he downed his drink and walked out
into the street. I turned back to Paddy who was fondling her shotgun
behind the bar.

"What can you tell me about that skinner?"

"Nothing much, lad. I just know his name was Leonard and he
fought with the Confederacy. Whenever he got drunk enough, he'd
brag about volunteering to fight with the Rebs when they invaded
New Mexico back in '61."

"The Confederates attacked New Mexico?"

"You didn't know? They came out of Texas and were led by Lt.
Colonel John Baylor. Their whole campaign lasted almost a year and
took about thirteen hundred lives. They captured Albuquerque and
Santa Fe and even set up their own territory capital in Mesilla. Their
grand scheme to attack Denver and the gold fields of Colorado came
to an end at the Battle of Glorieta Pass. The blue bellies sent them
running back to Texas. Some folks call that battle the 'Gettysburg
of the West'."

"Well thanks for the history lesson and for covering my bet. It's good to have you and your scattergun watching my backside."

Paddy fondled the Colt shotgun and smiled at me. "This little darlin' has been known to leave an oozy corpse too."

I was about to leave when something else came to me out of my drunken memories.

"I also seem to recall that you said Charles saved your life. How did he manage to do that?"

Paddy seemed hesitant but after putting down her shotgun and fussing with the bar top, she confessed.

"Most times in Santa Fe I dress in women's clothes and get along famously with the boys, especially if they've had a wee bit too much to drink. One night, however, I got ahead of myself and let one of 'em get too handy too soon if you get my drift. Well, right off, he found the extra plumbing… and… well, he got mad as a wet wildcat and with the help of his drunken friends; they tried to string me up. There I was, swinging from a sturdy tree limb when darling Charles comes along and cuts me down."

Paddy grabbed the ample flesh around her neck to reveal an ugly rope burn and proudly proclaimed, "Tis mighty lucky I had my three chins to protect me."

I was shocked by her frankness but amused by her silliness. She certainly was one of a kind or should that be two of a kind?

"It wasn't all for naught, laddie, don't you see? Now when I dress like a man and the ladies ask if I was hung, I can say yes and mean it."

Her raucous laughter faded away from my memory as I finally drifted off to sleep.

## SPRING 1886

The morning sunlight crept slowly across the dirt floor from the doorway to my face with just enough warmth to wake me up. I sat up with a start and tried to figure out where I was. The hard floor and thin blanket brought me back to reality. Further proof was provided by the leather bound journal that had served as my pillow. I wanted to talk with Toho and Chosovi but I had to read through the journal first.

The entries started on March 14, 1862. They detailed the travels of the Hiram Clifton family from the south side of Chicago. Hiram had a wife Johanna and two young children, William and Hillary. William was almost a year old and Hillary was a newborn of six weeks. Like thousands of other desperate souls, they sold or packed-up everything they owned and headed for "Californy" in hopes of finding a new and better life for themselves and their children.

Hiram kept track of every detail involved with their trip. Guess he'd figured it would make for good reading in future years. I paged through his descriptions of their travels from Chicago to Franklin, Missouri and on to Independence. There, they joined up with a wagon train led by a fella named Seth Adams. They paid dear for all their supplies as the market was best described as *caveat emptor* or buyer beware. Johanna had to discard much of her furniture, including her grandmother's cedar hope chest, to allow space for sufficient foodstuffs and water. No mention was made of them carrying any medical supplies which I was certain they would come to regret.

The trail led west across Kansas to Southeast Colorado before heading south into New Mexico territory. Sometime after leaving Santa Fe, the train was hit by prairie fever and the Clifton's wagon, along with several others, were forced to leave the train. William was stricken first and then little Hillary. Towards the end, Hiram wrote that he and Johanna had the fever too and were afraid they would all die from it.

The last entry, written by Johanna, spoke sadly of Hiram's death but ended on the optimistic note that the children seemed to be getting better. That entry was dated simply as August 1862 since she had no idea of the actual day.

It was pretty clear that after Johanna died, probably of fever, the children were found by the Hopi. The timeline was right and everything seemed to fit. The only thing left to chance was which boy child died and which one was taken to the Henrys. Hopi Joe was the only one that would know for certain.

I was about to leave my room when I heard what sounded like cries of alarm. I couldn't understand the words but I could tell they were warning the camp about something. The village came alive with Hopi men, women and children running every whichaway. Desperately, I searched through the chaos for Hopi Joe and Toho. When I found them, they were standing on the rim of the mesa along with a group of warriors and elders. I stood off to one side and waited while they talked over whatever was bothering everyone.

My curiosity finally got the better of me and I managed a glimpse down to the valley floor to see the source of all the ruckus. There were about forty or fifty Navajo warriors sitting atop ponies and they were made up for war. The leader was out front and waving his battle lance in the air as he shouted to the others. He was wearing the same style of cavalry hat that I'd seen before.

It didn't take a wise man to figure what was happening. Toho and I had left a clear trail across the Navajo reservation and there were a bunch of dead Navajos on the other end of that trail. We had brought more than treasure to the village; we'd brought fighting trouble too.

Toho finally took notice of me and broke away from the others. His face was a mixture of fear and anger.

"The Navajo have come for us, Henry. They followed our trail from Chaco Canyon. Somehow, they found the bodies of the young Navajo warriors we left behind and are demanding that both of us be turned over to them."

"Will they attack the village if your people don't turn us over?"

"No. Right now, they're trail-worn and would normally wait a day or two before mounting an assault. They are also aware that they would lose too many warriors trying to scale our mesa. I think they will simply surround the area to prevent us from getting food and water. It is the dry season and they know we have limited supplies of both. We must agree to their demands, fight them or die slowly from starvation and thirst."

Those choices were unacceptable to me. There had to be another way to handle the situation. If they wouldn't attack our position, maybe we could attack theirs.

"Maybe we could wait until darkness and surprise them. You and I could…"

Toho stopped me with a wave of his hand. "No, the elders wish to talk to them first and see what can be arranged. We are first a people of peace, not war."

"You know, for a couple of peaceful Hopis, you and your father are awful good at making war."

"The name Hopi comes from *Hopitu* which means peaceful people. We fight when necessary but never by choice."

I backed away from the group and watched from a respectful distance. After much discussion, one of the elders, accompanied by a young warrior, made the long descent down the side of the mesa and met with the leader of the Navajos. All of the other Hopis went about their usual business while Toho and I kept our eyes on the scene below. As I watched, I couldn't help wondering about the cavalry hat but I didn't have to wonder for very long. When the pow-wow was finally over, the elder came back and explained that the Navajo chieftain, *Ahiga*, was here to avenge the death of his son. That explained the hat.

The elder also said that only about a dozen of the Navajo were actually warriors. The rest were basically farmers and herdsmen that were forced to join the chase and they weren't any too happy about waiting for us to run out of food and water. They had crops and herds to take care of not to mention their families. The elder thought they might be willing to accept a tribute or gift in exchange for giving up the attack but Ahiga was adamant. For now, the talking was over.

Toho and I sat together at the edge of the mesa and talked about our options. Ever'thing we thought of seemed to be way too dangerous for us and the tribe. It was certain that as long as the Navajo leader was alive, he would continue to seek revenge and was willing to die to get it.  It remained to be seen if the others would endure a siege and stay as well motivated.

Soon enough, it was past midday and as the shadows started to lengthen, the tension mounted. Hopi Joe met with the elders and they counseled us on our options but made it clear that in the end, it was our decision to make.  The entire village watched and waited for us to decide what we were going to do.  There had to be a way to encourage the Navajos to leave but what was it?

All the while we were talking; I paid keen attention to the movements of the Navajo and finally got an idea.  Toho listened to my plan and agreed so while I went to fetch my Henry rifle, he gathered two lodge poles and some rawhide straps.

The Navajo encampment was about one hundred-fifty yards away which was way beyond the practical range of almost any rifle. Our three hundred foot elevation made a difference, but the 215 grain, 44 rim fire cartridges from a Henry would drop like a stone after about a hundred yards so we had to get closer by climbing part way down the mesa.   Next, we strapped the lodge poles into a large letter "X" which allowed me to cradle the barrel of the Henry in the crotch.  That shooting stand would help me gauge the drop of the bullets and hopefully hit what I was aiming at.

We never intended to shoot at the Navajos as that just figured to make things worse.  Instead, I was pretty sure I could cause a ruckus with their animals seeing they had a small *remuda* of extra ponies and pack mules that was probably within range.  I took careful aim about five feet above my target and pulled the trigger.  The bullet fell well short but ricocheted off a flat rock and did its job anyway. The sound of the shot and the whine of the ricochet scared the mules half to death.  They started snorting and honking which made the ponies fearful.

My second and third shots hit at the feet of the animals and managed to turn frenzy into chaos.  The pack mules started bucking off their bundles of supplies and water sacks.  The sacks broke open and the water was trampled into mud along with corn meal, beans and fry bread.  Many of the horses slipped their tethers and raced away in panic. Most of the Navajos swarmed the make-shift corrals to calm their animals but the few that had rifles starting shooting in our direction. Luckily, we were out of their range too and their bullets fell well short of our position. We beat a hasty retreat and watched the fun from the top of the mesa.

It took the better part of an hour for the Navajo to retrieve their ponies and quiet the rest of their stock. They had lost most, if not all, of their water and supplies and many of the warriors seemed pretty upset about it. Ahiga was running back and forth between different groups trying to retain control of the group and reassure them. He was losing his grip on his war party and he knew it. They could always forage for what they needed but their siege of our mesa had surely gotten a lot more complicated.

As the afternoon wore on, we watched as the struggle for dominance continued in the Navajo encampment. Finally, a large group of forty or more mounted up as if they were preparing to leave. The chieftain seemed to be pleading and threatening them but to no avail. As a final measure of his desperation, Ahiga mounted his horse and charged our position by himself. While screaming at the top of his lungs, he rode to the base of the mesa to display his courage. He wheeled his horse back and forth while being careful not to remain in one place long enough to present an easy target.

Toho seemed to think of something and raced back to his adobe. Quick as a wink, he returned with the Spencer rifle he'd collected from the dead Navajo. He handed the rifle to me and said "Ahiga means he who fights. He will never stop coming for us. If we are to live; he must die."

Toho was right. The only thing driving the Navajos was their chieftain's blind quest for revenge. As long as he was alive, we would always be in danger.

We set up the lodge poles on the edge of the mesa. Down below our elevated perch, the crazed Navajo clan leader continued to ride back and forth as if daring us to try to stop him. Since the Spencer had an overall range of five hundred yards and an effective range of two hundred yards, he was well within reach but his constant motion made an accurate shot very difficult.

Again, Toho sensed the problem and came up with an inspired solution. He picked up my Henry rifle and fired three rounds a quickly as he could. They landed well short of their target and seemed to embolden the Navajo chieftain. Ahiga reined in his pony and came to a complete halt with his arms raised in triumph. That's when I took a deep breath and slowly pulled the trigger of the Spencer. My aim was true and his chest seemed to explode with the impact. His lifeless body flipped ass backwards off the back of his pony.

Just like that, it was over. After a few minutes, two Navajo warriors came forward to retrieve his body and within an hour, they all rode off in the direction of their reservation. All that remained of the explosive standoff was a rumpled cavalry hat lying in the dust.

Once again, Toho and I were heroes to the Hopi people. Another celebration was hastily planned to mark the victory over the hated Navajo. Hopi Joe was beaming with pride in his two sons. I was just relieved that ever'thing worked out like it did. In all the excitement, I'd almost forgotten about my talk with Chosovi and the journal of the Clifton family.

The elders decided to hold the joining ceremony along with the victory party so Toho and Chosovi became the center of everyone's attention. They certainly made a handsome couple as they came before the council of elders. Toho wore a white wedding robe with a large white belt and white deerskin moccasins. They were topped off with colorful beaded necklaces and a white string tying up his hair. Chosovi was decked out like an Injun princess. She wore a similar white robe and belt but hers had a red stripe on the top and bottom. She also had white buckskin leggings and moccasins but her hair was held with a red string. Her light brown hair was waist length and braided in traditional Hopi style. She was absolutely beautiful and it was easy to see why Toho thought I was her brother as we did share many of the same features. Our height, pale skin, blue eyes and light colored hair really stuck out in the Hopi village.

During the ceremony, I stood next to Chosovi as a member of her clan or family would have. I couldn't help but wonder if I really could be her brother. Was it possible that I wasn't Charles' son after all? The suspense was killing me and the ceremony seemed to last forever. When it finally ended, the real celebrating began and I was swept away in the festivities. Toho and Chosovi left the gathering but I stayed put and was treated as an honored guest and given the best of ever'thing. I tried to speak with Hopi Joe but he always seemed to be surrounded by well-wishers. I caught his eye and he nodded as if he knew my thoughts but he never made an attempt to speak with me.

A young girl named Kaya kept me company and well supplied with food and drink. She seemed very young and unsure of her English so she spoke very little but I caught her constantly staring at me. I thought of it as a young girl's crush on a stranger but then it dawned on me. In her eyes and the eyes of her people, she wasn't a little girl but a young woman and I was a young man without a woman. She was even wearing her hair in a style that Toho called the "squash blossom" to show she was of age. To make things worse, I was being treated as a hero by the entire village and an honored member of their clan had just married a white woman. I was struggling with this new situation when a blood-curdling scream brought my thoughts and all the celebrations to an abrupt end.

I whirled around and saw a Hopi warrior staggering towards us with an arrow in his back. Behind him, in the shadows, I saw about a half dozen figures fanning out in an attempt to encircle the village. The Navajos were back.

The scene became total chaos as people seemed to be running in all directions at the same time. Everyone was screaming or yelling at the top of their lungs. My first instinct was to draw my Colt but I became suddenly aware that I wasn't armed. I'd left my pistol and rifle in my sleeping quarters.

I raced in sheer panic to get them as the conflict began in earnest. Gunshots rang in my ears and screams of pain and terror echoed through the adobe walls. I grabbed the Colt and Henry and ran back to fight the raiders. I was racked with guilt. This terrible attack was my fault. I'd brought the horrors of war to these people of peace.

The first Navajo I saw was shouldering a rifle and aiming at a Hopi warrior. Without waiting to stop and aim, I fired the Henry from my hip so the shot was low but it stirred up enough dust to scare him as he lowered his rifle and ran for cover. My second round was better considered and hit him in the back of his right leg. He tripped, hit the ground, rolled over and tried to aim his rifle in my direction. My third shot tore a chunk out of his skull.

Another Navajo made an attempt to retrieve the rifle and I put two bullets in his chest. I was so intent on what I was doing I plumb forgot how exposed I was. As I whirled around looking for more targets, I saw a muzzle flash at the same time I felt a burning pain in my right shoulder just below my armpit. At that moment, I was more scairt than hurt but I dropped the Henry and reached in my waist band for my Colt with my left hand. Luckily, I tripped over the body of a fallen Hopi just in time to avoid a second round that whizzed over my head.

Staying as low as I could, I fired my Colt in the general direction of the muzzle flash. All around me there were hand to hand battles going on and the screaming and yelling was deafening. I spotted another Navajo perched atop a wounded Hopi warrior and about to scalp him alive. I had a clear shot so I took it and was able to save another one of my Hopi friends.

I staggered to my feet and dropped my pistol just in time to see the Navajo rifleman coming right at me about twenty feet away. Wouldn't you know it; he was wearing that same damn cavalry hat. He had me dead to rights and fired before I could react. I braced for the impact that never came. Kaya had raced between us and took the bullet intended for me. She fell at my feet with a look of pain and terror on her face that I will never forget. Her last act was to look up at me and say the word, "Pahana" before she died.

The Navajo seemed to be amused at her sacrifice as he levered his rifle and took careful aim at me once again. I wanted to move or duck or something but I just couldn't. I was frozen in place awaiting my own death when a loud concussion behind me knocked my attacker off his feet and rendered him quite dead. The accursed cavalry hat landed in the campfire and was finally turned to ashes.

Naturally, it was Toho with the Spencer rifle to my rescue. I went to one knee and then pitched forward in a heap as I was losing consciousness. All around me, Navajo and Hopi alike were locked in life and death struggles. The difference was the Navajo fought to kill while the Hopi fought to stay alive. The last things I remember were more gun shots and lotsa whooping and hollering as I blacked out.

When I awoke, I was lying in my sleeping quarters and my right shoulder felt like it was afire. It was still dark outside and a wisp of moonlight illuminated the small room. The sounds of battle were silenced and replaced by an eerie calm. I was just able to make out the figure of someone sitting with his back to the wall and his head resting on his knees. Since he was dressed in a white wedding robe, it figured to be Toho. Since we both seemed to need rest, I decided to leave well enough alone and try to get back to sleep. What I hadn't figured on was my wild dreams. I replayed the entire battle over and over and it always ended with Kaya dying right in front of me. Fitfully, I drifted in and out of sleep for several hours before finally dosing off.

The next thing I remember was sunlight on my face. It was warm and bright and felt good. It also meant that it was full morning and the sun had made its way through the doorway to where I was sleeping. I looked around and was surprised to find that I was all alone. Toho had left sometime during the night. Guess that meant that they weren't too worried about my recovery which I took for good news.

My bullet wound still hurt a lot but not as bad as before. I wondered if the slug had gone through or needed to come out. My shoulder was wrapped in a soft deerskin bandage and had some kind of leaves underneath. From the stench of it, I could tell they'd put something else on the wound but I'd been healed by Injun potions before and was well aware of the gawd-awful smell. I wanted to get up but found that I was too weak to do anything but roll over and there it was, right in front of my nose, along with my other possessions… the Clifton's journal. I knew I'd have to speak with Hopi Joe to find the answers about my past but I was almost afraid of what he might say.

It wasn't long before I was visited by two older Hopi women. One was carrying a pottery crock with an herbal soup of some kind and with sign language; she insisted I try it. The other was intent on checking my wound and changing the dressing. She was as gentle as she could be but the pain was almost more than I could bear. I tried to ask if the slug was still in my shoulder but they didn't seem to speak any English so I let them perform their tasks and even swallowed some of the soup. It was spicy and bitter but I figured it would probably help with my healing. After they left, I slept for awhile until Toho walked in and woke me up.

"Well, my brother, how are you feeling?"

I tried to sit up but fell back down and felt a searing pain in my shoulder. That pretty much told me where the slug ended up. "It was a rough night and I don't seem to be getting any better."

Toho nodded his understanding and gently pulled back the bandage.

"The bullet must come out before you can get better. When you are strong enough, we will remove it."

"Tell me, how bad was it? Did many of your people get hurt?"

Toho's face tightened as he looked to the heavens for support and gave me the grim numbers. "Nine dead and eleven wounded. Two of them will not survive this day."

"What about the Navajo? How many were there?"

Toho turned back towards me with a face hardened by anger. "There were only seven of them and they are all dead. Their attack was without honor. They killed women and children without cause or reason. It was the act of cowards. We threw their bodies off the mesa to the canyon floor. They will be left to rot in the desert sun and to feed the many scavengers of this land."

"How about the rest of the Navajos?"

"We have sent scouts out to be sure that the rest of them have truly left our lands."

I couldn't believe the terrible numbers. I was suddenly racked with guilt about my part in the disaster. "It was my fault. If I hadn't fired on them…"

Toho interrupted my confession. "If you had not killed their chieftain, he would have led the attack last night with many more warriors. They might have wiped out our whole village. Ahiga cried revenge for his son but his only true mission was to kill Hopi. The Navajo have been and will always be the mortal enemy of the Hopi people. Last night was just another battle in a war that knows no end."

Toho finally relaxed a little and sat beside me. "You fought with much bravery, Henry; the people will sing songs about you around our camp fires."

Suddenly, I remembered that Kaya and Toho had each saved my life. "What about Kaya, she died trying to save me."

Toho nodded and lowered his eyes as a sign of sorrow and respect. "Kaya died of her own choice. She willingly gave her life to save yours. Two other women died trying to help the wounded. One was with child."

"And you… if I remember right you saved my life too. That has to make us even."

"Yes, I guess we are… as you say… even."

Toho clasped my left hand with his and we shared a moment in time. His strength and mine were one in the same. We were truly brothers.

Toho stood and walked towards the door as if looking for something or someone. When he finally spoke, he had trouble getting the words out.

"Can you walk with me Henry? There is someone waiting to see us."

All I could think about was the pain in my shoulder and having a slug dug out by some Hopi medicine man and he wanted me to walk with him: was he crazy?

"No, why can't he come here?"

From my angle and distance it looked like Toho had tears running down his face. "Because he is near death and cannot be moved."

"Who?"

"My father. The one you call Hopi Joe."

I went kinda numb. How could that be? A thousand conflicting thoughts raced through my mind. I had to talk with Joe before he died.

"Last night...the attack?"

"Yes. He was stabbed several times but managed to kill his attacker before passing out. He lost much blood and is unable to overcome his wounds. Our medicine man has done all he can to prepare Father for his spirit journey to the underworld. Soon, he will leave this world to join our ancestors. Come, we must go."

Toho helped me to my feet and it was quite a struggle but nobody or nothing was gonna stop me from seeing Hopi Joe. Then he gave me a buckskin sling of sorts and ran it across my left shoulder to help support my right arm.

"Let's go. I've wanted to talk to Joe ever since yesterday morning. I gotta ask him about..."

Toho interrupted again as he reached out to steady me, "Father may not be able to answer your questions, Henry. He is very near death."

I couldn't believe my ears but I could believe Toho's eyes. They were heavy with tears that were impossible for him to fake.

Toho put my left arm around his shoulders and helped me out the doorway and down the adobe pathways to Hopi Joe's lodge. The pain was bad enough to cross my eyes but I was almost unaware as we struggled along.

"Father has asked to speak with you before he leaves this world."

When we reached Hopi Joe, he was lying on his death bed with a medicine man chanting something I couldn't comprehend while gyrating around the room. The shaman seemed to be in some kind of trance and was completely unaware of us. There were small groups of elders in the room and I caught a glimpse of Chosovi off to one side. Still in her wedding robes, she sat cross legged with her hands in a prayer-like position. When she heard us enter, she looked up for a moment and her red and swollen eyes revealed the depth of her sorrow. It finally hit me that Hopi Joe was really dying and tears filled my eyes too.

Toho waved the shaman away as he knelt and spoke to his father. Joe seemed to be semiconscious at best and didn't respond at first. Finally he opened his eyes a little and gazed up at me. With great effort, he managed to smile and say my name as only he would say it, "Mon-roe."

"Yes Joe, I'm here. Is there anything I can do for you?"

With some measure of pain and discomfort, he reached out for my right hand and gently placed his on top of mine. His touch was cold and clammy and gave me the shivers from the feel of it.

"Go home to your father, Mon-roe. He needs you now more than ever."

"Why, what's wrong with Pa?"

"He has not been the same since Miriam took ill and died."

"But Ma died over 20 years ago."

"Not your mother, your brother's daughter."

Finally I understood. Joe was talking about my niece, Miriam. G.W. had named his daughter after Ma and she would have been around four or five years old. I was stunned. I'd never gotten word of her passing. It made me wonder if Taylor heard about what happened but never told me. I was suddenly ashamed of my failure to stay in touch with my family. I felt so sorry for G.W. and Susanna. What could they be thinking of me?

"When did she die?"

"About one year ago. They all thought you knew. Your father was heartbroken when you never answered any of his letters. He feared for you and Taylor and wonders to this day if you are still alive. He has aged beyond his years and looks very old and tired. You must go to him."

Joe winced as the pain got worse and he struggled to keep talking. He seemed to be losing his last battle and I didn't want to upset him but I just had to ask.

"Joe, please tell me which white baby died? I have to know once and for all who I really am."

Joe closed his eyes and didn't respond to my questions. Toho carefully released my left arm and knelt at his father's side. I managed to stay upright and back away a little as he leaned over his father and whispered to him in Hopi. Joe remained motionless for the longest minute of my life and then slowly opened his eyes. He spoke in a voice just above a whisper but his response was also in Hopi so Toho translated for me.

"Father says he simply can not tell you which white child was which. He truly wants to help you but he can not remember. It was a longtime ago and not important to him at the time."

It seemed to me that Hopi Joe said a lot more than he was sorry and couldn't remember. "Did he say anything else?"

"No, that was all."

Hopi Joe had closed his eyes after speaking to Toho and looked for all the world like he'd been laid out by a bone planter. The movement of his breathing was barely visible and his face held no expression. When Toho finished speaking, however, Joe opened his eyes and his mouth moved like he wanted to speak again. The sudden motion brought him severe discomfort and he winced from the pain of it. Toho tried to comfort his father and spoke to him again in Hopi. Whatever he said did the trick 'cause Hopi Joe relaxed and closed his eyes again. That was the last chance I had to speak to him.

Toho helped me back to my room and made sure I was as comfortable as possible. He returned to his death watch and I tried to sleep but the waiting was difficult. There was nothing further to be done so I was left to wrestle with my own thoughts. Why hadn't I spoken with Hopi Joe before the attack? Why didn't I have my guns with me? What else could I have done to prevent the massacre? A thousand "what ifs" ran through my mind.

To add to my frustration, I found I couldn't stop thinking about Kaya and the sacrifice she made for me. She was so young and so innocent. Why did she have to die? I also wished to talk with Chosovi and Toho about the Clifton journal but knew it was not the time. That conversation would have to wait until after Hopi Joe had passed and was properly buried.

I fell asleep somewhere around midnight and was awakened by Chosovi in the gray mist just before sunrise.

"It is over. He is *mokee*. Toho is preparing his father for the spirit journey."

"What can I do to help?"

"Toho wishes you would rest and gain strength. As the eldest son, it is his duty and honor to provide the things that are necessary for his father's trip. Hopi Joe will have his bow and lance to protect him as well as his prayer sticks and "cloud blower" to comfort him. Toho will wash the body with yucca suds and dress him in his best ceremonial robes. His favorite foods will be offered at his gravesite to sustain his spirit along the journey. We are left to pray and grieve for his spirit to help him on his way. The Hopi believe the spirit moves on a sky path to the west. Those who have lived a good life will travel with ease while those who haven't will encounter much suffering.

Chosovi left and my elderly Hopi nurses entered with soup and medicine. I drank more of the soup and endured the pain of the bandage being changed before losing consciousness. I drifted in and out of reality as the day wore on. Once again, I became delirious as wild and crazy dreams continued to haunt my mind. Images of Hopi Joe, Toho, Chosovi and Kaya came at me from all directions. I think I even dreamt of Taylor and the going-ons in Santa Fe. I do remember someone washing my face with a cool cloth and a woman's voice comforting me but it was all such a blur.

Finally, I came full awake as Toho was kneeling beside me with a bottle of whiskey in each hand.

"I brought your medicine, Henry."

He said it with such a serious face that it made me want to laugh but the pain in my shoulder quickly reminded me nothing was funny at that moment.

"The bullet must come out now.  This medicine should help you endure the pain."

I nodded my agreement as speaking seemed to be too much effort.  Toho slowly gave me as much whiskey as I could swallow.  It tasted as gawd awful as the Injun soup but I would have drunk anything to ease the pain.

Soon enough, I was "feeling no pain" as they say and ready for anything.  Toho seemed to be amused at my transformation from wounded warrior to happy drunk.

"Try not to enjoy this firewater too much, Henry."

"I told you it was good medicine."

"It may serve you now but it can become your master if you allow it."

I knew Toho was right but at that moment I didn't care.  I asked for more whiskey and he complied.  The spinning of my head was matched by the churning of my stomach as I hadn't eaten anything in almost twenty-four hours but the Kentucky sour mash was working its wonders.

Toho explained that the shaman was unwilling to work on anyone who was not a member of their clan and had never removed a slug anyway.  That left my Hopi brother with the honor of removing it.  When Chosovi knelt on my left side and bathed my face with a cool cloth, I realized it was her calm and soothing voice I heard during my delirium.  She looked like an angel looking down on me as her head was haloed by the afternoon sun that came through the doorway.

Toho gave me a leather strap to chew on as he made his cuts and dug into my shoulder with a red hot hunting knife.  He cautioned that the first cut would be the deepest and would cause the most discomfort  I thought I was beyond feeling any pain but that proved to be incorrect.  I screamed in silence until the shock of it mercifully knocked me out.

They tell me that I slept for most of two days after the extraction but the only way I could tell was my three day growth of beard. Since the Hopi men had little facial hair, I was the cause of much curiosity among my caretakers. My shoulder pain had been reduced to a dull throb which was a considerable improvement. Toho left the slug for me to see. As luck would have it, it was a small caliber, probably 32-20 or 38-40, and did a lot less damage than some big ol' forty or fifty caliber would have.

Chosovi fretted over me like a mother animal hovers over her newborn. I sure appreciated all the attention but worried about her honeymoon with Toho. They had little time together since their joining and a lot of sadness and misery. They deserved better.

As I became more alert and aware, Chosovi had a strange question for me.

"During your restless dreams, you cried out many names and places. You spoke of Santa Fe and the place of St. Charles. You called out for a Paddy, Beau and Taylor. Who is this Taylor? Is she your sister or your woman?"

That was a good question. Since I wasn't really willing or able to explain our complicated relationship at that moment, I gave her the same answer that Paddy had given me; Taylor was neither and both.

# CHAPTER IV

## "Sister wherefore art thou?"

**SUMMER 1882**

My second day in Santa Fe started out with a bang, literally. I awoke in a hurry with the sound of both barrels of a double barrel scatter gun going off beneath my window. I carefully peered out the window and saw two large and hairy men dressed in animal hides standing at the bottom of the stairs. They were both carrying shotguns and appeared to be buffalo hunters or worse yet, muleskinners.

My mind flashed back to the dead body from the night before and I almost got sick again. I hitched up my britches and was fumbling with my gun belt when one of men called out.

"Come on out here, gamblin' man. We know you're in there. We jus' want to talk to you about our good friend Leonard."

They had to mean the muleskinner that got killed and filleted in the alley. It figured he'd have friends just as big and ugly as he was. But who was the gamblin' man they were after? They couldn't know about me and Paddy said Beau had rooms of his own in some hotel though she never said where.

The voice from the stairs got louder and closer. "Don't make us come drag your black ass out here. We don't wish to disturb da girls."

Girls? What girls? I was still half awake and confused. With just my pants and gun belt on, I opened the door to the hallway and almost got rundown by a two hundred pound candy cane. It was Paddy, dressed in a red and white stripe night shirt. She was toting her Colt shotgun and cursing under her breath.

"God dammit, I told him. I told him they'd come looking for his worthless hide."

She stopped at the back door and opened it just enough to peek out. "One more step Caleb and you're going to meet your maker."

This was getting way out of control. I had to do something. "Wait. Stop. Let me try talking to 'em."

Paddy looked at me with unbelieving eyes. "You want to talk with Caleb and Luther?"

I gently pushed back the barrel of her shotgun and opened the door. I stepped out on the landing in the dawn's early light and saw, about fifteen feet below me on the wooden stairway, two of the ugliest and filthiest creatures that ever walked the earth. The smell of their awful breath, putrid body odor and the manure on their boots made an almost lethal combination. The one closest to me spit tobacco from his almost toothless mouth and growled at me. "Now who da hell are you?"

"I'm Henry Charles, the new owner of this gambling hall. What can I do for you?"

Caleb considered for a moment and then growled again. "You can get outta da damn way. We came for the little darky."

"Beau isn't here. I believe he has a room in some hotel."

Caleb spit again and toned down his voice a bit. "We've already been there and he ain't.

"Well he's not here either and won't be for a couple of days. I sent him to Albuquerque on business and he probably just left last night. Why are you chasing him?"

"We figure he kilt our friend Leonard."

"Well he didn't. I was here last night and Beau was in the casino all night. He kicked the crap out of your friend but he didn't kill him. Leonard was still alive when some of the boys dragged him out."

Luther finally spoke up. "You da one that took up his fight?"

"I just made sure that things didn't get too outta hand."

Caleb turned on his partner. "Shut up Luther, let me handle dis." He turned back to me and said in a slow deliberate voice. "Then you must be da man who posted da reward."

"Yes, one hundred dollars for information leading to the capture and conviction of the killer. I'll not pay for a necktie party."

"Well we're planning to collect dat reward."

"I'll be happy to pay but only under my terms."

That seemed to sooth the savage beasts and they went about their business. As I watched them walk away, I heard Paddy right behind me.

"Well, 'Glory Be'. You're Charles' son alright. That was the work of a silver tongue if I ever heard it. Oh, by the by, you do know that Beau stepped out for a little air last night. I'd wager he was gone for about five minutes."

Yeah, I know but I didn't think there was any reason for them to know. Do you know where Beau is now?"

She pointed back down the hallway. "Third door on the left. He'd most likely be keepin' company with Angelina."

It suddenly occurred to me that the hallway ran the length of the building and there were numerous doors on both sides. I quickly counted over a dozen doors.

"Who stays in all these rooms?"

"Just Maude and her girls. No all-nighters allowed with the possible exception of one Monsieur Didlet."

"Sporting girls? This here upstairs is a brothel?"

"Your father called it his pleasure palace. That gave the joint a touch of class don't ya think?"

"Well, I don't know nothing about running a pleasure palace or a gambling hall saloon for that matter. Now what am I gonna do?"

"Oh, I'd wager you'll do alright and you're gonna just love Maude."

By now, half the doors were open and young women, in various stages of dress, were peering at us. Beau, wearing only his underwear and smoking a stub of a cigar, walked out of the third doorway on the left and strolled down the hallway in our direction. He was small in stature but solidly built and his tight under garments left little to the imagination. Beau seemed to relish the attention he was getting from the other girls as he passed by and greeted us with a smug grin on his face.

"Morning Paddy, what's the ruckus about?"

Before Paddy could speak, I inserted myself into the conversation. "A couple of disgusting muleteers took offense at their friend Leonard being murdered and figured you were the one who did it."

Beau looked at me like we'd never met. "Who are you? Wait, don't tell me, I remember now. You're the new plantation boss man come to oversee his slaves."

"I'm sorry you see it that way but if at any time you wish to leave this plantation you're certainly free to go."

Things were heating up between Beau and me again and Paddy figured it was her cue to butt in as usual.

"Easy boys, there's been ruckus enough already."

We both took a couple of deep breaths but continued what my Pa used to call the long hard stare. Finally, Beau took the cigar from his mouth and looked away. "What did you tell them… fellas?"

"I told them I sent you out of town on business for a few days."

"Mighty white of you."

I had more to say and a physical way to say it but better judgment got the best of me and I returned to my room. At that moment I had no idea who killed the muleskinner but if it was Beau, I'd gladly see him hung for it.

I got dressed and went for a long walk to think about ever'thing. I stopped and had a breakfast of *chorizo* and eggs along with corn *tortillas,* green peppers and coffee. The sign outside said *"Pepe's Cantina"* but I only saw one Mexican senorita and she was as pretty as she was friendly.

Without conscious intent, I was slowly but surely wandering over to the dry goods store where I'd left Taylor. Paddy had mentioned I should get new clothes but that was hardly my reason for heading that way. I really wanted to see Taylor. I knew it would be better if I'd stay away for a few days but I had to make sure she was alright.

Soon enough, I found myself across the street from Olson's Mercantile and watched as a young boy about seven or eight years old swept up and restocked the sacks of feed and grain in front of the store. He worked up a thirst in the hot morning sun and a woman who looked to be his mother came out with a glass of water for him. It seemed natural enough for me to cross the street and strike up a conversation.

"Morning folks. I'm new to Santa Fe and am just wandering around getting to know the town. Do you own this fine store?"

The lady was tall and thick-boned with blond hair worn in a tight bun. She wore a red checked gingham dress and pointy toed lace up boots. Her manner suggested she was strong and confident and she shook my hand with the grip of a man.

"And good morning to you sir. Yah sure, my husband, Ole, and I own dis store. My name is Lena Olson and dis here is my son, Lars. Ve come six months ago from Sweden."

"Well, I'm proud to make your acquaintance. My name is Henry Charles and I just got here yesterday from the Arizona territory."

I bent down a little and tried to shake hands with Lars but he hid behind his mama's skirts. He was trying to be brave but seemed a little afraid of me. His eyes got as round as dollars when he saw the Colt revolver I was toting.

"Dat's strange. Ve had a young lady take a room with us yesterday and she was from the Arizona territory too."

What was I thinking? I'd barely opened my mouth before I stuck my boot in it. Taylor and I were to be strangers and I'd already told somebody we came to town from the same place on the same day. I had to correct my mistake.

"Oh, I'm actually from Animas City, up in Colorado, but I took the long way around and came this way after traveling across northern Arizona. I wanted to see the Grand Canyon and the Painted Desert. They're really something."

I finally stopped babbling as Ole Olson came out the front door of the store.

"Vell, hello dere young fella, vat can ve do fer ya?"

Ole was as large as a buffalo and almost as wooly. He had a face full of whiskers that extended from his double chin to his waist. Thick red suspenders held up his baggy trousers and kept his shirt from flying off his barrel shaped chest. When we shook hands I lost sight of mine within his huge mitt and for the moment was at a loss for words. Lena came to my rescue.

"Ole, dis here is Henry Charles. He is new in town and is out meeting his new neighbors. I believe he said he is from Colorado."

Ole continued to shake my hand up and down with increased vigor. "Velcome to Santa Fe. Ve vill vork hard to earn your business."

As I finally gained control of my hand and arm, I was able to speak. "And you shall have it sir. They tell me I'm in need of a new set of clothes."

Ole and I went in the store and I picked out two new pairs of trousers, three ruffled white shirts with pearl buttons, a black silk waistcoat and a new top hat. My boots were still in good shape but were badly in need of a shine. After settling up, we talked for a few minutes about the weather and local business conditions until it was time for me to leave. As I was walking away, I finally remembered to ask Lena about Taylor.

"Misses Olson, I believe you mentioned a young woman that just came to town. Is she here now?"

"No, bless her heart. But do come back and meet her. She is a lovely young woman and so full of the love of life."

"Where did she go?"

"Oh, she caught the eye of a young man who is also staying mit us. I think they went for a buggy ride to see the town and the countryside. I believe Victor rented one from the livery down the street"

"Victor?"

"Yes, Mister Victor Bodine. He has been boarding mit us for several weeks now and he told us he vas from New Orleans. He seems to be a nice young man."

With that, the Olsons went back into their store and left me with a head full of questions. What the hell was Taylor up to? When was she gonna get in touch with me? And who the hell was Victor Bodine and why did his name sound so familiar?

As luck would have it, there was a young Mexican boy a short ways down the street that shined boots and shoes so I completed my new wardrobe by having my boots conditioned. When I got back to the St. Charles around noon, Paddy was busy behind the bar as usual but Beau was nowhere in sight. There were two or three men at the faro tables and four or five active poker tables. Somebody completely wrapped in a *serape* was leaning agin the bar and a hung over piano player was slurping coffee as he tried in vain to make sense of some sheet music. I walked through the casino and took my spot at the far end of the bar. Paddy took note and stopped her scrubbing and scouring long enough to wait on me. She looked at my new clothes with approval in her eyes and with a straight face, said, "Well darlin', now you look like you just might be the owner of this fine establishment. What'll it be, whiskey, beer or me?"

"I think I'll settle for a cup of coffee if you've got it."

"Paddy looked over to the person concealed by the colorful Mexican shawl and laughed her fool head off.

"See what I told you, Maude, he's liable to be no fun at all.

Much to my surprise, the person beneath the *serape* turned out to be none other than Maude Dickers, or "Mother Maude" as she preferred to be called. She was the madam who ran Charles' pleasure palace.

Maude might have been a good-looker in her day but that day was long past and she looked to be rode hard and put away wet. She had enough paint on her face to double coat a good sized outhouse and her hair resembled a wasp nest. Her dress might have fit at one time but now it was several sizes too small and her heaving breasts strained the seams as she laughed along with Paddy.

"So you're my new partner. Welcome to Santa Fe. How're they hanging?"

My embarrassment musta showed on my face cause both of them started to laugh even harder. Paddy poured me a beer and slid it down the bar with just enough force to have it stop right in front of me.

"Fresh out of coffee, have a beer. I told you that you were gonna just love Maude."

Maude threw off her *serape* and strutted right up to me.

"Not unless he pays for it."

Now both of 'em were laughing again and Maude gave me a bear hug of sorts. She smashed my face into her breasts and rubbed my nose in 'em.

"Don't you fret now sweetheart, nose jobs are free."

When she finally let go, Maude leaned on the bar and looked me up and down.

"I see you're sporting new clothes. Well, you certainly look the part."

She was standing so close that I could almost feel her eyes touching me. It was an uncomfortable feeling I'd had before with a madam and I didn't cotton to it. To make matters worse, Paddy was directly behind her cleaning glasses and making funny faces at me.

After all the silliness, Maude got down to business. "Did your sweet daddy tell you all about his arrangement with little ol' Mother Maude?"

Before I could answer, she continued.

"You furnish the rooms and control the customers while I manage the girls and they provide the… 'services'. I run a clean house. The girls charge based on the service rendered from two dollars to twenty and beyond if it's warranted. With few exceptions, nobody rides for free. You and I have a fifty-fifty split and I take care of my girls. We settle accounts every Sunday morning instead of going to church."

"Who are the exceptions?"

"Well, Beau provides our security so he spends time with Angie whenever she isn't otherwise occupied. I take care of the mayor, three town councilmen and the sheriff, of course. We tolerate no smelly riff-raff or anyone who might hurt the girls."

"Is that it?"

Maude lightened up a little and put her hand on my cheek.

"I guess it goes without saying that your father… and now you… have your pick anytime. Charles used to call it quality control. You know, making sure the girls were properly educated in the ways of passion. I've already told the girls to 'be nice' to you."

As she was speaking, Maude ran her hand slowly down my chest and stopped on my left thigh. Then, she reached under her right breast and pulled out a wad of bills and handed them to me.

"This is your share for the last few weeks that Charles has been gone. I kept it safe and warm for ya in my 'booby-bank'."

She couldn't have smiled any sweeter if she'd had a mouth full of sugar. Behind Maude's back, Paddy rolled her eyes and shook her head. Then she put down the glass she was cleaning and held up six fingers as she pointed at me followed by four fingers as she pointed at Maude.

"I certainly agree on the division of duties but I do believe Charles said the split was sixty-forty in his favor."

Sweet went to sour as Maude considered my words. She flung a quick glance back at Paddy who had gone quickly back to cleaning glasses and looking off the other direction.

"Oh, silly me, that's right, sixty-forty. I wondered why I had this extra left over."

This time she scooped out a smaller wad of bills from under her left breast and handed it to me.

"There, that makes us square."

Paddy was laughing in silence and shaking her head again. She made hand gestures that portrayed turning the pages of a book.

I had to figure for a minute but I finally got her meaning. As Maude turned to walk away I gently restrained her right shoulder.

"Why don't we both take a look... at the book?"

This time sour went to bittersweet as Maude reached between her legs and located another wad of bills secured in her garter belt. Thankfully, she hadn't named that particular bank. She handed it to me with a look of regret and shame.

"You can't blame a girl for trying can ya? I had to find out if you really were Charles' son and now I know."

The aging madam threw the *serape* over her shoulders and walked out the door without another word or glance. Paddy stopped her glass cleaning and walked back to my end of the bar.

"Maude keeps an honest book but she has to be nudged ever so often. She respected and trusted Charles so she played him pretty straight. If you take care of her and the girls, she won't screw you... unless you want her to."

"Why aren't there stairs inside here so ever'one doesn't have to walk down that damn alley to the back stairs?"

"Tis a little deal Charles made with our town council. He figured gamblin' and drinkin' would always be legal but prostitution may not. With the way this place is set up using separate entrances, they can run the girls out of town without closing down the casino or the saloon. Everybody knows who runs what but Charles could claim he had no knowledge or connection with the shenanigans upstairs. And don't think some of the church-going ladies aren't already raising a ruckus with their men-folk about Maude and her girls. Luckily, most of the upstanding gentlemen in this town are among our best customers."

"Does Maude still work it or is she just a madam?"

"Most nights, she just collects the money and watches over the girls but she has her specials, ya know. There are repeat customers that are used to her and she to them. That's where she was this morning when all the ruckus broke out... entertaining Manual Garcia Gomez, one of our illustrious town councilmen. He comes by real early about twice a week. Tells his battle-axe wife he's going to early mass at St. Michaels but he's really going to mass at St. Mattress."

Paddy laughed at her own joke and continued. "He leaves when he hears that old mission bell ring."

"Mission bell?"

"The one at St. Michaels or San Miguel's if you will. They claim it was cast in Spain about 1356 and weighs over eight hundred pounds. You can hear it for miles."

"How many girls are there and what did Maude mean by telling the girls to 'be nice' to me?"

"That's just her way of saying give the man a poke, haul his ashes, or clean out his pipes… whatever you want to call it. The actual number of working girls varies from time to time. I think there's six or seven. Let me see…"

Paddy started counting on her fingers.

"Right now, there's Angelina, Nicole, Margarita, Jolene, Carlotta, Mei-Xing and… Renee, of course, she's the new one."

"Mei-Xing?"

"Chinese girl. Her name's supposed to mean beautiful star. She was brought over here twenty years ago as a sex slave for the Chinese railroad workers. I met her back in '69 when I was working for the Union Pacific. She was kept in one of them traveling brothels that followed behind the construction crews. The railroad workers called 'em 'Hell on wheels' and they were."

Paddy seemed disturbed by the memories that she was reliving. "When all the tracks were finally laid, I helped her escape and she followed me here. Would you believe after twenty years in this country she barely speaks a word of English?

"Well, it sure sounds like an exotic group of girls Maude has there."

"Believe you me, those names are just to impress the customers and most of the girls don't look half as good as they sound. With the exception of that young Renee, and Angelina they're more plow horse than filly. Good thing the boys get too drunk to care."

"When Maude said no smelly riff-raff, was she referring to our mule skinning friends?"

"Yeah, she tries to keep that crowd away from the girls but when it can't be avoided, she hands 'em over to Mei-Xing. The skinners call her 'old slant eyes'. I think Mei's beyond caring who or what she does."

"Have the customers ever hurt any of the girls?"

"Just the usual... slapping around mostly. Last year, we had a German gal named Gretchen that got herself beat up pretty bad. Had to quit the business and leave town. That's when Maude had them all conceal some kind of weapon in their rooms."

"What kind of weapons?"

"Differs from girl to girl. Most have some kind of shillelagh. You know, a length of pipe or a wooden cudgel of some sort. Mei-Xing has a fancy Chinese dagger with jewels inlaid on the hilt. They say she's had to threaten a couple of men with it."

"Where'd she get an expensive knife like that?"

"From a regular customer of hers. He was an elderly Chinese fella that ran our first laundry service in town. She said he never touched her. He only wanted to talk Chinese with someone. When he passed, he left it to her in his will."

Paddy seemed disturbed by our conversation again and walked away to go back to her chores. I tried to drink the beer she served me but my stomach wasn't up to it.

After a while, Paddy finished what she was doing and took me to a small office in the back. There, wedged in the bottom drawer of a small desk, she showed me a good-sized lock box and handed me the key.

"I put the daily take in the slot there and now you have the only key. Charles left it with me while he was gone so Beau and I could get paid and I could pay our suppliers. Normally, he settles up with us every Sunday. We get salary plus bonus depending on the volume of business. It's all there in his accounts book."

She handed me a well worn accounting ledger that I casually paged through. It was painfully clear that I needed to understand how Charles was running his business so I sat down to read and learn. Paddy was about to leave me when she remembered something.

"Oh, one more thing. Do you see that short rope hanging down there?"

I looked up to see a knotted pull-rope hanging from what looked like a trap door in the ceiling. I couldn't be sure since the wood was well fit and barely noticeable. The rope had a perfectly round piece of wood about two inches across attached to the end of it. Since the ceiling was at least ten feet high and the rope was only about one foot long, it took a pretty good jump to grab it.

"If you yank on that rope hard enough, the door opens and a ladder comes down. Charles had it made as an escape hatch. You can climb right up to his room. There's a moveable panel that opens somewhere in his closet or so he says. You see, I've never used it myself. I'm too broad in the beam to grab that rope or get through that tiny opening."

I considered trying the trap door but decided to look for a moving panel in the upstairs closet instead. I wondered why Charles felt he needed an escape hatch but reasoned that I'd probably find out.

When I started reading the ledger, it became clear that it was also a diary of sorts. Charles wrote about current events in his life and people he met at the bottom of the pages. Several entries mentioned the Pinkerton Detective Agency and its fruitless search to find his long lost son.

As I sat in his chair, I'd tried to imagine Charles' last day there. He hadn't heard about me yet so he was just off to Denver on business. When the "private eyes" wired him, he took the first train to Animas City. After that we traveled together to Flagstaff where he was shot. He had no idea that he would never make it back to Santa Fe.

In fact, I was hired by a woman who called herself Victoria Farley to pretend to be her son. She claimed to be Charles' widow since she thought he was killed in the wagon train massacre. My job was to fool the Pinkerton's into believing I was her son so she could cash in some railroad stocks. The "Pinks" told Charles and that's how we met. I thought I was pretending to be his son and then it turns out I really was.

The only sad part of the whole story is that Charles died before I knew I really was his real son. Somehow, he seemed to know what I didn't.

The next thing I found was a handwritten Will and Testament. Charles indicated that upon his death, should his sons never be found, all his worldly goods should be given to Paddy. She was to inherit the St. Charles and all his other assets. Now didn't that beat all. I wondered if she knew.

That Will made me consider my own death for the first time. If I died, who would end up with all my newly gained assets? Paddy? Legally, I had no family other than Charles since I was no longer related to the Porter Henry family. It certainly was something to consider.

As I continued reading, I found the numbers of two bank accounts he had in the First National Bank of Santa Fe which was just across the plaza. Next to the number he underlined the name Lucien B. Maxwell but didn't say why. Was it possible Charles had substantial funds in the bank? That gave me something else to think about as I sat back in the chair to rest my eyes.

I rested my eyes so well that I fell asleep until Paddy rudely woke me up.

"Henry, you might want to get out here. There figures to be trouble."

I shook myself awake and followed her back to the casino. Before I saw 'em, I could smell the trouble Paddy was referring to; the muleskinners were back.

Caleb and Luther were sitting at a table at the very back of the saloon. They sat with their backs to the wall so they could observe everything that happened. It seemed like they were waiting for someone and it was easy to guess who. Somehow, they found out that Beau was still in town and expected back here at the St. Charles. They were both cradling double barrel shotguns and chewing tobacco which they spit in any direction that suited them without ever looking for a spittoon.

Something had to be done as they were making the other customers edgy and nervous. Several anxious drummers and a couple of local shop keepers picked up and walked out. Eric, the piano player, kept looking at 'em over his shoulder and almost fell off his stool. Paddy looked over at me every once in awhile as if she were awaiting my direction about the matter. She kept tending to the customers at the bar but stayed pretty close to her shotgun.

I wondered what Charles would have done so I asked Paddy, "What would Charles do in a situation like this?"

"He'd try to avoid a shoot out as it usually makes a mess of the place and always disturbs the normal flow of business so he'd try to get them drunk and laid. First off, he'd send over a couple of free rounds of drinks and then he'd offer Mei-Xing to whichever wanted to go upstairs with her. That way they were split up and a mite easier to deal with."

"Okay, that sounds like it should work. You take the drinks over and make 'em strong enough to walk on. I'll find Maude and tell her to get Mei-Xing."

Paddy held up her hand to stop me. "Whoa there, hold your horses cowboy. This here ain't our first rodeo. They're eagerly swilling their second free drink and Carlotta already went out and around to warn Maude. Mei will be down here directly."

"If you've already taken care of things then why did you get me out here and ask me what to do?"

"Thought maybe you'd just walk over and plug 'em both. It would save a lotta time and good whiskey. Those two surely deserve whatever comes their way, just like their good friend, Leonard."

"Are these two regulars here?"

"Used to be. The three of 'em left town a few years back and ain't been back until yesterday. I was deathly afraid I might never see 'em again."

I was trying to figure what she meant by what she said when Carlotta and Mei-Xing came through the batwing doors. Everyone took notice as they sauntered in.

Carlotta was a tall and rather chunky redhead with a pasty white complexion in her late thirties if she was a day. Like Maude, her hair and makeup were overdone and her dress barely fit. She was in a surly mood and actually snarled at some of the men who approached her as she made her way to the bar.

Mei-Xing, on the other hand, was short and thin and wore her coal black hair long and straight down to her butt. She had no makeup of any kind and her expressionless face belied her age or intentions as she ignored all the other customers and headed straight for the muleskinners.

Carlotta slapped her hand on the bar and pleaded with Paddy.

"I know I've used up my ration but please, I really need a drink."

Paddy's answer was as cold as ice. "You know the rules. Get back to work."

Carlotta looked down at the floor for a second or two and then raised her head, put on her very best phony smile and returned to the game tables.

Meanwhile, Mei-Xing was concentrating on Luther rather than Caleb who was too busy drinkin' for free to want a woman. In a fashion I couldn't understand, she teased and cajoled him to down his drinks and follow her out the front door. I couldn't imagine how she could do that. I would have thought the smell alone would gag her but somehow it didn't.

The tension level in the gambling hall went down a little after Luther left and Caleb started to show the signs of too much alcohol. A half hour later, Beau wandered in and immediately caught the scent of muleskinner. There were enough customers in the way to block his view of the entire saloon so he immediately walked over to the bar. While nervously looking over his shoulder, he spoke to Paddy in a voice just loud enough for me to overhear.

"Caleb and Luther?"

"Yessiree bob. Here to see you about Leonard."

"We both know I had nothing to do with that but they'll never believe me."

Beau turned about and carefully looked around the room. He quickly located Caleb who was still sittin' and drinkin' in the back and hadn't seen him yet.

"I can see Caleb, where's Luther?"

"Upstairs with Mei."

Beau turned back around and spoke in a lowered voice. "You were right. They just had to come back didn't they?"

"Come to face judgment."

"Well, I reckon we should get this over once and for all. What do ya want to do?"

Suddenly Caleb recognized Beau and struggled to get to his feet. In doing so, he dropped his shotgun and fell to his knees when he tried to retrieve it. Ever'one in the room held their breath as they awaited his next move. Finally, he swore a couple of times and then started to laugh.

"I'll be damned. Guess I had too much of your hooch to walk upright."

Seeing an easy way out of our problem, I walked over to Caleb and gingerly applied my right knee to his left temple. This action rendered Caleb more compliant and then, leaving his shotgun on the floor, I steered him to the front doors and shoved him out into the street. He took two or three steps before falling flat on his face. A couple of moments later, I heard him heading around the front of the building and down the alley yelling after Luther. I sincerely hoped we had seen the last of 'em but I knew better.

Beau scorned me as I returned to the bar. "You just put off the inevitable you know. They're gonna come back and we're gonna have to kill 'em."

"The way you killed Leonard?"

"I should have and damn well could have but I didn't. It's true enough that I've hated white trash like him since I was a boy and would have gladly killed him face to face but not while he was passed out and helpless."

"Who did then?"

Beau smiled at me and then turned towards Paddy. "You got any thoughts about that Paddy?"

Before Paddy could answer, I jumped to her defense. "What makes you think she knows anything about Leonard's death?"

"Let's just say that I'm not the only one with ample reason to want him dead."

I looked for Paddy to refute Beau's accusation but she didn't. Instead, she looked at me and sighed.

"Remember me telling you about the time I was almost hung? Well, Leonard was the fella that started all the trouble and Caleb and Luther were part of the pack that strung me up. They left town right after that night and I thought I might never have a chance to repay them for what they did to me. It's my good fortune that they've returned.

I'll admit I thought about killing him last night but I never got the opportunity. I went looking for him and found his body in the alley just like you did. I figured Beau had done me the favor."

Beau stopped her story by interrupting. "And just why would I do that?"

"How about your fight with him last night? Was that just a co-incidence or were you trying to save me the bother?"

Before Beau could defend his actions, I interrupted. "Well if you two didn't do it, who did? Who else hated him enough to mutilate his body that way?"

They looked at each other and then seemed to have the same thought at the same time as they spoke in unison. "Mei-Xing."

I ran out the front doors and headed for the alley. It was already dark and I couldn't see very well but the smell was overpowering and I could guess what lay ahead of me. There were two more bodies in the alley. Both were gutted like Leonard's had been the night before. Luther's body was face down while Caleb's was face up with his eyes wide open. There was a jeweled dagger, covered with blood and remains, on the ground beside the bodies.

I overcame the urge to purge and raced to the back stairs where I found Mei-Xing. She'd tied a make-shift noose around her neck, secured the other end to the railing and flung herself off the landing. Her body was still swinging gently back and forth but there was no life in it.

We'll probably never know why she killed those men but then again, it didn't really matter. She might have been avenging her friend Paddy or protecting Beau. Most likely, she just had enough of their kind and decided her life wasn't worth living any longer.

Maude got Sheriff O'Reilly to come by and with his blessing; we carted the three bodies to the pauper's graveyard. It seems the good Irish sheriff was another of Maude's special customers. The two muleskinners were dumped in the common grave along with their friend Leonard but I saw to it that Mei-Xing was buried separately and with what little dignity we could muster.

We held a short ceremony the next day with a small group of mourners that included Paddy, Beau, Maude and most of the girls. Then we went back to the St. Charles and resumed business as usual. Paddy held her own little Irish wake and got herself drunker than a skunk while the red-headed piano player, Eric, composed a special funeral dirge for the affair that he called the "Muleskinner Blues". He meant it to be serious but we all took it as a joke.

I spent the next three weeks getting used to the daily routine of the saloon. I met many of our suppliers and got to know most of the regular customers. Paddy cheerfully showed me the behind-the-bar side of the business and Beau reluctantly took me through the gambling side. Now and then I wondered about Taylor but was too busy to chase after her. After all, she knew where I was and could get in touch with me if she needed anything.

Maude and her girls were a constant source of irritation. The competition and jealousy between them caused cat-fights at all hours. Angelina, or "Angie" as she was known, was a tall and slender half-breed of some sort with long black hair and a caramel complexion. Because of her relationship with Beau, she considered herself to be somehow better than the others which only made things worse. Angie only worked when she wanted and then only with a very select group of customers.

Nicole and Jolene were common-looking girls that were really jealous of Angie's superior status. They deeply resented being paired with some of the seedier customers once Mei-Xing was gone. Margarita, the feisty Latino, was a favorite of Mexicans and white men but for some unknown reason, she would balk at servicing Negroes or local Injuns. Carlotta had a serious drinking problem and seemed to despise all men so their skin color never mattered much to her.

While Maude was busy trying to find another oriental girl to satisfy that part of her clientele, I was trying to figure out Renee and her part of the operation. She was very young and seemed to be performing the tasks of a scullery maid. I never once saw her with a customer but she was kept busy cleaning and fetching for the others. One morning when she was returning from the laundry, I tried to speak with her but she ignored my words and just went about her duties in silence. Since Maude wasn't around, I went to Paddy for answers.

"What's the story with Renee? Is she one of the girls or just their maid? I never see her with a customer."

"Don't get involved with Renee, laddie. Maude has special plans for that one. She's been parading her around here for over a month but hasn't let any man get near. I think Maude intends to auction her off to the highest bidder. Her tender age makes her a prized commodity around these parts. It's not often a man gets to 'poke' a virgin."

"Renee's a virgin?"

"Well… she may look the part but she ain't. The way I hear it, her darling father put an end to that condition years ago. After her mother died, Renee became 'daddy's little girl' at the ripe old age of nine. At thirteen, she started to fight back and that's when he sold her to a traveling boot salesman out of El Paso. Think Maude said he was a Scotsman by the name of McLean. Anyway, she finally got away from him last month and was living with the rats on the street. Maude gave her the clothes on her back and food in her belly. I reckon she'd do most anything for Maude right about now. Renee has the look of a cherub but the cold heart of the devil himself and who could blame her?"

"If she's not a virgin, won't the winner be able to tell?"

"Oh, my word. You are such an innocent lad. Women have ways to 'tighten' themselves up and a small bottle of pigs' blood will give a man the bloody sheet he so dearly desires."

"And Renee is willing to do that?"

"I don't think she cares one whit or another. She already hates most men so anything she has to do for them or with them won't change that opinion. Right now, Maude is the only one keeping her alive so if she's smart, she'll do as she's told."

I could certainly see why Charles let Maude handle the sporting girls. After what I had watched and heard, I wanted no part of any of 'em. I'd gladly take my cut and leave the rest to her. My romantic notion of the whore with a heart of gold had been stepped on once before but now it was completely stomped to death.

I spent my evenings watching the comings and goings in the casino. Things were generally quiet and the business flowed in a predictable fashion. Beau and Paddy were true professionals and quite capable of running ever'thing all by themselves. I began to wonder just what I was supposed to contribute to the operation of St. Charles Place until Paddy gave me the answer.

"Charles built this business to pass along to his son. It's your lot to do the same. I watch the bar and Beau watches the gambling so you should watch us. There's no trusting anybody when it comes to money."

Thinking about having a son made me think about Taylor once again. I knew I was just being stubborn and should go to see her but I couldn't imagine why she didn't feel the same. What could she be doing that took up all of her time?

As it turned out, the answer to that question walked in the door just when I was asking it. I looked up to see a rather handsome and dapper young gentleman about my size and age. I judged him to stand six feet three and about two hundred pounds. His coat, shirt and pants where fresh-pressed and his derby hat was steamed to perfection. He had a dark complexion with a well trimmed mustache and dark curly hair that trailed off his collar. If he was trying to make an impression, he succeeded.

Paddy had also noticed his entrance. "Welcome back Victor. Where have you been keeping?"

Victor looked around the room and nodded at Beau and several other customers as he made his way over to the bar. His gaze swept by me without any sign of recognition.

He spoke in a decidedly Louisiana accent. "I have been busy, my love. It seems that I have acquired a new lady friend that must be attended to."

Paddy feigned anguish. "You've been stepping out on me?"

"No more than you've been stepping out on me, I'll wager. But you know, Miss Paddy, you'll always hold a very special place in my heart."

With that line, Paddy actually started to blush so she adopted a southern accent.

"My dear sir, what you won't say to turn a young girl's head."

"Young no, girl maybe and your head has been turned more times than there are stars in the sky but I love you anyway. Will you set me up with my usual?"

"Of course I will darlin'. You know me too well."

Paddy went to making some special drink while Victor carefully looked around the room again. This time he held his gaze with Beau and nodded again. He deliberately avoided looking my way and directed his attention back to Paddy.

"The word on the street is that you had a little problem with some of our charming muleskinners. I do hope it's been resolved to everyone's satisfaction. And how about the new owner? I hear he's Mister Charles' son and he's taken over the running of the business."

Paddy placed his drink on the bar and pushed it in his direction. "Well, aren't you just burstin' with questions tonight? The problems with the skinners have been laid to rest, so to speak. And, as far as the new owner goes, why not introduce yourself and find out first hand."

With a sweeping gesture, Paddy pointed to where I stood at the end of the bar. Victor slowly sipped his drink and looked at me for a moment or two before he made his way through the crowd. We sized up each other as he approached. His movements were smooth and well coordinated while his handshake was just the right combination of strength and grip control.

"Welcome to Santa Fe, sir. I am Victor Bodine. Like you, I have recently arrived in this fair city. I hope you will find it as hospitable as I have. And, if I might say so, you have a delightful and well run establishment here."

"It's a pleasure to meet you, sir. I'm Henry Charles. Are you here to try your luck at our tables?"

"Yes I am, sir. There's only one thing in life that I enjoy more than a game of cards with congenial gentlemen."

"And what would that be?"

Victor leaned closer and spoke in a lowered tone. "Why, the attention of a beautiful young woman, of course, Henry... or is it Charlie or perhaps Monroe? You'll have to excuse me; I'm terrible at remembering names."

After his deliberate use of those names, Victor made his way to a poker table and sat down with his back to me. He was, however, facing Beau who was busily dealing cards at the adjacent table.

I was so shaken by what Victor said that I finished the beer I was nursing and headed outside. Under the light of a brilliant full moon, I looked to the stars to help me understand what had just happened. Now that I had a face to put with the name Victor Bodine, I was more certain than ever that I'd heard it before. But for the life of me, I couldn't remember where.

My bigger concern was Taylor. It was obvious that she had revealed our secret to Victor and that could prove to be very big mistake. Had she been spending time with him ever'day since we got here? Just how well did they know each other? My head was swimming with possibilities.

"Perhaps I could be of assistance, Gove' nor."

I turned around and was confronted by a gnarly little man of middle age with an unlit cigar in his mouth. His body was bent and twisted and his clothes were thread bare and filthy. Only the gray woolen tam on his head looked to be fit for clothing. He walked with the aid of a wooden cane and was shod with well worn sandals.

"And what makes you think I need help?"

"I make it my business to know. I sell information and I believe you might be in need of some right about now."

"What possible information could you have that I might want or need?"

"Now that you've met Victor Bodine, I thought you might want to know about his relationship with a certain young woman named Taylor Henry."

I tried to conceal my surprise and concern but wasn't successful.

"Relax, Mister Charles, I was a friend to your father and I can be a friend to you.

"How were you a friend to my Father?"

"As I said before, I sell information. Your Father was one of my best clients. It was to his advantage in the gaming business to know everybody else's business. Many twas the time…"

I wasn't in the mood for war stories so I interrupted. "What can you tell me about Taylor Henry?"

The little man seemed taken aback by my interruption and snapped back. "I can tell you that she rode into Santa Fe with you and that you paid for her lodging above Olson's Mercantile."

I was dumbfounded. "How do you know this?"

"The stable hand at the livery is in my employ from time to time. I believe he said he was quite impressed with both of your horses.

They were a mustang stallion and a pinto filly if I remember correctly and I can see by your expression that I am correct."

"I also know that you returned to that same store this morning and bought the new clothes you're wearing this evening."

"And how do you know that?"

"A young shoe shiner might have mentioned it."

I couldn't believe my ears. Ever'one in this town seemed to know ever'thing about ever'body else. I decided I had to trust the little man and started over again.

"Let's back up. My name is Henry Charles."

I extended my hand but all I got was the end of his cane as his badly deformed hand was unable to shake.

"You can call me "Mutt" and as you can see, I'm not one for shaking hands."

"Mutt?"

"Yes, I seem to come from questionable lineage so the sobriquet applies. As a babe, I was abandoned on the streets of Liverpool but I survived. Then I became a beggar's crutch on Penny Lane and again, I managed to survive. Some years later, four young lads threw me aboard a ship bound for America as a joke but I earned my passage by climbing the mainsails and survived again. New York was cold and wet so I found the means to get to Santa Fe and here I will survive once more. Don't waste your pity on me."

"Mutt" was small in stature but large in spirit and determination. I decided right then and there that he would be a welcome friend and a fearsome enemy.

Now, if you have a silver eagle to spare, I'll tell you all about Miss Taylor Henry."

# CHAPTER V

## "The games people play"

**SUMMER 1882**

It quickly became apparent to me that Mutt and his small army of tattletales and snitches were remarkably well informed. A silver eagle bought me a wealth of information about my little sister and her relationship with Victor Bodine. What they had done together, including the when and the where of it, was carefully detailed along with impressions of their flowering friendship. His informers reported the couple had separate rooms at Olsen's, of course, but no one could speak to the actual sleeping arrangements. I had just met Victor and already I hated him. How could Taylor be taken in by a green felt rider from Louisiana?

After hearing all that Mutt had to relate, I was fit to be tied. Why was Taylor acting like that? Was she using Victor to taunt me or had she really fallen for him? I knew I had to see her first thing in the morning and find out where we stood. If her goal was to make me crazy it was working.

I couldn't go back in the gambling hall and face Victor so I decided to call it a night and go up to my room. As I made my way down the alley to the back stairs, a tub full of cleaning water came showering down just in front of me. I jumped back just in time to keep from getting drenched.

"Hey, watch where you throw that water."

I heard a woman's voice from the landing above.

"Watch out yourself or you'll get doused again."

I walked slowly and deliberately over to the stairs and started climbing. The moon was peeking in and out of the clouds but there was enough light for us to see each other clearly. Renee changed her tone when she realized who I was.

"I'm so sorry, Mister Charles, I didn't know it was you. I thought you were just another one of the local drunkards that come back in the alley to pee, crap or throw up. I take great pleasure in soaking them every chance I get. (Laughter) Most of the sots think its raining soap suds."

"Well, no harm done although you might consider that those same drunkards are some of our best customers and shouldn't be chased away."

"I doubt if a little sudsy water will curb any of their appetites."

When I reached the landing at the top of the stairs, Renee and I were face to face. She was an attractive young girl of medium height and build with mousy brown hair cut short like a choir boy. Her tattered dress was that of a charwoman and her feet were bare and filthy. She did look rather young and innocent in the flickering moonlight but I could tell she was neither. A hard and cruel life had aged her way beyond her years.

"I was told to be 'nice' to you so I will if you wish it."

"Who told you that?"

"Maude. She says since you're the new boss, all us girls have to be 'nice' to you any time you want."

"That might have been the rule for my Father but not me."

"Is there something the matter with you or aren't we good enough for ya?"

"It's not that. I'm just not interested in having a woman that's been bought or ordered to my bed. I'm looking for one that comes willingly and wants me as much as I want her."

"You sound like the kind of fool who believes in love."

"I reckon I am."

"Well, I think its rubbish. Men are nothing more than feral pigs and women are forced to slop them and that's all there is to life."

I couldn't change her mind or ease her pain so I just walked through the doorway and headed down the hall. As I unlocked the door to my room, she had one final caustic comment.

"I might hate doing it but they all tell me I'm damn good so if you ever change your mind…"

I wasn't gonna change my mind, at least not that night. I had Taylor and Victor to worry about.

The next morning found me up and dressed at first light. The air was cool before the sun could heat it up and the skies were blue in every direction. I had a quick breakfast of *Huevos rancheros*, corn cakes and coffee at *Pepe's Cantina* and headed off for Olsen's Mercantile. It turned out the pretty little Mexican gal was Pepe's daughter, *Solana*, and she was truly his "sunshine".

Lars was outside doing his usual morning clean up and restocking. Lena was running in and out making sure everything ended up where she wanted it. I wanted to ask about Taylor and wasn't really sure how to do it but Lena relieved me of the problem. When she came out and saw me, she yelled back into the store.

"Taylor, here's da young man dat was asking about you last veek."

Lena took me aback with her openness and honesty but when Taylor came out the door, I was stunned silent. She was absolutely beautiful. I had never seen her in anything but saddle-worn jeans, checkered shirts and boots but there she was wearing a new blue dress with matching shoes and a bow holding her hair in a ponytail. She was all smiles and sweetness as she came up to me to be introduced. Lena did the honors and I removed my hat in a gentlemanly fashion.

"Taylor, dis here is Henry Charles. He is also new to town and was asking about you. He's from Colorado if I recall."

Lena smiled at both of us and then went back into the store and took Lars with her. Taylor watched them leave and then turned her bright smile my way. She seemed to relish my confusion and really played it up.

"I'm pleased to meet you, Henry. What brings you to Santa Fe?"

I was fighting for words that were slow in comin'.

"Ah, I'm here on business sort of... I mean... I'm the new owner of a business here in Santa Fe."

"And what business would that be?"

I'd had about enough of the play acting. "Taylor Henry, you know full well who I am and what my business is."

"Come on, Monroe, don't spoil the fun."

"The name is Henry and this maybe fun for you but not me. I want to know what you've been doing these last few weeks and who you've been doing it with."

Taylor turned away from me but kept an eye on the door of the store.

"Listen... Henry... What I do and who I do it with is none of your concern. In case you've forgotten, you're not my brother anymore."

"Maybe not but it seems like you've forgotten who you are and why we're here. I paid for the room your staying in."

"Well, I'm working here at the store part time to pay for my own room so you won't have to bother with that any more."

"Where'd you get that new dress and shoes?"

"Not that it's any of your business but I received them as a gift from a gentleman friend of mine. He said they were made for me and brought out the blue in my eyes."

While Taylor was parading around in front of the store to show off her blue dress, I was trying to control the urge to throw her over my knee and spank her.

"And I suppose your new friend would be Victor Bodine, am I right?"

"Have you been spying on me?"

"Do you have any idea who and what he is?"

"Well I know he's a real gentleman for starters. He's also a businessman and sporting promoter, whatever that means."

"It means he's a professional gambler. That's what it means."

"Well aren't you the pot callin' the kettle black?"

She had me there. I was the owner of a gambling hall and saloon as well as a partner in a sporting house and Victor was just one of my customers. I had no good answer for her.

"That's different."

"How is it different?"

"Well it just is. You know I ain't no gambler."

"So does Victor."

"And that's not all he knows. How could you tell him all about me?"

"I didn't."

"Yes you did."

"No I didn't!"

"Then who did? He called me Charlie and Monroe instead of Henry. He knows all about who I used to be."

For the first time, I saw a glimmer of the old Taylor Henry I used to know. "He called you by both of those names?"

"Yes he did. Last night in the casino and he did so very deliberately."

"Believe me Monroe, I didn't tell him anything about you or us. I don't know how he could know or why he would care."

"Then you'll stop seeing him?"

"No. Why should I?"

"But I thought..."

"Until I have a new boyfriend, I'll stick with the one I've got."

Taylor spun around and walked back into the store.

"And a good day to you sir."

There I stood with my hat in my hand and my heart in my throat. There was so much I wanted to say but it just wouldn't come out. Part of me wanted to be her new boyfriend while another part wanted to be her older brother and lock her in her room.

I walked around for several hours of sight seeing before returning to the St. Charles. When I reached the plaza, I saw the First National Bank of Santa Fe and it reminded me of the note in Charles' ledger. I didn't have the actual account numbers with me but figured the manager might be able to tell me something about the accounts Charles had.

The bank was a well built building of stone and mortar. The front doors were large and thick which gave the place a look of safety and security. Inside, it was fancy as all get out with oak paneled walls, overstuffed chairs and the largest double door safe I'd ever seen. There were several teller stations and a highly decorated office in the back. I remembered the name Lucien B. Maxwell from the ledger and asked for him. A clerk gave me a strange look and then directed me to the manager's office.

I was introduced to and shook the hand of the vice president of the bank, Richard Dixon. Sensing a new customer for his bank, he was full of bluster and blarney. He pointed to a large portrait of a man on the wall and explained to me that Lucien B. Maxwell was the founder of the bank but had died back in 1875.

"Did you know he was called the 'Emperor of the West'? They say he once owned one million, seven hundred thousand acres in New Mexico and Colorado. He started out with Kit Carson, you know. They were scouts and hunters for John C. Fremont on his many expeditions throughout the West. He was well known as a rancher, farmer and businessman but I'm told he was always a mountain man at heart. Bet you didn't know that Billy the Kid died in Lucien's home in Fort Sumner. I have it on good authority that Billy and Lucien are buried just a few feet apart."

Dixon finished his sales pitch and sat back in his chair.

"Tell me, why were you asking for Lucien?"

"I never knew about the man or his death but I reckon my Father did. I found his name in an old ledger along with some bank account numbers."

"And who was your Father?"

"Farley Charles. I'm his son, Henry."

With that bit of news, Mister Dixon rose from his chair to shake my hand again.

"Your Father was a friend of mine and a long time customer of this bank. I'll wager his accounts were established years ago when Lucien Maxwell was still running things here. I was greatly saddened to hear of his untimely death. Is there anything I or the bank can do for you?"

"Nothing special. I was just curious about those accounts."

"I am familiar with your Fathers accounts. He had two saving deposits and a rented lock box but I will need written proof of his death and proof of your identity as his sole heir before I can allow you access to them. Sorry, but we have very strict regulations regarding these matters."

"No matter. I have all the documents you need and will return in the near future. I was just passing by and thought to come in and introduce myself and see about continuing our financial affairs."

"Let me assure you that the First National Bank of Santa Fe will be very happy to continue our relationship with St. Charles Place and its new owner."

We shook hands again and I left the bank with a new sense of urgency regarding the accounts. Why two different savings accounts and what was in his lock box?

It was a little after the noon hour when I entered the gambling hall and the place was damn near empty. Beau sat by himself at a poker table playing solitaire. He looked up when I came in but didn't say anything. I looked for Paddy but she wasn't around so I pulled up a chair and sat across the table from Beau.

"I'd like to ask a favor and this isn't an order from your boss. Please feel free to say no."

Beau stopped playing his game, looked over at me and smiled. "No."

"But you haven't heard the favor yet."

"Alright. Ask me the favor and then I'll say no."

"I want to learn to play poker. Really play poker. I know all the rules of the game but I want to learn to play the way Charles played. I want you to teach me to be as good as he was."

Beau seemed frozen in thought for about thirty seconds and then he continued fooling with the cards.

"Your Father was the only man to ever beat me at poker. I can still see him sitting there chewing on his unlit cigar, drinking his phony alcohol with two of the girls posed behind him. I could never read the man. He was born with a gift and that can't be taught."

"Well, I'm his son. It stands to reason that I might have the same gift."

Beau stopped playing again and looked me straight in the eye.

"You asked the one favor I can't turn down. Charles taught me all I know about the finer points of card playing and I owe it to him to do the same for you."

"When do we start?"

"Now's as good a time as any. Paddy takes a lunch break every day about this time so I watch the bar for her. I'm generally alone in here so we won't be disturbed."

"Good. Let's get to it."

Every afternoon for the next two weeks was spent with Beau and the poker table. Paddy teased us both for getting along so well. I wouldn't say Beau started to like me but at least he didn't hate me anymore and I was learning all about the finer points of poker.
I quickly found out it was so much more than a card game. Knowing when to hold 'em and when to fold 'em was just the starting-out point. Poker was a game of personality and strategy combined with elements of chance and pure dumb luck. A professional card-sharp played the other players as much as he manipulated the cards. Though a truly skillful player never had to cheat to win, many did. Knowing all their tricks and watching the ebb and flow of the game was half the fun.

To start each lesson, we practiced card shuffling and stacking. My hand coordination was good and I was able to master the basics pretty quickly. Beau was much better, of course, and showed me how to watch for a false deal, a second deal, a bottom deal and marked cards. He was really good at a "false shuffle" where he could stack the cards to cut an ace every time.

According to Beau, the first rule of poker was "one vice at a time". Never mix poker with alcohol or women. Either can cloud your mind and ruin your concentration. Beau told me that Charles always drank "tea-skey" which was a mixture of ninety-five percent dark brewed tea and five percent whiskey splashed on top. By sipping off the top, he could get "whiskey breath" without any whiskey symptoms. The girls from upstairs always stood well behind Charles and struck provocative poses to distract the other players.

The second rule was to never develop a "tell" unless you did do so deliberately to fool an opponent later in the game. A "tell" was a change in your behavior or routine while playing a hand. It could involve actions such as touching a certain part of your face, blinking too often or "fingering" with a stack of chips. Any repetitive routine at a specific time might give away your hand or strategy to other players. For example, an inexperienced player might develop a nervous "tell" whenever he bluffed. On some occasions, Charles would remove his unlit cigar from his mouth whenever he bluffed until he had a sure winner and then he would take it out to fool the others into calling his bluff. It was a risky but often profitable maneuver.

Beau's third and final rule was never count your money when you're sitting at the table. There would be time enough for counting your winnings when the game was over. Nobody liked a loud winner or a sore loser. Whenever Charles won every dollar a man had, he would always give the man a double eagle as seed money. It eased his pain and brought him back when he had more money than sense.

My evenings were usually spent in the casino just watching and learning. Once or twice a night Beau directed me to play and I got involved using house money. I won more than I lost but still had a lot to learn. The following afternoons we would talk about how I played and what I should have done or not done. I was amazed and impressed with the depth of his knowledge of human nature. He "read" gamblers right about eight out of ten times.

There was always an exception like Victor Bodine, who was a person that Beau found hard to characterize. He could detect no discernable strategy to Victor's game. Sometimes he played fast and loose while other times he was slow and tight. He rarely bluffed or bet large amounts of money and seemed content just to play for the sake of passing time. What bothered Beau the most was that Victor resisted all attempts to draw him into bigger games and that didn't match with his attitude and attire. He wished to dress and act like a professional gambler but he never actually played poker like one.

During my two week training session, Victor came in five times. He never stayed long and avoided playing against Beau or me. Instead, he got into penny-ante games with cattlemen, drifters and drummers. Once he made "walking around money", he'd pack it in and head out. He usually acknowledged me with a smile and a tip of his hat but we never spoke. Paddy was the only one who was able to break through his secretive shell and actually have a conversation with him. From what I could tell, it was always the same horseshit every time as he ordered his usual drink.

Mutt paid me a timely visit every day or two with tidbits of information regarding my dear ex-sister, Taylor. She was still seeing Victor but not as much since she was working more hours at Olsen's Mercantile. The missionary school had opened and Lars was no longer able to work so Taylor took over his duties. Twice I walked over to speak with her but stopped midway and gave up. I had to accept her desire for independence and trust that somehow, things would work out.

On Tuesday of my second week, good old Maude did exactly as Paddy predicted and put Renee up for auction. She said the bidding would last four days from Wednesday through midnight on Saturday night and the high bidder at that time would win his "virgin". She wrote the bidder's name and the highest bid amount on a chalkboard for all to see. The bidding was fast and furious for two days until Friday, when the price reached the princely sum of three hundred dollars. A corpulent German rancher by the name of Herrmann looked to be the winner as few could afford to match his bid.

Each afternoon when I came in for my training session with Beau, I saw Renee walk through the casino and look up at the chalkboard. As usual she showed little emotion but I could see apprehension in her eyes. I couldn't begin to imagine the conflicting emotions running through her head. Herrmann was a disgusting bacon-fed German with a bearded hoglike face who enjoyed the idea of besting the others in the bidding more than he relished the prize. He got stupidly drunk each night and taunted the others for their inability to outbid him.

To confuse matters even more, the other girls all started showing signs of jealousy and got ornery as all get out. They had spats with their customers as well as each other. Margarita punched out a local Injun when he belittled her non-virginal condition. Even Angelina, who usually stayed aloof and separate from the others, got into a cat fight with Jolene and Nicole. It took Beau and me, along with three customers, to break 'em up. Carlotta drank way too much and actually passed out at one of the tables and had to be carried up to her room. The aging trollops had a belly full of being told that Renee was the gold standard and they didn't measure up.

Maude got mad as hell and tore into the whole bunch of 'em. She warned that if they didn't get back to business as usual, they'd find themselves selling it for quarters out on the street. The whole deal with Renee and the auction was getting out of control. I was relieved to see Saturday night roll around so we could put an end to it.

As might be expected, the gambling hall was overstuffed with customers. All the tables and chairs were taken and it was standing room only. Many were strangers since word of the event had spread south to Albuquerque and north to Taos and Angel Fire. But the one who'd traveled furthest was the Scottish boot maker from El Paso, Drummond McLean. Paddy spotted him right off and warned me of trouble brewing.

McLean was a tall, thick-built man of fifty with a drooping mustache and sour expression. His hands and forearms spoke of many years spent hammering leather. Somehow, he musta heard about our auction and was surely here to reclaim his property. To ease the situation, I sent over a free drink and opened a spot for him at Beau's table. At first, he was suspicious of the hospitality but no good Scotsman could rightly refuse an open chair or a free drink.

During the next half hour, I sent over three more drinks and watched while boot maker McLean repeatedly broke the first two rules of poker. The free whiskey clouded his mind and raised his voice to a volume where ever'one in the place could hear him bragging or cursing about his cards. I figured that if he ran out of gambling money he'd have to leave, so at my direction, Beau skillfully relieved him of ever' last dollar. For a moment, it looked like the burly boot maker had had enough.

At exactly the wrong time, Maude came through the front doors to check out the action and went straight to the bar to speak with me and Paddy. In a deliberately loud voice, she said Renee was gonna parade around the bar at ten o'clock to stir up the bidding for the two remaining hours. A cheer went up from the crowd and that got McLean's attention. We watched with amusement as he staggered over to join us. The drunken and broke boot maker was cherry-faced and mad beyond all reason.

"I've come a long way to see your so called virgin Renee so where is she? If she's who I think she is, she's my property and certainly ain't no virgin."

Maude was livid. "You can't possibly believe that you can own another human being? That's slavery and against the law"

Paddy had her say too. "And didn't we just fight an uncivil war to settle that very question?"

"Well I don't answer to your law. I answer to the word of God and in the old testament of the good book it says a man can sell his daughter into slavery and that's what her Father did. I paid good money for her and will have what is mine…so shut up you old whore."

At that point Maude slapped him across the face and he instinctively back slapped her. The old madam was stunned by the blow and fell to floor. Paddy hurriedly reached for her shotgun so it was left to me to calm things down. I stepped between Paddy and McLean and tried a new tactic.

"So tell me, Mister McLean, just how much did you pay for the young lady in question?"

The boot maker was just befuddled enough by the drinks and the slap to be confused by my intrusion and my question. His eyes were red and watery and his tongue had started to thicken.

"Aye...Her Father asked for five gold double eagles. That's... ah... what I paid... one hundred dollars. But now that I see that fine chalkboard, I figure she be worth at least three hundred dollars."

"So if I gave you three hundred dollars you'd leave town?"

"Aye that I would, laddie"

I looked over at Beau who was just leaning back in his chair and taking in the show.

"Beau, do you have three hundred in cash in front of you?"

Beau riffled the greenbacks in his stack. "Yes I believe I do."

"Then kindly bring it over here and give it to Mister McLean."

Beau tipped his hat and picked up the money. "Yes boss."

When Beau handed the cash to McLean, the besotted boot maker got flustered and angry.

"What's this? You're giving back me own fookin' money."

"I do believe you lost that money at the table so it is no longer yours. Either way, you've been paid as you requested and are now obliged to leave."

"But...but...this ain't enough. I want more I tell ya."

If you want more, then you'll have to cut the deck. What do you say...double or nothing?"

His good sense almost overcame his drunken rage but he couldn't help himself.

"Alright, laddie, we'll cut for it."

Beau produced a cold deck and laid it on the bar. Then he offered to break in the new deck and did so by running a quick riffle shuffle to mix the cards. McLean started to cut them when he had a minute of cold sobriety and backed off.

"I think maybe we should give 'em another mixing, what do ya think?"

Before I could stop him, he performed a very sloppy overhand shuffle, slapped the deck back on the bar and glared at Beau.

"Now neither of us will know just where the aces are."

Then, he cut the cards very slowly and deliberately from about the middle of the deck and turned over the knave of spades. He was delighted with his selection and taunted me with his good fortune.

"See if you can beat that one gambler man."

I calmly turned over the top card from the remaining half-deck and revealed the queen of hearts. McLean's face fell like a boulder off a cliff.

"You cheated me but you did it well. I'll go back to El Paso with a lesson learned."

With that rational response, McLean turned and walked towards the door. I knew it was too good to be true so I watched and waited. When he reached the swinging doors, he went for his pistol and turned to fire. I drew my Colt and plugged him dead center in the chest. His six gun hit the floor and he stood there for a second or two as the shock of being shot finally got through to his alcohol soaked brain. When he finally hit the floor, he rolled over to utter his final words.

"I guess you ain't no virgin neither."

The acrid smell of gunpowder filled the casino and ever'one held their collective breath for a second of two until the place erupted in hootin' and hollarin'. Like it or not, I was an unwilling hero once again because I was fast with a shootin' iron. I hadn't planned for things to end that way but it did settle the matter without any loose ends. McLean would never be coming back to claim his property so Renee was free of him at last.

Sheriff O'Reilly must have been making his rounds 'cause he came through the door about thirty seconds after the shooting. Maude deftly took him aside and explained things to his satisfaction while a couple of the regulars carted the body away. To the delight of the crowd, Paddy announced a drink on the house. But before she attended to the drink requests, she left Beau with something to think about.

"I warned you he might be pretty handy with that Colt revolver."

Even Beau was impressed. "For once I must agree with your assessment. I don't think I've ever seen it done with such speed and accuracy."

Maude had other thoughts. "Well I want to know how you knew that queen of hearts was there. I thought you were gonna loose that bet for sure."

"That was easy. After Beau gave the deck a false shuffle, McLean's overhand shuffle didn't change a thing. All the face cards were still in the center of the deck. I couldn't lose."

Beau got a concerned look on his face and turned over and spread out the remaining part of the cut deck. All the bottom cards had faces but those towards the top were a mixture of numbered cards. Now Beau was visibly embarrassed and had to clear his throat.

"Ahem... well... I guess it wasn't quite like that. I didn't figure on his sloppy shuffle. I thought he would let the deck be and cut first and deep so I put all the high cards on the bottom. Somehow, his shuffle separated that jack and queen from the others. Picking that lady was a hundred to one."

Beau's comments made me queasy and weak in the knees. I was so sure I was right and all along I was so wrong. I guess I learned a lesson too.

Paddy had the answer. "What was it that Charles always said? Skill always wins over time but in a showdown hand you can never beat dumb luck."

Maude put her arms around me and held me close enough to whisper in my ear. "The queen of hearts is always your best bet and luck always runs in pairs. Maybe you'll be lucky in love tonight too."

After things had quieted down and returned to normal, Renee came downstairs for her ten o'clock showing. When she came through the doors accompanied by Jolene, Nicole and Carlotta, she looked like a shiny new penny in a stack of old nickels. Her new hairdo and make-up made her look a little older but the skin tight red dress really made her out to be a full grown woman. I couldn't believe my eyes and neither could the rest of the crowd. Herrmann was so surprised when he saw her that he spilt beer down the front of his shirt. In rapid succession I heard three ascending bids that raised the ante another sixty dollars. Not to be outdone, the beer-soaked German called out "four hundred" and the crowd went nutty.

When Renee saw me at the bar, she broke away from the others and made her way to where I was standing. Her eyes met mine as she walked up to me. She was the damndest combination of innocent child and seductive siren I'd ever seen. She took my hands in hers and leaned closer so that no one else could hear.

"I heard what you did for me this evening and I will never forget." Then she quickly kissed my cheek and backed away. "Maybe I was wrong. Maybe all men aren't pigs after all."

We held eye contact for a few more seconds and then she whirled around the casino one more time and went upstairs to await the highest bidder. The other girls stayed and trolled the crowd for those who lost out in the bidding. I was suddenly in bad need of a drink and ordered whiskey from Paddy. She complied but did so with a stern warning.

"I told you not to get involved with Renee. I've seen her likes before and if you give 'er a chance, she'll ruin your life… mark my words."

"It's not that…"

"In a pig's eye. I've seen that look on men's faces all my life. I'll wager it's been there ever since Adam and Eve were in the garden. That little vixen's got her hooks in you and she'll reel you in if you let her. I'll say no more."

Part of me knew Paddy was right but the rest of me didn't care. I had to get Renee out of my head. I downed the whiskey and it burned all the way. I grabbed my beer and went to find a game of cards.

For the next two hours I played poker while breaking the very first rule. Thoughts of Renee clouded my judgment to the point I could barely remember what I was doing. Paddy watched me with motherly concern but Beau watched with an ever widening grin on his face. I was supposed to be winning but I was barely staying even.

In the background, Maude was urging the rowdy crowd to raise the ante with additional bids. Herrmann was likewise taunting all the young men with his guttural remarks about what he was about to do with Renee. It was almost midnight when fate stepped in and dealt me a pair of eights with an ace kicker.

I was instantly reminded of Wild Bill Hickok's so-called "dead mans hand". He died with two pair, aces and eights. Some inner feeling told me it was time to take a chance.

We were playing draw poker with a ten dollar ante. There were six of us at the table and ever'one was about even and itching to do better. I was fifth in line and double raised the opening bid of twenty dollars to forty. That raised a few eyebrows and drew some restrained chuckles from the others. I guess they were also aware that my head hadn't been in the game. They musta thought I was trying to buy the pot and they weren't gonna let me so all five called my raise.

On the draw, I pulled another pair of eights to go with my ace. Four of a kind was almost impossible to beat and I struggled to keep my composure.

I took a deep breath and feigned disappointment with the draw before offering a weak opening bet of ten dollars. As luck would have it, two players folded but the other three got good cards so the call bet was sixty dollars when it got back to me. I raised the bet to one hundred dollars and changed the mood at the table. Two of the three tossed in their cards in disgust but one hung in there and raised the bet again to one hundred and fifty.

It was time to depend on rule number two. My opponent was a middle aged drummer with an alcohol habit. He'd been playing tight all night and this was his first venture into a big money pot. Seeing that he drew three cards, the best he coulda had was a pair going in so the odds of him holding a better hand than mine were minimal. Since he was also fidgety as all get out and sweating like a live frog on a hot griddle, I figured him for a bluffer and upped his raise another hundred dollars.

He swallered hard and riffled his remaining chips. Another hundred would clean him out and he knew it. When he tried to sip his drink, he was so shaky that it spilled on the table and never reached his mouth. The pressure was mounting and he couldn't stand it any longer. He shoved in all his chips and called my bet.

By this time, our continued betting had attracted the attention of a lot of the bystanders. They gathered around the table like buzzards around a water hole. There was more than a thousand dollars on the table and most were waiting for the winner to buy a drink for the house. Beau halted his game to watch, Paddy stopped pouring drinks and Maude actually stopped pushing her auction to join the crowd. I enjoyed the moment.

Without showing my cards I answered the call.

"I've got two pair."

The crowd groaned and the drummer beamed. He turned over his cards to reveal a full house, tens over threes. He started to reach for the pot when I tossed in my cards face up.

"Yes sir, two pairs of eights."

The crowd went wild and the drummer collapsed. Paddy yelled out "drinks on the house" and Beau tipped his hat to acknowledge a hand well played. I pulled in the pot and grabbed Maude by the arm.

"What's the current price for Renee?"

"Mister Herrmann still has the high bid of four hundred dollars and time is running out."

I handed her five hundred dollars in chips.

"Cash these in and announce you have a bid of five hundred."

"Should I use your name?"

"Sure. It will show that even the boss has to pay to be first."

"But surely you know that she isn't..."

"Yeah, I know but I'm betting she'll be worth it. Didn't you say I might be lucky in love tonight?"

When Maude announced my bid, the crowd cheered and Herrmann fumed. He downed his drink and stomped out of the place. Paddy gave me a disgusted look and Beau just kept on grinning.

When the auction was officially over, Maude handed me a big brass key which was supposed to open Renee's door upstairs. Truth be told, except for my door, the rooms upstairs had no locks at all but it was a fine prop and the crowd hollered their support and encouragement as I left to go out the front and down the alley.

As I walked up the back stairs and down the hallway, my heart was pounding with anticipation. I had no idea what was going to happen when I entered Renee's room but I was hell-bound to find out. The hinge gave a pathetic squeak as I opened the door and there she was, still wearing that skin tight red dress and staring out the window at the midnight sky. The room was barely illuminated by the moonlight but I could see her body stiffen with apprehension. Her back was to the door so she had no idea who had just entered. She spoke in a defiant voice.

"So, you must be the grand prize winner."

"And you must be the grand prize."

Renee froze for a minute and then turned around with a face full of questions.

"You? Why would you bid four hundred dollars when you could have me for free any time you wished?"

"Actually, I bid five hundred and I told you before that I don't cotton to an unwilling or purchased woman."

"Then why?"

"I'm really not sure. I guess I couldn't stand the thought of you with Herrmann."

She thought about what I said and then returned to the window.

"Well, tomorrow night anyone can have me for the usual price and that includes Herrmann."

"Unless you're not here."

"Where else would I be?"

"You could leave Santa Fe. Go somewhere far away to start a new life."

She whirled around full of anger and spite.

"And just how do I do that without any money?"

"What was your split with Maude for tonight's auction?"

"A lousy ten percent."

"O.K., that's $50.00. My split with Maude is sixty-forty which means she owes me three hundred. I could throw in that amount and that would give ya three hundred and fifty dollars. A girl or excuse me, a young woman could get quite a ways with that."

"Why would you do that for me?"

"Let's just say I think you deserve another chance at life. You can just walk away Renee. Go back to your old name or pick out a brand new one. You could start over."

"Are you trying to save me from a life of prostitution?"

"Maybe…I don't know. I just want to give you that chance."

"What would I do? I have no schoolin'. I can't read or write."

"It won't be easy but you could learn."

"That's easy for you to say. What if I want to stay a prostitute?"

"That would be your decision. Either way, the money is yours."

I walked over to the bed and pulled back the covers so I could strip off the sheet. Renee knew what I was doing so she tossed me a small glass bottle of pig's blood she had concealed somewhere under her dress. I poured most it out in the center of the sheet and rolled it back up.

"That should keep the boys downstairs satisfied."

Next, I counted out three hundred dollars and tossed it on the bed.

"If you pack your things tonight and leave early in the morning there should be a train or stage to take you wherever ya plan to go. Don't give Maude a chance to talk you out of it."

We stood in silence for a minute or two as we were both lost in thought. Renee sat on the edge of the bed and just stared at the money. Tears rolled down her face and she tried not to cry. In the pale moonlight she looked so young and beautiful it was hard to imagine what she had lived through. We said good-by and I left her room.

I waited on the back landing for about ten minutes and then I went downstairs to show off that damn bloody sheet. When I got there, I was surprised and disappointed to see Victor Bodine standing at the bar. Now why did he have to be there to see that bloody sheet? It suddenly occurred to me that Taylor would certainly find out. I could only imagine what she would think.

Maude held my "trophy" up for inspection and the remaining crowd of drunks cheered their approval. After accepting congratulations, I snuck away and hurried back to my room. It had been a day I wouldn't soon forget. I killed a man in a gunfight, won my first big poker hand and like some knight in shining armor; I tried to rescue a fair damsel. I was pretty pleased with myself as I tried to get to sleep.

A short time later, as I was about half asleep, I became aware of the presence of someone else in my bed. I jumped a little when I felt a soft hand on my shoulder and heard Renee whisper.

"Don't worry, Henry, I'm not here to hurt you."

"How did you…?"

"I learned how to pick locks so I could get away from McLean. Your door was simple enough."

"I told you before, Renee, I really don't want…"

"But I'm here to give you exactly what you do want. You told me you were looking for a woman to come to you willingly and I am. You also said you wanted a woman to desire you and I do. The only question left is… do you still want me?"

That turned out to be a moot point as she wrapped herself around me in a fit of passion. After that, there wasn't anything left to say.

We shared a wonderful evening together and watched the sunrise in each others arms. Renee got up before I did and wasted no time getting cleaned up and dressed.

"Guess I better get going, today's another day."

"Are you planning to leave?"

"Here? Yes. Santa Fe? No. Why should I? Thanks to you, I don't have to worry about Mclean anymore and now I won't have to work for old horse-face. I can be my own boss and decide who, when, and for how much without having to split any of it."

"But last night…"

"Face it Henry, last night was a dream for both of us but today is reality. I'm just a girl with nothing to sell but her body while I'm still young enough to get a decent price for it. If you want to spend another night with me, you'll pay like anyone else. Last night will never happen again. Some dreams can only be dreamt once."

With that, she picked up her small valise and walked out the door. Paddy tried to warn me but I just had to find out for myself. Renee could "put-on" sweet and innocent like a satin dress but inside she would always be cold and ruthless underneath. From the window, I watched her walk down the back stairs without hesitation and never look back.

I caught a glimpse of Mutt watching it all from the alley. I wondered if he was watching for her or me and if he'd been there all night. It was a sure thing that I wasn't his only paying customer in Santa Fe.

# CHAPTER VI

# "Headin' for the Flagstaff"

## SPRING 1886

"Henry, are you awake?  Can you hear me?  Who is Taylor?"

I could hear Chosovi speaking but for some reason I wasn't responding.  Guess when I started thinking about Taylor I sorta drifted away for awhile.  I assured her I was alright and then tried to answer her questions.

"Taylor was my baby sister and I was her big brother when we were growing up.  That's when I thought I was the natural son of Porter and Miriam Henry.  Four years ago, I found out that I wasn't.  That meant we weren't really blood kin so I began to look at her with different eyes.  When we went to Santa Fe, we tried to be jus' friends but that didn't work out so well.  It's for certain she's not my little sister anymore and never really was my woman.  Right now, I couldn't even call her a friend.  That's all in the past."

I could tell Chosovi wanted to ask more questions but respected my feelings and let the subject drop.  She talked about her life growing up with the Hopi and her hopes for the future until I was too tired to listen.  After attending to my wound in silence, she left me with worries and concerns about my own future.

## SUMMER 1886

Spring meandered into summer before I fully overcame the effects of the gunshot and the bullet removal. Fever and infection came and went as I rasseled with the grim reaper to stay in this world and not enter his. Through it all, Chosovi was by my side and Toho was never far from hers. Finally the battle was over and I could eat on my own and take short walks without assistance. With the aid of Injun medicine, the wound healed over and I finally regained my strength and endurance. My Hopi friends had been great to me and saved my life but I knew it was time for us to part ways.

Toho could sense and understand my desire to leave. Just as he could never be completely at home in the white man's world, he knew I couldn't be content living with the Hopi. One night after we had eaten, he questioned me about it.

"Will you leave us now that your wound has healed?"

"Yes, it is time. I must return to the Box H ranch and try to explain what has happened to Taylor and me since we left."

"We will always think of you as one of us. You are to be known as *Pahana*, our lost white brother. You will always be welcome."

With that settled I packed my gear and had a good nights sleep so I was up and ready to leave the following morning. I considered shaving but thought better of it. I'd never grown a full beard before and kinda wondered what it looked like. Did it really make me look older or was that another tall tale told around the campfire? Since there were no mirrors in the Hopi village, I would have to wait until I got to Flagstaff to see if I liked it or not but I sure didn't miss shaving.

Toho and Chosovi prepared plenty of food and water for my trip across the Painted Desert. I had made the same trip four years earlier and was confident I'd be able to find my way again but it was certain to be a challenge.

While I was checking the loads in my rifle and pistol, I could sense there was some tension between Toho and Chosovi. They were unusually silent and seemed to avoid looking at each other. Finally Chosovi spoke out.

"Henry, will you tell us what was in the book?"

"Book? Oh, you mean the Clifton's journal. I thought you knew."

Toho reluctantly explained. "None of our people, including my Father, could read the words in the book. We cannot read any language. Chosovi wishes to know what the book says about her white family. I tell her that the Hopi people are her family but she yearns for more. She wants to believe that you are her brother."

We all sat down on the dirt floor as I tried my best to explain what I'd read. Chosovi was excited and anxious to hear while Toho was apprehensive.

"The book was written twenty-four years ago and tells about a family by the name of Clifton. A man named Hiram, his wife Johanna and their two children came west along the Santa Fe Trail. When they caught the fever, they were forced from the wagon train and left to fend for themselves or die. I guess you know the rest."

Chosovi was eager for more information. "How old were the children? What were their names?"

"The boy was a little older than the girl but both were less than two years. His name was William and hers was Hillary."

"Hillary? What does it mean?"

"I don't know if it means anything. White folks name their kids in many ways. I was named after a dead president."

Toho just had to ask. "So your real name may be William Clifton?"

"Yeah, and that would be a new one for me. I guess that's something we'll never know for sure. Hopi Joe was the only one who might have known the answer and now he's gone. There's no other way to figure which boy baby died.

Toho looked like he'd swallowed a frog and got up to leave. Chosovi grabbed his arm and said something in Hopi that I didn't get. She seemed to be pleading with him but I couldn't be sure. Finally, he gave in and sat down again.

"Before my Father entered the spirit world, he did remember one more thing about the boy that died. He said the baby had a scar or dark colored shape on his buttocks."

"A birthmark?"

"I do not understand."

"A different colored shape or scar on the skin when a baby is born."

"Yes…birthmark."

"What shape was it?"

"Father said it looked like a small *yongosona*, a little turtle."

"Did he say anything else?"

"Only that he was sorry he could not remember more."

That was an interesting piece of information but seemed of little use. Toho and Chosovi left me to my packing and my wandering thoughts. What possible help could a birthmark on a long dead baby be?

I walked to the far side of the mesa where all the horses were kept and reunited with Goner. He seemed glad to see me but balked at leaving the pony herd. The herdsman explained that Goner had been very active with the mares and that his bloodline would be welcome in their herd. No wonder he didn't want to leave.

When ever'thing was loaded, it was time to say good-by to Toho and Chosovi as well as the rest of the village. It was kinda awkward because he saw me as his blood brother, Henry, while she saw me as her real brother, William. For my part, I wasn't sure just who I was.

I wished them well and promised to return as soon as possible but truly wondered if I ever would. I reminded Toho that they could visit us just like his Father used to and he accepted the invitation. It was an emotional moment but thank goodness Goner got road-eager and took off down the trail before I had a chance to tear-up and make a darn fool of myself.

I left the First Mesa heading in a southwest direction. I could see the San Francisco Peaks in the distance. They were over twelve thousand feet high and made a great trail marker to aim for.

Franciscan monks living with the Hopi supposedly named the mountains after Saint Francis of Assisi. The peaks were sacred to many of the pueblo tribes including the Hopi who considered them to be the winter home of their Kachina Gods that lived in the clouds. The Hopi called the peaks *Nuvatukaovi,* meaning the place with snow on the very top.

Since we had food, water and plenty of time, Goner and I took our good-natured time and enjoyed the journey. Although barren and lifeless, the Painted Desert was a beautiful landscape made up of a rainbow of colors. They ranged from lavenders to shades of gray with vibrant layers of red, orange and pink. The badlands were a seemingly endless expanse of hills, buttes, sand dunes and lava beds. Rock pinnacles rose from the desert floor to form rough sculptures shaped by the wind and rain. Each one had its own pattern of colors that layered the stone like a barber pole.

We crossed the Little Colorado River at Grand Falls. The river dropped almost two hundred feet to a muddy pool at the bottom. The spring runoff had provided some fresh water but it was so thick with sediment you could call it flowing mud. Because of the rich brown color, some folks even called it the "Chocolate Falls". We camped overnight and let the sound of the falling river put us to sleep.

In the morning, I spent some practice time with my Colt revolver. My shoulder was a little stiff and sore but after awhile, I got my rhythm and coordination back. It was fun shooting the seed pods off the prickly pear cactus. In fact, I was having so much fun playing shoot 'em up that I damn near ran myself out of ammunition. I was down to only four bullets when I finally stopped. That meant I'd have to stop and see my old friend Jonah at Goldman and Son Dry Goods Store and fill up my loops. It also occurred to me that I needed another good shirt since my spare had gotten shot up and bled on.

The ponderosa pine territory of Flagstaff was a welcome sight after the barren desert we'd been through. The juniper trees, the mulberry bushes and meadows of green grass all provided scents of home. I saw a good-sized herd of deer drinking out of a small creek and watched a golden eagle fly overhead as the day just kept getting better. I let Goner feast on the spring grass and drink the mountain water from a gushing stream as we meandered our way to Flag.

As I remember it, Flagstaff got its name following a Centennial celebration held on July the 4th, 1876. Some adventurous folks from Boston lopped all the top branches off a tall ol' pine tree and ran up an American flag. They were commemorating the first hundred years of our country's history. That waving flag was up there so high you could see it whippin' in the wind for miles around. Travelers used it as a guidepost to keep the right trail heading. "Head for the flag staff" were the only directions necessary.

It'd been four years since I left Flag and I could see the changes as I rode in. What had started out as a muddy crossroads in the middle of a pine forest was rapidly becoming a fair sized town. New homes and businesses were springing up ever'where but I could see the remnants of a real bad fire in the center of town. The area down by the railroad tracks seemed to have gotten the worst of it but they were rebuilding. It was fairly early in the morning when I arrived but folks were already comin' and goin' like ants around an anthill. I was trying to decide what to do first when I spied the old Wells Fargo office.

When Charles passed away, he left me an account with Wells Fargo that held twenty-four thousand dollars. It seemed like a good idea to make sure it was still there. Mister Quincy, the resident agent, seemed like a real nice fella but four years was a long time and I'd learned you could never get too comfortable in your dealings with lawyers or bankers.

I tied Goner to the hitch rail and was busily brushing trail dust off my clothes when I heard a child's voice.

"See Mama, there's another fella wearing a six gun."

I turned around to see a pert young mother crossing the street with her two sons in tow. They were yanking on their bits but she seemed determined to hang on to each so they didn't get stepped on or run over.

She was speaking to her older son with her back to me but I could overhear.

"I don't care what he's wearing. A real gentleman would never display such a weapon in public. Pay no attention to him. He's just a ruffian like those others."

I hadn't realized just how civilized Flagstaff had become. A quick look around confirmed that no other men on the street were wearing guns openly. To these city slickers, I must have looked like a savage coming in off the trail from the reservation. I took off my hat and tried to apologize in the flowery English I'd learned while running my gambling hall in Santa Fe.

"I'm sorry if I offended you, madam, but I just a rode in from the Hopi reservation and haven't had time to clean up and change clothes. Let me assure you and your children that I am not a ruffian."

She appeared so flustered and obviously taken aback by my words that she actually tried to apologize to me.

"Maybe I was mistaken about you, sir, but not those others. They were simply barbarians."

"What others?"

"Why, those two that just entered the Wells Fargo office. They made rude remarks to me and one of them even had the nerve to spit his vile tobacco on my shoes."

I dropped the high brow words and slipped into my normal conversation. "What did you say that got 'em so riled up?"

"I just told them what I thought of guns being displayed in public and the men who brandished 'em."

The older boy interrupted. "Then he called Mama a strumpet... what's a strumpet?"

The woman was deeply embarrassed by the question and yanked her son's arm. "You shush up, Billy, enough is enough."

I had questions of my own. "They went into the Wells Fargo office with their guns drawn?"

"Well, one of them was carrying a two-barrel shotgun and the other one, the one who spit at me, drew his pistol as he walked in the door. I saw that very clearly."

Well, it was clear to me too. I'd wandered into a hold-up in broad daylight in the middle of Flagstaff. I waved the remaining bystanders away and rushed to the window by the front door of the building. Inside, I could see one man with a double-load, short barrel shotgun holding a group of terrified customers at bay. There were a half dozen of 'em, four men and two women, huddled together on the far left side of the counter. I could just make out the other would-be bank robber behind the counter with Mister Quincy. He was waving a pistol around so it figured Quincy was being forced to open the safe. It suddenly occurred to me that they were not only stealing Wells Fargo money; they were trying to steal my "future money".

I gently tried the door handle and could tell it was latched from the inside. My only chance was to shoot the lock mechanism and smash the door open with my shoulder but first I needed a diversion. The Wells Fargo building had a rolled tin roof that sloped off to the back so I pulled off my right boot and hurled it over the top of the roof so it would land on the backside with a loud bang. When it did, the man with the shotgun whirled around and provided the opportunity I was waiting for.

I shot the door lock and hit the door as hard as I could with my left shoulder. The door gave way easier than I thought and I caught my sock foot on the threshold and fell into the room. It turned out to be a good thing since the shotgun rider turned back around and without taking time to aim, just fired both barrels at the open doorway.

Needless to say, I was several feet below his line of fire and was assaulted by the blast from the powder but none of the buckshot. I returned the favor by placing two perfect shots from my Colt revolver in the middle of his chest. He dropped the empty gut-buster and fell backwards into a growing pool of his own blood.

I rolled over on the floor to get a better angle when I saw the second robber was coming out from behind the counter using Mister Quincy as a shield. The bandit was holding a pistol to Quincy's head and didn't see me until I'd already lined him up in my sights. When he finally caught sight of me and turned my direction, I squeezed the trigger and gave him a third eye right smack dab in the middle of his forehead. He let go of his hostage and kinda slid down the side of the counter with a look of wonderment on his face. His unfired pistol slipped from his lifeless fingers and "clunked" on the floor. The last little bit of tobacco spittle drooled off his lips as he completely collapsed in a heap.

The leather satchel he was toting hit the floor about the same time and came open to spill greenbacks and gold coins ever'where. Suddenly, it occurred to me that bullet was my last shot. My Colt revolver was empty. What if I'd missed? I was mindful of the old gamblers phrase, "Lady Luck was riding my backside", and it certainly applied.

All the shooting was over in less than five seconds but it seemed like an eternity when it was happening. Quincy had been cowering agin the book cases on the right wall but when he saw the loose currency on the floor he overcame his fear and got down on his hands and knees to retrieve it.

"You're a sure-fire hero, young man. You saved our lives and… of course, all this money."

The huddled customers had crouched down at the far left side of the counter and were slowly standing upright and coming forward. The two women were crying and clinging to each other for comfort while the four men were collecting themselves and trying to look as if they had ever'thing under control.

About this time, I looked up to see Billy, the kid from the street, standing right behind me with eyes as big as pie plates. His Mama wasn't far behind and grabbed him by his right ear.

"You come away from there, Billy Joe. Didn't I tell you guns were good for nothing but killing?"

As she yanked him away, she had one more thing to say to me.

"And you, sir, are no gentleman. Why, you're nothing but a murderer. Look at those poor men."

I let her drag her sons away without further comment. I'd met a woman like her once before and there was no reasoning with 'em. A minute ago, those two dead hold-up men were barbarians and now they were victims and I was a killer. How could you figure?

I started to get up when I was offered a helping hand. I took it gladly and was pleasantly surprised to see the man behind it was an old friend, Kenny. He was the desk clerk at the Beaver Street Hotel when I stayed in Flagstaff four years before. At that time, the hotel was brand new and so was Kenny. His excellent service was exceeded only by his enthusiasm to please his customers.

"Thank you, Kenny."

At first, Kenny was surprised that I knew him but then he took a closer look into my bearded face and broke into a knowing smile. As I stood and holstered my pistol, Kenny spoke in a lowered voice. "My pleasure, Mister 'Kid'... or should I call you Henry James?"

Now that really took me by surprise. I hadn't heard either of those names in a long time. It'd completely slipped my mind that when I first met Kenny; I was pretending to be the "Navajo Kid". That was part of my scheme to deceive the Pinkerton agency into believing I was Charles' son. Later, after a little shootout in town, lotsa folks, including Kenny, thought I fit the description of "Henry James", a notorious gunfighter from Virginia City.

Before I could answer, Mister Quincy, who had been on all fours corralling the escaping gold coins, also recognized me and suddenly stood up.

"Wait, I remember who you are. You didn't have that beard but aren't you young Mister Farley? Don't you have an account with us?"

I gave Kenny's hand a short but deliberate squeeze and gave him a wink before I responded to Mister Quincy and shook his hand. "Yes, that's right. And I believe you're the resident agent, Mister Quincy."

"What has it been, three or four years?"

"Almost four years. My father, Charles Farley, set up the account for me."

"Yes, I remember. Wasn't he shot in some gambling dispute right after that?"

"Yes, unfortunately."

About this time, we were getting stampeded by customers trying to get out and bystanders trying to get in. Quincy went back to rounding up the money and Kenny and I squeezed our way out the door. The street looked like a stomped on ant hill with folks running every whichaway. Kenny shook my hand again and tipped his bowler hat.

"Don't you worry Mister Farley; I won't tell a soul about your 'other names'. Having more than one name is pretty common in my business, ya know. If you're planning to stay in town, you have a free room anytime over at my hotel."

"Your hotel?"

"You see, I'm not just a desk clerk any longer. I'm the assistant to the new owner so now I tend to think of it as 'my hotel'."

"Well, good for you, Kenny. I'm sure you deserve that fine title."

"And its Kenneth now, not Kenny... if you don't mind."

"I don't mind... Kenneth."

As Kenny turned to leave I saw another familiar face coming towards us. It was a man I knew as Sheriff Bradford Mullins. I'd know that square jaw and bow-legged walk anywhere. He was only about five and a half foot tall but he was built like a brick. His stubby legs were so bowed that it looked like he could straddle a water trough without getting his pants wet. I turned my face away so he might not recognize me and managed to step on a sharp rock with my sock foot. Suddenly it seemed like a great time to go behind the office and retrieve my other boot.

Eight years ago, Sheriff Mullins had been the town drunk in Grasshopper Flats. When the locals got us both liquored-up enough, we held a mock shootout which sent me running from the Flats and sent him down the long road to sobriety. He turned his life around and became a County Sheriff in Cottonwood. That's where we met four years ago and I learned his identity. He seemed to be a fair and honest man but a real stickler for the letter of the law. I wondered how he'd become a lawman in Flagstaff.

I took my time and waited about five minutes before getting my boot on and returning to the front of the building. There I saw Sheriff Mullins and Mister Quincy talking with the remaining customers that hadn't yet fled the scene. When I came around the corner, Quincy was quick to point me out.

"There he is, Marshal, that's our hero."

I wanted to talk to the Marshal alone so I waited right where I stood. Once the witnesses and bystanders drifted away, Quincy went back inside and my old friend approached me with a questioning look on his face.

"Is there a problem, Marshal?"

"Not with the shooting. You're either very good with that pistol or very lucky and frankly, I don't care which. You did the town a big favor when you killed Bert and Ernie. They were bound to get shot sooner or later and as far as I'm concerned, sooner was better.

"So what's the matter?"

Marshal Mullins was staring me straight in the eye and his intense gaze made me nervous and edgy.

"I never forget a face young man. Even with that scruffy beard I can recognize you from Grasshopper Flats. And I remember you from four years ago in Cottonwood when you showed up at my office with your brothers' body. He was snake-bit as I recall."

The lawman in him was watching my reaction to his words but he was smiling as he spoke.

"Now Quincy there thinks you're someone named Farley but I know you to be James Monroe Henry so... which is it?"

Since I didn't seem to have a choice, I spent the next few minutes trying to justify my change of names to the Marshal. I told him how I found out I was really born Charles Ulysses Farley even though I grew up as James Monroe Henry. Then I explained Charles' death and the inheritance I received which included the account with Wells Fargo. Finally, I mentioned that Cecil Abernathy, the local lawyer, could verify ever'thing I said. He seemed to believe me but said he would check with Cecil anyway.

While he was chewing on my story, I asked him a question.

"How'd you come to be the Marshal here in Flag?"

"The old Marshal got a three slug retirement about six months ago so I applied for the job. I like the cooler weather up here and the smell of pine trees. As you can see, we had a pretty bad fire last February but the town's coming back strong. They do keep me pretty busy on weekends but the room and board is top notch and the pay is better. So what brings you to town?"

"Actually, I'm just passing through on my way home. I just thought to check with Wells Fargo here and make sure my account was still in order."

"Well it's a damn good thing you did. They might have gotten away with all that money and maybe even killed some innocent by-stander if you hadn't."

"So I gather you knew them?"

"Sure. Everybody in town knew Bert Simmons and Ernie Tubbs. The last I heard, they both got fired from their jobs over at the S Diamond Ranch. That's probably why they were desperate enough to try and rob this Wells Fargo office. If I'm not mistaken, Bert's older brother still works on the ranch. Reckon that's where we'll cart the bodies."

That was just what I needed; a big brother coming after me to settle the score. And why did they have to work for the S Diamond? Hadn't I already had enough run-ins with the owner of that ranch? It seemed a mighty good idea to get shed of Flagstaff as quick as I could.

As I started to walk away, Marshal Mullins had one more piece of advice.

"I wouldn't be in a hurry to leave town if I were you."

His words were threatening but his manner suggested otherwise.

"Why? I thought you were satisfied with what happened."

"I am but Wells Fargo isn't. Quincy tells me that the company will be sending you a reward of five hundred dollars as soon as he wires them the details. Shouldn't take more than two or three days."

"Couldn't they just send it to me?"

"They want the publicity. For that, they need a picture of you receiving your reward from Quincy on the front page of the Arizona Champion. It's good for business and serves as a warning to other would-be bank robbers."

I thanked Marshal Mullins and prepared to leave. I still needed to check my account but figured there'd be plenty of time in the next two or three days for that.

Next stop was the livery where I could board Goner. I saw to it that he got the best grain as well as a clean stall and rub down. Then I walked with my gear over to the Beaver Street Hotel. It seemed like a good time to take "Kenneth" up on his offer.

Four years ago, the hotel was brand spankin' new and just like Kenny, it had aged some since then. I missed the smell of fresh cut wood and varnish but the hotel had aged gracefully. A young desk clerk was all set to help me when "Kenneth" came from a back office with a quick stride and a big smile.

"I see you're gonna be able to stay with us and that's great. It will be our pleasure to provide you the very best of lodgings at absolutely no cost whatsoever."

That was the Kenny I remembered. He was still wound tighter than a two-dollar watch and plumb full of bluster. He was bound to go far in the hospitality business.

Kenny pulled a fancy brass key from under the counter and handed it to me. He looked as proud as a pup with a new collar.

"Here ya go. This is for the Napoleon Suite and that's the finest accommodations we have. When I told the new owner what you did today, she insisted you get our very best. Is there anything else we can do for ya?"

"No, not now, but thank you and please thank her for me. I think I'll just clean up a little and stash my gear right now."

Kenny turned the hotel register around and gave me his widest smile.

"Would you do us the honor of signing your name?"

There I was, stuck again. Four years ago, when Kenny asked that question, I made up the name "Navajo Kid". Now he was eagerly awaiting what I would sign and I had to act natural doing it. So, for the first time in my life, I actually signed my name as Charles Farley.

Kenny looked at the signature and smiled again. I could tell what he was thinking so I thought to stop him before he got started.

"The Navajo Kid was a made-up name that I used as a joke but I have never called myself Henry James so please keep both of those names to yourself. We don't need a herd of name chasers coming here looking for a famous gunfighter, do we?"

Kenny immediately got defensive. "No sir, I wouldn't tell another soul."

"Who did ya tell?"

"Just the new owner. When she heard about the shooting she wanted to know all about you. She promised not to tell anyone else."

I picked up my gear and headed for my room. "Well, let's hope she doesn't."

The Napoleon Suite consisted of two adjoining rooms with a doorway between. There was a canopy-topped bed, a chest of drawers, two over stuffed chairs, a large desk and a sink with two porcelain pitchers of water for clean-up. Adorning one wall was a massive portrait of the famous French Emperor himself aboard his white horse and heading for some battle. The furnishings were mighty fancy for the time and place and made me feel like a fish outta water but I figured "what the hell"; if I had to stay in Flag for two or three days, I might as well try to enjoy it.

After washing some of the trail dust off, I tried out the bed and found it to my liking. It reminded me of another canopy bed I'd slept in but that was years ago in Animas City and this one didn't have mirrors looking down on me. The goose-down pillows were a real treat since I'd been using my saddle as a pillow ever since I left Santa Fe and the silk sheets made me wish to stay in bed all day.

As I lay there, I considered my options. First off, I needed ammunition for my Colt pistol and my Henry rifle. And rather than send my dirty clothes to be cleaned, I figured to buy new. After all, I was getting a $500.00 reward so I could afford to outfit myself in style. That meant I should hightail it over to Goldman's and see Jonah right away. Then, I could wander around Flag and renew some old acquaintances and maybe try my luck playing poker in the Kaibab Saloon. Eight years ago in Grasshopper Flats, I was a greenhorn kid that got skinned at a poker table but my years in Santa Fe had sharpened my gambling skills considerably so I was confident I could hold my own in Flagstaff.

It was mid afternoon when I finally hit the streets of Flagstaff. The skies were bright blue, air was crisp and the wind was blowing the scent of pine from the surrounding forests. It really felt like I was home again. As I made my way to Goldman's, I drew unwanted attention because of my six-gun rig but there was no cure for it. The fact that it was unloaded went unnoticed but made me walk a little faster. Over and over again, I'd learned to be safe rather than sorry when it came to packing my hog leg. If it offended some folks, then so be it.

Goldman and Son Dry Goods Store looked just like I'd remembered it. The fire from the previous February damaged some of the buildings up the street but left them untouched. Jonah Goldman was just finishing up with a lady customer when I entered the store and started wandering through the men's clothing area. He muttered something about being "right with me" but didn't show any sign of recognition.

Jonah seemed pretty much as I remembered too. He was four years older, of course, but he was still a roly-poly fella with a round face and bushy mustache. He still had a twinkle in his eye and a musical way of talking to his customers that made them feel right at home.

"There's your laudanum, Misses Adamov. Tell little Sammy I hope he's feeling better real soon. That son of yours is a very special boy, yessiree."

As the woman left the store, Jonah turned his charm on me.

"And what can I provide for you, young man?"

"I'm in need of new clothes."

"Well, you've come to the right spot. Let me help you find the right sizes."

As Jonah walked over to help me, he took a closer look at my face and saw something he recognized.

"Don't I know you?"

"I'll bet you never forget a face."

"Faces I can forget but a good customer, never. You were here a few years ago and bought some clothing and ammunition for your Henry rifle. You were hunting a wrangler's job and got involved with Miss Megan Shaw if I'm not mistaken. I seem to recall something about a fist fight and shootout too but that might have been someone else."

"Well, you're right about the clothes and ammo. In fact, I need both today. How's your supply of 44 rimfire?"

Jonah reversed his direction and hustled behind the counter to where he stored the ammunition. He carefully inspected his stock but kept talking the whole time.

"Like I told you last time, I still keep 'em in stock for my old customer out at the Box H, Porter Henry, although Trace Cummings usually picks them up. How many do you need? I've only got five boxes left."

Over the years, I'd almost forgotten about Trace. He stood by my side during a big shoot out and took a slug in his leg so when I left the ranch; I talked Pa into giving him a job. It was good to hear he was still with 'em.

"I'll just take two for now. You best grab a couple boxes of 45's too. My Colt ran dry this morning."

As I made my way over to the counter with two new shirts, some underwear and a pair of jeans, Jonah developed a hitch in his "git-a-long" and seemed lost in thought. I started fishing in my pocket for my spending money when he stopped me cold.

"*Oy Vey*, I should have known. That was you this morning over at the Wells Fargo office. You're the one who shot those bank robbers. Well, your money's no good in here today. Everything you have there is already paid for. I will personally replace the bullets you expended and Misses Langley told me to put anything else you wanted on her account. You're a real hero in this town."

I was really taken aback by what Jonah had to say. I was grateful, of course, but also confused.

"Well, thank you very much but who the hell is Misses Langley and why would she wish to pay my freight?"

"The 'who' is easy. For starters, she's the richest woman in Northern Arizona and maybe the whole damn territory. She recently bought out the Beaver Street Hotel just down the street. The 'why' is her business but now that I know who you are; I reckon I can guess the rest."

I couldn't imagine what he was jabbering about. I didn't know any Misses Langley or did I? That surname itself was familiar but not the Misses part. The Langley I remembered was Sampson and he died the day before he got married. I was about to ask about the lady when the store started to fill with folks. They all came in at the same time. There were two families with kids, an older couple and a drummer fella dragging a carpet bag full of samples. Jonah excused himself and went to wait on 'em while I pondered.

I figured to stop by later so I picked up my clothes and ammo and started for the door. One last thought crossed my mind and I passed it on to Jonah.

"If Trace comes in during the next few days, don't tell him I was here. I'm gonna pay him a visit out at the Box H and I want it to be a surprise."

Jonah hollered back. "He might not be back for awhile. I hear they got a problem with rustlers."

"Rustlers? At the Box H?"

"Just passing along gossip. The Marshal would know for certain."

I couldn't imagine rustlers around the Box H. I had to find out if it was true and just how much trouble they'd had. I decided to return to my "suite" before chasing down Marshal Mullins and was lost in thought as I approached the hotel.

I regained my senses when I saw a freight wagon that was parked out front and a huge man with his back to me liftin' and totin' a large cast iron stove all by hisself. That cooker had to weigh two hundred pounds but the man showed little strain. He looked to be seven foot tall and three foot wide with untamed shoulder length hair. I was shocked to see a man with that size and strength but what happened next was even more shocking.

"Well, I do declare; if it isn't Charles Farley. Look "Ogger", here's the man that killed your brother. Don't you have something to say to him?"

It was a woman's voice and one I would surely know anywhere but I wasn't so concerned with her at the moment as I was with the giant standing in front of me holding that heavy stove. He was truly a fearsome creature with a full beard and one great eyebrow across his overly wide face. One eye was completely closed with a scarred piece of skin covering it and his oft broke nose was bent like a dog's hind leg. He spoke with a gravel voice that rumbled from his almost toothless mouth.

"Uh, thank you, sir."

I almost forgot to breathe as I was damn near overcome with fear and then relief. You could've knocked me over with a feather. I couldn't believe the huge hairy man in front of me had just thanked me for shooting his brother.

"That's very good, "Ogger". Now, please take that new stove back to the kitchen."

"Yes, Miss Megan."

"Ogger" lumbered past us and through the front door without further comment. Megan was grinning at me like a cat that just swallered a canary.

"Now wasn't that something?"

My tongue was still tangled. "Why did you...how did you?"

"Ogger thinks he's in love with me so he'll do or think most anything I tell him. I simply told him that his brother Bert was hurting little puppies and kittens and you had to kill him to make him stop. Ogger really loves little animals so he wanted to thank you."

"And that's all there is to it?"

"Oggers' great physical size and strength is matched only by the weakness of his mind. They tell me he was such a huge baby that the midwife had to yank him out with a set of fireplace tongs which distorted his face so badly. I guess when she saw what happened she musta dropped him on his head too."

"You called him 'Ogger'... is that a name or a description?"

Megan laughed out loud. "I guess it's both. His real name is Homer but everyone called him 'Homely' so he came to hate that name. The first time I saw him all I could think of was the mythical ogre and since he had no idea what a real ogre actually was; I guess it's become his nickname."

"So you keep him around like a pet?"

"More like a draft horse, actually, although he is housebroken and allowed in the ranch house on occasion. But enough about him; how about you? I almost didn't recognize you with that scruffy beard. Should I call you the Navajo Kid, Henry James, the gunfighter or plain old Charles Farley?"

"Charles Farley will do. The others don't apply anymore. How did you become Misses Langley? Didn't Sampson die before your wedding?"

"Well he died before the wedding but not before the marriage. I had the Justice of the Peace perform a civil ceremony the night before just to be certain. Your tall friend gave Sampson an awful beating and I wasn't sure he would make it to the wedding. In times like these, a girl has to provide for her future you know."

Now I understood. Miss Megan Shaw was the girl I fell in love with eight years ago in Grasshopper Flats. I was barely sixteen and drunk as a skunk and she was...well, young and beautiful. Her father, Clayton, owned a large cattle ranch just south of Flagstaff called the S Diamond. Four years later, when we met again, she was the widow Megan Black. She'd become known far and wide as the Black Widow because so many men in her life had died mysteriously. She was engaged to a wealthy, powerful and ruthless business tycoon named Sampson Langley. Sampson met his just reward before their wedding could take place and Megan was left with nothing, or so I thought. Now I knew better.

"So I guess I have you to thank for the Napoleon Suite and the account over at Goldman's."

"And free meals and drinks in our hotel restaurant and bar, if you so chose. You did our little community a great service by killing those ruffians and I want to apologize for the way I acted four years ago."

Four years ago, Megan blamed me for Sampson's death and actually tried to shoot me. If it hadn't been for Taylor…

Megan interrupted my thoughts. "Would you join me for dinner this evening, say around eight o'clock, in the main dining room? Perhaps we could start over or at least relive the good times we shared when you were pretending to be the Navajo Kid."

I was thinking "no thanks" but I heard my mouth say "sure thing, eight o'clock will be fine."

I quickly excused myself before Ogger could return and raced past Kenny and up the stairs to my suite. I stashed my new clothes in the chest of drawers and quickly reloaded my pistol and gun belt. I sat there for almost an hour ready to shoot anyone or anything that came through the door. Mostly, I was thinking of Ogger but Megan or Kenny might have gotten shot too.

I couldn't imagine why Kenny just had to tell Megan all about me. 'Specially the part about me being known as Henry James. I'd run long and hard to rid myself of a gunfighters reputation and now it might be coming back, If that news got out, young gunslingers would be coming this way from all directions. Two or three days could turn out to be a lifetime.

Since I had a couple of hours before dinner, I lay down for awhile and thought about the next few days. I was forced to remain in Flag if I wanted the reward which I did. That meant I had to play whatever games Megan had in mind. Meanwhile, I could talk to the Marshal about the rustling that was going on over at the Box H. It might even be a right smart idea to pay Cecil a visit to find out how I stand legally what with all my name changes. I wondered if he still worked part time for the Pinkerton Detective Agency. Either way, it would be good to see him and renew our friendship.

No matter how I tried, I couldn't get over the thought of seeing Megan and Ogger together. They reminded me of the story about the Beauty and the Beast. And that reminded me of Taylor because she had read Beaumont's tale many times since childhood and told me the story when we were riding to Santa Fe. She said every young woman was looking for her handsome prince. That lead me to fret about Victor and Taylor which was the last thing I wished to do.

# CHAPTER VII
## "Bear down and bull up"

### FALL 1882

After Renee disappeared down the alley, and Mutt crawled out of the shadows to follow her, I went back to bed to consider my situation. Thanks to Victor Bodine, my little stunt with the sheet was surely gonna be related to Taylor and I could rightly guess what her reaction would be. I might be able to justify that incident with the sheet but what happened afterwards would be a lot more difficult to explain. I was desperately hoping that would remain between Renee and me but then I saw Mutt. I had to find out who else he was working for and how much he knew.

I finally decided to face the day, ready or not. When I was getting dressed to go downstairs, I remembered Paddy telling me about the hidden panel in my closet. It seemed like a dandy time to try and find it. I searched around until I found a lever carefully carved into the molding that released a section of the side wall. Behind it was a steep and winding staircase that descended into darkness. I noticed a short fat candle on a shelf along with a box of stick matches so I lit the candle to light the darkness as I gingerly made my way down the stairs. The steps finally ended on what I assumed to be the ceiling of my office.

As Paddy had described, there was some sort of fold-up ladder stacked atop the trap door. I carefully released the hasp on the door lock and let it open downwards. The ladder was made in two foot sections and hinged together so that when the door opened, it unfolded and locked into place when fully extended. It seemed to work perfectly and I was very impressed with the workmanship. I found a cable attached to the ladder that when pulled, unhinged the whole thing and allowed it to be retracted. Charles had indeed made himself an escape hatch.

When I pulled the ladder up and the trap door with it, I could see that the round piece of wood on the end of the pull-rope would fit like a knot in the bottom of the trap door when the rope was completely pulled up. Once you did that, there would be no evidence that there was a trap door at all when looking up at it from the office. The entire mechanism was a work of genius.

I lowered the pull-rope so that the ladder would release if tugged on from below. Then I scrambled up the stairs and into the closet before the melting candle wax could burn my fingers. With the sliding panel put back in place, everything was returned to normal. I had no idea if I would ever have the need for an escape but it was comforting to know it was there.

When I finally got to the casino, Paddy was hard at work and the bar was already half full of imbibing customers. She excused herself from her regulars and directed me to my office. Once there, she looked long and heard into my eyes until she saw whatever she was looking for.

"What happened between you and Renee last night? Didn't I warn you…?"

"Nothing happened. I just didn't want Herrmann to be the first, that's all."

"If nothing happened then why the bloody sheet? You knew full well that neither of you would be first with the likes of her so why…."

"To satisfy the other bidders and make 'em think the auction was on the square. I gave Renee my share of the auction money so she could go somewhere and start over. You know, have a second chance at life."

"Well, that explains her sudden arrogance and independent airs. She came in here this morning demanding her percentage of last night's auction and I had to roust Maude from her satin sheets to get it for her. Then, out of the blue, she announced she was leaving Maude's employ and going out on her own. The snippy little bitch had the nerve to call Maude a dried up old tramp right to her face. I was afraid Maude's head might explode from the pressure of her anger. The poor dear went back upstairs to lie down and calm herself down."

"Maude's a tough old broad, she'll get over it."

"I wouldn't be so sure of that. She had plans for that sweet young thing. Hell, Maude was going to auction her off again tonight."

"The 'virgin scam' only works once."

"Aye, but Maude was planning to say that the second time would be better than the first. Can't you just hear her shouting, 'All the pleasure without the bloody mess'."

"Well, Renee's gone so we'll be spared another Roman circus like last night."

I'd had all of that conversation I could take so I left Paddy to her customers and took a long walk. I stood outside Olson's Mercantile for almost an hour before Taylor came out to sweep the sidewalk. I was across the street partially hidden in the morning shadows but she finally saw me. She stared at me for a few seconds and then ran back inside. It was sure-fire certain that she'd heard about Renee and the bloody sheet. I wondered if she'd ever forgive me.

I stopped by the livery stable and took a short ride on Goner. I tried to do that every day or two as he needed the exercise and I figured there was always a chance that I might run into Taylor when she tended to Domino. This time, like all the others, found the stable empty when I returned.

My wanderings back to the casino took me past the bank and I went in to renew my business relationship with Mister Dixon. This time, he was much friendlier and somehow managed to overlook the banking formalities he was so insistent about before. He handed me two savings books and showed me to the vault where they stored the lockboxes. It was a small room with three walls that housed small numbered doors. In the very center was a massive oak table but only one solitary chair. Once the box was unlocked, Mister Dixon discreetly left the room. Although I was alone, I could almost feel Charles looking over my shoulder.

First off, I looked over the two savings accounts. They held the exact same amount, five thousand dollars. Each account was made out in his name but both were followed by the notation "for my son". That made little sense to me at the time so I proceeded to open the lockbox. Instead of the gold and jewels I'd hoped for, I found a cache of papers bound with a rawhide string. The papers seemed to be a collection of deeds and bills of sale along with another hand written Will and Testament. I hastily read through it and found that Charles repeated what he had written in the other Will; Paddy would inherit all his worldly goods if his sons could not be found.

Suddenly, it hit me. It said "sons" and not son. I couldn't believe what I was reading so I reread it just to be certain. It made me wonder about the Will I'd read in the office. Had that one said "sons" too? Was I so taken by Paddy being the beneficiary that I missed the plural? As far as I knew, Charles never made mention of another son.

At least that explained why there were two savings accounts. I was so stunned by the news that I ignored the rest of the papers and put them back in the lockbox along with the two savings books. I returned the box to its resting place in the vault wall and left the bank as quickly as I could. Mister Dixon seemed hurt by my haste but there was no way I could pass the time of day with him. I had to get back to the office and read the other copy of the Will. Then, I would need to have a long talk with Paddy and find out what she might know about Charles' having a second son.

I rushed into the gambling hall without a word to anyone and headed straight for my office. Once there, I quickly took out the Will and read what I'd missed before. The two Wills were exactly the same. Both times Charles had deliberately written "sons".

Paddy was no help as she claimed to know nothing about any second son. I asked her about any other women in Charles' life while he was in Santa Fe but she could not remember any. As far as she could recall, he only indulged himself with Maude's girls once in awhile and none of them ever got pregnant enough to show. Paddy seemed as concerned and confused as I was.

"Your Father remained in love with your Mother, Henry. He always said Lacy was the one real love in his life. That's why he was so determined to find you. Since she died giving you life, you were his only connection to her. He did mention another woman's name, I think it was Vicki, but she was a part of his past that he preferred to keep in the past...if you get my drift."

I knew what she meant and I knew who Vicki was but that didn't solve the mystery of the second son. Since I had nowhere to go for further information, I let it drop. If there was another son, I would surely find out about it in due time.

## WINTER 1883

For the six months or so, things settled down in Santa Fe and life took on a steady if not exactly exciting routine. Business at St. Charles Place was good and trouble was held to a minimum. There were numerous arguments and fights as well as a few minor shootouts but nobody died and no one got hurt too bad. Beau flashed his "pick" on occasion but only stuck those who needed sticking. Gamblin', drinkin' and fightin' just seemed to go hand in hand with a casino. The St. Charles even had three bullet holes in the wall left by the notorious "Doc Holliday" to attest to the conflicts that arose from his gamblin' and drinkin'. He was said to have killed three men in Santa Fe for questioning his honesty at cards.

I rather enjoyed gambling once or twice a week but normally I left the card playing to Beau. Gambling and liquor were like one in the same to me. I'd learned to only indulge in either with moderation.

I continued to get along with Paddy and Beau and we worked pretty well as a team. Paddy functioned as our bartender bouncer and she handled all the common drunks. When things got too physical for her, Beau was more than willing to crack a few skulls. I only got involved when gunplay was imminent. My reputation as an able gunfighter got around after the McLean incident and most folks gave me a wide berth.

Maude and her girls were my only constant source of irritation. The daily drama of their jealousy and backbiting was tiresome but my share of her gross was substantial so I put up with it. However, what happened to Renee was a sad example.

After leaving Maude's menagerie, Renee went on her own for about a week before getting badly beaten and robbed by one of her clients. The rumors flew but nobody was ever arrested or charged in the case. In fact, our good Sheriff O'Reilly seemed quite indifferent to the whole situation. Renee lost all the money I had given her and the injuries to her face kept her out of work for several months. When she came crawling back to the casino, Maude sent her packing. The ruthless old madam told her she never would have gotten beaten or robbed if she'd stayed put and not gone on her own. I took that to be a veiled threat to the other girls but maybe it was just a statement of fact.

The last I heard Renee was selling herself on the streets and barely making enough to stay alive. Then, they found her body a week before Christmas. She was beaten again and this time, her neck was broken. With no evidence or witnesses, our seldom sober sheriff closed the investigation and the case was quickly forgotten. He showed little sympathy for a disfigured prostitute and no interest at all in finding her killer. Maude feigned sorrow but shed only crocodile tears at Renee's funeral before she was dumped in a pauper's field.

Taylor continued to avoid me like the plague up to and including the holidays. In hopes of renewing our relationship, I left a Christmas present for her at Olson's. It was a signed first edition of "The Adventures of Tom Sawyer" by Mark Twain. She had mentioned the book to me several times and I was sure she would love it however I received no acknowledgement. Her hurt and anger were displayed by her stony silence. She simply acted as if I was no longer alive.

Mutt kept me apprised of Taylor's activities which seemed to be centered around her job at the mercantile and Mister Victor Bodine. They appeared to be a happy couple and were seen together on many social occasions including the big Valentines dance in February. I respected her wishes and kept my distance although it was killing me to do so. For his part, Mutt claimed that he wasn't currently working for anyone else in Santa Fe but wouldn't comment on whether or not he used his informants' information for blackmail purposes. I was certain his wares were always available for the right price.

Victor continued to be an on again off again customer in the casino with no other visible means of support. His puzzling and often contrary ways confounded Beau and made me more certain than ever that he was up to something. Maybe I was just jealous of his relationship with Taylor but I couldn't shake my suspicions. Mutt was of little value as Victor remained a mystery to him and his legion of snitches. We finally got our answer on the Ides of March when he started being seen around town shilling for Boris and Natasha Godunov.

### SPRING 1883

Boris and Natasha billed themselves as Russian royalty that were touring America and fostering goodwill between our respective nations. To that end, they were promoting a physical battle to the death between a Russian bear and an American bull. According to Boris, they had been traveling the western states for almost a year and had held many such contests. He boasted that his Russian bear had always been victorious as evidenced by his still being alive. I had trouble understanding just how this was fostering goodwill but I didn't ask.

Their Kodiak bear was a huge creature named after a former Tsar, "Ivan the Terrible". "Ivan" stood almost ten feet tall and supposedly weighed around fifteen hundred pounds. After seeing him in person, I had no reason to doubt either of those claims. He traveled by rail in a specially constructed steel cage which had been built on a flat-bed railroad car. It was the same shape and dimensions as a freight car so Ivan had plenty of room to move around. Iron rods could be inserted across the middle of the cage to separate it into two parts. This would allow two animals to be caged but unable to make contact with each other. With that done, the cage provided a safe and secure arena for the brutal contests of life and death. Ivan bore a few scars of his previous battles but seemed to be in overall excellent condition.

Boris was a large barrel shaped man with an equally huge hunger for life. He ate and drank to excess and it showed all over his body and face. His unkempt hair and beard framed a bulbous nose and rotted teeth. He surely looked much older than his years and seemed to have trouble breathing on occasion. He spoke in a thick accent and with the exception of Ivan, had the loudest voice in all of Santa Fe.

Natasha was the complete opposite of Boris. She was tall and rail thin, stately in manner and aloof to all about her. She claimed to be the cousin of Princess Dagmar of Denmark who was married to the current Russian Tsar, Alexander III. While she might have been cut from royal cloth, traveling with Boris had given her a fondness for vodka which she drank to excess. When drunk, she referred to Boris as a little *muzhik* or Russian peasant. She did not say it as a term of affection.

Now being a cousin of the Tsarina might be a big deal in Russia but it didn't mean squat in the West with the possible exception of San Francisco. Folks were curious and courteous in Santa Fe but there were no fancy dinners or special events held in their honor.

The Godunovs did meet with our mayor and town council but that was only to introduce themselves and their grand contest. Boris offered a five hundred dollar prize to any rancher who could provide a bull, large enough and mean enough, to challenge Ivan. They intended to charge admission to folks who wanted to watch the contest and attend the big barbeque afterwards. Boris assured everyone that they would be served American beef rather than Russian bear.

What they failed to mention was the gambling involved. Boris was offering three to one odds on Ivan and was accepting all bets. To make things even worse, his banker was none other than Victor Bodine.

Since Victor was involved, I smelled a polecat under the porch right off but few would listen to me. Folks got caught up in the patriotism of the moment and rushed to bet on an American bull to beat the Russian bear. There were some that were still incensed that America gave Russia seven million dollars back in sixty-four for that wintry wasteland called Alaska.

To maintain a high level of enthusiasm, Victor organized a contest of sorts to select a suitable challenger for Ivan. He had flyers printed and distributed to all the ranches around Santa Fe. It became an affair of honor for many of the cattle barons to see their own bull selected. On the day before the actual contest, nine surly bulls were penned up in the stockyards so they could be appraised by the local ranchers.

There were many breeds represented and all were rather large and menacing. I saw a ponderous old Holstein sire that looked like, win or lose, he was barbeque bound, two young Angus studs that had great confirmation but short stubby horns, a hefty Hereford that was well past his prime and favored his left foreleg, a really beautiful rust colored Simmental and four of the toughest looking Texas longhorns I'd ever seen.

With the exception of the longhorns, the rest of the bulls looked like they were more suited to eating and breeding rather than fightin'. The longhorns looked like they could handle anything on four feet but not necessarily in the confined space. Their huge horns could easily get hung up in the cage and leave them helpless to a bear assault.

In turn, each bull was presented to the crowd much like a cattle auction. Victor was about to declare a winner when a late entry was turned loose in the arena. It was a magnificent black Spanish fightin' bull that probably came out of old Mexico. He was almost six feet at the shoulder and had to weigh more than a thousand pounds. His horns were massive as they faced forward with a noticeable uplift and the tips looked to be honed to a fine point. His very presence in the pen silenced the cheering crowd and seemed to "cow" the other bulls. Even the defiant longhorns seemed intimidated. There were no dissenters when Victor chose *El Toro Grande* to represent America.

The winning rancher was none other than Herr Herrmann. He had lost his dignity and standing among the other cattlemen over the bidding for Renee so he was determined to regain his status by providing the bull for the contest. He boasted that he had imported *El Toro Grande* all the way from the Mexican state of *Tlaxcala* which was home to 40 bull-breeding ranches, or *ganaderias*.

Once the pairing was set, the betting became fierce. Ever' red-blooded American wanted a piece of the three to one odds offered by the "Ruski". I saw Victor wearing a big smile as he left the stock-yards with a carpet bag full of money.

On Saturday, March 24th, the day before Easter, Santa Fe was alive with visitors and locals eager to pay five dollars a head to watch the spectacle. The railroad car cage had been rolled to a side track and the area roped off so only those who paid could gain admittance. Victor had dropped off two tickets at the St Charles so Beau and I decided to take in the show.

We arrived early so we could watch them get set up and saw Ivan being fed by his two Russian handlers. They tossed a good sized deer in the cage and Ivan made short work of it, bones and all. Boris referred to the men by their nicknames of *Losi* and *Belka*. He laughed as he explained their names referred to his "moose and squirrel". One look at 'em and I could understand.

*Losi* was a tall, muscular man with droopy eyes and a large bulbous nose. He stumbled along with the off balanced gait of a moose and seemed to be all kneecaps and elbows. *Belka* was short and rotund with a furry face, curly brown hair and a long thin snout. His chubby cheeks were usually chuck full of chewing tobacco so in many ways he did resemble a squirrel.

Beau and I were commenting on Ivan and his handlers when I looked over at the entrance gate and saw Victor selling tickets. And there, standing right beside him, was Miss Taylor Henry. It had been several months since I'd seen her but I was once again taken by her striking appearance in a Sunday dress. She looked much more like a full grown woman than the young cowgirl I used to know.

I figured she would try to avoid talking to me so I dragged Beau along to make it appear like we were engaging in a more normal conversation. She saw us approaching but couldn't find a reason to run away.

"Well, hello Miss Henry. How are you this fine morning?"

Taylor was trapped and had to answer me. "I'm just fine, Mister Charles, how are you?"

"I'm equally fine. Miss Taylor Henry, may I present Mister Beau Didlet. He is a business associate of mine."

"Pleased to meet you, sir."

"It is my pleasure to meet such an attractive young lady. How do you happen to know Mister Charles?"

Taylor flashed me a look that coulda peeled paint from a barn wall. "Why he's a customer at Olson's Mercantile. That's where I am usually employed."

Beau was on his best behavior. "Then I shall become a customer too. Are you here to watch the classic struggle between bear and bull?"

"I'm here as a guest of Mister Bodine. He's handling the ticket sales and making sure that everything goes smoothly. By the way, if you are betting men, you should put your money on Ivan. From what Victor has been told, that bear has learned how to fight bulls and simply cannot be beaten."

Victor heard his name and turned around to join us. He greeted Beau and me like old friends and explained to Taylor that he visited our establishment on occasion. When Victor went back to selling tickets, Taylor clung to him and effectively ended our conversation.

Beau and I pushed our way into a good position from which to observe the fight. The cage had been partitioned into two sections and Ivan was in the left or west side. We watched as *El Toro Grande* was coaxed up a ramp and prodded into the right side.

Suddenly, the two combatants were face to face, separated by only those two iron bars. Ivan roared his challenge and defiance while the big bull paced and snorted. The tension was building between them and throughout the crowd. Folks were cheering and calling for the contest to begin although it was scheduled for noon and it was only eleven o'clock.

In traditional bullfights, the bull was stabbed with a lance or *vara* and then stuck with *banderillas* to make him mad enough to fight. In this case, none of those were used as the sight and smell of his antagonist was more than enough to provoke *El Toro Grande*. He actually rushed the bars on two occasions and slammed into them in an attempt to get to the bear. Ivan was content to growl ferociously and stand on his hind legs to make himself appear even larger than he already was. The crowd went crazy and was almost as wild as the two animals.

Herr Herrmann was standing on the far left side of the cage and seemed to be watching Ivan very closely. He drew my attention because of his large silver buckle that reflected the sunlight in my eyes. Besides the amount he'd spent on *El Toro Grande* and it's transportation to Santa Fe, I heard he'd made a two thousand dollar bet with Victor. At three to one, he stood to make back all of his expenses and then some if his bull won. But if he lost, it would be a very expensive attempt to regain his bragging rights around Santa Fe.

Boris and Natasha were sitting in a wagon on the edge of the arena as if wanting to watch from afar. Perhaps they'd seen this so many times that they were bored by it.

At their direction and to the delight of the impatient crowd, "Moose and Squirrel" came out on opposite sides of the cage and pulled out the two iron bars while the sun was still in the eastern sky. The cheering stopped for just a second or two as the bear and bull glared at each other and then the life or death struggle began.

Both animals reacted instinctively. Ivan stood on his hind legs and roared while the infuriated black bull put his head down and charged. The thundering charge was thwarted by a powerful swipe from Ivan's right forepaw. It was potent enough to spin the bull halfway around and tear a chuck of meat off the side of his snout. Stunned and confused, *El Toro Grande* backed off to get another run at the bear. The left side of his face was bloody and the smell of his own blood seemed to enrage him even more.

His futile charge was repeated three more times with the same result each time. The bull was getting his face clawed off and the bear wasn't injured at all. I remembered what Taylor had said about Ivan knowing how to fight bulls. I wondered if he'd actually been trained to react like he did. I was immediately relieved that I hadn't bet at all because I wanted to bet on the bull.

The fifth charge started like the first four but *El Toro Grande* shied away and turned his head at the last second. From where we were standing, it looked like the sunlight that reflected off Herrmann's buckle had flashed right across his eyes and halted his advance. I'll never know for sure if it was intentional or not but the result was immediate. Ivan swung as before but this time he hit the left horn rather than the snout. The blow was so powerful that the horn pierced all the way through his paw and blood spurted all over the ringside crowd. Oddly enough, they seemed to revel in the dousing.

Ivan screamed in agony and tried to pull his paw free but the struggling bull was backing off and the two were momentarily locked together. Ivan was leaning forward and off balance when the bull shook free of the paw and charged once again. This time he caught the big bear full in the mid section as Ivan was trying to recover his balance. The impact knocked Ivan back against the cage and left him with two deep punctures in his midsection. Blood from the wounds flowed down his hairy torso as the bull backed up to charge another time. It was the moment of truth as they say in bullfighting.

Ivan showed his breeding, strength and determination as he somehow righted himself and charged the bull. He managed to grab the bull by his head and horns but only for a moment. *El Toro Grande* used leverage and his incredible strength to come up from under the bear and actually lift Ivan almost off the ground. Then he pushed forward with such force that Ivan couldn't resist him. Together, they crashed into the west end of the cage and this time the horns penetrated deep into the bears' chest.

Ivan continued to claw at the back of the bull and bite at its neck but his strength was waning. The Spanish giant bellowed his triumph and backed away from the dying bear. The great Kodiak made one final attempt as he swung wildly with his left paw but missed and fell on his face. *El Toro Grande* finished him off with crushing blows from his hooves as he appeared to dance on Ivan's head.

The crowd exploded with a frenzy of emotion. It was New Years Eve and the Fourth of July all wrapped into one. Hats flew in the air, gunshots rang out and the crowd started singing "The Battle Hymn of the Republic". I looked for a reaction from Boris and Natasha but they were long gone. Their wagon was nowhere in sight. Even the Moose and Squirrel had vanished. When I searched for Victor, I saw him standing at the gate with a decidedly sick look on his face. The crowd was already demanding their winnings from the betting and it was plain to see Victor didn't have it.

What happened next could only be described as bedlam. Victor took off running with his carpet bag full of money and Taylor right behind. The horde of jubilant bettors turned into raving savages as they raced after 'em demanding their money. The mob could have hung Victor from the tallest tree in town for all I cared but Taylor was right in the middle of it all and was certain to get hurt in the process so I ran after 'em too. Beau joined the chase as we raced down Rodeo Road towards the plaza.

"I'm just following them to make sure that Taylor doesn't get caught in the middle. Why are you running along?"

Beau laughed at me and shouted over the noisy crowd. "I bet a hundred on that damn bull and I want my winnings."

Victor and Taylor had a pretty good lead on us but I had a good idea where they were headed so Beau and I took a short cut. We got to the livery stable just after they did. Both of 'em were trying to get to their horses but there just wasn't enough time. When the angry mob came charging through the doors, Victor and Taylor climbed a wooden ladder into the hay loft and pulled the ladder up after them. They were safe for the moment but they were also trapped. Some of the crazed bettors tried to start a fire to burn them out but they were confronted by the proprietor of the livery and his helper. Things were about to get way out of control so I pulled out Colonel Colt and fired into some hay bales to get the crowd's attention.

"Hold it... just hold up a minute. Burning this place down won't get you your money. Besides, there's an innocent young girl up there with Mister Bodine. I'll personally guarantee you'll get your money back but let's take Victor to the sheriff's office and try to get things straightened out first."

There's nothing like the sound and smell of gunpowder going off to get people to listen. Once the outraged throng reluctantly backed off, Victor and Taylor came down from the loft and we all marched towards the sheriff's office. Once inside and protected by a locked door, I figured we could find a solution to the fiasco.

Sheriff O'Reilly was sitting at his desk busily reading telegrams when we arrived. The flurry of activity and the threatening horde outside of his office aggravated his hangover and he was in a foul mood.

The sheriff informed us that Boris and Natasha, along with all the loot, had made it to the noon train and hightailed it out of town. He wired the Marshal in Albuquerque to pick them up but was informed the Marshal and most of his deputies were here in Santa Fe to watch the damn show. It seemed doubtful that anyone there was capable of taking them into custody.

After a quick accounting, we found that all Victor had in his carpet bag were the gate receipts that totaled about a thousand dollars.

From his betting tally sheets, he figured almost seventeen thousand dollars had been wagered. Five thousand that had been bet on the bear was considered lost and forgotten but that left twelve thousand that was bet on the bull. Since Victor only had about a thousand in cash, not only was he thirty-five thousand short of paying off the winnings; he was also eleven thousand short of repaying the original amount that was wagered.

Sheriff O'Reilly wasn't sure where the law stood in the situation so he sent one of his deputies to round up the circuit judge for a legal opinion. We could do little but wait and worry till they got back. Victor looked like he was going to get sick and Taylor was beside herself with excitement and fear.

Judge Ambrose Chesterton Judy was an elderly white haired gentleman with a pompous attitude matched only by his formal black suit and top hat. I knew him to be a fire and brimstone judge from the old Baptist tradition who mixed the law and his religion as he saw fit. Since Judge Judy was dead set agin any form of gamblin', he held little concern for the angry bettors or their demands. The way the judge saw it, Victor could be charged with fraud if the bets were not repaid but if the crowd wanted their winnings, they'd have to take it up with Boris and Natasha. His version of the law would have no part in supporting gamblin'.

So it was settled. If Victor could reimburse the mob for the betted money, he would go free. Until the financial arrangements could be made, Sheriff O'Reilly decided to keep ol' Victor in jail for his own safety and protection. The crowd was still in a surly mood and considering a necktie party with Victor as the honored guest but the sheriff talked most of 'em into giving up and going home. Taylor was allowed to leave so the three of us snuck out the back door. Beau made his way back to the gambling hall while I walked Taylor back to Olson's.

At first, Taylor was too shocked and scared to say anything but when she started, she couldn't stop talking… about Victor.

"How dare they keep Victor locked up in jail? He's completely innocent. Boris and Natasha are the guilty parties. They assured us that damn bear would destroy that bull and Victor would get a share of their winnings. We had no idea they would run off. They stole the money and left poor Victor holding the bag."

When I didn't comment, she continued. "How do they expect him to raise that kind of money? Victor has no money. He's practically broke. Now he's stuck in that damn jail and it's all your fault."

"My fault!?" I couldn't believe my ears. Her worthless boyfriend partnered-up with a couple of cons to steal thousands of dollars and when he got caught it was my fault? Somehow, I kept my big mouth shut for once.

"Victor thinks that you and I were involved romantically at one time and now he's competing with you for my favor. I told him we were nothing more than friends but he doesn't believe me. Since you own St. Charles Place, Victor thinks you're rich and can give me so much more than he can. I told him I didn't care about being wealthy but he won't listen."

I still had nothing to say so Taylor continued with her raving.

"That deal he made with Boris and Natasha was his chance to make some real money and be successful in his own right. Aren't you gonna say anything?"

"So now I'm responsible for his lack of money and status?"

"Victor grew up in an orphanage. His mother abandoned him when he was four years old and he's trying so hard to make something of his life. You've got to help him."

"Help him to compete with me? Now why would I want to do that?"

"Because he's my boyfriend and you're my brother. You'll never be any competition for him after what happened between you and Renee."

Well, that was plain enough. My worst fears were realized. Taylor heard some version of what happened and was gonna stay mad forever.

"What do you expect me to do?"

"Do what you said back in the livery. Make up the money he owes so he can get out of jail."

I thought of the ten thousand dollars that Charles had left in the two savings accounts. It was unexpected money and I could afford to use it.

"You're right. I guess I did guarantee ever'one would get their money back. I can get my hands on ten thousand as soon as I can get in the bank."

"Then I'll make up whatever difference there is."

"You'll pay the rest? Where would you get that kind of money?"

"Don't you worry, I'll get it."

At this point we had arrived at Olson's and Taylor ran up the stairs without looking back. I headed to the bank to get the ten thousand dollars Taylor needed,

I got to the central plaza at ten minutes after three and the bank was locked up tighter than a cheap drum. Since most all businesses were closed on Sunday, Victor would have to remain in jail until Monday morning. I kinda liked that idea but I was sure that Taylor wouldn't. Bankers hours or not, I was sure to get blamed for that too.

Sunday brought more bad news about Boris and Natasha. The Marshal from Albuquerque and his deputies took the same noon train back home and found their two remaining deputies tied-up, gagged and locked in their own cells.

The four Russians overpowered them and got away scot-free. They took rifles and ammunition from the Marshal's office as well as the two pistols the deputies had. Next, they tied up the stable hand and made off with a buckboard and four horses. Lastly, they stopped at a dry goods store and loaded up with food and water for two weeks and left without paying. The owner said they were headed west towards the Navajo reservation. The Marshal got up a posse to go after 'em but the Russians had a full day's head start and he wasn't too hopeful about catching up.

On top of everything else, when Taylor went to visit Victor on Sunday, he refused my help. Taylor thought he had too much pride to accept it but I had my doubts about that. Instead, he had her send a telegram to his Mother in New Orleans asking her to wire him the money. I walked with Taylor as she went to the Western Union office.

"I thought you said Victor was abandoned by his Mother."

"That's what he told me. It seems she came back to New Orleans last year and reunited with him. In fact, it was her idea that he come here to Santa Fe. I guess I'll have to thank her someday for sending Victor to me."

It seemed like Taylor was going a long way out of her way to throw Victor and their relationship in my face. It was almost like she was trying to make me jealous but why would she?

"Can she get her hands on that much money?"

"Victor says she had a lot of cash with her as well as a new husband when she returned to New Orleans. She must have married well."

After sending the message, Taylor decided to wait around for an answer so I went for a long ride on Goner. I had a lot of thinking to do and didn't get in until after dark. Wouldn't you know, this time Taylor was waiting for me at the livery?

"You sure took your good natured time."

"Didn't know I was gonna be missed. Did you hear something from Victors' Mother?"

"Yes. She has the money but wants to come here in person rather than sending it by wire."

"So what's the problem? Why are you waiting on me?"

"She can't be here for almost a month and Victor just can't stay in jail all that time. He… we… still need your money. He says he'll repay every cent plus interest when his Mother gets here."

"I guess when a person is faced with a month in jail his pride lessens a mite."

That comment earned me another "curdlin'" look as Taylor stomped out of the stable.

Monday morning found me at the bank when it opened. I closed both savings accounts when I withdrew the ten thousand dollars and threw the contents of the lockbox in an old leather satchel that I found under the desk in the office. I planned to review all of the documents when I had the time but right then I had other things on my mind.

I met Taylor at the sheriff's office and we went over the amount Victor collected against the amount that was due. The mob from Saturday afternoon was reforming and as restless as a herd of cattle in a thunder storm so we hurried our counting. The final difference was ten thousand, seven hundred and twenty dollars. I had the extra money just in case but Taylor was as good as her word and produced the seven hundred and twenty dollars. I was amazed and more than a little curious.

"Where did you get that kind of money?"

"It's none of your business but I'll tell you anyway. Pa gave me some money as a dowry or wedding present. He and Ma set up an account for me when I was born. Pa has been putting a little in it each month like he promised. He said I could use it for anything I wanted but he hoped it would be for my wedding. I guess he was afraid he might pass before I got married or I might even get hitched right here in Santa Fe without him being able to attend."

"And you're using your dowry to bail out your boyfriend? Pa would tan your hide if he knew."

"That may be true but he won't find out cause you're not gonna tell him. Besides, Victor has promised to repay every cent as soon as his Mother gets here."

For the first time in a long time, I felt like an older brother. I wanted to throw Taylor over my knee and "brown her backside". Better judgment took over and I simply walked out of the office. I could hear Taylor calling after me but I was too mad to answer. She made her bed and she could damn well sleep in it.

The following month was filled with stormy weather. Santa Fe got more than its annual rainfall in a three week period. Business reflected the weather as commerce slowed and the flow of settlers was down to a trickle. I stayed around the gambling hall and seldom ventured out. Mutt kept me apprised of the relationship between Victor and Taylor but I felt less urgency than I did before. Victor didn't come in the casino at all and I went out of my way to avoid seeing Taylor so when they walked together through the doors of the St. Charles one afternoon, they took me completely by surprise.

Victor looked calm and confident while Taylor looked like a balloon about to burst. She was dying to tell me something that I probably didn't want to hear.

"What are the two of you doing here? Did your Mother arrive in town?"

I addressed the questions to Victor but Taylor was first to answer. She was almost too excited to speak.

"She's not coming. Victor's figured out a way to pay you back without using her money. Tell him Victor."

Taylor had turned towards Victor and was waiting for him to tell me his great plans. He was far less enthusiastic and more business like in his approach.

"Can we speak privately?"

I took notice of Paddy, Beau and several customers that were within earshot so I reluctantly led them to my office. Once inside, Victor opened a briefcase he was carrying and placed some newspapers on my desk. He spoke like a man who was describing a sure thing.

"We are going to promote a fisticuff tournament. The winner will represent the Western Territories in a championship bout against none other than John L. Sullivan, Heavyweight Champion of the World. With your permission, it will be held right here in your gambling hall and you'll make a fortune."

Victor paused his presentation to let me consider what he'd said. I resisted the temptation to laugh in his face but sarcastically offered that he might consider inviting Bill Cody and his Wild West Show to perform instead. Victor ignored my suggestion and pulled a folded telegram from his pocket which he handed to me. I unfolded the message and read it as Victor continued.

"As you can see, I've been in contact with Billy Madden who is Mister Sullivan's manager. He has agreed in principle to such a bout to be held here sometime before the end of the year. The champ is currently on a barnstorming tour of eastern cities and about to move into the Middle West. They are traveling by train so Mister Madden has assured me that it would be no problem for them to ride the rails all the way to Santa Fe. The "Boston Strong Boy" is currently taking on all challengers by offering a thousand dollars to anyone who can last four rounds with him using the new Marquess of Queensberry rules. They claim he's knocked out more than two hundred challengers so far. He's so famous they even named two piece underwear after him. They call 'em 'Long Johns'."

I thought Victor was crazy but decided to play along. "How did you get involved with this Madden fellow?"

"My Mother's current husband has had dealings with Mister Madden before and is involved in promoting Sullivan's Chicago appearances. He suggested we might be able to do the same here with the added bonus of having an actual heavyweight championship fight."

"How do Sullivan and Madden make money? Do they sell tickets?"

"Yes they do and they take all bets from those who think some local pugilist can get the better of the champ."

"Sounds like the bear and the bull all over again."

"Yes it does but with one very important difference. Before the Championship, we're going to hold a tournament to decide who will represent the Wild Wild West and the contestants will have to pay for the privilege of competing."

"I don't follow."

Now Victor was getting excited as he laid out his plans. He had done a lot of figuring and was proud of his ideas. He handed me a sheath of papers from his case and continued as I tried to look them over.

"We have laid out a plan for one hundred and twenty-eight challengers to fight elimination bouts until we have one clear winner.

He will then be crowned The Western Heavyweight Champion and fight John L. for the World Championship."

"You expect them to pay for the chance to get the crap beat out of 'em?"

"Yes, that's the beauty of this deal. None of them think they'll lose. Don't you imagine there are at least a hundred and twenty-eight men in the West that think they're the toughest man alive?"

I had to laugh as I thought of the men I knew who felt exactly like that. "I suppose you're right. How much are you planning to charge?"

Victor directed my attention to the papers in from of me. I was looking at columns of figures and trying to make sense of them.

"Each man pays one hundred dollars. When we get all one hundred twenty-eight entries, we'll have twelve thousand and eight hundred dollars. That's enough to repay you and Taylor with more than two thousand to spare and two thousand is exactly what Billy Madden wants before he'll commit to the big fight."

"If, and I mean if, you get all this money, who takes care of it?"

Victor held my attention for a few seconds with his cold confident stare. "You do. Every cent will come directly to you. Taylor felt that was the only way you'd agree to go along with us."

I glanced at Taylor and she looked like she was holding her breath waiting for my opinion. I pretended to look at the papers as I thought about all the things that could go wrong with their plan.

"How do you plan to publicize this tournament and what will it cost?"

At this point, Taylor jumped into the conversation with both feet. "We already are publicizing it and it hasn't cost a dime. Look at those papers."

She was pointing at the newspapers that Victor had tossed on my desk when he came in. I picked them up and scanned the front page of each. I saw the "Tombstone Epitaph", the Dodge City Times, and the Daily Boomerang from Laramie, the Abilene Daily Reporter, the "San Francisco Daily Examiner", and the "Rocky Mountain News" from Denver as well as the "Territorial Enterprise" from Carson City.

As I was paging through the papers Taylor was still promoting. "It's been reported everywhere in the West but these are the areas we're really interested in."

All of them had the same headline that basically said "John L. Sullivan to hold Championship fight in Santa Fe". The article varied in content and length but all detailed the proposed fight and elimination tournament. I was impressed and confused.

"How did all this happen?"

Taylor was only too willing to explain.

"It was all my idea. I sent out telegrams to every newspaper in the west asking if they had any information about the big fight that was coming to Santa Fe. That was designed to get them curious and interested. Then I walked over to the "Santa Fe New Mexican" and told them all about what we were planning to do. When our local reporter put a small article on the wire, every newspaper sent follow-ups asking for more information. He was only too happy to respond with all the details. All at once, it was a news story and you don't have to pay for news."

I still had my doubts. "I notice there's no information on how to enter the tournament or how much it costs."

"Exactly right. If we asked them to print that information, it would be an advertisement and they would try to charge us. Once those headlines create a demand, they will come to us for the information as a service to their readers. If we feed them the story in small amounts, they'll keep coming back for more and treat everything as news."

"And this was all your idea?"

"Yeah, aren't you proud of me...?"

Taylor almost added "big brother" but caught herself just in time. We spent a few awkward seconds trying to think of something to say before Victor jumped in.

"Well I'm proud of you. We make a great team."

Victors comment made me angry and I directed the big question to him.

"I just have one concern. If all the tournament money goes to repaying your debts, how do you make anything out of all this? Do you plan to get involved in the gambling on the fights?"

Again, Taylor interrupted. "Victor has promised me that he wouldn't. Repaying his debts and having a successful promotion is enough for now."

Taylor was living in a dream world and I could see it in Victor's eyes. He went along with what she said but clearly, his heart wasn't in it. I agreed to collect the money if and when it came rolling in and provide a venue for the local fights if and when they started. I had my doubts but it was certain that they had come up with a hell of an idea. Seeing all those western newspapers reminded me of the "Arizona Free Press" from Yuma. I figured that they must have run the article too and wondered if Zack James had seen it. He would be my choice for the toughest man in the West but he probably wouldn't even enter such a contest.

# CHAPTER VIII
## "Second time's a charm?"

When I finally stopped fretting about Taylor and Victor, eight o'clock rolled around and I was more than eager for dinner. What with all the excitement, I hadn't eaten since my breakfast of hard tack biscuits and coffee. I cleaned up and put on my new shirt and jeans so as not to embarrass Miss Megan but strapped on my old gun belt just in case.

The dining room was where I remembered it was but bore no resemblance to the old one. The walls had been decorated with fancy paneling and paintings and the chandelier overhead was dramatic to say the least. It was so damn bright that you'd think the sun came inside to have dinner with us.

The tables and chairs were brand spankin' new and looked to be hand-carved by a master carpenter while the tablecloths were made of fine linen rather than plain old spun cotton. The few folks having dinner were dressed way beyond my means and made me feel like a saddle bum. Even my new clothes were no match for that place and I felt so uncomfortable I turned to leave.

"Where are you going, Charles? Didn't you agree to have dinner with me?"

I looked up to see Megan coming towards me in a fancy gown of lavender and pale pink that made a futile attempt to conceal her physical attributes. Her hair and makeup were overdone and her smile seemed like it was painted on but she was still an undeniable beauty. She was outfitted for a battle for which I was completely unarmed.

"I thought about sending up some other clothes for you but I suppose what you're wearing will have to do. May we at least place your gun belt behind the bar while we eat? I doubt if you will have to shoot anyone during dinner."

If her purpose had been to humble and humiliate me then she had done a fine job of it. I unbuckled my gun belt and passed it to the bartender who looked down his regal nose at me and sneered at my Colt pistol. Megan took my arm and directed me to the fanciest table in the room. All the while, she went on and on about the changes she had already made and those that were a'comin'.

We sat at the table and a waitress came over to take our order. To my surprise and delight, she was an old friend named Glory. She was the same little blond girl I remembered but I hardly recognized her in a French maids outfit. Although it was a cute get-up and suited her feisty personality, it seemed out of place in Flagstaff. She didn't seem at all surprised by my presence so I gathered that I must have been expected.

Megan stopped talking about the remodeling just long enough to order what she called *hors d'oeuvres*. The first *entree* Glory brought out was something named *Escargot de Bourgogne* but they sure looked like plain old snails to me. No matter, they weren't to my liking and I left all of them on the plate. I coulda swore Glory snickered under her breath when she picked up my plate.

Next we got some weird looking wild mushrooms that were introduced as "white truffles". They were swimming in some sort of salty brine but I forced a few of 'em down. Glory sarcastically recommended that I might have more but I declined.

I was about to starve to death when a thick creamy potato soup was served. It turned out to be something called *Vichvssoise* and was served cold. Glory suggested that I might enjoy it but she was wrong. As with the snails and mushrooms, Megan praised the cold potato soup as being *Magnifique-superbe*. I gathered someone had been taking French lessons.

The main course, *Chateaubriand* Steak, was served for two. It was lucky that Megan wasn't much for beef cause by that time I was more than ready to eat a whole steer by myself.

While I was finally enjoying something that tasted like real food, Megan explained that fancy cut of beefsteak was named after some French author and diplomat who served Napoleon and Louis XVIII. Somehow, she seemed to think that made it taste better.

The worst part of the meal was the wine. Now I've always felt that most wines were just a waste of good grapes but that French Burgundy was gawd awful. And giving it a fancy name and pedigree didn't change my opinion one little bit. Glory kept coming by to refill Megan's glass and politely ask if I wanted more which I did not. Megan was obviously disappointed with my "cowboy palate". She acted as though she pitied my ignorance of French culture and cuisine but I couldn't have cared less.

Through the entire fiasco, Megan kept babbling about her hotel, her dining room, her French chef Philippe and her entirely new kitchen that allowed for the creation of such wonderful meals as the one we were being subjected to. I couldn't wait to excuse myself but was informed that no French meal was complete without dessert.

Philippe, the portly chef, came out of the kitchen with a large plate containing some skinny flapjacks Megan called *crepes*. They were marinating in some sort of sugar, butter and liquor concoction that he set on fire. I was sitting so close to the plate that the flames almost singed off my eyebrows. At first, it looked like he was trying to burn the joint down but the fire died out pretty quick. After considerable urging, I tried the *crepes suzettes* and found them a sight better than the snails or mushrooms but hardly worth the effort.

As we finished the dessert, Megan excused herself so she could go to the kitchen and compliment Philippe in person. As soon as she left the table, Glory appeared with a tray full of cigars.

"A fine cigar to finish off your meal, sir?"

"No thanks, I don't smoke much."

"Evidently you don't eat much either or wasn't the dinner up to your usual standards?"

"Listen, I spent the last few weeks on the res and enjoyed ever' meal more than this one. Although, I must admit, the "Chatto-steak" was pretty good."

Glory laughed at my description. "You are such a cowboy."

"I thought you used to like cowboys."

"And I thought you hated Megan. I guess time heals all wounds."

"Nothing has changed between Megan and me. I don't have any use for her or her French food."

Glory pushed the tray closer to me and lowered her voice.

"Just take one of these damn cigars, will ya. Misses Langley is watching us from the kitchen window and I can't afford to lose this job."

I picked out the biggest stogie, unwrapped it and bit off the tip. Having no where to spit it, I stuck the tip in my shirt pocket while Glory struck a match and lit the damn cigar for me. I took a drag and almost threw up my fancy French meal. That damn thing smelled like burning manure and tasted worse. Glory laughed out loud and seemed delighted with my reaction.

"I take it you aren't much of a smoker. You might want to get some fresh night air to clear your lungs."

Glory turned to leave but hesitated a moment and looked back.

"If you're serious about hating Megan, I could meet you out back in a half hour and we could take a little walk. Clear the air, so to speak."

If I remembered correctly, Glory offered me that same walk four years ago and I didn't take her up on it. I figured it might be the right time to see what I missed.

Megan returned from the kitchen and feigned great concern for my discomfort after sampling the cigar. I just wanted to be shed of her and that dining room.

"Are you alright? I hope that cigar wasn't too strong. They're imported from France, you know. The very best money can buy.

I'll wager you didn't know our word "nicotine" comes from a Frenchman, Jean Nicot. He was the French ambassador to Portugal from 1559 to 1561."

That figured. It seemed like I had no use for anything French.

"Well, in the Arizona Territory we call these "Stogies", not cigars. That word comes from Conestoga, Pennsylvania where they make a bunch of fine quality American cigars. You might be aware of the fine overland wagons that are made there too."

My cutting comments kinda stalled the conversation. Given that opportunity, I overdid the coughin' and hackin' as an excuse to return to my suite. Megan politely pretended to understand and allowed me to leave. I retrieved my gun belt from the bartender who stood there with his palm extended for a tip so I fished out the cigar tip from my shirt pocket and gave it to him. I don't suppose he'll ever get over that.

As I tried to leave, Megan caught my arm and pretended to pout.

"If you're feeling better in the morning, perhaps we could have breakfast together. Silly me, I've been going on and on about my life and I never got to hear about what you've been doing these past four years. I'm also interested in your future plans. We may have mutual business ventures that would benefit us both."

I promised to consider breakfast and headed back to my room coughing all the way. I couldn't imagine why Megan was trying so hard to be nice to me. We had nothing in common except for mutual hatred. I knew one thing for certain; whatever Megan had in mind had nothing to do with the Wells Fargo shooting. I suspected her reason had something to do with our past relationship and I knew I wasn't gonna like it.

After rinsing the sour taste of the dinner and cigar out of my mouth, I cleaned up a little and went downstairs. I made sure no one saw me make my way to the rear entrance of the hotel. As I snuck past the kitchen, I saw Ogger devouring a huge plate of what I assumed to be leftovers. I think he ate the snails, shell and all.

The moon was full in a cloudless sky and the wind was whipping the evening air about as it always did in Flag. It seemed like a perfect night for a walk.

When Glory came out, she had shed her French maids' outfit for a lacey blouse, jeans, and boots. She looked just like the cute little blond I remembered. When she saw me, she put on her brightest smile, walked right up in my face and slapped it as hard as she could. Before I could protest, she explained herself.

"That's for standing me up four years ago. Now we've cleared the air and we can start over again. I liked you better without the beard."

"O.K., I guess I had that comin'. What happened to your little maids' outfit?"

"You don't think Megan would trust us to launder them ourselves do you? She collects every uniform each night and sends 'em out to be cleaned and pressed fresh every morning, even the damn bellhops and bartender. I think she's taking this 'French thing' of hers way too far."

"Why is she doing it?"

"Oh, that's right, you wouldn't know about her trip."

"What trip?"

"When Sampson Langley died, they were legally married and she inherited all his money and property. He musta had a lot of money 'cause she's been spending it like it was water. She went on a two year trip to Europe and came back with Philippe. She says she hired him away from some big time French restaurant in London called 'The Savoy'. I guess she thinks the Arizona Territory needs to be exposed to French culture and she's been appointed the one to do it. She bought the Beaver Street Hotel so she could turn it into what she calls her "little piece of Paree".

As we walked down the street, I continued asking questions and Glory kept on answering. I found her to be a fountain of local knowledge and gossip.

"Whatever happened to her father's ranch, the S Diamond?"

"Now that she lives here at the hotel, she hardly ever goes out there. Before she left on her trip, she hired a man named Jonathan Winters to manage the ranch. He's known as 'Big Jon' and supposedly rode with Quantrill's Raiders during the war. He brought in a tough bunch of cowhands they call his 'rat pack' to handle the spread and terrorize the town every other Saturday night. 'Whitey' Winters killed our town marshal a few months back and so far, nobody's done a thing about it."

"Who's 'Whitey'?"

"That's Big Jon's son. When he was born, they named him Johnny after his Pa but he turned out to be an albino with those awful pinkish eyes and white hair so folks just naturally called him 'Whitey'. He's rattlesnake mean and real quick with his six guns."

"What about Marshal Mullins?"

"The Marshal seems like a good and decent man but when he got here, there was no hard evidence to go on and no witnesses that dared to testify against Whitey or the S Diamond. He ran the whole bunch of 'em out of town a week ago Saturday when they got drunk and rowdy so they spread the word that they're coming back this week to kill him too."

"What day of the week is it?"

"It's Thursday, why?"

"That means there's a good chance I'll still be here on Saturday night. Maybe I can help him out."

"I heard about what you did at the Wells Fargo office. And I remember that shootout you were in four years ago. Are you really the famous gunfighter, Henry James? You have those pretty blue eyes and everyone knows that all the famous gunfighters have blue eyes."

"Well, thank you but no. People called me Henry James but that has never been my name. In Virginia City, almost eight years ago, I avenged the murders of my friends, Mal and Josh James and folks somehow assumed I was their brother, Henry. Actually, their real brother is Zack James. You met him, remember?"

"You mean that big good-looking cowboy you had breakfast with? That very morning that Miss Megan tried to shoot you
both?"

"Yup, he's the one and that was the morning."

"Too bad he had to leave so soon. I would have liked to know
him better. Didn't he live in Yuma?"

"Yeah, and I haven't seen hide nor hair of him in…"

I was about to say two years because I had seen Zack in Santa
Fe but I didn't want to start Glory thinking about him anymore than
she already was.

"…I guess it's been four years already. Bet he's married with a
passel of kids by now."

For the next few minutes, we walked in silence up and down
the streets of Flagstaff just looking in the store windows. Both of
us were lost in our own thoughts. Finally, Glory could not contain
her curiosity.

"How about you, Charles? Are you married with a couple of
kids too?"

"Nah, I spent the last four years in Santa Fe but never got serious
about anyone."

"So whatever happened in Santa Fe stayed there?"

"Yup. How about you? Have you got yourself a beau?"

"No one that's special. I refuse to settle down and raise a family
just to placate my parents. When the time is right, I figure Mister
Right will come along. Until then, I'll have as much fun as I can
with Mister Wrong."

As usual, Glory made me laugh. "That sounds like a reasonable
attitude."

She looked up at me with a big smile and then stuck her arm
around mine so we could continue walking arm in arm down the
wooden sidewalks.

"Well, I hope Mister Right hurries up 'cause I'm not getting any
younger ya know. I'm damned near twenty."

We walked and talked for another half hour before heading down her street. The conversation had remained general in nature until Glory made it personal once again.

"I hope we have time to see each other before you leave. There's a barn dance on Saturday night if you're interested. I would love an escort. You are planning to shave that awful beard aren't you?"

"We'll see."

"About the dance or the beard?"

"Both."

Glory and I parted ways outside her parent's home. I think we both thought about a good night kiss but decided against it. We'd become friends again and that was plenty for one night.

Friday morning was bright and sunny with the usual crisp breeze in the air. I had just gotten dressed when Kenny knocked on my door and handed me a message from Megan. She requested that I join her for breakfast in her suite. I could tell by the smirk on Kenny's face that he knew what was in the note so I told him that I would be right along. Without much enthusiasm I finished cleaning up and went to Megan's suite. I didn't figure to need my pistol over breakfast so I took it off and hid it behind a planter in the hallway. My arrival was announced with a huge brass knocker that sounded like a church bell going off. I guessed it was probably imported from France.

When the door opened, I figured that I musta got there early since Megan wasn't even dressed yet. Her hair and make up were done to perfection but she met me at the door in an emerald green satin robe that barely covered her obviously naked body underneath. If her intent was to get my undivided attention, she surely had it.

"Come in Charles, I'm so glad you could join me. I hope you don't mind but I prefer to take my breakfast here rather than the crowded dining room down stairs. *Le petit dejeuner* can be such a personal meal."

"I don't mind. That's a right smart robe you got there. It really sets off your red hair."

Instead of acknowledging my compliment, Megan recoiled in mock horror.

"This dressing gown is a copy of one presented to Marie Antoinette by Louis XVI of France. It cost over five hundred dollars and is most definitely not a robe."

Then, quick as a wink, Megan caught herself and dismounted her high horse.

"I'm sorry; sometimes I get a little carried away with everything European. I must learn to be satisfied with what we have here in the American West. Please sit down. I would love you to sample the French roast coffee and Philippe's superb *croissants* or perhaps the *pain au chocolat*. It's that sweet pastry filled with chocolate and is very decadent."

If Megan meant to bore me to death with her French breakfast, it was working. The coffee was good but the rolls were kinda over baked and flakey. While I was waiting for the steak and eggs to be served, I tried that chocolate thing but it was way too sweet for my taste. After a few minutes of chit-chat, I finally figured out that there would be no steak and eggs so I tried to excuse myself gracefully.

"I'd like to thank you for this fine French breakfast but I really should be going."

"Wait, please. I am sorry. This wasn't what you were expecting for breakfast, was it? I shouldn't have expected you to enjoy it like I do. But, before you leave, I have two business offers for you to consider."

Megan swiveled in her chair and exposed her right leg all the way to the hip while that fancy dressing gown somehow opened up a mite to show off all of her cleavage. It was clear she was getting down to some kind of business.

"What could I possibly do for you, Misses Langley?"

"Megan, please call me Megan. I am in real trouble, Charles, and you may be the only one who can help."

"You better start from the beginning."

Megan went back to the beginning alright. Back to that fateful night four years before when Sampson Langley died and left her his fortune. They had only been married for a couple of hours but in the eyes of the law, she stood to inherit ever'thing. Once the funeral was over and the legal papers signed, she was sitting on a mountain of cash and property.

Thanks to Glory, I already knew most of what was coming but it was fun to listen to Megan bemoan her situation.

In her haste to travel abroad, Megan hired "Big Jon" Winters to run the S Diamond while she was away. He certainly had a questionable background but was a close friend of Sampson's so she took him on. Next, she gave him free reign to buy and sell livestock as well as tend to repairs and additions to the ranch. That meant giving him access to the ranch bank account which turned out to be her second big mistake.

When Megan got back from Europe, she found a large amount of money missing from that account which "Big Jon" could not or would not explain. When questioned, he became abusive and told her to shut up or get off her own ranch. He said he was doing just what Sampson would have done and she should mind her own damn business.

Megan fled to town and sought help from the law but there was little they could do. She had given him the legal right to use her money and no territorial sheriff or judge wanted to bring any charges against "Big Jon" if they could avoid it. His well known association with Quantrill's Raiders had a chilling effect on folks.

To make matters worse, Jon's albino son, Whitey, came to the ranch and his menacing presence just added to the problem. His manner was rude and crude as his hideous features and his gunslinger reputation scared away any assistance Megan could find. Her daddy's ranch had been stolen away from her in broad daylight and she wanted it back.

I just had to ask. "Why come to me? What would you have me do?"

"It's simple; I want you to kill Whitey Winters and Big Jon, too, if he gets in the way. Whether you wish to admit it or not, your actions of four years ago and yesterday convinced me that you are Henry James, the famous gunfighter from Virginia City. I will pay you one thousand dollars to call out that albino bastard and shoot him legally dead."

"Why one thousand dollars?"

"I've been told that's the going rate for a top flight shootist and I'm willing to pay for the best. There will be another thousand for Big Jon if it becomes necessary."

That's when things started to get interesting. After talking with Glory the night before, I'd kinda planned on shooting Whitey Winters for nothing but I liked Megan's idea better. Added to the five hundred from Wells Fargo, that thousand would go a long way at the Box H ranch. Big Jon would be like a bonus.

"What else would you have me do?"

"So you'll do it? You'll kill Whitey?"

"I'll think about it. What else?"

"I want you to find a man by the name of James Monroe Henry."

At first I thought she was joking and then I realized she was serious. I had a hard time keeping a straight face and had to bite my lip to keep from laughing out loud.

"Who is this Henry fella and why do you want to find him?"

"That's my business and no concern of yours."

"Then my answer is no. If I don't know why I'm looking I won't know what to look for."

"Alright, I'll tell you but you have to promise to keep my reasons between us even if you can't find him."

Megan went through another story that I already knew most of but once again, it was fun to listen.

Among his many properties, Sampson owned two very promising mining claims in Calico, California. They were silver mines called the Blue Belle and Silver Lady. Although both were good producers, he shut them down to buy out the minor shareholders so he could own them all by himself. He was successful with every one but James Monroe Henry who refused to sell his ten percent ownership in each. Based on what she told me, Megan simply wanted me to find Mister Henry so she could buy out his shares.

There had to be more to the story than that. "Why buy him out now, hell, why buy him out at all? Those mines could be worthless?"

"That's my business."

"Then why not hire the Pinkertons to find him? It could take me forever to track him down while they have the manpower and resources to do it in a week or two. They even have an office right here in Flagstaff."

"Because they're so damn thorough they'll find out why I want to buy him out. Once they have the information everybody else will know and..."

Megan caught herself and thought a few moments before continuing.

"I trust you to keep all of this confidential. Will you try to find him? There's another thousand in it for you if you can."

"Another thousand? You must really want to buy his shares."

"That's true. Will you do it?"

"Do you mean after I've killed Whitey Winters?"

"Yes, Whitey's death is much more important at this time."

"Well, I hear he's due to be here tomorrow night so we'll see what happens."

"Are you sure you can beat him? I'm told he's awful fast."

"Your concern is heart warming but I wouldn't test him if I wasn't sure."

I got up to leave but Megan had other ideas.

"Now that our business is settled, wouldn't you like to get reacquainted in a more personal and intimate way?"

Megan stood up very slowly and her fancy dressing gown sorta slipped off her shoulders and floated to the floor. There she was, the one-time girl of my dreams, standing completely naked in front of me. I was momentarily stunned by her boldness as much as I was impressed with her beautiful body. She enjoyed my confusion and walked towards me with a suggestive motion and sultry look. Part of me wanted to stay but the rest of me knew better. I admired the view, tipped my hat and left her suite in a hurry. I heard her calling my name as I went down the hallway to retrieve my pistol but I never looked back.

Once on the street, my heart rate returned to normal and I headed off to see my old friend and attorney, Cecil Abernathy. Pa always warned me to keep skunks and lawyers at a distance but Cecil was different.

When we first met four years ago, he was a lawyer, Justice of the Peace and part-time agent for the Pinkerton Detective Agency. By deceiving him, I was able to convince the agency that I was Charles' son when at the time, I was just pretending. Later on, Cecil wrote out Charles' Last Will and Testament which gave me all of his worldly assets. Finally, and most important, he transferred the old deed to the Box H ranch from Charles to Porter Henry. Now I had other legal matters to attend to as well as soliciting the help of the Pinkertons.

Over the years, Cecil had moved to a newer building and had a real live secretary outside his office. She recoiled from me at the sight of my six gun and when I told her the "Navajo Kid" was there to see Cecil she reluctantly relayed the message. I think we were both surprised when Cecil came hustling out of his office to greet me.

"Well, if it isn't the 'Navajo Kid'. It's good to see you. I hardly knew you with the beard. Come right on in this minute."

Cecil ushered me into his office and closed the door behind us. This office was a far cry from his old one. The walls were painted, the desk and chairs were new, and a large Pinkerton Private Eye Logo was on the wall behind him. It was easy to see which of his three professions was paying the freight.

As I watched him retreat behind his desk, I took notice of how much Cecil had changed. He was still short in stature but not nearly as thin. His thick spectacles, brown suit and bowler hat were about the same style as I remembered but they were much newer and in better shape than before. Even his manner was different. Success had given Cecil a confident attitude that he had lacked. He spoke more like a salesman and less like an attorney.

"How have you been, Henry?  How are things in Santa Fe?"

Cecil was the only person in town that knew I had legally changed my name from James Monroe Henry to Henry Charles on the day before Taylor and I left for Santa Fe.  To ever'one else in Flagstaff I was Charles Farley but that was never a legal name.

"I've been well but things in Santa Fe didn't exactly go as planned.  I'll only be in town for a few days and I have a couple of things I want you to do for me in your capacity as a private eye."

"How can the Pinkerton Agency be of service?"

Briefly, I reminded Cecil of the wagon train massacre twenty years ago and their discovery that I was Charles' son.  Next, I told him about Hopi Joe and the two white boy babies.  When I started to tell him all about the Clifton family, he started taking notes.  I referred to the journal which was still in my saddle bags back at the hotel and he said he would like to see it.  Finally I mentioned the turtle-shaped birthmark that Hopi Joe had seen on the baby that died.  That all led up to my request.

"I'd like your agency to contact any living members of the Clifton family in Illinois to find out if any of them remember the little boy named William and whether or not he had such a birthmark."

"After all you've been through you're still not sure you're Charles' son?  What do you hope to find"

"I'd just like to know for sure one way or the other."

"What if we can't find any relatives or friends of the Clifton's?  Where do we go from there?"

"Maybe you can run down a nurse that took care of Charles' son before they left Chicago.  Victoria paid her to suffocate the baby but she couldn't do it.  Even if your agents found her, I'm not so sure she'd be willing to talk about what happened.  I figured the Clifton's family might be easier to find."

Cecil agreed and wrote down all the details I could give him.  I promised to bring the journal over to him when I got the chance.  He made no promises about solution or time frame but said he would do his very best.

As I rose to leave, Cecil leaned back in his chair and commented. "I heard about your exploits over at the Wells Fargo office. You're the town hero right now but the bad thing is that folks are whispering the name of Henry James again and that's bound to cause trouble. I don't need to know if you are or were ever called Henry James but that name will travel fast in these parts. Everybody remembers that shootout four years ago and now this…?"

"Thanks for the warning but I was already expecting it. A good friend once told me that there was no rest for a known gunfighter short of the grave and he was right. I'm hoping to be out of here before they arrive."

"Well, good luck, Henry. I'll hold whatever information we get until you contact me. Oh, by the way, Marshal Mullins paid me a visit yesterday afternoon and asked about Charles Farley. I told him about the Will and the Wells Fargo account but nothing more."

I thanked Cecil for his discretion and paid him in advance for his service as he walked me to the door. His young secretary finally warmed up enough to say "Good-by, Kid" as I left but her heart wasn't in it. Why did a pistol make some people so skittish?

The day was heating up and I wanted to see Marshall Mullins next. Being aware of my regained gunfighter fame led me to make my way with extra caution. I thought I saw someone following me but it turned out to be my over active imagination. When I got to the Marshal's office a young lad with a Western Union cap was just leaving. He was so intent on his next delivery that he ran right past me without taking notice. The Marshal was reading the message when I entered.

"Good Morning, Marshal."

"Ah, the young Mister Farley. Just the man I was about to go looking for."

He held up the telegram along with two others that were lying on his desk

"This here is the third one of these I got this morning asking me to confirm the report that Henry James is actually in Flagstaff. That jackass reporter over at the newspaper put a story out on the wire last night and every paper in the West seems to have picked it up. You're gonna get a heap of company if you stick around and I would not recommend that you do."

"I'm just staying around long enough to get the reward. Do you think you can put off answering those for a day or two?"

"Sure, but that won't stop any name hunters who are in the area. They'll be here like flies on horseshit. You might want to lay low over at the hotel just in case. I admire what you did yesterday and owe you a favor from Grasshopper Flats but I won't have a bunch of yahoos shooting up my town just to make a name for themselves. If I have to run you out of town to stop 'em, I will.

Glory was right. Marshal Bradford Mullins was a good man and a straight shooter. More than ever I wanted to help him with his handling of the Winters gang.

"I figured to do some poker playing but I see your point. I'll stay close to the hotel and keep outta sight."

"Thank you Charles or Henry or whatever... I'm obliged."

I happened to notice a deputy badge on his desk and had to ask. "Are you short a deputy around here?"

The Marshal frowned and looked down at the badge. "Yeah, he quit last night. He heard the Winters gang was gonna come in here tomorrow itching for a fight and he didn't have the stomach for it. Can't say as I blame him. He's got a young wife and three kids to think about.

"Say the word and I'll stand by your side."

The Marshal gave me a long hard look before answering. "I hope it won't come to that but if it does... I'd be proud to have ya."

His words hung in the air as we both considered what we might be up against on Saturday. He tossed me the badge and said, "Just in case".

I turned to leave when I remembered what Jonah had told me the day before.

"Do you know anything about rustling out at the Box H ranch?"

"Only what Trace Cummings has told me. He thinks they're some of the riders from the S Diamond but he has no proof. He and G.W. chased a couple of 'em but it was neigh onto dark out and they never got close enough to make a positive identification. Is that where you're headed once you leave here?"

"Yeah. I still think of Porter as my Pa and G.W. as my brother. The Box H will always be home. If Trace thinks the Winters gang is doing the rustling you can take it to the bank. I reckon that makes two good reasons to stand up with you tomorrow."

"Two reasons? What's the first... a lack of good judgment?"

I was thinking about Megan's offer but I couldn't tell him so I just made a joke. "Yeah, something like that."

We shook hands and I walked out on the busy street. As I slowly made my way back to the hotel, I kept a close eye on all the young men on the street. I saw very few with side arms but that didn't make me feel any less nervous. I got that feeling again like I was being watched but I couldn't see anyone that seemed out of place. I wasn't afraid of getting shot but I was unwilling to shoot any amateurs if I could help it.

The last thing I expected was a young girl with a gun. When she stepped from the shadows and called out "Henry James", I was shocked. She was dressed like a tom-boy with an old fisherman's cap, a wool coat about three sizes too big, stitched up dungarees a blue flannel shirt and well worn boots. She couldn't have been older than fourteen and her hands were shaking like a willow tree in a windstorm as she pointed a big old Walker Colt percussion pistol at my head. I hadn't seen one of those nine inch cannons in a long time. I had to think fast.

"Hold up there, young lady, I'm not Henry James. My name is Charles Farley and you're about to make a big mistake."

"You're Henry James, there's no mistake."

"Why are you after Henry James?"

"He... you... murdered my Father and my brother."

"If that's true he deserves to be shot. Where and when did all this occur?"

I figured that as long as I could keep her talking she wouldn't shoot and that Walker Colt was so heavy that she couldn't maintain her aim for more than thirty seconds. It was my only chance as she had me dead to rights otherwise.

"My brother, Preacher Daniels, was killed in Virginia City almost eight years ago. My Father, the Deacon, was shot in cold blood about four years ago in a little town south of here called Grasshopper Flats. He left Ma and me to tend the ranch so he could chase down Henry James and kill him but he got hisself dry-gulched instead."

My plan was working. She looked to be about one hundred pounds soaking wet and the Walker Colt was too heavy to hold up. Her aim was wavering along with her resolve.

"You just gotta be Henry James. You look just like people say."

"Did he wear a beard like mine?"

"Well, no... not that I know of."

"See? I can't be Henry James can I?"

By now, we had gathered a fair sized crowd and folks held their breath as she considered what I said. The young girl couldn't make up her mind but the weight of the Walker got to be too much and lowered itself as she broke into tears.

I approached her with great caution and gently took the heavy pistol from her hands. The crowd seemed to have mixed feelings. Some were glad no one got hurt while others wanted to see her shoot me. I told 'em all to go about their own business and I directed the young girl to a bench seat in a small park just off San Francisco Street. We sat there for a while as she tried to get control of her emotions. I could see she was a tired, hungry and scairt little girl so I tried to help.

"What's your name?"

"Magdalene Daniels... but folks call me Maggie."

That figured. Her Father was a self-styled Deacon who named his son Preacher so it followed that his daughter be called Magdalene.

"Where did you come from, where do you live?"

"I usually stay with my Ma near Silverton, Colorado but I left home two months ago to find my Pa. I've been camping in the woods over by McMillan Spring ever since I got here."

"When's the last time you had anything to eat?"

"Guess it's been a day or two."

"Let's get on over to the hotel and get you the biggest lunch you've ever had."

Since "Maggie" wasn't exactly dressed for the hotel dining room, I convinced Glory to bring a selection of food outside so the three of us could have a little picnic on the lawn behind the hotel. The girls were wary of each other at the start but quickly became friendly as the soup and sandwiches broke the ice between them. After considerable prodding, Maggie finally told us her story.

Her father left home almost eight years ago after Preacher was killed. Like Captain Ahab, in Melville's "Moby Dick", Deacon was obsessed with hunting down and killing Henry James. Four years later he sent them a telegram from Flagstaff which stated he was close to ending his quest but then they never heard another word. Her Mother gave up on his returning but Maggie kept her slim hopes alive. Being "almost fourteen", she felt she was old enough to try to find him.

She hitched a ride from home on a freight wagon that took her to Durango. From there, Maggie "rode the rails" on the train to Flagstaff. After weeks of searching and asking around, she ended up in Grasshopper Flats. A kindly bartender named Deke showed her to a shallow grave outside of town which contained some gnawed-on bones, worm eaten clothing, a torn-up bible and the Walker Colt. There was no telling for certain but Maggie just knew it was her Father. Everyone in town agreed the man had been shot by Henry James so she set out chasing her own "white whale".

When Maggie finished her incredible story, she wiped the tears off her face and said, "When I find Henry James I will kill him."

Glory and I looked at each other without knowing what to say. Maggie was too young to be consumed with hate and vengeance so I tried to reason with her.

"Your Father and brother were known to be gunfighters... did you know that?"

Maggie grudgingly nodded her head "yes".

"Could it be that they just ran into someone that was simply faster than they were?"

Maggie started to protest but then she acknowledged it was possible. It seemed like she was looking for a good enough excuse so she could give up her quest.

I picked up the old Walker Colt to check it out and had to laugh. It was shy two rounds and the other four were moss green. The cylinder was covered with mold and the hammer looked like it was rusted tight. I explained to Maggie that the old gun was useless so she couldn't shoot anybody with it even if she got the chance. With that additional piece of depressing news, Maggie wandered off by herself and eventually fell asleep under a big piñón pine.

Glory had to go back to work so I was left alone with the would-be assassin. After two hours of fretting, I came up with a solution. I rousted Maggie from her slumber and made her an offer she couldn't refuse.

"Wake up Maggie I've got something to say to you. It's almost September and you should be getting back to school. How about I buy you a ticket on that Durango train so you can go on back home? I'm sure your mama is sick with worry."

Maggie resisted but couldn't find a reason to decline my offer. "It would be more fun to 'hop the train' but it's a sight more comfortable riding in the club car than the cattle car."

We talked about her future as I walked her to the train station. I tried to make her see that she had to get on with her life and forget about things she couldn't change. Since her Father and brother were gone and nothing she did would ever bring them back, hating Henry James and chasing after him would just ruin her life. I sure hoped she understood. And could accept what I was telling her cause I didn't cotton to the idea of looking over my shoulder for her the rest of my life.

As luck would have it, when we got to the station, there was a scheduled train to Durango within the next hour and they had an open seat. While I waited with Maggie, I saw Kenny talking to the station master as the incoming train unloaded a couple of well armed and hungry-looking desperados on the platform. I was reminded once again of the gunslingers curse as I watched them walking down the street with their hands near their pistols. Talking worked with Maggie but I didn't imagine for one minute I could talk those two gunslingers out of anything.

Maggie hugged me when we said good-by and whispered in my ear so nobody else could hear. "Thank you for everything... Henry."

With that she walked up the stairs and disappeared in the passenger car. I wasn't sure how I felt about what she said but I was certainly relieved when the train pulled out and I saw her waving from the window.

I took back streets to reach the hotel and went in the rear door, through the kitchen and up the back stairs. I hid by the stairs as Ogger lumbered past on his way to the kitchen as I still wasn't sure if I trusted his feelings about his brother. I found no reason to tempt his wrath.

I found a note from Kenny that was shoved under my door and read it as soon as I got inside. He wanted me to know that several fellas had been asking around town for Henry James. Just the sorta news I wanted to hear.

I relaxed in my fancy canopy bed and thought about my eventful day. It started with an interesting breakfast of two business offers and one sexual advance. Megan offered me a thousand dollars to kill Whitey Winters which I would have been willing to do for free and then she tossed in another thousand if I could track down myself. Things really got crazy when she offered herself to sweeten the deals... so to speak.

After taking care of my legal business with Cecil, I met with Marshal Mullins and somehow volunteered to be his deputy when the Winters gang came to town. I had plenty of reason to do so after learning they were probably involved with the rustling at the Box H.

Last but not least, I ran into Maggie and spent the rest of the day getting her set straight and on the road back home. All in all, not a bad day.

My day-dreaming was rudely interrupted by the sound of three rapid gunshots and then one more some two or three seconds later. I ran to the window but could only see folks scattering in all directions. The shots had come from the next street over and I couldn't tell anything from where I was perched. I strapped on my gun belt and ran down the stairs without actually thinking about what I was doing. As I was running out the door, Kenny was running in and we collided with a thud.

"Sorry Kenny, I didn't see you comin'."

"Mister Farley...I was just coming to tell ya. Two of the men that were looking for Henry James got into a scrape over at the Kaibab Saloon and they shot it out. One of 'em is dead and the other is pretty badly wounded. The bartender said they were fighting over who would get the first crack at you."

Well wasn't that a pleasant little fairy tale? Two name chasing morons shoot each other over the right to get shot by me. What was the world comin' to?

From behind me came a very familiar female voice.

"I'm glad to see that you weren't involved in that shooting, Charles. I would be very disappointed if you were injured before you could fulfill the first part of our agreement."

It was Megan and she was about a foot behind me with Kenny standing in front and unable to keep his mouth shut around his new boss lady.

"Good evening Misses Langley. I was just telling Mister Farley all about the shooting. Two strangers shot it out over at the Kaibab... one of 'em is dead and the other is wounded."

"That's enough Kenneth. I overheard your conversation as I walked up. You may return to your station."

Kenny looked crestfallen as he slinked past us and back into the hotel. He was trying so hard to win her approval. Megan had a sharp tongue with her employees and I didn't like the idea of being one of 'em.

"It's a beautiful evening is it not, Charles? Do you have any plans? In case you're wondering, I saw your little picnic this afternoon and sent Glory home early as punishment for leaving her station during work hours. She's a capable little waitress but one more incident like that and she will be fired. Do we understand each other?"

"Yeah, I guess we do."

I pushed past Megan and started for the stairs when she called out. "I don't suppose you've found out anything about James Monroe Henry have you? I trust that you didn't mention his name to Cecil or the Marshal."

I retreated to my room with my head spinnin'. I couldn't believe it. That feeling I had about being watched was not just my imagination. Megan had someone watching me all day and now I could easily guess who it was. She had good old Kenny following me and he had certainly been earning his wages. Megan knew my every movement and that gave me something else to worry about. It reminded me a little of good old Mutt in Santa Fe but this time I was the one being watched not the one paying for the information.

I drifted off to sleep thinking, once again, about Santa Fe.

# CHAPTER IX

## "Saturday night fights"

### FALL 1883

The dog days of summer came and went before I heard any more about the big fisticuff competition. According to Mutt, Victor and Taylor were busy as bees 'round a hive but they stayed away from the St. Charles and I avoided any casual contact. Just when I thought they might have given up their grand scheme, Taylor came by with more newspapers and an update of their progress. She was dressed like she just came from the ranch which made me wish that she had. Jeans, boots and cotton shirts just seemed to suit her.

Since Taylor didn't wish to be seen hanging around the gambling hall, we retreated to my office where she was "bubbling" over with news.

She handed me a short stack of newspapers. "Just look at these papers, they're full of stories about our Championship Prizefight. We've selected promoters in each city and they've already scheduled their preliminary bouts. We're in business."

From what I read, it sure seemed she was correct. All the local newspapers papers from Dodge City, Abilene, Denver, Laramie, Carson City, San Francisco and Tombstone, detailed the contest rules and dates of local competitions. From what I could gather, most were sold out with additional challengers clamoring for their chance.

"How did you get all these promoters? Who are they?"

Taylor looked to be proud as a pup with a new collar as she explained the details of the success. She talked as she paced around the office.

"My news stories got everybody talking and the high rollers in each city wanted to be a part of the big show. We didn't have to go lookin' for them, Monroe; they came to us. They'll make money on their local fights and then follow their champions here. It'll be like a party and should be a big winner for everybody."

I chose to ignore her use of my name "Monroe" since I had other concerns.

"What about the money? I haven't seen any money."

Taylor looked out the office door to make sure no one else was within earshot. "Here ya go, big brother. Didn't we promise that you would handle it?"

From the rear pocket of her jeans Taylor produced a handful of folded Western Union wires. Each one authorized the transfer of funds from some bank to my business account in Santa Fe. Four promoters had paid in full while the other three managed partial payments. I was holding over nine thousand dollars in my hand. I couldn't believe it.

As I looked at the promoters and the amounts I noted that I'd heard of many of them including Horace Tabor from Denver, John Mackay from Virginia City and George Hearst from San Francisco. They were well known as rich and powerful men with the exception of one Archibald Slack from Laramie. When I asked about him, Taylor gave me a short history lesson on Wyoming and woman's suffrage.

"His mother is Ester Hobart Morris, the first woman Justice of the Peace in the whole damn country. I'll have you know that Wyoming was the first state to allow women the right to vote way back in 1869. Women serve on juries there and run for political office. The Arizona and New Mexico territories are far behind the times."

I sensed a real sore point so I remained silent until she ran out of steam. I had no idea she was so adamant about women's rights.

"Anyway, I chose him as our promoter to help his mother and the suffrage movement in Wyoming. You'll notice he paid the entire sixteen hundred dollars in full."

Either Taylor was changing right before my eyes or I hadn't known my little sister as well as I thought I had. I continued to look at the figures and wonder at her accomplishment when it occurred to me that there were only seven cities involved and not eight as promised.

"There's one missing. What about Santa Fe? Weren't you planning on having a preliminary round here?"

Right about that time she really got smug and pulled a roll of greenbacks from the other rear pocket of her jeans.

"I thought you'd never ask. Here's sixteen hundred in cash that Victor and I have collected. Our prelims start in one week right here in your casino. What have you got to say about that, big brother?"

Taylor was really flying high so I measured my comments but I wasn't happy about her and Victor doing anything let alone trying to promote boxing matches. When I'd agreed to stage their boxing matches, I never really thought they'd do it so now I was forced to put up or shut up.

"I'd say you've done a mighty fine job of it so far. I'll make sure these funds got deposited in the bank and build a boxing ring so we can hold the fights in proper fashion. They are to be held in accordance with the Queensberry rules, aren't they?"

"Yes. The ring should be a twenty foot square or as close to it as possible. Victor can provide you with the details of the construction. Mister Sullivan and his manager are insistent on putting an end to the bare-knuckle, toe-the-line fisticuffs of the past. Following these strict rules, boxing will become more civilized and less barbaric."

"Are all the preliminary fights being held under the same rules?"

"They're supposed to be but in the end, it's really up to each promoter."

"Alright. I guess I better get to work. Thanks for the update and the money."

Taylor started to leave the office and then she turned to face me.

"I wish things were different between us. Maybe someday we can go back to being brother and sister again."

I had so much to say that I couldn't speak. I just let her walk away without comment. I had no idea what the future held for us but I seriously doubted if I would ever consider us brother and sister again.

It took a lot of work and about two hundred dollars but one week later we had a jim-dandy boxing ring in the middle of the casino in St. Charles Place. I hired carpenters who worked round the clock for three days once we had all the building plans and materials. As promised, it was a twenty foot square inside the ropes with a two foot "apron" all around the outside. The ring itself was built on a platform that was three feet off the floor and had four corner posts or "turnbuckles" that were five foot tall. We had three one inch ropes secured to each post at different heights that made a "fence" around the ring. I wondered if that "fence" was to keep the fighters in or the crowd out.

With the assistance of Beau, Paddy and Maude, I was able to beg, borrow, or steal every folding chair in town to place in rows for the spectators. In all, we had room for two hundred and fifty seated and another fifty or so standing in the back. Since all of our gambling set-ups were pushed out of the way, I was depending on ticket collections to more than make up for my lost business.

As Beau and I were admiring the newly constructed ring, a strange thought occurred to me.

"Have you ever wondered why they call this a ring when it's square? I mean, rings are usually round and not square."

As always, Beau had an answer. "I reckon it goes back to when men fought bare-knuckle inside a circle or ring drawn in the dirt. A fighter lost a match when he was knocked out of the ring and couldn't get back in. It might also refer to when spectators surrounded fighters in a loose circle or formed a 'ring' around them. Now that they have the new fancy set-up I guess they call it a ring because of tradition. I've heard tell that some folks have taken to calling it a 'square circle'. Now don't that beat all?"

I guess what we called the damn thing didn't matter as long as it was completed in time for the first eight fights. I was just hoping the boxing matches would be worth all the fuss and expense.

Victor was set up and ready at seven o'clock and the fight fans were damn near beating down the doors. Folks were so starved for entertainment and excitement that the response was overwhelming. At two dollars apiece, we sold over three hundred tickets in about forty-five minutes. Some traditions were hard to break as only a few women were allowed in the casino to watch the spectacle but weren't permitted to smoke or drink. I was reminded of what Taylor had said about New Mexico Territory being so far behind the times.

We were doing a landslide business at the bar so I helped Paddy to keep up with the demand. Each of the sixteen contestants seemed to bring his entire family and all of friends to root for him which made for a boisterous and belligerent group. We had to separate some of them to stop impromptu fights in the audience. With fifteen minutes to go before the first fight, we had our hands full trying to contain the expectant crowd. Finally Victor took over as Master of Ceremonies and the show began.

The first three bouts were pretty run-of-the-mill affairs and the crowd started getting agitated. The fighters were non-local Mexicans and Injuns that fought with guts and determination but little fighting skill or common sense. In each case, the winner was determined when the loser finally gave up after taking a severe but uninspired beating. The crowd wanted blood and knockouts and they were sorely disappointed. The third winner was booed out of the ring and chased by several empty beer bottles. What we needed was a real knock-down drag-'em-out fight and we finally got it.

The fourth match featured a huge teamster named "Rocko" Mancini and a big cowboy callin' himself Texas Slim. Now Slim might have been from Texas but he was anything but slim at six foot four and at least three hundred pounds. He was represented in the crowd by a half dozen rowdy cowhands that got into a shouting and shoving match with some of "Rocko's" Italian backers. When the fight started, they finally broke up their little dust-ups and devoted what energy they had left to rooting for their favorite.

The match lasted almost three full rounds of three minutes each before it ended in a dramatic knockout. The cagey Italian wagon driver had been getting the worst of it but he suckered the big cowboy into a wild miss and hit him with a left uppercut and a right hook that ended the contest. It took two buckets of ice cold water to revive Slim to where he could be helped out of the ring. Rocko won the fight but looked like he'd lost it as much of his face had been rearranged by the big Texan. The crowd gave both fighters an ovation and eagerly awaited the next four bouts.

The next three fights ended with first round knockouts by local favorites with large local followings. An Irishman known only as Skully, a German blacksmith named Wilhelm Mulder and a crazed mule skinner called Doggett advanced to the next round. By that time, the crowd was really getting it's monies worth and the evening looked to be a big success.

As it turned out, Victor had saved the best for last and the eighth bout promised to be the best. A Mexican half-breed with long red hair was the first one in the ring. He was known all over Santa Fe as *"Rojo Grande"* or Big Red. He was a very large man that stood over six feet five and weighed upwards of four hundred pounds. His movements were slow and ponderous but his immense size alone made him a formidable opponent. I couldn't imagine who or what would get in that ring with him.

The crowd was ripe with anticipation as several minutes went by before Beau walked through the batwing doors to announce the challenger to Big Red.

"Here he is, ladies and gentlemen, the next Boxing Champion of the World, Charlemagne Brown."

The boisterous and rowdy crowd fell deathly silent as a large and extremely well built Negro walked in the doors. I judged him to be six feet four and about two hundred-fifty pounds. He was so much bigger than Beau the two of them standing together looked like father and son. His head was completely shaven and his only clothing was a ragged set of short-legged pants. The hushed on-lookers started to whisper their amazement at his size and obvious strength. For his part, the African was completely focused on Big Red. His defiant stare was returned by the big Mexican and the crowd let out a loud cheer as he approached the ring.

Beau walked over next to me and gloated. "How do you like my fighter? You might want to get a bet down on him because he's gonna be the next champ."

"Where did you find him?"

"I had some old friends send him here from New Orleans. He actually hails from Saint Charles Parish. Now don't that beat all?"

"I thought you were from Martinique, not New Orleans?"

Beau shot me a knowing grin and continued. "How do you like the name Charlemagne? I thought it sounded more intimidating than his given name, Charlie."

Now the thought of that really made me laugh. Charlie Brown, from Saint Charles Parish, was fighting in St. Charles Place which was owned by me, Henry Charles. Our conversation was interrupted by Victor shouting above the din.

"Here we go with the last contest of the evening. Let's have a big hand for '*Rojo Grande* and Charlemagne Brown."

The two antagonists stood in opposite corners and glared at each other as the crowd clamored for the fight to begin. When it did, the yellin' and cheerin' was so loud I couldn't hear myself think.

It was immediately clear that the African had boxing experi-ence. He fought with speed and grace and easily avoided all of Red's clumsy attempts to wrestle or clench. For three solid minutes he pummeled the big Mexican with punches that were as powerful as they were lightning quick and well placed. The big surprise was that they had so little effect. Big Red was bloodied and battered but still on his feet and in control of his senses.

The second round was much the same except when Charlemagne slipped on the bloody canvas and went to one knee. Red seized the opportunity and tried to pounce on or "pancake" him. The tactic almost worked but the Negro fighter blocked his charge and rolled out of the way. At the end of the round, both men looked dog-tired; One from punching so much and the other from taking all those same punches.

Beau leaned closer so I could hear him. "I told Charlie to carry the big fella till the third round. Makes for a better fight and doesn't make him look invincible. I wouldn't want to scare off any potential bettors, you know."

If Beau was telling the truth, he was setting-up the boxing bettors just like he did the players at the poker tables. I had to admit that from what I'd seen; backing his fighter seemed a right sensible idea.

The third round was almost over before it began. As Big Red trudged to the center of the ring, "Charlie" took two quick strides, stopped his advance with several hard left jabs and then hit him with a incredible right hook right on the end of his jaw.

For the big Mexican, the lights went out and the party was over. His legs buckled and he crashed to the canvas so hard he dislodged one of the turnbuckles. Charlemagne Brown was declared the winner by knockout. Beau quickly escorted him out of the casino and that was that. Folks calmed down, finished their drinks and went about their business leaving Paddy and me to clean up the mess.

All in all, we had a great night. I counted almost seven hundred dollars in ticket sales and the promise of more to come in the next three weeks. I was about to concede that Victor and Taylor had been right all along when I caught sight of Victor collecting bets outside. As a professional gambler I couldn't fault what he was doing but he'd promised Taylor he wouldn't. It made me wonder what other promises he'd broken and how far his gambling was going to go.

One week later we were set up for four more fights. Taylor provided many newspaper accounts attesting to the success of similar contests in seven other cities. All of the matches were supposed to be chosen by lot but I heard Victor had hand-picked them here in Santa Fe. It was clear to me that he was setting up his bets and making sure he was going to win. Taylor was so excited and happy that I decided not to spoil her fun by telling her the truth. It also occurred to me that she might not believe me and it was certain Victor would never admit it. I asked Mutt to keep tabs on him so I would know about how much money was involved and bided my time.

Skully, Wilhelm Mulder and Rocko Mancini easily won their bouts against gutsy but overmatched opponents. Skully, the Irish loudmouth, showed signs of boxing skills while Herr Mulder and Mancini just overpowered their opponents with sheer mass and muscle. All three fights ended in first or second round knockouts but the crowd didn't seem too impressed. They finally came alive when the final bout was announced. The crazed muleskinner known only as Doggett was set to face Charlemagne.

All week long, the "smart talk" was whether the crazy muleskinner would show up at all. He was in one saloon or another every night trying to drink his courage up and not doing a good job of it. I believe he was half drunk when he finally got into the ring.

Beau had kept his fighter away from the bars and out of sight until the night of the fight so when Charlemagne made his entrance, the place exploded with cheers. He had clearly become the home town favorite.

The bout itself turned out to be closer than most people expected. Doggett might have acted crazy but he had some boxing skills and protected himself pretty well. He didn't hand out much punishment but he avoided it until the fourth round when "Charlie" hit him in the stomach so hard that he collapsed on the canvas and never got back up. The referee called it a "TKO" or technical knockout as Doggett was never knocked out but was clearly unable to continue. The crowd was a little disappointed by the lack of a dramatic knockout but otherwise satisfied with the outcome.

I couldn't help but wonder how much influence Beau had on the fight and whether his fighter had carried Doggett all those rounds. As with the prior week, Victor was busy collecting his winnings after the fights while trying to keep anyone from seeing him doing it.

On the third Saturday night we were limited to just two bouts. In accordance with the rules that Victor set up, we raised the ticket price to three bucks but it didn't seem to limit the crowd. In the first contest, the cocky Irishman, Skully, was matched against Rocko Mancini and all week long the Irish and Italians in town had been going at it. Both men were cast as champions for their native homelands and their supporters were driven by patriotic passions. The contest itself lasted six rounds as Skully danced and slapped his way around the ring while the Italian plodded after him. The brazen Irishman taunted and teased the "wop" teamster which infuriated the crowd but had little effect on Mancini. Finally, Rocko trapped the "mick" in the corner and knocked him through the ropes with a combination of lefts and rights. The bout was officially over but several fights got started in the crowd and we had to escort some of their supporters out into the night.

The second bout featured Wilhelm Mulder, the stout and sturdy German blacksmith against Charlemagne. I'd never met a blacksmith that couldn't crush your hand when he shook it so I wasn't surprised when Herr Mulder was able to hold his own for almost eight rounds. The burly German took a punch pretty well and even handed out a few of his own but they appeared to have little effect. The African seemed to be waiting for his chance and not taking any unnecessary ones himself. In the middle of the eighth round, Charlie finally exploded with a flurry of punches that just overpowered Wilhelm. The rapid punches and overall exhaustion proved to be too much. The German blacksmith sunk to his knees on the canvas for the count of nine and then struggled to his feet with help from the referee. Since he was unable to continue, it was considered a technical knockout but a great fight none the less. I was satisfied if the crowd was and they were.

When Beau was escorting his fighter out the door, I heard him questioning why the bout had lasted so long. I didn't hear the answer but I could tell that something was going on with Charlemagne Brown that Beau didn't like. I could only guess what it might be.

As we neared the fourth weekend and the final match, the entire town seemed caught up in the boxing hysteria. The "smell" of battle was in the air and most of the young men in town walked around like bull elks during the "rut". An unintended brush of a shoulder, a casual slip of a tongue or the dreaded return of a defiant stare started numerous confrontations and fights.

The betting was five to one that the African would win. The only person that was actively backing the Italian teamster was Victor and that rang a warning bell in my head. What the hell did he know or think he knew that made him so sure Mancini could win?

My able confidant, Mutt, estimated that Victor had bet almost three thousand dollars at the current odds and was willing to take all comers. I had no idea he had that kind of money and wondered if Taylor had any clue as to what he was up to.

Paddy thought Victor had lost his mind but Beau saw it differently.

"He's gonna try to fix the fight but I won't let him. I'm two steps ahead of that 'Bayou bandit' but he just doesn't know it yet. Trust me, my fighter will win."

One thing was for certain; both men thought they were right and only one of 'em was. Saturday night might be right for fighting but the real drama would be taking place during the week and outside of the "square circle".

On Saturday morning, Taylor brought me the remaining wire transfers from the contestant's registration. As she promised, we had the grand total of twelve thousand-eight-hundred dollars. I took ten thousand as repayment of the money I'd advanced to Victor while Taylor counted out her eight hundred. That left two thousand for Victor that my naïve little sister thought he was going to send to Sullivan's manager. I figured he had to be counting on that money to back his bets. Only time would tell that tale.

With tickets going for five dollars a head, we were packed to the rafters on Saturday night. The Italians in the crowd were waving their tri-color Sardinian flags and raising a ruckus from the time they got there. Side bets were being made everywhere as each side thought they had a sure thing. The Italians bet out of pride and passion while everyone else bet based on their assessment of the two fighters. One group or the other was bound to be deeply disappointed so I brought in some extra help in case things got out of hand when the fight ended.

Mancini entered the ring to a tumultuous ovation of cheers and boos. Some of his Italian supporters started singing their national anthem, "*Marcia Reale*", but were quickly shouted down by the majority of the spectators. Beau and Charlemagne Brown finally entered the St. Charles and the mob erupted in even louder cheers and fewer boos. When the two fighters faced each other across twenty feet of canvas, the stage was properly set.

Beau stood by my side as Victor introduced the pugilists to the audience. My Cajun friend seemed as nervous as a long-tailed cat in a room of rocking chairs. His eyes flashed between the ring and the front doors. It was obvious he was waiting for someone to enter and he didn't seem none too happy about it.

With the crowd teased and taunted to a fever pitch, the fight was about to start when Beau sprung cat-like towards the doors. He spread out his arms and bared entrance to an Italian mother with her brood of five children. She was a heavy set woman in her forties and the children were a mixture of boys and girls in ascending ages from about three to eleven. She began calling out Rocko's name and pleading in her native tongue. It was pretty evident that this was Mancini's family and Beau was doing his damnedest to keep them from watching the fight. He looked kind of funny leaping back and forth trying to keep the kids from getting around him.

Paddy raced around the bar and had a short but tense conversation with Beau before gently pushing the entire family back into the street. Beau tried to straighten his clothing and regain his dignity as he walked back to stand beside me. His wave to the referee signaled the bout to begin.

I just had to ask. "What the hell was that all about?"

"Watching this here boxing match is no place for that woman and her children."

"Wasn't that Mancini's family?"

"What if it was? All the more reason they shouldn't have to see their daddy get "whupped" by my fighter. I did 'em a favor by running 'em off."

"Maybe. But that's not why you did it."

Beau gave me a look that said the conversation was over. "Mind your own business and watch the fight."

From a pure pugilistic standpoint, this final bout figured to be a classic struggle between a brute puncher and a skilled boxer. In most cases, such a fight would go many rounds with each fighter gaining and losing the advantage until one of them made a fatal mistake.

This time, however, the mistake that Rocko Mancini made was getting in the ring at all. Charlemagne was as focused as I'd ever seen him. He made no pretense of boxing as he stood toe to toe with the Italian teamster and just beat him into the canvas. I don't think the fight lasted thirty seconds including the referees count to ten. The entire crowd was stunned to silence when Mancini went down but erupted into hysteria when the count was finished. The celebrating was so loud that I stepped outside to get away from the din.

The next thing I knew, Victor was pushing his way through the mob and heading towards me with an anxious group of bettors climbing up his backside. I pushed the bat wing doors together and leaned against them to keep 'em shut so when Victor got to the doors he had no where to go. He was forced to turn and face his fate.

It took almost ten minutes and over four thousand dollars for him to exhaust the line of his creditors. When everybody was paid, I backed off and let the doors swing open. At long last, Victor walked out, gave me a look that could curdle fresh milk and walked off into the night. I wondered what tall tale he would tell Taylor about his evening but figured that was his business and none of mine.

When I went back to the St. Charles, Beau and Charlie were celebrating his victory at the bar where they had been joined by Angelina and a young Negro woman named Lucille. "Lucy" was introduced to me as Charlie's wife but she looked young enough to be his daughter. She wore the look of a frightened fawn as the crowd surged around her. Angelina took notice and tried to shelter her as much as possible.

Beau started crowing about the fight and promised every-body that would listen that Charlemagne Brown would be the next Champion of the World. To further his point, he sprung for a drink on the house and paid for it with a handful of bills he'd just received from Victor. I was tickled to see Victor get skinned but I was a little worried about how Beau had managed to do it.

I finished the free drink and made my way out of the casino. The crowd had broken up and we had plenty of extra workers to handle the clean-up. I planned on a lonely walk in the night air but Mutt slithered out of the shadows and joined me.

"Quite the fight, 'eh, Gove' nor?"

"Yes it was. I imagine ever'body but Rocko and his Italian had a good time and got their monies worth."

"I don't think young Victor Bodine had such a good time but he had it coming."

"What do you mean?"

Mutt stopped walking and stared at me with the look of a canary with a mouth full of feathers. "Are ye asking for conversation or information? One is freely given but the other will cost you a gold eagle."

I considered his proposition and reluctantly produced a gold coin and flipped it to him. "This information better be worth the weight of it."

"That it is, Gove' nor. Worth its weight in gold."

Mutt gave me chapter and verse about Victor's gambling and fixing of the fights. He had carefully matched the fighters so he could always pick the winner and thereby win all his bets. He paid three of the earlier fighters to "take a dive" and intimidated two others into losing those first bouts. Mutt's best guess was that Victor was ahead about three thousand dollars going into the final match. Then, he backed Mancini and risked all his earnings only to lose all he'd won plus half of the two thousand that I'd given him.

"I can't imagine why Victor would bet ever'thing he had on Mancini. What was he thinking?"

"He thought he had that fight rigged too but as it turned out; he didn't. Beau beat him to the punch, so to speak."

"How?"

"Did you see Beau turn away that family?"

"Yes. I believe that was Misses Mancini and her children."

"Aye that they were. Victor had them brought to the fight to distract the African fella. He knew all about him from New Orleans. Charlie Brown might be a great mass of a man but he has a soft side and can't bring himself to hurt anyone that doesn't dearly deserve it. That's why he went so easy on the muleskinner and the blacksmith. Big Red was the only one he felt needed a beatin'. If he'd a' seen those poor miserable Italian children rooting for their papa, well, it would have been a different fight. And that's what Victor was banking on."

So that was what Beau had been talking about. He knew what Victor was up to all along and called his bluff. It was a classic poker strategy to let the sucker get over confident and then clean him out with a single hand.

I thanked Mutt for his useful insight into the affairs of others and slowly meandered back to my room. I had no idea how the rest of the boxing tournament was gonna go but it sure had been fun up 'till then. The casino had made a good deal of money on the exhibitions and stood to make even more if the fights continued but the best part was that good old Victor Bodine lost his shirt in the process. There was no telling how his gambling problems would affect his relationship with Taylor but I figured they couldn't help. Sooner or later there was a piper to be paid and it could cost Victor more than he could afford.

## WINTER 1884

The Western Championship bouts were to have been held around Christmas and New Years, 1883 but the uncommonly cold weather put a damper on everything. What came to be known around the country as the "Long Winter" started when it snowed in New Orleans on June 5th, 1883 and the uncommon cold lasted until the spring of 1885. The "mini ice age", as they termed it, ruined crops, froze and starved cattle and drove some folks to travel back east on the same trails that brought 'em west. Travel from the other seven cities was nearly impossible so the finals were put off 'till spring. In Santa Fe, we didn't get hit as bad as some of the western states and territories but the snow and cold made daily life quite a chore.

Charlie Brown and his wife, Lucy, became local celebrities as they patiently waited for the other challengers to arrive. They kept to themselves but were still the talk of the town. Everybody wondered if they'd stay around Santa Fe after the fighting was finished.

In each of the other cities, the local paper boasted that their local champion would win the final competition. Since all we could do was wait, I read each paper and tried to imagine what each man looked like as well as how he might measure up to the others.

Right off, I was delighted to see that I knew the winner from Tombstone. He was none other than my old friend, Zack James. Back in 1878, when I ran away from Grasshopper Flats and joined a trail herd, I became best friends with his younger brothers Mal and Josh. When they were gunned down by a drunken miner in Virginia City, I avenged them by killing the sot. Folks thought I was a third brother named Henry so I became a gunfighter known as Henry James. Two years later Zack found me in San Bernardino, California and saved my life in a bar fight. We became close friends as he considered me a replacement for his own brothers. Two years after that, he appeared in Flagstaff just in time to save my bacon once again. I owed Zack my life and was eager to renew our relationship when he finally made it to Santa Fe.

According to the Tombstone Epitaph, my six foot eight "brother" demolished the competition with three straight first round knockouts. Having seen him in action, I wasn't even a little bit surprised. I'd back Zack against anyone else I'd ever seen, and that included Charlemagne Brown.

The other six finalists were likewise described in glowing terms by their local newspapers. The San Francisco Examiner devoted two entire pages to their champion who called himself "Kronos the Great". He was Greek by birth and a fisherman by trade that was known to drink massive quantities of ouzo before each fight. They marveled at the fearless and vicious way he attacked his opponents.

The Territorial Enterprise in Virginia City seemed equally proud that their fair city was represented by a recent immigrant from Cornwall, England. His name was given as Kenan Trehane and he'd been employed as a hard rock miner in the Ophir mine. Since I'd tried my hand at that occupation in the very same mine, I had great respect for the man and his potential strength. Swinging an eight-pound sledge for ten hours a day could turn a man into a monster.

The Daily Boomerang in Laramie boasted that their Cheyenne half-breed was surely the toughest and scariest man in the West. His Injun name was "wolf-man" but he claimed his Christian name was "Jack". He was described as a man of "prodigious strength and guile" but was also accused of biting two of his opponents about the head and neck. Seems the referees had allowed it because there was no specific rule agin it.

Not to be outdone, the Rocky Mountain News out of Denver offered an extra prize for anybody who could last three rounds with their mountain man. They said he could neither read nor write and rarely spoke but was kin to a grizzly bear when he got in the ring. His so-called manager, named "The Colonel", did all the talking and just referred to his fighter as "Griz".

The Abilene Rancher was sending us a big cowboy by the name of Billy Bob something or other. The paper was torn and his last name was missing. He was also their local rodeo king and claimed boxing was pretty tame after riding the big bulls. He was quoted as hoping the competition was better in Santa Fe since he'd had such an easy time of it in Abilene.

The Dodge City Times seemed in awe of their local strongman named Dimitri Plushenko. Being a paper of few words, their article claimed that he was too big and strong to ever be beaten. They also mentioned that he hailed from the Russia territory known as the Ukraine and spoke no English at all. Somehow, however, the town fathers came up with enough money to send a local school teacher along with him to act as a translator.

Sporting such a colorful group of combatants, our Western Heavyweight Championship promised to be a successful venture if we could ever get it going. It wasn't 'till a week after Easter that the weather let up a little and Victor sent out the telegrams notifying the promoters that the fight was on. The first elimination bouts were to start on Saturday, the 4th of May, and continue for the next two Saturdays whereupon the champion would be crowned.

What Victor didn't mention was that he'd been unable to send the two thousand dollar front money to Billy Madden. It followed that he had no idea if he could ever get John L. Sullivan to come to Santa Fe. Oh, he pretended that he had ever'thing under control but I knew better. He was seen taking even more bets on the upcoming fights since that was the only way he could ever hope to recoup his losses. Since Taylor was still smitten with the man and wished to believe his lies; I let her. His day of reckoning was coming and I just wanted to be around to watch.

The first of the pugilistic challengers arrived the 28th of April. There he was, the fighter known only as "Griz", clinging to the roof of the Denver Stage as it pulled into town. Among the passengers aboard the stage was his manager, Colonel Rufus King. He exited the stage with a plumed three corner hat, a loud plaid suit and an even louder mouth. With a regal flourish, he introduced his fighter.

"Here he is, ladies and gentlemen, the next Heavyweight Champion of the World. Climb on down here, boy, so the folks can get a look at the size of ya."

Griz leapt from the roof of the stage and landed neatly on his feet in front of the stunned audience of onlookers. He was a man of massive proportions covered with bearskins and leather trappings. While the Colonel had a neatly trimmed white beard and mustache, Griz had a face full of unruly brown hair that had never seen a scissor or comb. His deep-set eyes darted back and forth as he nervously confronted his audience. As advertised, the Colonel did all the talking in a manner of a snake-oil salesman.

"Yes sir, ladies and gentlemen, this man is as wild as they come. He was raised by grizzly bears high in the Rocky Mountains. He stands almost seven feet tall on his hind legs and weighs four hundred pounds most of the year. As you can see, his neck is as thick as a telegraph pole. He cannot read or write and barely speaks beyond his unusual assortment of growls, snarls and snorts but he will eagerly take on all challengers in the ring and emerge as the next Heavyweight Boxing Champion."

The Colonel preened his mustache and observed the crowds reaction to his little speech before speaking under his breath to the stage driver. "Can you direct me to the nearest stable, my good man? I'd like to find a comfortable stall for my furry friend here so I can get settled in the Palace hotel."

I doubted the dimensions that the Colonel boasted about but there was no doubt that Griz was a formidable opponent given his size and strength. His shoulders and arms were twice as thick as mine and his legs were massive. Others agreed and the betting started to favor Griz. He went from even odds to three to one by nightfall. I figured if the matches were "no-holds-barred" affairs, he might win easily but the fighters were limited to the formal Queensberry rules which severely limited his wrestling and mauling abilities. Either way, there were no conditions under which I would care to get in the ring with him.

The next fighter to arrive, a day later, was Billy Bob Morton from Abilene, Texas. He had been accurately described by his local paper as a blow-hard rodeo cowboy with an elevated opinion of himself and his abilities. He rode into town upon a beautiful palomino stallion with two guns blazing and his mouth working overtime. He was tall and fit with a big smile and an eye for the ladies. He slid off his horse and landed right in the first saloon he saw. Luckily, it wasn't the St. Charles Place so I didn't have to put up with his blather. In a normal athletic contest with normal opponents Billy Bob may have stood a chance but not in this one. He appeared to be seriously overmatched against any of the others. Some of the local ladies might have been impressed but the savvy fight bettors wrote him off as an early loser.

April 30th saw the arrival of two trains and two more contestants. "Kronos the Great" arrived from San Francisco on the morning train. He traveled with two suitcases and a carpet bag. The bag held his extra clothing and the two cases were crammed with bottles of ouzo. He'd been warned that his drink of choice would be hard to find in Santa Fe so he came prepared. He was not a physically imposing man to look at but his dark eyes and long black hair seemed to give him a sinister air that was felt like a winter chill as he walked by. Personally, he reminded me of drawings I'd seen of the pirate "Blackbeard" but, once again, the bettors weren't impressed by his "evil stare" and he stayed at even odds.

The afternoon train delivered the Russian strongman, Dimitri Plushenko, and his translator, Sasha Petrova. She was billed as a school teacher and translator but I saw her in a much different light. He looked to be strong and dumb while she was beautiful and smart so they made a good paring. With her pinned-up hair, thick spectacles and peasant clothing, Sasha didn't brook any nonsense from the local fans as she immediately got two rooms for the two of them and rented an old warehouse building so Dimitri had a place to train. Of all the fighters that had arrived, he looked to be the best boxer given the new rules and all. His odds went up a mite to two to one.

While I was patiently waiting for Zack to arrive, May 1st brought the Laramie "wolf-man" to Santa Fe. He traveled with about a dozen Cheyenne Injuns that brought their tepees with 'em and set up a little village about a mile out of town. "Jack", as he was known, was the shortest of the contestants but broad and powerfully built. Dressed in a red blanket and leggings, he plodded around town like a stoic Injun and quickly became the favorite of the local Pueblo tribes. They saw him as representing all Injun tribes against the white invaders and bet accordingly. His odds soared to four to one for a time until they came back down to a more reasonable two to one.

I started getting anxious about Zack on May 2nd when the only new arrival was Kenan Trehane from Virginia City. He rode in on a very large gray mule which caused quite a stir as the big ugly critter honked and snorted like a locomotive. Kenan was young and eager to please everyone he met. He was overly polite and seemed genuinely proud to be representing his adopted city in his adopted country. He almost apologized for his boxing abilities and said he'd just been lucky in the preliminary fights but his thick build and broad features suggested otherwise. At six foot five, his long arms gave him great reach and I'll bet he could crush walnuts in the palm of his hands. Smart bettors smelled a ringer and his odds went up to two to one in spite of his youth.

I was going over some bookwork in my office on the night of May 3rd when I heard a commotion in the bar. I started to go out to see what the fuss was about when Paddy stuck her cherubic face through the door.

"Come out here and see what just walked in the joint. I think I've fallen in love again."

There he was, bigger than life, my good friend and "brother", Zackary James. Two years hadn't changed him much and I could see why Paddy was all a'flutter. Zack was about as tall and handsome as a man could get. He stood a full six-foot eight and a solid two hundred-fifty pounds. He was broad shouldered and narrow at the hip and had hands that looked like sledge hammers. His big

smile seemed to assure ever'one that everything was gonna be alright now that Zack James was there. I'm not sure how fast his odds
rose but he was five to one at fight time. Only Charlemagne, at six
to one, held higher odds.

Zack and I had a lot of catching up to do so we retired to my
office to get away from his growing group of admirers. Paddy kept
the rest out but let herself in ever so often just to make sure we didn't
need anything.

After winning the local competition in Tombstone, which included knocking out one of the Clanton clan, Zack had gone back
to Yuma and wasn't aware of the finals until the last minute or he
would have arrived sooner. It'd just been a coincidence that he was
even in Tombstone when the competition started. Zack had made
a hobby out of chasing after Beale's camels and was following up
a sighting near Bisbee. The camels had been released by the Army
after trying them out as pack animals. Zack always said that chasing after 'em was like looking for lost Spanish treasure. They were
always out there, just beyond the horizon and out of reach.

On the personal side, he said the ranch was doing fine, his folks
were getting along and his recently married baby sister had made
him an uncle already. He was still free and single and asked about
my sister, Taylor. They had met two years prior in Flagstaff. I said
she was fine and left it at that. Somehow, the thought of competing
with Zack for Taylor's attention was more than I could handle.

On Saturday morning I was busy directing the final set-up for the
first round of fights when Victor came through the doors. He was
full of self congratulations over the apparent success of his grand
scheme but seemed eager to speak with me alone. We sat at a table
in the back and Victor started his sad story.

"I trust that you will do very well what with the ticket sales, the
liquor and all."

"I'm sure we will. I guess I do have you and Taylor to thank for
that."

I knew what was coming but I had to ask. "Is there something I
can do for you?"

"Now that you mention it, there is. I had to sweeten the deal with some of the local promoters to get them to send their winners here and now I don't have the money to settle up."

"How sweet are we talking?"

"I had to promise five hundred a piece. Tombstone, Virginia City and Denver didn't squawk so there's just four that need to be paid."

Two thousand dollars seemed like an awful convenient amount so I could figure what he was up to. "Is that the money you need to send back East?"

Victor looked like he was trying to swallow a clump of horseshit as he tried to come up with another tall tale.

"No... I mean yes, well...not really. I gave them the advance money and now I'm short the money for Billy Madden so, yes, I will be sending the money back East."

"And you expect me to just give it to you?"

"You could raise the ticket prices and cover that amount easily."

"Yes I could but I won't. Ticket prices are too high already."

The clump must have gone down cause Victor suddenly became panicky. "Then how am I to complete the deal for the Championship?"

"Maybe you could get lucky and win all the bets you've made. You know, all that gambling you promised Taylor you wouldn't do."

"How do you...?"

"A little bird-dog told me."

"You haven't told Taylor?"

"No, I haven't. I figure that's your business and not mine. But, eventually, she will find out."

"Not if I can win my way out of the hole I'm in."

"Well good luck to ya. My Pa always said the first step in getting out of a hole was to stop digging."

Victor started to leave and then paused as if his nimble brain had concocted yet another scheme I couldn't wait to hear.

"How about you, Henry? Are you betting on the fights?"

"I hadn't planned to but I might, why?"

"How about we make a winner-take-all bet on the eventual Champion?"

I was about to decline his offer when I had to reconsider. Zack was a sure winner in my mind so why not bet with Victor? If I cleaned him out, then he might have to leave town with his tail twixt his knees and that would suit me just fine.

"How much money are you talking?"

"I was thinking about ten thousand."

"Ten thousand?"

"If that's not enough, how about twenty?"

I knew I was being suckered in but I just didn't care. Jealousy, envy, and ego all got involved and I spoke without thinking. "Twenty it is."

Victor called Beau and Paddy to our table so they could witness our bet. Paddy was aghast at the amount but Beau figured he knew what I was up to and just sat there with a big grin on his face. He did come up with a big question.

"What if you're both betting the same fighter? Someone has to choose first and the other will have to select someone else."

Beau pulled out a deck of cards and offered them to us. "Wanna cut for it?"

I knew Beau made the comment 'cause he thought we'd both might wish to bet on his fighter, Charlemagne but I knew better so I wasn't concerned.

"Victor can have first choice. I'll pick from whoever's left over."

Victor looked mildly surprised but Beau seemed amazed by my concession.

Paddy couldn't stand the waiting. "So Victor, darlin', who are ya chosing?"

"I should probably go with Beau's man from the bayou but I'm gonna go with that big fella from Tombstone, Zack James.

You could hear a pin drop at our table as Beau and I were both in shock. Paddy was the first to speak. "Well, he's my choice too."

Victor's attitude changed completely and his vicious smile told me that I'd been had. Our whole conversation had led up to that moment. He hadn't come there to beg for two thousand dollars and he never intended to send any money back East. He was there to trap me into betting against Zack.

"Why did you choose Zack James?"

"It was Taylor's idea. She says she saw him fight in Flagstaff once and thinks he will be a sure winner. And we both know that girl can sure pick 'em."

I finally caught on. Wittingly or not, Taylor had given Victor all the information he needed to bamboozle me out of twenty thousand dollars.

Beau couldn't imagine my hesitation so he chose for me.

"Well, Henry will take Charlemagne, wouldn't you?"

"Yes, I guess I will."

Victor had the last word and then left us to our druthers. "Then it's settled. If neither man wins, we call the whole thing off. Good day gentlemen and lady."

I had been left with the impossible choice of rooting for my close friend or my twenty thousand dollars. Either way, I was bound to lose.

# CHAPTER X

# "All hail the champ"

## SPRING 1884

Saturday night found the St, Charles filled to the rafters once again with folks eager to witness the first round of elimination bouts. The room was filled with cigar smoke and loud piano music as Eric tried in vain to garner attention from the boisterous crowd.

The first match, as selected by a blind draw, pitted Charlemagne Brown against Kronos the Great. I could just imagine Beau filling Charlie's head with terrible stories about the Greek fisherman to make him out to be a villainous character like the famous "Blackbeard". Although, given Kronos' excessive drinking and generally sinister appearance that shouldn't have been too difficult.

The San Francisco champ entered the ring in a manner best described as "marinated". He was certainly living up to his hard-drinking reputation. He even brought along a fresh bottle of ouzo to sustain him through the fight. I figured that liquor was his way of combating fear so it helped him to get in the ring with the likes of our beloved Charlie Brown.

The Examiner had stated that as each of his fights progressed, he got drunker, meaner and tougher but we'll never know if that was true or not since his bout with Charlemagne didn't even last a single round. Before the fight began, he swore at, cursed and taunted the African which only made things worse. After about thirty seconds of constant pummeling, a knockout upper cut from a huge right hand deep-sixed the Greek fisherman. He remained in "Davy Jones' Locker" for several minutes before being revived. Wouldn't you know that his first act upon regaining consciousness was to ask for another drink? While the semi-conscious drunk was being helped from the ring, Beau shepherded Charlie away from the crowd. It looked like my bet was a solid one for the time being.

The second bout promised to be the most exciting of the evening based on the personalities of the fighters. Griz was set to do battle with "Wolf-Man Jack" as he had come to be called. The growlin', snarlin' and stalkin' that went on before the fight began was really something to hear and see. If that weren't enough, the flamboyant Colonel King strutted around the ring in his splendid attire and hardily encouraged the craziness.

I couldn't imagine those two semi-humans following a civilized set of rules and my suspicions proved to be correct. Along with the fisticuffs, there was bitin', gougin', kickin', and good old mud wrestlin'. I think the wolf-man bit off a chunk of ear. The referee went crazy trying to stop all the violations and was about to declare both of 'em disqualified when in the middle of the sixth round, Griz landed a fearsome left hook and followed it with a right cross that knocked several canines from the mouth of the wolf-man. Jack stood there trying to remain upright but a left upper cut to the stomach and yet another right cross took away all his options and he fell to the canvas like a tall oak tree in a Texas twister.

The Colonel jumped into the ring to raise the right paw of his fighter and the audience loved it. The match was more theatrical than athletic but no one seemed to care. The unconscious half-breed was carried from the ring and his Cheyenne friends were forced to cart him back to his tepee on a *travois*.

At this point, the ring needed to be cleaned up so we took a short intermission and I got a chance to talk to Zack. He was fighting in the last match but had arrived early to watch his competition. We both agreed that the winner of the fight between Charlemagne and Griz would be a rugged opponent when Victor announced the third bout. As I left to help behind the bar, Zack had some last words for me.

"Hope you have your betting money on me, Henry, cause I intend to win."

"Who else?"

My bravado was unconvincing and short lived as I turned to face Paddy.

"You really stepped in it this time, didn't you, laddie?"

"Yeah, it looks like I got the bitter end of the stick."

The third bout ended up as a toe-to-toe slugfest between the Cornish miner, Kenan Trehane and the Russian strongman, Dimitri Plushenko. For the first three rounds the two of 'em just stood in the middle of the ring and hammered away on each other. Both men were so big and strong that no matter how many punches were landed, there seemed to be little effect on either of 'em. They were bloody from facial cuts and smashed noses but showed no signs of lettin' up or givin' in.

To the delight of the mostly male audience, Sasha Petrova made an appearance at ringside in an obvious attempt to encourage Dimitri. She scolded him in Russian for a few seconds and then played to the rowdy crowd by removing her *babushka* to reveal her waist length blond hair. I couldn't imagine her teaching school but I'd bet she surely held the attention of any young men or boys in her classroom.

The crowd which had been pretty neutral during the match was suddenly heavy in favor of the Russian. Dimitri responded by starting to box rather than just slug it out. His conversion was well received by the audience and devastating to poor Kenan who chased and swung wildly at Dimitri as the Russian danced away and counter punched with great effectiveness. A strong and accurate left jab turned the Englishman's face into bloody mush. Kenan desperately tried for one big knockout blow but Dimitri wisely stayed away and let him punch himself out. Once the Cornish miner was exhausted, the Russian moved in and finished him off with an overhand right to the temple. The count ended after the bell sounded but it didn't matter. Kenan wasn't going to be in any shape to fight anyone for a long time and ever'one knew it. Sasha appeared again and paraded around the ring with Dimitri. The crowd was in such a frenzy that Victor could hardly be heard announcing the final bout that featured the two cowboys.

Billy Bob entered the ring with his cowboy hat on his head and boots with spurs on his feet. He was accompanied by four young ladies that hovered around him like mother hens 'round a chick. He called out to the audience for support and got a rousing ovation from the onlookers. Zack remained quiet and calm until the bell rang and the fight started. Billy Bob actually lunged across the canvas in an attempt to surprise Zack but instead, ran into a very hard left jab that not only stopped him but stunned him for a moment. That was all the opportunity Zack needed. A rapid delivery of right, left, and another right ended the bout almost before it began. The big Texan never knew what hit him and said later on that he'd run into the business end of a thousand pound bull that hadn't hit him as hard as Zack did. No matter, Zack James was an instant hero and favorite, along with Charlemagne and Griz, to win the title.

The week before the semifinal bouts was awash with fond farewells, mystery and intrigue. A sullen and subdued Kronos boarded a train bound for San Francisco with his one remaining suitcase full of ouzo while Texan Billy Bob galloped back to Abilene on his palomino and Kenan rode his big gray ass back to Virginia City.

While wolf-man Jack was being treated by his Cheyenne friends, they discovered a white face under the "mask" of the wolf-man. Turns out he was a Pentecostal tent preacher by the name of Foster and not an Injun at all. He used the disguise of an Injun so he wouldn't disgrace his religion by seeking fortune and fame. He must have been one hellacious preacher cause the Cheyenne forgave him and he returned to Denver with three baptized converts and a new lady friend.

Beau kept his fighter out of sight and thus, out of trouble. The whereabouts of Charlie and Lucy were a well kept secret and that made folks crazy. They all wanted to drink and celebrate with their favorite but Beau had other ideas. He wanted to keep Charlie safe from outside influences and focused on his next fight.

Colonel Rufus King, on the other hand, was not hard to find. He strutted all over town and told anyone who'd listen that his fighter was going to be the next champ. Griz, however, was pretty much confined to various stables around town. I found him in one as I was about to go riding with Goner one morning.

"Griz, what are you doing here?"

"Colonel say to stay put so I stay put."

"Why do you let him treat you like an animal? You're a man. You have the right to do what you want. You don't have to obey the Colonel."

Griz seemed uncomfortable with my words and headed back towards his stall. I knew I should let it be but I couldn't resist trying to help so I followed after him.

"Why do you do the Colonel's bidding? What is he to you?"

"He found me in the mountains and taught me to speak. He says if I win fights, I get to live with people and never return to mountains. I want to live with people."

It was clear that the hulking half-man and half-bear was nothing more than a scairt little boy underneath it all. As terrifying as he appeared, I still felt sorry for him. As I rode out on Goner, I saw him watching us from his stall. When we returned from our ride, Griz was gone.

Meanwhile, Sasha Petrova had become a celebrity in Santa Fe. She accompanied Dimitri wherever he went and acted as his translator and watchdog. Whenever he got too close to anyone or anything, Sasha put herself in between. She kept him from socializing too much and restricted his drinking to beer only. She seemed determined that Dimitri become the champ and equally willing to do whatever she had to just to see that he was. For his part, the big Russian appeared content to enjoy his new found fame and freedom in Santa Fe.

Zack and I spent the week getting to know each other better and share stories from the past. We reminisced about his brothers, Mal and Josh, and how much we both missed 'em. Since he wasn't much for gamblin' or drinkin', Zack spent little time around St. Charles Place. Instead, he preferred that we saddle up and take long rides to see the countryside.

Paddy added to his discomfort in the casino by hovering around us and making crude suggestions about what she'd like to do with him. Even Maude and her girls were a bother with their offers of a "free ride" for the big cowboy. Zack took it all in stride and was content to enjoy Santa Fe and await his next bout.

When we were talking about his upcoming fight with Dimitri, I got to wondering just how "blind" the blind draw had been since Victor had been involved. It sure seemed like Zack had gotten the best of that draw. Billy Bob and Dimitri were perfect opponents for him while Charlemagne had to face Kronos and now Griz. Then it finally dawned on me; Victor not only wanted to trick me into a bad bet but he also wanted to beat Beau. He'd lost all his bets when Charlemagne won the local contest and now he was making sure it didn't happen again. What a brilliant and twisted plan.

I decided to swallow my pride and tell Zack the whole truth about what had happened but knowing what Victor was up to was one thing and knowing what to do about it was another. We discussed all the possibilities and came up with an if-all-else-fails plan. Beau was made aware of our suspicions but not our plans. After all, he was the one who taught me to never divulge my "hole card".

The evening of Saturday, May 11th was marked by a near blizzard in Santa Fe. The temperature dropped like a rock and several inches of snow fell when a blue northern swept down upon us. We thought about canceling the fights but the majority of the fight crowd weathered the storm and demanded we go ahead as planned. Normally folks had enough good sense to stay indoors during such a winter assault but the scent of blood brought them out in spite of it.

The Colonel and Griz arrived early and entertained the crowd with feats of strength. Griz squeezed an empty whiskey keg until the slats caved in and bent railroad spikes in his teeth with his bare hands. Our prizefight was starting to look like a carnival side show.

When Beau and Charlemagne walked towards the ring, the boisterous crowd held its collective breath and waited for the explosion that was bound to come. Griz continued to pace up and down on his side of the ring while the tall Negro stood passively and stared at him. After Victor introduced the fighters, the bell rang and the crowd roared its approval.

The first two rounds went pretty much as expected. Griz stalked his opponent and tried to engage him in a wrestling match but Charlie danced away and punched just enough to keep the mountain man at bay. Neither man was hurt but Griz showed signs of being out of shape as he was gasping for air before round three began.

Charlie started out with his defensive footwork and then seemed to hit a wet spot on the canvas which caused him to slip and lose his balance. Griz lunged across the ring and body-slammed him into the ropes. That move was illegal under the Queensberry rules so the referee tried to get between the fighters to stop the action but Griz proved too big to move out of the way. He had the elusive Charlie Brown pinned against the corner turnbuckle and hit him with a flurry of right and left hand blows that might have killed lesser men.

When the referee finally separated them, Charlemagne was barely conscious and looked like he might be done for. Griz walked around the ring with his arms raised in anticipation of victory. The referee counted to nine before the Charlie showed signs of recovery and was allowed to continue the fight. Luckily for him, he was able to duck and dance his way out of trouble so he could survive the rest of the round.

The fourth and fifth rounds continued the same pattern as the tortoise and the hare. The slugger chased the boxer and neither left much of a mark on the other. The restless crowd wanted blood and started shouting for more action.

Clearly, the pressure was rising for both fighters as the sixth round began. It was easy to see that Griz was running out of steam while the younger and heartier Negro seemed to be getting stronger.

When his recovery from round three was complete, Charlie stopped running away and met his oversized opponent head-on. Griz was so surprised by the direct assault that he failed to defend himself properly and got rocked by several very hard punches to the head. They were followed by numerous body blows that bent him over in pain. A crossing combination of right and left hooks knocked the huge mountain man to the floor for a count of seven. Griz wasn't hurt badly but he had learned to respect the power of his African opponent.

Round seven and eight featured several toe to toe battles where each fighter gave as good as he got. Their faces were bloodied and cut-up from the many punches they'd received. Both men showed signs of exhaustion and collapse but neither showed any sign of quitting.

Griz was slow to leave his corner at the start of round nine. He found his bulky frame to be both advantage and curse. The big man was running out of the strength he needed just to stand up for another three minutes. In a clumsy attempt to slam into Charlie, Griz missed him completely and collided with the turnbuckle head on. He turned around with an ugly cut on his forehead and a stunned look on his face only to be greeted with the hardest right hand blow that I'd ever seen. Charlie hit him with everything he had left and it was just barely enough. When Griz hit the floor this time, the whole room vibrated and the crowd went nuts.

The Colonel jumped in the ring and tried to silence the count but the referee persisted and finally reached ten without any movement from Griz. The big mountain man was out cold and stayed that way for several minutes. He was finally helped up by several volunteers from the crowd and led out of the ring by a disconsolate Colonel King. I could certainly imagine him threatening to send Griz back to the mountains because of his failure.

After all the excitement, the folks in the audience were almost as exhausted as the fighters had been. An intermission was taken so the ring could be cleaned-up and the ropes retightened. I was thankful that Charlemagne had won but sorry that Griz had to lose.

After witnessing such a titanic struggle between two evenly matched opponents it almost felt like a let down to imagine Zack going up against Dimitri. It looked to be a classic mismatch although the Russian strongman had proven to be pretty tough in his opening fight with Kenan. In a contest between two punchers, the biggest one usually won and no matter how massive Dimitri was, Zack was just bigger and faster. Of course, I hadn't figured on Sasha Petrova and her part in the fight.

The so-called schoolmarm appeared to be anything but as she led Dimitri to the ring. She wore a dress of red velvet that barely concealed her firm and athletic body. Her long blond hair was down and her spectacles were nowhere to be found. I was enjoying the view when I felt a tug on my left arm. It was Mutt and he wanted me to follow him outside. Since the fight hadn't started yet, I reluctantly went with him.

"What's so important that you'd take me away from all the excitement?"

"Are ya betting any money on your friend from Tombstone?"

It bothered me to admit the truth but I shook my head and replied, "No."

"Well it's a good thing ya didn't, Gove'nor. I just found out that Russian in there is a ringer."

"What do you mean?"

"He's a Heavyweight Champion from the Ukraine, yessiree bob. He was imported by some wealthy Russians back there in Kansas. They want him to beat John L. Sullivan and become World Champ for the glory of 'Mother Russia'. I hear he's won over two hundred fights and most of 'em were of the bare knuckle variety. He's tougher than a two-bit steak; I tell ya."

"What about Sasha? Is she really a school teacher?"

"Well, as you can see for yourself Gove'nor, she's no schoolmarm. She works for the Tsar Alexander III's secret police. They call the outfit the *Okhrana*. She's here to make sure Dimitri does as he's told and wins... legally or not."

"I can't believe..."

"You better believe. Have I ever been known to give false testimony?"

"No you haven't. I know better than to doubt you."

I tossed Mutt a gold eagle which drew a long low whistle from my little English bloodhound. "Many thanks, Gove'nor. I'll have more information for you tomorrow on an entirely different matter. Good evening to ya."

Mutt slipped off into the shadows and I made my way back into the casino to warn Zack. He was just about to enter the ring when I was able to get his attention and relate the story I heard from Mutt. He was as skeptical as I was but it gave him pause and reason to be aware.

While Victor was introducing the fighters, Sasha made her way around the ring and spoke briefly with Zack. It looked like she was wishing him "good luck" but knowing what I did, I saw it differently. Zack looked to be amused by her comments but shook 'em off and concentrated on Dimitri. When I asked him about it later, he said she offered herself to him if he would take a dive.

The first five rounds of the final match were fought as the Marquess of Queensberry had wished. Both fighters battled fairly and demonstrated the boxing skills of footwork and defense. There were plenty of hard and fast exchanges but each man took a punch as well as he gave it. The crowd seemed to gain a whole new appreciation of what journalist and sportswriter Pierce Egan had dubbed the "Sweet Science of Bruising".

During the one minute rest between rounds, Sasha hovered over Dimitri and encouraged or threatened him as she deemed necessary. Then she would turn to the audience and lead them in cheers for her fighter.

After every round Zack just stood in his corner and waited without any sign of emotion. As the next round was about to begin, he would ladle water from a pail and rinse out his mouth but that was it. I think he was truly surprised by the skill and toughness of his opponent and maybe just a mite tuckered out.

During the sixth and seventh rounds I could see Zack was getting the best of it. Dimitri was clearly hurt and dropped his guard several times. The bell to end the seventh round found the burly Russian flat on his back as Zack recorded the first knock down. When Dimitri was slow to get up and return to his corner, Sasha clearly berated him for his performance. While doing her darnedest to rally the crowd, she walked around the outside of the ring all the way to Zacks corner. As she turned back the way she came, I could have sworn she tossed something in his water pail.

I was about to question her actions when Zack ladled some water to rinse and spit. The answer came to me immediately and to Zack about two minutes later. He had knocked Dimitri down for an eight count and was waiting for the bout to resume when I saw him shaking his head as if to clear it. Whatever Sasha had dropped in the water pail had made him groggy and wobbly on his feet.

During the last minute of the eighth round Zack had all he could do to stand upright. Dimitri rocked him with several combinations and a constantly stiff left jab. When the bell finally sounded, Zack had trouble locating his corner and had to be directed by the referee.

I grabbed a pail of fresh water from behind the bar and made my way to ringside. I replaced the "tainted" pail and tried to explain to my "foggy" friend what had happened. I encouraged him to rinse several times in hopes that he might dilute the effects of whatever Sasha had given him. Across the ring the Russian vixen watched everything we did with a sly smile on her face. Dimitri looked away as if ashamed of her actions.

The ninth round would have been scored as even. Dimitri had recovered from being knocked down and Zack seemed to be overcoming his drug hangover. The round ended with both fighters flaying away at each other. The tenth and final round would have to tell the tale.

During the rest break I chanced to look at Victor and he was grinning at me like a canary-fed alley cat. At first it made me wonder why Taylor never came with him and then it suddenly hit me that I'd just saved Zack and that was exactly what Victor would have wanted me to do. I was aware that I was betting agin myself but when it came down to a choice between friendship or money, my choice had been clear.

From an audience viewpoint the last round was just magnificent. The slugging never stopped until the fight did. Both fighters were knocked down but only one got back up. Dimitri knocked Zack down for a six count in the early going and Zack knocked the Russian boxer all the way out of the ring just before the final bell. Dimitri flipped over the ropes and collided with Sasha before the two of 'em fell off the apron and crashed into the crowd.

Dimitri was unable to continue, the bout was officially over and Zack was the declared winner. Victor waved a cynical "thank you" my way before entering the ring to make his final announcements.

"The Championship of the Western Territories will be held right here, one week from today and will pit Charlemagne Brown against Zack James. You'd better get your tickets tonight cause we'll be sold out by tomorrow."

Paddy and I helped Zack to my office as he seemed to be near collapse. She provided hot water and towels to clean him up as well as a barefoot root salve to cleanse and close his cuts. It was as plain as the sunrise that Zack was gonna need a full week to recover if he planned to fight for the championship.

I heard later on that Sasha had received a broken arm when Dimitri fell on her and was recovering over at the Santa Fe Inn. Meanwhile, Dimitri had skipped town and his whereabouts were unknown. Guess he wasn't too interested in returning to Russia to explain why he'd lost.

I guess things turned out pretty well after all. Zack won the fight, Dimitri got his freedom which is all he really wanted and Sasha got some of what was comin' to her. There was still the little matter of my bet with Victor but I figured we'd burn that bridge when we got to it.

The seven days leading up to the Championship fight were cold, wet and miserable. The temperature hovered around freezing so we received an annoying mixture of snow, sleet and rain to go with the howling winds that came in from the north. All modes of transportation were interrupted so we ran short of almost all supplies. It was fortunate that we had an ample storehouse of alcohol since folks came to depend on us so they could drink the weather away.

Mutt showed up late on Sunday to deliver the additional information as he'd promised. He'd found out where Beau had hidden Charlie and Lucy. They were staying in a room above Olson's Mercantile, right next door to Victor and to Taylor. There was something that was very wrong with that set-up. Victor and Beau couldn't be working together, or could they?

Now I knew why Taylor had been out of sight for the last few weeks. She was busy caring for Charlie and Lucy as well as performing her regular duties for the Olsons. I had to find out if she was involved in whatever scheme the "bayou boys" were hatching.

Mutt promised to keep an eye on all of them as I was sure there was treachery in the air. It was becoming clear that winning the prizefight was not the only game in town. Zack, Paddy and I talked things over and made plans of our own.

Everyday Beau assured me things were fine with his fighter and I shouldn't worry about my bet. "Sure as sunrise tomorrow" he was wont to say. On Thursday evening he even suggested that I double down and increase my bet to forty thousand. He assured me that he had already bet every cent he had and was looking to borrow more. "How many times does life deal you a royal flush?" became his favorite saying.

Coincidently, Victor came in on Friday morning to check the ring and mentioned that he was willing to "up" the bet if I was interested. I didn't say yes or no but lead him to believe I was thinking about it. He sarcastically thanked me for taking such good care of "his fighter".

I had stashed Zack in an extra room we had upstairs so he could recover and get the rest he needed. He received round the clock attention from Paddy, Maude and the rest of her girls. Zack never wanted for anything and got himself pretty spoiled by the day of

the fight.  He said it felt like he had his own personal harem but I'm
pretty sure he was just funning with me.  No matter, he was being
well cared for.

The sun broke through the clouds on Saturday, May 18th to raise
spirits and restore souls.  The town was full with folks comin' and
goin' for the first time in nearly a fortnight.  The big news from the
day before was that Alaska had become a Federal District.  I couldn't
believe some folks still referred to the 1867 purchase of Alaska as
Seward's Folly even though we got the whole shooting match from
Russia for about two cents an acre.

The calendar said it was late spring or early summer but old man
winter still held us in his icy grasp so a sunny day, no matter how
brief, was a welcome sign of better times to come.

Every boxing fan throughout the West was in Santa Fe if he
could afford to be.  Silk suits, top hats and big cigars were suddenly
the fashions of the day.  Sold-out tickets were being resold for twice
and the St. Charles was wall to wall with gamblers and drinkers.
Things were playing out just like Victor and Taylor had planned or
had they?

An hour before the bout was to begin; Beau strolled in by himself and joined me at the bar.  The first words out of his mouth were
to remind me that I still had time to double my bet.  When I asked
about Charlie I was told he was "just fine" and "they" would be
along later.  I found that to be a very strange set of circumstances.
Beau always came and left with Charlemagne before so why not tonight?  I couldn't begin to imagine who "they" were or why "they"
were with Charlie now.

Victor was the next one through the doors and he made his way
over to us.

"Well gentlemen, are you ready for the big fight?

Without waiting for an answer, he reached over Beau's shoulder
to grasp the drink that Paddy was handing him and spoke to Beau in
a low but clear voice.

"If you haven't found any more money to bet why not ask Henry
here?  I'm sure he'd be glad to lend you a grand or two."

Beau pulled away with a feigned look of embarrassment and anger so Victor turned in my direction.

"And how about you, Henry? Are you ready to risk forty thousand on Beau's 'boy'?"

His deliberate use of the racial insult drew an immediate response from Beau. A pretty decent right hook sent Victor and his drink crashing to the floor. Beau pounced on Victor until cooler heads pulled them apart but the war of words continued.

"Who in the hell are you callin' 'boy'? Charlemagne is a man and he'll destroy Zackary James tonight. I want to raise my bet by five thousand dollars right now if you're man enough to match it."

The pre-fight crowd surrounded the two of them and urged even larger and crazier bets.

Victor rose from the floor and carefully rearranged his clothing before lighting a cigar and throwing more fuel on the fire.

"I'll take your bet, sir, and I'll even double yours, Henry, if you have the stomach for it."

Now the crowd reacted like a pack of jackals 'round a fresh carcass. They were ravenous for any kind of action and screaming at me to accept his challenge. In response, I called his bluff and raised the ante again.

"Why stop at forty? Let's make it an even fifty thousand, Victor; what do you say to that number?"

I saw a moment of terror flash across Victor's eyes but he had gone too far to back down.

"Fifty thousand it is."

With the bets finally settled, everyone started to clamor for the final bout to begin.

Zack came in and I walked with him to the ring. Behind me, Beau and Victor shook hands as if to settle their little scrap or was it something else? No matter, I told Zack what had just happened and he just smiled and nodded his approval.

The only real surprise of the evening occurred when Charlie came through the doors with Lucy and Taylor and joined Beau and Victor at the bar. Seeing all of them together answered all my questions about who was involved in the con game. Little sister had to be in on it from the start.

At some time between the local competition and the finals, Beau and Victor cooked up a scheme to swindle me out of forty thousand dollars. They tricked me into backing Charlemagne and then made it appear like I couldn't lose. Their phony staged fight was meant to goad me into doublin' my bet. The beautiful part of their scheme was using my friendship with Zack against me. I couldn't wait to see how they intended to play it out.

Victor took center stage and introduced the fighters. The two men met in the middle of the ring and exchanged pleasantries before the battle began and Zack did most of the talking. Charlemagne wore a look of pure hatred as he returned to his corner

The crowd was whipped into a fever pitch by the time the bell sounded for round one and the fight was finally on. Both fighters relied on speed and footwork as they felt each other out in the early going. Neither was hurt nor tuckered out as round one came to an end.

During the one minute rest, Victor strolled over to Charlemagne and they spoke a few words. Judging by his reaction, Victor wasn't pleased with what he heard and he tried to continue the conversation but the bell sounded for round two.

The second round was full of raw and violent moments where each man hit the other and got hit in return. Zack either slipped or tripped and went down but only for a count of three. A cut was reopened above his left eye and his lip was split. Charlie managed to stay on his feet but suffered a cut on his forehead and a puffed-up right eye. While awaiting the third round, he ignored Victor's pleas and didn't speak with him. Over at the bar, I could see that Beau was concerned and Taylor seemed to be consoling Lucy.

Round three belonged to Zack. He knocked down his African opponent three times. The counts were all stopped by eight but the accumulated damage showed on Charlie's face as he stumbled towards his corner at the end of the round. I took notice that Victor had relaxed and Beau was back to his usual smiling self. I found his manner to be confusing since his fighter was clearly losing.

Round four was as one-sided as the third round except Charlie wasn't actually knocked off his feet. Zack trapped him against the ropes and pummeled his midsection for most of the round. At the end of the round, Charlie was doubled over in pain and Zack looked exhausted from the effort of inflicting it. Victor and Beau were grinning like possums eating persimmons but Taylor and Lucy were nowhere to be seen.

The fifth round started with a roundhouse right thrown by Charlie that caught Zack off guard and off balance. He went down for a count of nine in the first few seconds of the round and spent the rest of it trying to shake the cobwebs from his head. Charlie used the round to recover from the last two so there was little excitement after the early knock down. Victor looked confused and made his way over to the bar where he had a heated discussion with Beau. They were headed ringside when the bell sounded for the sixth round.

Round six started like round one with each man feeling the other out but it ended like round two with both fighters slamming each other with all they had. Neither wanted to quit at the sound of the bell and the referee had to step between to get them to stop scrapping. Strangely enough, both of 'em got their second wind and were getting stronger in spite of the beatin' they were taking. Beau and Victor made it to ringside but were ignored by Charlie as he waited for the seventh round. Victor tried to climb up on the apron but Beau pulled him back down and that started another spat.

Round seven almost ended the fight for both of 'em. Each hit the canvas twice as the battle royal continued. Zack had the best of it early in the round but was knocked down for a nine count that would have been ten had he not been saved by the bell. For his part, Charlie looked exhausted as he continued to ignore both Beau and Victor as they clamored for his attention.

Round eight began with Zack summoning all his remaining strength to flatten Charlie one more time but at the count of seven the resilient Negro got back up and returned the favor. He caught Zack with an unexpected body blow and followed it with a tremendous right uppercut and devastating left hook. Zack struggled to get to his feet at the count of nine but fell forward on his face and was counted out.

The fight was over, the crowd was hysterical and Victor was white as a sheet. Beau pushed his way through the crush of the audience in an attempt to make it to the front doors but Victor just remained in his seat and stared into the empty ring. I climbed into the ring and rolled Zack over on to his back only to find him winking at me through his one open eye.

"How'd I do, Henry?"

"You were so convincing even I thought you wanted to win."

"To tell ya the truth, until the seventh round, I did. I couldn't help myself. But Charlie is one hell of a boxer and he surely deserves the Championship."

"What did you say to make him so angry?"

"I just told him that I knew he was supposed to take a dive and I wouldn't be too hard on him. Really did the trick didn't it?"

I helped Zack to his feet and we made our way behind the bar to my office. Paddy had it all set up with hot water, bandages, ointments and salves. Once he was safely in her care and away from the crowd, I went back to find Victor.

Most of the crowd had dispersed by that time but Victor was still in his seat while Charlie was receiving medical attention in the ring from Taylor and Lucy who must have come back when the fight was over. When I reached the stupefied Victor I spoke loud enough for all to hear.

"I believe you owe me fifty thousand dollars."

Victor continued to stare into space but Taylor whirled around to face me.

"What did you say?"

"I said your boyfriend here owes me fifty thousand dollars and I aim to collect."

How could he...?"

"Oh, hasn't he told you about all the betting he's been doing ever since these fights began? He did pretty well for awhile... didn't you Victor?"

Victor reacted to what I said but didn't speak. Taylor stepped through the ropes, jumped down off the apron and sat next to him.

"What is he talking about, Victor?"

Victor still acted like he was in shock but he tried to respond. "It wasn't supposed to be like this. Charlie was supposed to lose. We were gonna be rich. Beau said..."

Victor's comments incensed Charlie who leapt over the ropes and landed next to him. He grabbed Victor by his lapels and lifted him off the ground so they were nose to nose. Taylor tried to get him to put Victor down but Charlie was mad enough to chew nails and spit tacks. I figured my work there was done so I left 'em to sort things out by themselves. I knew Victor didn't have the money but it was gonna be fun holding it over him. *Monsieur* Beau Didlet was a different story. I'd have to plan something special for him.

In the weeks following the big fight a bunch of things changed in Santa Fe. When local fight fans found out Victor couldn't pay off his bets, a lynch mob actually attempted to tar and feather him. They let him off when he promised that his Mother would pay off all his losses.

When it became known that John L. Sullivan wasn't coming for a World Championship Match, the threats got worse and Sheriff O'Reilly was persuaded to let Victor stay in a jail cell so the locals couldn't string him up. He wasn't arrested but he wasn't going anywhere either.

Charlie caught up with Beau before I did and beat him senseless. Beau was overcome so quickly he never got to use his famous "pick". Afterwards, Charlie bound and gagged him before placing his unconscious body in a large canvas sack. With my assistance, that heavy squirmy sack was shipped by rail back to New Orleans with instructions to dump it in the bayou where it belonged. I'll always wonder how far he traveled before being released from the sack.

Charlie and Lucy decided to stay in New Mexico and found a little place outside of town where they could raise cattle, crops and children. He would always be the boxing champ to locals and they treated him with the respect he richly deserved.

Zack recovered from his various cuts and bruises and returned to Yuma. I think Paddy's pestering hurried him on his way. Once he knew the "Boston Strong Boy" wasn't coming to Santa Fe, he didn't give two hoots in hell whether he won the Western Championship so he volunteered to lose the final match so we could beat Victor and Beau at their own game. His competitive nature got the best of him and he almost won the fight but in the end he was satisfied with the outcome. We had agreed to split whatever money I might get from Victor as extra cash was always a welcome guest around his family's ranch.

Good old Colonel King slipped out of town one night and left Griz to fend for himself. He was holed-up in the stable one morning and I saw to it he got a haircut, shave and bath which made him so presentable that folks barely recognized him in spite of his size. With the help of Rocko Mancini, we got him a job as a teamster and a whole new lease on life. He came into the casino whenever he was around and seemed to form a friendship with Paddy.

Taylor continued to work for the Olsons but refused to see me. I had no idea how she felt about Victor or how much she was involved in all the "shenanigans" that went on and I was beginning not to care. I just figured if I left her alone long enough, she'd come around eventually. It was pretty clear that we had little if anything to talk about anyway. Paddy and I continued to run St. Charles Place by ourselves. With Beau gone, I took over the gambling side of things and handled it the best I could. I think we both kinda missed him but were equally glad he was gone.

Maude and her ever-changing cast of sporting gals kept the joint jumpin' but the gamblin' and drinkin' paid all the bills. Angelina stayed around for awhile but disappeared one night and was never heard from again. We figured she went to Louisiana to find Beau but we never heard for certain.

I hadn't seen any of the fifty thousand dollars that Victor owed me but then I never really expected it. I wasn't getting rich but I was able to put money away for that ominous "rainy day".

# CHAPTER XI

## "All good things must end"

### FALL 1884

The long cool summer stretched into a surprisingly chilly autumn but Santa Fe remained a safe and comfortable place to live. Settlers were always passing through on the Santa Fe Trail and many of 'em stopped and stayed so our little pueblo always continued to grow. Although New Mexicans couldn't vote, November 4th saw the election of Grover Cleveland as the twenty-second President of the United States. He beat Republican James G. Blaine in a hotly contested race. Many of our newcomers celebrated the first Democrat to win the presidency since the Civil War.

After six months of hiding in a jail cell, Victor Bodine informed all interested parties that his Mother was finally coming to Santa Fe by train and she would cover all his gambling debts in full. The date of her arrival was scheduled for Tuesday, Nov. 25th, two days before Thanksgiving. I was as curious as the rest of the town to see this wealthy woman from New Orleans who came all the way out here to rescue her wayward son so I followed the crowd to the train station on that Tuesday afternoon.

When the passengers got off the iron horse, I got the greatest shock of my young life. Victor's Mother was none other than the woman I knew as Victoria Bellemont Farley. She was a madam in Animas City who claimed to be Charles Farley's widow. I suddenly heard Charles' voice echo in my mind, "When I met her, her name was Vicki Bodine and she was a sportin' girl in a New Orleans brothel with a five-month-old 'whorehouse bastard' to take care of." That child had to have been Victor. Now everything made sense. It was Victoria that sent Victor here because of Charles and his money. He was sent here to spy on Charles but ended up reporting on me. Victoria didn't know that I really was Charles' son. She musta thought I was merely the imposter she paid to act the part of Charles' son. There could be no doubt that she planned all along to reclaim all the assets of Charles Farley which included St. Charles Place.

Following right behind Victoria and carrying their luggage was none other than Arthur L. Finch, the former senior agent with the Pinkerton Detective Agency in Denver. He had to be her new husband that Taylor mentioned and he would have also been the contact Victor had in Chicago. The last piece of the puzzle fell into place when I thought of Charles' wills which referred to him as having two sons. Victor and I were half-brothers and at that very moment, I was the only one who knew the whole truth of it.

As I watched from a safe distance, I saw Victor greet his Mother and Agent Finch. To my chagrin, Taylor was with him and hugged Victoria like they were kissin' kin. I had to get back to my office and I needed to talk with Mutt. I left before anyone saw me and made my way back to the St. Charles Place.

I reread all of Charles' papers and confirmed what I remembered from his two original wills. He was clearly admitting that he had two sons and not just one. I could only imagine how this new information would affect my legal claims to Charles' property since his final Will and Testament was drafted in Flagstaff just before he died and left me ever'thing. I reckon his claim that Victoria already had a child when he met her must have been wishful thinking on his part.

I happened to browse through the cache of papers that Charles had in his lockbox and ran into an old friend, "Grasshopper Flats". Along with a bunch of worthless bills and receipts, there was a deed to a small property called the "Doodlebug Ranch" and it seemed to be located somewhere near "the Flats". At the time I doubted I'd ever see it but I did roll up the deed and place it in the butt stock of my Henry rifle. Since the stock of that rifle had concealed the deed to the Box H for so many years, it seemed like natural enough hiding place.

We were closing in on Christmas before I actually had a meeting with Mister and Misses Finch. Victoria and Arthur had avoided me for three weeks but I knew what they were up to. According to Mutt, they were staying at the Palace Hotel and had paid off all of Victor's debts right away with the exception of mine. The total was only around three thousand dollars so that part of his problems had been handled with ease. My English bloodhound also kept me informed of their social activities and I was well aware of their blooming relationship with Taylor. Since the sheriff had released Victor from custody, the four of 'em had been seen all over town. Meanwhile, I waited patiently for what I knew would be a very enlightening and exciting reunion with "Miss Vicki".

When they walked into the casino, I noticed that although two years had passed since our last meeting; Victoria hadn't changed one little bit. Arthur, however, looked to be a shadow of his former self. While she was still an attractive and seductive middle aged woman, he was no longer the commanding and confident Pinkerton Agent he'd once been. Two years serving under her thumb had reduced him to a lackey. There was no doubt which one was the trail boss and which one was the steer.

"Well, if it isn't Victoria and Arthur. Welcome to St. Charles Place. Can we get you anything to drink?"

Victoria met my greeting with a "too-sweet" smile as Arthur held a chair for her to sit down.

"No, thank you. We won't be here that long."

"Then I guess you've come to pay off your son's gambling debt."

"Hardly. We've come to inform you that we consider that matter closed. Remember, I know who you really are. So does Arthur. He knows all about our little deception up in Colorado. We can prove you are not Charles' son and thus not entitled to this fine establishment or any of Charles' other financial assets. We've started legal proceedings to claim what rightfully belongs to Victor."

"His last Will and Testament makes my claim pretty much iron clad."

"We have a judge..." Arthur interrupted but Victoria cut him off.

"Shut up Arthur. I'll handle this."

She collected her thoughts and continued. "His Will left everything to you based on his assumption that you were his son. Since you are not his son, we're confident that the law will see fit to disallow the last Will and rule that Victor is his only heir."

"You might find it hard to believe but I really am his son. I know it doesn't seem possible but you hired me to pretend to be who I already was but it's true. I survived the wagon train massacre just like Charles did but I was raised by the Henry family. I didn't even know the whole truth until after Charles died."

"I told you..." Arthur tried to interrupt again and this time Victoria slapped his face.

"I told you to shut up now stay that way."

After her unladylike display of temper Victoria stared at me for several seconds before speaking. Slowly her old seductive smile came back and she laughed to herself.

"I knew you looked too much like him. You have those deep blue eyes and that damn Farley clef in your chin. I should have known better."

"It might also surprise you to know that I may be willing to forget Victor's gambling debt in light of the fact that he might very well be my half brother."

"Might be?"

"Charles said you already had a bastard when he met you and we both know Victor is a bastard."

"That's not true."

"Which part?"

Victoria laughed at my jest. "I had my 'child' after living with Charles for two years. He was the boy's father although he was loath to admit it."

"Then you concede that Victor is a bastard?"

Victoria stopped laughing and gave me her hardest stare. "I guess it takes one to know one."

I conceded the point and we just sat with our own thoughts for about a minute. I guess each had said all there was to say. When Victoria and Finch stood to leave, I had the feeling I'd won the day so I offered a consolation of sorts.

"Charles had two savings accounts in the amount of five thousand dollars made out to each of his sons. I will release that amount to Victor as a Christmas present."

Arthur seemed delighted with my concession but Victoria took it in stride.

"Good day to you, Henry."

I met with Victor the day before Christmas and gave him five thousand dollars in cash. I also gave him an English publication of the "Adventures of Huckleberry Finn" by Mark Twain. It wasn't due for publication in the United States until February but thanks to Mutt, I had been able to secure an advance copy of his sequel to "Tom Sawyer". It was a gift for Taylor that I knew she would cherish. I dearly wished to give it her myself but that didn't seem likely.

When we parted ways, I asked Victor if he felt like we were brothers and his answer was an immediate "No". That was the one thing we had in common besides Taylor.

Some four months later, on the ides of March, I received a summons to the territorial court to defend my ownership of St. Charles Place. Victor and Victoria were contesting Charles' Last Will and Testament so I had to be prepared to defend myself.

Eschewing a lawyer, I represented myself in court. I was fully prepared with documents to prove who I was along with copies of Charles' wills. Judge A.C. Judy dutifully looked over my paperwork before giving any consideration to the claimant's arguments.

Arthur Finch, who was supported in court by Victor, Victoria and Taylor, spoke for Victor and made only one claim.

"Your Honor, we concede that Henry Charles is indeed the lawful son of Charles Ulster Farley. We simply contend that Victor Bodine is also fruit of his loins. As such, we contend that Mister Bodine is entitled to one half of his estate.

Mister Charles has already admitted as much by giving Mister Bodine half of the deceased's savings accounts. We estimate the remainder of his estate to be worth approximately one hundred thousand dollars and would like this court to direct Mister Charles to cede us half that amount."

I was immediately reminded of my Pa saying "no good deed goes unpunished". I never should have given Victor any money. It was their concession of my identity that caught me off guard but I wasn't done just yet. I produced Paddy as a witness to verify about the fifty thousand dollar bet that Victor lost. She reluctantly admitted she only heard the amount of forty thousand and not fifty. Arthur suggested that as my employee, she had to back up my story no matter what the amount. I produced a telegram from Zack that confirmed the amount but Arthur objected to it based on the lack of proof that it actually came from Zack. I called Charlie Brown to relate what he heard after the prizefight but his testimony was deemed hearsay and thus inadmissible. The court room was about to explode with tension when the self-righteous Judge Judy made a biblical ruling; he split the baby.

"In the normal course of my judicial proceedings, I rarely give credence to any form of gambling. This case, however, involves an admitted gambler and his two ill-begotten sons who are undoubtedly gamblers too. Therefore, I will admit the testimony involving the bet but only in the amount of forty thousand dollars. Since half of the estate would be fifty thousand, Mister Bodine is due an additional ten thousand. To make up that amount, I hereby order the gambling establishment known as St. Charles Place to be of split ownership. One half interest to each son with management left in the hands of Mister Charles. I declare this case to be over."

I was stunned. I still ran the gambling house but now Victor was my partner. On top of that, I didn't get a dime out of my bet with him. If Victoria had bought herself the judge like Arthur intimated, she sure got her money's worth.

## SUMMER 1886

Saturday morning dawned bright and early but I was hesitant to get out of the warm and cozy canopy bed. The Napoleon Suite had everything a man could want but a Josephine to share it with. That thought caused me think of Renee who made me sad and Megan who made me mad. Before I got more confused by thinking about Taylor and Glory, I got out of bed.

I knew Cecil wouldn't be available for a few hours so I hid out in my suite and ignored a knock on my door from Kenny. I also ignored the slip of paper he slid under the door which invited me to another breakfast with Megan. Instead, I browsed through the Clifton journal and reread some of what I'd seen before. Theirs was a compelling story of American settlers giving up everything they knew to come out west and seek a better life for themselves and their children. It almost made me wish that I was their son.

At nine o'clock I was bored and starved so I snuck down the back stairs and went hunting for food. I knew my "shadow" was following me but I found his efforts to be more amusing than threatening. When I found a small café further down Beaver Street, I had a real American breakfast of beefsteak and eggs. I watched Kenny hiding across the street and thought about sending him something to eat but decided agin it.

When I got to Cecil's office I was welcomed by his secretary Clarice, who, as it turns out, was his fiancé as well. We had an amiable chat while waiting for Cecil to be available and for once she didn't seem quite so put off by my wearing a pistol.

Cecil welcomed me with open arms and bad news. His queries to the Chicago office had led the Pinkertons to the remaining members of the Clifton family alright but only one member of the family could even remember little William Jefferson. The old man stated he never saw the baby's backside so he couldn't comment on the birthmark. Since they'd hit a stone wall with the Cliftons, the "Pinks" were starting to search for the nurse in Chicago. Cecil wasn't encouraged by their efforts as twenty-four years made people and memories hard to locate. I left the journal with him and he agreed to read it over for any possible clues he might find.

I suddenly remembered the other thing I needed Cecil to do for me. I handed him the deed to the Doodlebug Ranch and asked if he'd get it signed over in my new name, Henry Charles. He said that was a simple matter and he could draw up the proper papers right away.

I walked out of his office into bright sunlight and straight into a gunfighter's worst nightmare... a wet-nosed kid with a big gun and little sense.

He called out "Henry James" as he stood in the street with his shaky legs spread wide and his sweaty hand poised over his six gun. He was pimple-faced, dressed in ill-fit black clothes and looked to be so nervous that he might just pee his pants but that was his problem. My problem was that he looked about to draw his gun. I tried to think of some reasonable way out of my predicament but couldn't think of any.

At that exact moment, good old Kenny walked out of the doorway from the Apothecary Shop and saw what was about to happen. For some reason he shouted out.

"No, don't do it."

I'll never know who he was calling to but it worked. The "kid" drew his gun, whirled around and shot at Kenny who fell on his back upon the wooden sidewalk. I drew my gun and carefully shot the "kid" in the right hand as he held his smoke pole. That served two purposes as he dropped the gun and screamed in agony at the mutilation of his shooting hand. He learned a valuable lesson and it hadn't cost him his life. I was certain he would thank me some day.

Marshal Mullins took care of the "wanna be" gunslinger after Doc Watson stitched the gaping hole through the middle of his right palm. Although he was hurt and scared, he was really lucky he hadn't shot poor Kenny. His .45 slug hit the Apothecary sign over Kenny's head and Kenny just fell down or fainted. Either way, the "kid" was gonna be sent home sadder but wiser for his eventful day in Flagstaff.

I could tell Marshal Mullins was having second thoughts about me staying around to be his deputy so I tried to ease his fears.

"Tell you what, Marshal, I'll go back to the hotel and stay indoors until that gang from the S Diamond comes to town. Then I'll come out and back your play."

"Can I depend on that?"

"Yeah, I've had enough of being Henry James today. Besides, I have to get "Kenneth" back to work as soon as he's able."

Kenny was still in shock but otherwise unhurt. I helped him back to the hotel and scurried up to my suite. I was stuck in a trap of my own making. If I'd just forgotten about the damn reward and left Flag for the Box H, none of this would have happened. Now, one man was dead, two more wounded and all because of the gun-fighters curse.

A little after noon, Kenny was at my door bearing a sheepish smile and unexpected eviction orders.

"How are you feeling, Kenny?"

"I'm just fine, sir, but I'm afraid I have some bad news. Misses Langley has requested that you vacate this suite for other lodgings so we can provide this suite to her new and very important guests."

"She's kicking me out of these rooms?"

"That's the gist of it. You'll be moved to the second floor in room nine. It's a nice room but it's not a fancy suite like this. Did I mention that we have a French Ambassador and his wife arriving by train?"

"I might have guessed there would be a Frenchman involved."

"Actually, they're Russians. He's an ambassador to France from the court of Alexander III, the Tsar of Russia. His wife is rumored to be a cousin of the Tsarina."

"Let me guess, the Tsarina is a Danish princess so her cousin would be European royalty and Misses Langley is thrilled beyond words to have them stay here."

"Well that's right. How did you know?"

"Let's just say it was a good guess."

With Kenny's help, I gathered up my belongings and moved over to room number nine. It was as advertised, clean and neat but nothing special. When Kenny asked if there was anything else he could do, I reminded him that someone might bring me some food since I was not planning to leave the room. He sarcastically suggested that Ogger might be available but I asked him to reconsider and he said he would. As he left, I gave him one more thing to think about. "Hey Kenny, tell Boris and Natasha that I say 'howdy'."

At last I had something to laugh about. Besides confusing the crap out of Kenny, the thought of Boris and Natasha running a gambit on Megan was *Magnifique-superbe* as she would say. I put my gear away, tested out the bed and waited for lunch.

As luck would have it, my lunch was served by none other than Glory. When I saw her I expected warm and friendly but instead; I got cold and business-like. She brought me hot chicken soup and a turkey sandwich but no acknowledgement. She didn't return my greeting and headed straight out the door after she put the food on my dresser. I caught her by the arm as she sped past me.

"Hey, come on. What's the problem? You're acting like you don't know me."

Glory said she was sorry with her eyes but her lips told a different story.

"I'm really quite busy and must return to the kitchen, sir. Misses Langley…"

"Say no more, I understand."

Glory nodded and left. Megan had her on a short leash and Glory couldn't afford to lose her job. I'd have to see her when she wasn't working if I wanted to talk.

The lunch was great and I spent the rest of the afternoon watching the comings and goings from my second floor window. The crowds on the streets finally thinned out as the sun set in the western sky. If the Winters gang was heading to town from the S Diamond, it figured they'd be along soon.

I took special care to clean and reload my Colt and consider what was about to happen. I knew all I needed to know about Whitey Winters and was quite willing to send him straight to hell but I didn't really know anything about the rest of his rat pack. I figured Brad could give me all the details and since it was time to join up with Marshal Mullins anyway, I pinned on my deputy badge, left my room and headed down stairs.

My arrival in the lobby surprised Kenny so I told him where I was going if he wanted to catch up later but he said he was awaiting the arrival of the Godunov's and wouldn't be watching over me anymore. He mentioned their train was due in about a half hour but I told him I couldn't wait.

I found Marshal Mullins sitting in his office with his feet on his desk smoking a corn cob pipe. The wisps of smoke hung above his head like the storm clouds on the horizon. The tobacco smelled awful but he seemed to be enjoying himself. I almost hated to disturb him.

"Heard anything 'bout the Winters gang?"

"Not yet, but they come in every second Saturday just like clockwork. I've got a couple of young boys watching the roads into town so they'll let me know when they're comin'."

"I know about Whitey but who's liable to be with him?"

"Well his father, Big Jon, is bed-bound most of the time. Doc says he's weak as a kitten but I don't believe it for a minute. If the old man's not with 'em, Whitey'll just have the usual pack of rats that run with him.

First off, there's crazy Frank. He's far and away the toughest and the meanest of the lot. He's a born instigator who surely loves to start bar fights. He's not much with a pistol or his fists so he carries a sawed-off double-barreled shotgun hidden under his slicker that he uses like a war club.

Next, there's little Joey. He's Jon's nephew and the youngest member of the gang. He's got a big mouth with nothing to back it up so he drinks more than he can handle. Whenever he's drunk, he becomes a sneaky little back stabbing son-of-a-bitch. I wouldn't put anything past him.

Apache Pete is their knife guy. Folks that know say he carries about five of 'em on him and can throw accurately with both hands. He stays pretty much to himself and doesn't drink too much but seems to have an insatiable blood lust. Never turn your back on him cause he can go off at any moment."

"That's three, are there more?"

"Just one, a Negro fella named Slim. His given name is Sammy but they call him Slim cause he's so damn skinny. He's pretty handy with any kind of weapon and smarter than the rest of 'em. They tell me he likes the ladies and sings and dances with 'em when he's riding the bottle. To my way of thinking he shouldn't be hanging with the rest of that crowd but he will be."

The Marshal rose slowly, dumped the remains from his pipe and checked the loads in his pistol and shotgun.

"If you're ready, I guess we might as well walk the rounds and get a feel for the area. We might stake out the high ground so to speak."

As we walked down the city streets, I could feel the tension building around us. It seemed like every person in town was aware of what was happening and wasn't the least bit interested in helping. If I wasn't at his side, Brad Mullins would be making this lonely walk alone while facing an almost certain death. I couldn't imagine what drove men like him to become lawmen. When I asked about it he just shrugged it off as being part of the job. I was amazed and in awe of his courage.

When we saw two breathless boys running towards us, we knew the Winters gang was almost in town. Brad gave them each a quarter and sent them home to their parents.

"Their favorite watering hole is the Kaibab Saloon. We might as well head over there and see what we're facing."

Outside the Kaibab, we counted eleven horses. Only six of 'em were sweaty and breathin' hard so they figured to belong to the gang. That was one more than we planned for so we had to find out who else was involved. I volunteered to go in and scout the party but Brad brushed me aside and bulled his way right through the swinging doors.

Once inside, we created quite a stir. The locals all knew what was going down so they scampered out every opening they could find. The customers that didn't know or were too drunk to care just milled around and wondered what all the fuss was about.

At the end of the bar towards the back of the saloon stood the group of new arrivals and it was immediately clear who the sixth rider was; it was none other than Big Jon Winters himself and he looked nothing like a "weak kitten". No formal introductions were necessary as I would have known him anywhere. The old man stood at least six foot five and had to weigh close to three hundred pounds. He wore a rumpled Confederate Cavalry hat pulled down low over one eye that partially concealed a face that was criss-crossed with deep scars and a scraggy beard. His skin was white and pasty not unlike his son who was sitting next to him.

Whitey Winters looked the part of a cocky gunslinger. His white hair, pale skin and pink eyes contrasted with his all black outfit which included his gloves and hat. The only exception was a blood red bandana tied round his neck. He carried two pistols in separate gun belts crossing at his waist. His worn boots sported shiny silver spurs with big Mexican rowels that "jingled" when he walked.

Little Joey had a long pointed nose and deep set eyes of a weasel. His face had a ruddy complexion and his pudgy and shapeless body looked like skin stretched over fat. When we walked in the Kaibab, he left the bar and walked over to Big Jon as if seeking his protection. I noticed he broke into a sweat right off while nervously chewing tobacco and looking for a place to spit.

Apache Pete had his back turned but he was watching us over his shoulder just the same. He wore buckskin britches and leggings like an Apache but had a flannel shirt and cowboy hat. I noticed his belt held a couple of sheaths I could see and probably a couple of more that I couldn't. He had one foot up on a chair and was trimming his leggings with a bone handled hunting knife.

Crazy Frank was sitting at the table with his back to us. When he saw Big Jon's reaction to our arrival he moved his right hand from the table and placed it in his lap. All I could see was the backside of his well worn leather duster but I figured that sawed-off shotgun had to be in his lap too.

I looked around until I located the Negro fella they called "Slim". He'd left the others and was talking to one of the saloon gals at the bar. For the moment he was too busy to notice what was going on.

Big Jon was not one to be at a loss for words.

"Well howdy Marshal. I see you've brought a deputy along on your rounds. I'd call that mighty good thinkin'. You never know what dangers lurk in the night."

Big Jon was letting his gang know there were two of us to deal with. Whitey put down his cigar and slowly pushed his chair away from the table while Frank downed his beer and turned to look at us over his shoulder. Joey casually walked behind his uncle and Pete stopped his trimming.

I was to the left of the marshal and I moved two steps further away from him to get a better line of sight. Brad was cradling his shotgun as he talked to Big Jon.

"I'm glad to hear you're concerned about my welfare. There's been an ugly rumor going around that your boys here wanted to put a bullet in me and pin my badge on a donkey."

"I reckon that there was just liquor talk. We're just here to have a good time with our friends and wash down the trail dust."

"Then you shouldn't mind checking your sidearms while you're in town."

The Marshal was pushing his luck and they both knew it. Big Jon looked around at his gang and slowly stood up to unbuckle his gun belt. He rolled the belt around the holster and made like he was gonna toss Brad the whole kit and caboodle but he held on to the pistol as the holster and belt flew across the table.

"Here ya go Marshal, catch."

His first shot followed the leather and hit Brad in the left shoulder. The Marshal was driven backwards by the concussion but both barrels of his shotgun discharged and most of the buckshot hit crazy Frank right in the back as he was trying to stand up to get out the line of fire. The rest of the pellets hit Big Jon and he dropped his pistol on the table and fell back in his chair. He was down but not out.

Whitey pushed away from the table and tried to stand up at the same time but his spurs caught the chair leg and he fell over backwards. Apache Pete whirled to throw his knife at me but I drew and hit him dead center in the chest before he could let go of it.

Meanwhile Joey ducked behind Big Jon and fired at me from behind his wounded uncle. His shot was poorly aimed and broke a window behind me but I didn't wish to give him a second try so I put a well placed round clear through Big Jon and into him.

Joey squealed in surprise and agony and went to the floor but was only wounded. I was fixing to put another round into him for good measure when Whitey managed to stand up and face me man to man. His two handed draw was lightning-quick but I already had my Colt drawn and cocked so it was no real contest. My first shot hit him in the throat and my second and third tore his chest apart. He managed a shot with each hand but only succeeded in busting the bar-back mirror and winging a whiskey drummer from San Antone.

It was then that Joey, that fat little weasel, got to his knees behind his dead uncle and shot me through my right thigh. I wasted no time in using my last round to punch a hole in his forehead but I was losing blood and fading fast

I heard Brad shout a warning and I looked up to see Slim aiming his six gun at me and grinning like a mad man. I ducked to the floor behind an overturned table and heard the sound of a liquor bottle bustin', a body hitting the floor and Brad saying, "Oh, thank God."

When I dared to open my eyes, I saw my brother G.W helping the Marshal to his feet and my good friend Trace Cummings standing over Slim's unconscious body. They may have gone unnoticed standing at the bar but they sure stood out now.

The acrid smell of gunpowder and wisps of blue-gray smoke filled the room but the silence was deafening until Trace finally spoke up.

"That there was a waste of good whiskey but I reckon you're worth it."

With the silence shattered, the crowd burst into conversation while I tried without much success to stem the bleeding from my leg. I remember Trace took over and tied off my wound with his bandana but then I musta passed out from the shock of it.

When I came around, I was abed in my hotel room. G.W. was tending to me and was surely a welcome sight. My right leg was still throbbin' but I was relieved to see Doc Lewis had been quick to respond to the gunshots and had already plugged up the hole. I was in dire need of some hundred proof pain killer.

"Glad to see you're comin' around, little brother. You know, I hardly knew you with that scruffy beard."

"How long...?"

"You've been out for the better part of two days and lost a lot of blood. Doc Lewis says you're lucky that bullet wasn't an inch or two over or you'd had your manhood shot off. As it is, I figure you're doing pretty well for a dead man."

"A dead man?"

"It was Marshal Mullin's idea. There were a whole bunch of dead bodies to be buried after the shootout and he reported that Henry James had been one of 'em. He figured that way you could rid yourself of the gunfighters curse and not spend the rest of your life looking' over your shoulder."

"Tell Brad I'm mighty pleased to be dead and I really would be if you and Trace hadn't been there. What in the world were you do-ing in the Kaibab?"

"We came to town for supplies and Jonah told us all about the shootout. Since Trace had a hankerin' to wet his whistle anyway, we figured to stay around and watch the show."

"Tell Trace I owe him for that bottle of whiskey."

"I'll be sure to mention it. Lest I forget, I've got a message for you to contact that lawyer fella, Cecil, and here's an envelope addressed to you from a Misses Langley. Oh, there's been a cute little waitress name of Glory that's been asking about your condition too. She'll come by with soup and sandwiches whenever you're up to eating."

I opened the envelope and found ten one hundred dollar bills and a short note simply saying "thank you". It was signed "Megan". I guess Whitey Winters was worth a lot more dead than alive.

I told G.W. how sorry I was about little Miriam but he told me we could catch up on all the news, good and bad, when I was stronger. I started feelin' kinda woozy and about to fall back asleep when G.W. asked me a question.

"Can you tell me how Taylor's doing?"

I closed my eyes and thought of nothing else.

## WINTER 1885

It was nudgin' the holiday season once again. The snow and cold threatened to shut down the whole area. Even the trains trudging up the spur line from Lamy had trouble comin' and goin'. I was reminded that it had been just a year since that damn train brought Victoria to town and ruined my life.

I was lonely and miserable. Not only had I been forced to put up with Victor being my partner for nine months but I also had to suffer all the intrusions into our business by Victoria. Being a former madam, she made life equally miserable for Maude by continually threatening to set up a competing sportin' house if things weren't run to her satisfaction.

Arthur made a pest of himself by requesting to audit the books every month and ran afoul of my payment arrangements with Paddy. She started to receive a straight salary and no bonus which didn't set at all well with her. I got tired of fighting over every little detail and stayed busy working the gamblin' side of things but my heart wasn't in it.

To make matters even worse, Victor and Taylor announced their engagement on Thanksgiving and planned a spring wedding. I'd had almost no contact with Taylor since the day that Judge Judy made Victor my partner but I'd been informed she quit her job working for the Olson's and was spending all her time with her new family. I was hurt and jealous but it was her life to live and I was no longer any part of it.

Christmas came and went without incident as I declined to send Taylor a present for the first time. Since I'd never received an acknowledgment of my gift of "Huck Finn" I was loathe to repeat that mistake. I heard from Mutt that she thought it had been a present from Victor. I could only imagine how that happened.

On New Years Eve day, Victor walked into my office with a proposition I just couldn't refuse. He proposed a winner-take-all poker game on New Years Eve to settle once and for all the complete ownership of St. Charles Place.

Word spread about our face to face all-or-nothing poker contest and the casino was packed on New Years Eve. Everyone who was anyone was there to witness the competition. I saw Charlie and Lucy, Sheriff O'Reilly, Councilman Gomez, Mister Dixon from the bank and even the pompous Judge A.C. Judy. They were all making side bets and I wondered how my odds were going. Mutt told me that I started at three to one but lately the betting was getting down to even.

The audience was complete when Victoria and Arthur entered the casino with Victor and Taylor. Since the "family" had ringside seats behind Victor, I was forced to look right into the eyes of both Taylor and Victoria as we played. Could it get any better than that?

We each started the match with twenty-five thousand in chips just to make the night last longer and sweeten the pot even more. The game was to be five-card stud with no limit up to and including our half interests in the casino. Maude had been chosen as the dealer so without any further delay, the game was on.

For three long and agonizing hours, we traded chips without either of us really gaining much of an advantage. Twice I had Victor "sweatin' his chips" only to let him come back and once he had me the same. When we finally took a break to stretch our legs, I happened to run into Taylor as I was walking outside.

"I suppose I should congratulate you on your engagement."

Taylor gave me a hard look and then backed off. "I didn't think it mattered to you one way or another, big brother."

Without intending to, I spoke straight from my heart. "I stopped being your big brother long ago and it matters more than you could ever know."

"Then why did you let it happen?"

"I didn't let it happen. It wasn't my doing."

"Victor told me how you carried on with Renee and all those other saloon trollops. You even murdered poor Mister McLean. How could you, Monroe?"

I tried to answer but the words got tangled. "I didn't....that's not what happened."

"And how about the way you goaded poor Victor into betting on the fights and then fixed the final bout with your so-called brother. You wouldn't even acknowledge Victor's birthright, Monroe. He had to take you to court to get what was rightfully his. Victoria told me all about..."

Taylor was nearly shouting by that time and I had had enough,

"If that's the way you see it, then we have little more to say."

"That's the way I see it."

"Just consider one thing. How in the world did Victor get the English publication of "Huckleberry Finn" two months before it was available here in America? And if he's lying about that, what else is he lying about?"

I left her to think about what I'd said and went back to the table where Victoria had a hard question for me."

"You once told me that your dream was to have your own cattle ranch. Why are you running this casino and pretending to be a gambler?"

I had to admit she was right. What was I doing there?

The game continued for another hour and the crowd started getting restless. They had hoped for a winner and loser so they could settle their bets and get to celebrating. For my part, I was building a set of "tells" to throw Victor off his game. I led him to believe that I twisted my ring whenever I had a bad hand but was going to bluff anyway. I let him win several small and medium-sized pots while misleading him in that fashion. I was patiently waiting for the perfect hand and it finally came my way.

I was dealt four jacks with a seven kicker. I tentatively opened for a thousand dollars. Victor scanned his cards carefully and watched my hands. I casually twisted my ring before questioning his intentions.

"What do you say, Victor? Are ya in or out?"

Victor rechecked his cards and raised my bet by two thousand. Quickly, I called his two thousand and raised him another two. My sudden aggression caught the dapper Mister Bodine off guard so he slowed things down by drinking his drink and considering his cards again. I knew he was waiting for my ring twist so I made him wait and simmer for awhile before I did it. When I finally twisted my ring, he let out a noticeable sigh of relief and called my bet. At that moment, there was already ten thousand dollars on the table.

Maude called for cards and I threw in my seven spot and asked for one card. It was dealt face down and stayed that way. I deliberately refused to look at the card.

Victor asked for two cards and quickly picked 'em up as they came to him. He added them to his three cards and did a hand shuffle before fanning out all five. His raised eyebrow was a sure "tell" that he liked what he saw.

Without comment, I pushed ten thousand dollars in chips to the center of the table and a hush came over the room. Ever'one sensed that something big was about to happen. If Victor called that bet, there would be a thirty thousand dollar winner.

Once again Victor was shaken by my bet so he turned around to look at Victoria. She leaned forward so as to see the cards he was showing her and gave him a nod of approval. When Victor turned back, I was twisting my ring.

"Aren't you gonna look at your last card?"

"Don't need to. Are you prepared to call?"

By now Victor was certain I was trying to "buy" the hand and he wasn't about to let my four card hand bluff him out of it.

"Tell you what Mister Henry Charles: I'm gonna call your ten thousand and raise you my half interest in this here casino."

A roar went up from the crowd. The folks had finally got what they came for. The moment of truth had arrived and Victor was riding his high horse.

"Are you proud enough of that four card hand to call?"

I let the crowd cheer its self out before answering. It was a funny feeling to know I had maneuvered Victor right where I wanted him. He didn't know it yet but he had just lost ever'thing that he'd lied and cheated to get.

"I'll call your half interest and raise you all the rest of your chips. Winner takes all."

I saw the look of panic flash in Victor's eyes and Victoria's face. At that very same moment they both realized what I'd done. The crowd was in a frenzy as they urged him to go all in so the game would finally end. Victor was in too deep to fold and he knew it. He reluctantly pushed in his remaining chips and turned over his hand which revealed a full house of kings over treys.

The crowd finally quieted down and awaited the showing of my cards. The tension was so thick you could cut it with a knife.

"Before showing you my cards, I would like to ask Miss Taylor Henry a question."

Taylor was overwhelmed by the sudden attention and buried her face in her hands. The crowd was abuzz with questions and Victor couldn't stand the suspense.

"Well don't just sit there...ask her!"

I stood up and walked the few feet between Taylor and me and spoke to her very softly.

"Win or lose...do you still plan to marry Victor?"

She looked into my eyes for the longest few seconds of my life and answered.

"Yes, I do."

I had my answer and that's all I needed. I walked away from the table and left my cards face down. Victor was the winner.

# CHAPTER XII
## "Back to the Flats again"

### SPRING 1886

Victor allowed me to stay in my room until the weather got warmer so I took my good natured time settling my personal and business affairs. About a week after the big poker game, I was in the office collecting my personal items which included my Henry rifle. It was comforting to know I had the deed to the Doodlebug Ranch hidden in the stock but strangely disturbing that I was returning to Grasshopper Flats. That deed was the one part of Charles' estate that Victor wouldn't get.

Suddenly I heard Victor and Taylor coming my way and they were surely arguing about something but I couldn't make out the words. Since I didn't wish to get in the middle of their affair, I decided to try out Charles' escape hatch. I tugged on the rope, yanked down the folding ladder and climbed up into the false ceiling. I managed to pull the ladder back up just in time as they entered the office below.

Taylor was really upset. I could tell by the tone of her voice. Victor was clearly defensive and back-pedaling as fast as he could. I felt kinda funny about listening in but I just couldn't help myself.

"Why won't you tell me how you got it?"

"What does it matter? I knew you would like it so I made some inquiries...you know...and found a copy."

"And just how did you know I would love that book?"

"I don't remember.  Maybe Mother suggested it."

"Your Mother?  How would she know?"

"Can we just get the account books we came for and leave?  You know how Arthur gets when we keep him waiting."

"Go ahead and take him those damn books.  I'm going to stay here for awhile and clean up the mess."

"Alright.  Remember Mother expects us for tea this afternoon."

"How could I forget?"

Victor left the office and everything went silent for about ten minutes.  I was about to climb up to my room when I could have sworn I heard Taylor crying softly but I couldn't be sure.  After waiting another few minutes, Taylor walked out to the bar so I lowered the ladder and climbed back down.

There was no sign Taylor had cleaned up anything but the writing paper and ink well had been moved around.  While looking around, I carelessly knocked a ledger book off the desk which made a noticeable sound that might have been heard in the bar.  Not wishing to be discovered, I grabbed my Henry rifle, went back up the ladder once again and climbed the stairway to my room.

By the time the weather broke and I was ready to leave Santa Fe, almost ever'thing had changed around the gambling hall.  The St. Charles Place had been renamed the "Victorian Palace" and the inside had been completely redecorated in New Orleans style furnishings.  Maude had been sent packing since Victoria put herself in charge of the girls.  Arthur and Taylor were trying their level best to manage the bar since Paddy up and quit right after they took over.  That left Victor to run the gambling side of things so they seemed to be one big happy family.

I didn't think Paddy would ever forgive me for walking away from a winning hand but she came to understand.  It was past time for her to move on and she knew it.  She decided to try her hand at driving freight wagons so she became a teamster and went to work with Griz.  I sure hoped those two social misfits could find some kind of happiness together.

Goner and I left Santa Fe on a day filled with sunshine and re-grets. I had little to show for my time spent in New Mexico but bittersweet memories and now I was heading back to Arizona. With one last look at the *Sangre de Cristo* Mountains, we were on the road again.

## SUMMER 1886

The next thing I remember was waking to see the comforting face of Doc Lewis. He explained that I had gotten some kind of in-fection which damn near finished the job that the bullet started. I'd been delirious with fever for over a week and he was relieved to see me awake and aware. All I knew was that I was hungry enough to eat a grizzly bear while it was still alive.

G.W. and Trace had gone back to work at the Box H ranch but I was still in good hands with Kenny, Glory and Megan to fuss over me. Kenny ran errands about town and saw to it that Goner was well taken care of. He had a hard time keeping the secret of "Henry James" being alive but he managed.

Glory kept me well fed and well informed as she always knew the latest local gossip. She heard that several young gun fighters had come to town hunting fame and fortune but left with the disap-pointing news of my death. She also told me that Boris and Natasha Godunov were still around and they were thinking of investing money in some silver mines that Megan owned. That little bit of in-formation explained why Megan had wanted to find "James Monroe Henry". She needed to buy him out before she could accept money from the Russians.

Megan came by once a day to see how I was doing. She was paying the freight for my recovery since she felt responsible for sending me after Whitey in the first place. Her spirits were high since she had the Godunovs to entertain and the added bonus of get-ting her daddy's ranch back after Big Jon died.

Marshal Mullins dropped in every day and saw to it that I finally got the five hundred dollar reward money from Wells Fargo. I just wanted to get up and out of the hotel so I could hightail it to the Box H.

After a couple days of being bed-bound, I dared to walk around my room just to test my injured leg. After a few minutes I felt woozy and about to faint when a pair of strong hands supported me. To my surprise and delight, those hands belonged to none other than Zackary James. He'd heard about the supposed death of Henry James and he'd ridden all the way here from Yuma to pay his respects. When he ran into Glory in the hotel, she told him the good news and brought him straight to my room.

We sat around and talked of old times and I couldn't help but notice how Glory and Zack looked at each other. They were both looking for something they seemed to find in each other. When it came time for them to leave, he asked her to join him for supper and she agreed. I smiled my approval and told 'em to have a great night and I reckon they did.

One week later, their whirlwind romance resulted in a marriage proposal and a no-frills wedding in the hotel dining room. With the help of crutches, I stood up for Zack as his best man while Megan reluctantly agreed to be matron of honor. Glory's parents, Kenny and a few other hotel employees filled out the audience. The pair of lovebirds were up and gone the next morning on their way to a new life in Yuma. I was happy for them but sad for me as I watched 'em ride away.

When Doc Lewis said I was ready to travel, I was more than ready to go but I had some unfinished business too. The first thing I had to do was be straight with Megan so I sent a message asking her to come to my room.

"So, I see you're about to leave us. Are you certain you're able?"

"I'll be alright. It's not too far to the Box H and I'll rest up there till this leg is completely healed."

"Do you intend to find James Monroe Henry for me?"

"That's what I wanted to talk to you about. You see, as it turns out, you've already found him."

I thoroughly enjoyed her look of confusion but I just had to tell her the truth.

"I'm James Monroe Henry. At least, I used to be. My name has changed a few times but I'm the fella you're looking for."

"Now I remember. You asked Sampson about the Blue Belle and the Silver Lady and I didn't know what you meant. Why didn't you tell me right off?"

"I wanted to find out what you were up to and now I think I know."

Megan got red-hot angry and looked about to spit venom but she took a deep breath, corralled her emotions and spoke slowly and softly.

"I just wanted to buy out your ten percent interest in each of the mines and I'm prepared to offer a fair price."

"Well, normally I'd be glad to take your money but I think you want my ten percent for the wrong reason."

"How could you possibly know that?"

"Because I reckon it has something to do with Boris and Natasha."

"How dare you? They're my guests and I'll have you know he's an ambassador and she is..."

"Danish royalty...I know the whole story. They staged a bull and bear battle in Santa Fe when I was there. They're a pair of "grifters" who travel 'round the country with a couple of henchmen nicknamed Moose and Squirrel. They freeload off folks and swindle them out of their money. What did they promise you?"

Megan was aghast at the prospect of her honored guests being thieves so she tried her very best to defend them.

"You must be mistaken. How could they possibly be common criminals?"

"I didn't say they were common. I just said they were criminals so I'll ask you once again, what did they promise you?"

"Boris said he would purchase my silver mines with funds sent directly from the Tsar Alexander himself. He confided in me that Russia was running out of silver and needed new sources. They needed to keep things quiet and to do that they wanted to deal with only one owner. That's why I had to buy your shares. Once I had complete ownership, I could sign the mines over and..."

"To whom?"

"Well, Boris said they had to be in his name so foreign powers wouldn't know the Russian government was involved. He told me that international politics were involved and the sale simply had to be kept a secret."

"When and how were you to get paid?"

"I was to be wired the money in about six...oh, my God. I was never gonna get that money was I?"

"Not one dollar. Once the Blue Belle and Silver Lady were in his name, Boris would sell 'em off to the highest bidder and they would be on their way."

Megan finally saw the light and booted Boris and Natasha out of her hotel. I mentioned to Marshal Mullins they might be wanted in Santa Fe so he caught them at the train station along with Moose and Squirrel and tossed all four of 'em in his jail awaiting a wire from Sheriff O'Reilly.

Megan tried to thank me for saving her from the confidence game but I declined all of her offers. She even asked me to ramrod the S Diamond Ranch for her. When she offered once again to buy my shares, I informed her that I gave them to Zack and Glory as a wedding present with the hope that the mines became prosperous enough to provide financial security for my friends.

My last unfinished piece of business was to see my old friend and attorney, Cecil Abernathy. I walked to his office with the help of a cane and met him on the street outside. Cecil was just getting back from lunch with Clarice so we all entered his office together.

While Clarice got my file, Cecil and I discussed their upcoming marriage and I wished them well. First Toho, then Zack and now, Cecil. It seemed like all my friends were gettin' hitched.

First off, Cecil handed me the new deed to the Doodlebug Ranch. He'd had the county judge sign and seal it in proper fashion naming Henry Charles as the new owner. Then he returned the Clifton's

journal and looked over the file for a minute before handing me a
sealed envelope.

"According to our Chicago office, they found the nurse that was
hired by Charles Farley to watch over his son. She's an older lady
now but still had a clear memory of the baby boy. Her detailed description is in that envelope."

"Do you know what's in it?"

"No. I told them to seal it for your eyes only."

"Thank you."

I stood up to leave when Cecil continued the conversation.

"I'd think long and hard before opening that if I were you. You
might read something you don't want to see and that could adversely
affect the rest of your life."

"Are you speaking as my friend or my lawyer?"

"Both."

"I'll give it some thought but you're right: some truths are better
not known."

Kenny brought Goner 'round to the hotel so when I was packed
and ready to go I said my good-byes to Megan and the rest of the
hotel staff that had tended to me. Even Ogger came out from the
kitchen long enough to see me off. Megan gave me a long and sen-
sual hug and whispered in my ear.

"I wish things were different between us. There was a time
when...."

I stopped her wishful thinking with the cold hard truth.

"That was a long time ago. You were right when you said I
could never afford you. I couldn't then and I can't now. We're in
the same country but we live in different worlds. I left her with the
only French phrase I knew.

"*Au revoir*."

On the way out of Flagstaff I stopped at the Wells Fargo office
and checked on my account. Mister Quincy was delighted to see me
and treated me like a king. I deposited the thousand dollars from
Megan but kept the five hundred dollar reward since I figured Pa
and G.W. could always use extra cash 'round the ranch. That ac-

count was my future and I would surely need it once I got settled in Grasshopper Flats.

## FALL 1886

Goner and I took our time returning to the Box H ranch. Mount Humphrey was a comforting trail marker as I rode through the rolling hills of pinion pines, juniper trees and scrub oak. Southbound Canadian Geese flew overhead and a turkey vulture abandoned a carcass as I passed by. Old friends like deer, coyotes, elk, bobcats and wild turkeys showed up along the way to make me feel at home. I relived moments of my childhood as well as the time spent here as an adult four years ago. I couldn't help but think about my parents, my brothers and, of course, Taylor. We'd left the ranch for Santa Fe filled with dreams of success and happiness and now I was coming back full of sadness and remorse.

The Box H looked better than I'd remembered it. The extra money I'd given Pa four years ago had allowed them to paint the house and barn as well as rebuild fences and plant a good sized garden. The stock looked well fed and cared for and the smoke from the chimney meant supper was on the stove. For once, it seemed, my timing was perfect.

G.W. heard me coming and came out to see who it was. Trace was busy in the barn shoeing a horse but he stuck his head out far enough to see it was me so he just waved and went back to work. My nephew, Franklin, followed his daddy outside and ran to greet me when I got down off Goner.

I wasn't prepared for a seven year old to jump atop me but Franklin did anyway. Somehow I managed to stay standing till G.W. pulled him off and we made our way to the house. Once inside, I found Susanna, G.W.'s wife, tending to her one year old son named William Harrison Henry or "Billy" for short. I couldn't believe they had another child already. I was very happy for them and more than a little bit jealous. I kidded G.W. about his son's name.

"If you keep having boys, we'll run out of dead Presidents to name them after."

"Nah, there's still a half dozen or more we ain't got to yet. Mister Lincoln would be next, I believe or shall I save that one for you?"

I laughed at his joke but inside I was crying. There was no telling when or if I'd have a child to add to our list. After playing with Billy for a minute or two I had to ask G.W. about Pa.

"Where's Pa? Is he alright?"

"Pa's in his room. He's taken to napping before supper. We'll wake the old man when it's ready and you can surprise him. Why don't we step out on the porch so we can talk?"

I didn't like the sound of that. Talking outside usually meant talking about serious things we couldn't share with Susanna and the kids.

"How are ya doing, Monroe...or should I call you Henry?"

"The leg is coming right along and you can call me whatever pleases you."

"Doc Lewis said you had a pretty fresh hole in your right shoulder. Would you like to tell me about that?"

"I got it fighting the Navajo. I was siding with Hopi Joe and his son, Toho. I'm sorry to say that Hopi Joe was killed in the same battle."

G.W. took the news easier than I thought. Since he was five years older, he'd spent much more time with our Hopi Uncle and was closer to him than I was. I told G.W. the whole story so he would understand the hows and whys of it.

"Pa's been wondering why Joe hasn't come around. This news will damn near kill him. It'll help that you're here 'cause he's really been upset about not hearing from you and Taylor. How is she doing, anyway? You drifted off before you could tell me at the hotel."

"I reckon she's fine but she's not the Taylor we used to know."

After that statement I was obliged to give G.W. all the details of our time in Santa Fe. I left out some things he didn't need or want to hear but he came to understand what I meant.

"I can understand your confusion. It's easy for you and me to remain brothers but the feelings between you and Taylor are harder to sort out. I'm sorry it worked out like that."

"And I was so sorry to hear about little Miriam. I know you and Susanna must have been heartbroken."

"We were and we are but life goes on. The good Lord saw fit to give us a fine healthy son to replace our sickly daughter and for that we must be thankful."

We were silent for a while as we both thought long and hard about our lives. I'd been feeling sorry for myself about losing Taylor and here my brother had truly lost his daughter. No matter how you sliced it, life wasn't fair.

"How about you, Monroe? What are you planning to do?"

"I'll show ya."

I walked over to Goner, pulled my Henry rifle from the scabbard and went back to the porch. I pried open the keyhole opening in the metal butt plate and shook the rifle so the cleaning kit would fall out. Next, I stuck my finger inside and pulled out two rolled up papers.

I was only expecting to find the deed to the Doodlebug ranch but there was another paper inside. It was a letter from Taylor. She must have stuck it in the rifle stock when she was alone in my office. Without reading it, I folded the letter carefully and put it in my shirt pocket.

I handed the land deed to G.W. and told him how I'd come to have it. After reading the details and description, he agreed that Doodlebug Ranch might turn out to be a fine piece of land as it bordered Oak Creek. We both laughed about the irony of my going back, once again, to Grasshopper Flats.

When Susanna called G.W. to help her in the kitchen, I was left alone on the porch with a letter I was almost afraid to read.

Dearest Monroe,                                        1-9-1886

I'm writing this letter because I'm ashamed to face you. I've come to find out that you were right about Victor all along. When I asked about "Huck Finn" he was evasive and defensive. I finally learned the truth from your friend Mutt. After talking to him and Paddy, I now know the truth about a lot of things.

It's clear to me now that Victor has never really cared for me. He merely used me to get to you. As you probably know, it was all his Mother's doing. Victoria is a vicious jezebel and she controls Victor's life. She was determined to get all of Charles' property and now she has it. I hope she chokes on it. I don't know where I'll go or what I'll do but I will never marry Victor.

I don't know if you can ever forgive me but I pray you will. I wish you the best of everything life has to offer and hope someday we can at least be brother and sister again.

With all my love, Taylor

I reread the letter three times and tried to read between the lines. Why hadn't she just come to me? Where was she now? How could I find her? My head was swimming with questions without answers and then I heard her voice.

"Can you forgive me, Monroe?"

I wheeled around so fast I dropped my cane and almost fell off the porch. There they were, my whole family, awaiting my answer. Taylor was standing next to Pa while G.W., Franklin, and Susanna were on one side and Toho and Chosovi on the other. I was struck speechless until Trace walked up behind me and slapped me on the back.

"Supper's waiting for your answer so get to it."

"Yes...Hell yes I forgive you. We embraced in a family hug that lasted for several minutes before Trace insisted that we move to the supper table. I can't remember what we ate but it musta been good since we stayed at the table for almost three hours. We laughed and cried and shared stories to bring everyone up to date on the events in our lives. I felt so good my leg stopped hurting.

Evidently, the news that the gunfighter, "Henry James", had been killed spread like wildfire all across the West. Taylor left Victor and Santa Fe as soon as she heard. Toho found out at the Day and Damon trading post in *Chinle* so he and Chosovi decided to come to the Box H to express their sympathies. The three of 'em had been at the ranch just waiting for me to get there. No wonder G.W. hadn't acted surprised about Hopi Joe; he already knew. They were all waiting in Pa's room 'till I read the letter.

Trace, being an adopted member of the family, gave a toast that put us all in stitches but left me to answer.

"Well here's to your safe and successful homecoming Monroe Henry...or is it Henry Charles? It can't be Henry James 'cause we all know he's dead but how about the Navajo Kid...or maybe Charlie Farley? Chosovi thinks that you might be someone named William Jefferson Clifton. Just who the hell are you anyway?"

When the laughter subsided, I stood up and answered his question to each person at the table.

"I plan to keep the legal name of Henry Charles. But to my Pa, Porter Henry, I will always remain his son, James Monroe Henry. To my brother, G.W., and his family I'll be plain old Monroe or Uncle Monroe to his boys. To my blood brother, Toho, I will be *Pahana*, his white brother and to Chosovi I will be her long lost brother, William. To Trace, I reckon I'll always be the Navajo Kid so what I call myself won't matter."

Everybody laughed along with Trace but they were all wondering what I would say to Taylor. For once, words didn't fail me.

"To Taylor Henry, my one time sister and forever friend, I want to be known as her husband and father of her children...if she'll have me."

Taylor's reaction left little doubt as to her answer. She hugged and kissed me so long and hard that we both fell on the floor. The cheers and clapping from everyone else was proof they approved and my homecoming was a complete success.

Trace and G.W. rounded up a Justice of the Peace the next day and we made it all legal like. Taylor wore Ma's wedding dress that was stashed in the attic and I even shaved off my beard before the ceremony. Ever'thing went off without a hitch and Taylor finally got her third name; she was officially Taylor Henry Charles.

The celebration afterwards lasted for the better part of two days and nights. When it came time to say goodbye to Toho and Chosovi

I gave them the envelope that Cecil had given me. I told them that I chose not to open it but they could if they wished and I would read the description of the baby to them. I explained that if the baby boy had a small *yongosona* birthmark then I was indeed born William Clifton and if not, then I was the son of Charles Farley. Chosovi thought about it for a few minutes and then spoke to Toho before placing the envelope in the fireplace. Then she walked over to me and took my hands in hers.

"It does not matter what the paper says. In my heart, you will always be my brother."

## FALL 1886

Taylor and I left for Grasshopper Flats a week later. We had a wagon full of building materials and supplies for our new home so I borrowed Pa's draft horses to pull the load. Goner and Domino were tied behind as we made our way down Oak Creek Canyon.

I was once again awestruck by the natural beauty as we slowly and carefully made our way down the steep and rocky slopes. The crimson cliffs framed Oak Creek with its mixture of rocks, trees and critters that called the canyon home. The air was scented with pine and juniper and the fall leaves were an ever changing display of color.

We stopped, as we had four years earlier, at the cabin of Rufus, the old bear hunter. We were saddened to hear that he'd been "kilt and eaten by a bear" two years earlier but I was delighted to be reunited with Rufus' younger brother and my old friend, Cleetis Dunbar. He'd set up shop in his brothers' cabin with two Injun wives and his two "Blue-eyed redskin" children. It was good to have Cleetis for a neighbor.

When we finally rolled into Grasshopper Flats, I was disappointed to see that it could hardly be called a town any longer. The sun was setting in the west and the pink-bottom clouds were overhead but the "Flats" seemed to be all but abandoned. Most of the false-front buildings were in some stage of collapse. The few businesses that weren't boarded up looked to be close to it. The rows of shacks and tents behind the buildings were mostly vacant and dilapidated but oddly enough, the "Rainbow's End" saloon was still open for business. I just had to go in and see if Deke was still around.

I wasn't disappointed. Deke was in his usual spot behind the bar but he was all alone in the saloon. He was still tall, lean and butt-ugly as I remembered him to be. His roving eye still gave me the yips but he was friendly as ever as he walked up to my end of the bar.

"Can I get you something Mister?"

"What have you got to drink, Deke?"

"Should I know you?"

"Sure as shooting. I come back here every four years just like clockwork."

"Well. I'll be damned if it isn't James Monroe Henry. I hope you're not gonna shoot up the place like you did four years ago."

"If you remember correctly, that was Henry James, the gunfighter, that did all the shooting and I heard he got himself a bullet hole up in Flagstaff."

"That's right. I heard the same thing. Like the good book says; live by the sword and die by it."

"I'll pass on the drink but I could use some directions. Can you tell me how to get to the Doodlebug Ranch?"

"Well sure, but it's abandoned and has been for over twenty years. You gotta go back down to the creek and cross over to the other side. Then head south about a mile to that red butte that kinda looks like an elephant. Off to your right, you'll see the old ranch house next to the creek. There used to a sign but it fell apart years ago. They say it was owned by some fella from Chicago but he let it go to seed."

"Well, my wife and I are the new owners and we plan to raise horses, cattle and kids on it."

"Well I'll be... welcome back to Grasshopper Flats."

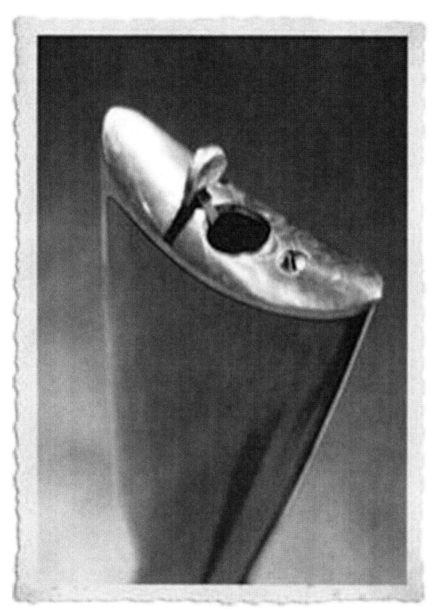

"I pried open the keyhole opening in the metal butt plate..."

# EPILOGUE

Henry Charles and his wife, Taylor, both lived well into their eighties and died a week apart. They had seven children although one died in infancy. They were blessed with seventeen grandchildren and thirty-five great grandchildren. With the last name of Charles, they started over with dead Presidents by naming their first boy G.W. Their five sons continued the tradition but their eleven grandsons ran out of names since the Charles boys came along quicker than Presidents died.

James Monroe Charles, their youngest son, fought in World War One, became an attorney and eventually an Arizona state senator. Their lone surviving daughter, Tyler, had seven children of her own before becoming the first registered mid-wife in the state of Arizona.

Andrew Jackson Charles, a grandson, was a journalist and novel writer while another grandson, Wesley Charles, became a well known singer-songwriter in Southern California.

Grasshopper Flats eventually returned to the ground it sprung from but the nearby area around Oak Creek continued to flourish. On June 26th, 1902 it became officially known as Sedona, Arizona.

The Doodlebug Ranch was subsequently homesteaded by the Chavez family and in later years by Ira Owenby. It was eventually separated into two real estate subdivisions in Sedona.

The author of this novel currently resides in Doodlebug Ranch II.

CPSIA information can be obtained at www.ICGtesting.com
Printed in the USA
LVOW090048241011

251740LV00002B/1/P

9 781937 600327